M000306733

# ROAD

A JOE TIPLADY THRILLER

# ROAD

## JOHN SWEENEY

**THOMAS & MERCER**

This is a work of fiction. Names, characters, organizations, places, events, and incidents are either products of the author's imagination or are used fictitiously.

Text copyright © 2017 John Sweeney
All rights reserved.

No part of this book may be reproduced, or stored in a retrieval system, or transmitted in any form or by any means, electronic, mechanical, photocopying, recording, or otherwise, without express written permission of the publisher.

Published by Thomas & Mercer, Seattle

www.apub.com

Amazon, the Amazon logo, and Thomas & Mercer are trademarks of Amazon. com, Inc., or its affiliates.

ISBN-13: 9781503940932
ISBN-10: 1503940934

Cover design by Mark Swan

Printed in the United States of America

*For Agim Neza, RIP, Marie Colvin, RIP, and the
doctors of what was, once, Free Aleppo*

*[Thunder. Enter the three Witches.]*

*First Witch: Where hast thou been, sister?*

*Second Witch: Killing swine.*

*Third Witch: Sister, where thou?*

*First Witch: A sailor's wife had chestnuts in her lap,*
*And munch'd, and munch'd, and munch'd:—*
*'Give me,' quoth I:*
*'Aroint thee, witch!' the rump-fed ronyon cries.*
*Her husband's to Aleppo gone, master o' the Tiger:*
*But in a sieve I'll thither sail,*
*And, like a rat without a tail,*
*I'll do, I'll do, and I'll do.*

*—Macbeth*


*The most abominable savagery should continue until*
*the anticipated chaos breaks out.*

*—Abu Bakr Naji, The Management*
*of Savagery (2004)*


*. . . all around us, though*
*We hadn't named it, the ministry of fear.*

*—Seamus Heaney, 'Singing School'*

# MOSCOW

Grozhov's electric wheelchair whined as it conveyed its master to his desk in the large office in the Lubyanka, the headquarters of Russia's secret armed fist since 1917. He took out the memory stick, inserted it into his computer and pressed play. A grainy image, black-and-white, not colour. Three separate pinhole cameras captured the scene.

The black prostitute, the most expensive to be found in South Africa – flown in, business class, from Joburg – was wearing a simple white dress, and a black choker around her neck attached to a chain. She was led in by two blonde goddesses, one from Russian Karelia, one from Siberia. They ripped off her clothes, spanked her – not too heavily – and chained her ankles and wrists to the bedposts so she was quite helpless.

Then the show proper began. At the end of the performance, the humiliation of the black woman was complete. The customer, hair of spun-sugar and skin of marmalade, was clapping and laughing heartily. Grozhov pressed stop, extracted the USB stick, picked up his phone and gave orders for the black woman to meet with a fatal road accident on her return to South Africa. Nothing in this operation should be left to chance. That done, he called a number in the Kremlin. The other party answered on the second ring. Grozhov explained the content of the secret film in some detail and concluded his report. Silence from the man in the Kremlin. Then four words: 'So Washington is ours?'

Grozhov sighed. 'Not yet.'

# TROPOJË, NORTHERN ALBANIA

A storm to remember the night before: the small town that nestled in the mountain range dividing the Serbian plain from the Albanian hinterland had been enveloped in its own bespoke thundercloud, sheets of lightning warping darkness into electric-blue day, trees cleaved asunder, roofs ripped up, torrents of water cutting the hideously expensive road the construction mafia had built, cheating the European Union rotten. A lightning bolt had taken out one of two electrical substations feeding High Albania; the other one was out of commission, awaiting repairs. The moment all the lights died, Tropojë warped back to the Middle Ages. Tourist-friendly alleyways became places for thieves to lurk; local vendettas were settled for good and shops looted; lovers took their chances, leading to enraged husbands and suicidal wives. And so it took the best part of a day before Police Lieutenant Agim Neza could follow up on the farmer's report of a shepherd discovering a body after the storm.

Agim was in his thirties, a thin, diffident man, dark-haired, clean-shaven, not unhandsome, in stature short for Europe, tall for malnour-ished Tropojë, a slight cast in one eye. He had a civility and a love of irony that was, well, quietly impressive for someone from the poorest part of the poorest country in Europe.

The farmer had said the body was high up in the mountains. 'High up' wasn't the half of it: the storm rain had washed away the dirt road in several places and it was only Agim's ingenuity and deep knowledge of the lie of the land that enabled him to weave a path in his four-wheel drive up to the farm where he'd arranged to meet the shepherd. Twice, Agim had had to edge the jeep along the knife-slash of a precipice, looking down on the eagles coiling in the thermals below, the wheels sending clods of earth and pebbles whistling down to the bottom – a thousand feet, more. It was towards the end of the afternoon when he got to the farmer's shack.

The storm had cleared the air and the breeze carried with it the scent of pine. The view was extraordinarily beautiful: even though it was high summer, mountains capped with snow charged towards the eye – black patched with white, like a herd of piebald ponies – above them fantastic whirls of cumulonimbus clouds soaring into an intensely blue sky. In the foreground was a dirty grey concrete bunker from Enver Hoxha's time, when the paranoid Communist ruler who fell out with everyone – the West, Stalin's heirs, eventually even Chairman Mao's successors – built three-quarters of a million pillboxes, the better to defend a country no one in their right mind would ever want to invade. (Mussolini, who did so, was not in his right mind.) Inside the bunker and outside it, in a pen built of stones, thirty thin sheep or fat goats bleated their devotion to 'Enver, our Enver' – or, at least, they bleated. The farmer, a white-haired peasant – tough, lean and so old, people said, that he could remember the time before Enver – made it clear that he was just the messenger. He hadn't seen a damn thing, on account of the discovery of the body taking place somewhere a bit higher than the farm. He warned Agim that the shepherd – well, he spent time, too much time, on his own and may have seen things that weren't there. But he added that he had never seen the poor fellow so agitated.

The farmer invited Agim inside his shack. After the brilliant light of the mountains, it took a while before Agim's pupils refocused to read the gloom: two chairs, a table hewn out of rough wood, a cot for sleeping in, a fire for cooking; a poor, mean, nine-inch square of window looking out on a view to die for. The farmer offered Agim a cup of coffee, served black and gritty, washed down with a glass of his homemade *raki*. They drank the coffee and brandy in companionable silence, only the sound of the wind in the pines disturbing the stillness. After a time, the door flung open and in walked the shepherd.

By the look of him, his father had been a wolf. Leastways, the whole of his face – forehead, too – and the back of his hands were covered in fine black hair, poor man. Agim had read somewhere that there was a disease that caused too-white skin and hair all over the body: a malfunction of the blood, not enough red blood cells, so the body compensated by growing too much hair and compelling the wretched victim to hide from daylight. The disease meant they couldn't see well, their gums receded and they were ostracised by their fellows and, so fearful of the sun burning their bloodless, thin skin, they only came out at night. The best nights were when they could see by the light of the moon. Driven half-mad by the disease, outside the world of language, they'd only be seen howling at the moon. One more thing, it had said in this article: if a carrier of the disease bit another person carrying a silent copy of the disease and drew blood, it could trigger the disease in the bite victim. So that's how the legends of werewolf and vampire were born: a disease of the blood parlayed into myth and nonsense.

Agim smiled at himself: for all his fancy university education in Tirana – never mind his trip to London, to Scotland Yard – he was a local, too. Tropojë was in his blood.

He said to the shepherd, 'May I ask, sir, what is your name?'

Conditioned to people ogling his body hair, this simplest of courtesies pleased the shepherd a great deal, and he smiled at Agim and said, shyly, 'Sotir.'

'May I ask, Sotir, how far away is the body? How much walking time? An hour? Two hours?' He really didn't like the idea of making the trip back to the capital in the dark. The jeep could easily tip over in the darkness and then Tirana would be looking for a new police officer to cover the country's least popular beat.

Sotir the half-wolf grunted something in the mountain dialect. Agim was mystified. 'Not far,' translated the old farmer, adding, 'He'll show you the way.'

Joined by an old sheepdog with rheumy eyes who seemed more human – or, at least, less of a wolf – than the shepherd, they set off at a punishingly fast pace: Sotir lolloping along, Agim hurrying to catch up with him, the dog trotting on behind.

Higher and higher they climbed, far up past the tree-line, into a land of lichen and dwarf shrubs, where slivers and fingers of snow and ice still lingered in sunless clefts of rock. In the end, it took them two whole hours before they found the body where the shepherd had left it. Agim shivered, cursing his luck. The sun was sinking low in the west and he would have to pass the night in the farmer's shack. They would be lucky if they got back even to that before nightfall.

Was it worth all this walking? Death was everyday up here. Not his job to record every death of every villager. But the farmer had explained that Sotir was insistent that the police officer should attend, and Agim was, if nothing else, a dutiful police officer.

He made a casual inspection of the corpse and ran off to a rock and leant forwards, hands on knees, vomiting three times.

After a time, Agim wiped his mouth with a paper handkerchief, took a series of pictures with his phone of the mutilated thing in front of him, steeling himself to do so. The corpse was Mediterranean in appearance, thought Agim – not Albanian, not local. Someone had removed the man's fingernails, he noted, but that hadn't been the reason he'd vomited. Looking at the man's hands, Agim realised that some of the nails had started to grow back, so if he'd been tortured, it had been some time – months – ago. Something else, too: a fine tracery of red on his right arm, like a tattoo, but not like any tattoo he'd ever seen before.

When Agim had finished taking the photographs, Sotir barked something in the dialect Agim didn't get, then pointed his finger uphill, to the west. Agim squinted into the dying sun in vain. Sotir pointed at the corpse and held out three fingers.

Mystified, Agim nodded vaguely, to fob Sotir off, and made to go back down the mountain. The shepherd barked a negative and, tugging at Agim's leather jacket, set off uphill. Reluctantly, Agim followed him. This time it wasn't that far at all: nothing more than a sheet of thin rock, some kind of slate, over a cleft in the mountainside. Sotir shifted the slate, and Agim took out his phone and switched on the torch. As he did so, the stink of the dead assaulted him. Three more corpses; these had all been burnt – no, fried, somehow electrocuted. But up here? How was that possible? These bodies, too, had the strange red tracery of the first corpse.

The half-wolf studied Agim, saw his befuddlement and handed him a lump of rock; it was not heavy, around two inches long, gnarled and knotted, the like of which Agim had never seen before. The policeman put the rock in his leather jacket but still didn't understand what the gift signified. Sotir's eyes shifted, coyly, to an old Enverist lookout post, standing on top of a jutting rock, thirty feet away: a metal ladder, a metal frame, an open-sided metal box. Climb that thing in a thunderstorm and you would fry, no question. But lightning doesn't mutilate.

None of it made any sense.

# THE CALIFORNIAN DESERT

Grass burnt the colour of bad gold, leaves crinkling in the wind, the land beyond Pyramid Lake ached for rain. Joe turned his Beetle off the interstate onto a grade running up through a valley with neither life nor end. The blades of a windpump bit against a cobalt sky, but the homestead the pump watered was nothing but a tin roof lying topsy-turvy on a hillock of rubble. A Ford tractor had been dumped in a bone-dry ditch, its skinny front wheels and toothsome radiator grille dating its manufacture to the fifties. Folks had moved out of the valley back in '73 when they built the dam, so that made a kind of sense.

The news was on the radio: a report of a rally in the election, a man's voice, soft, wheedling, then a crowd roaring, 'JayDee! JayDee! JayDee!' Joe grimaced and switched it off. Ninety minutes' driving north of LA and this valley was remote as the sunny side of Mercury and twice as hot.

The Beetle's soft top had jammed open and the heat smacked Joe in the head like a bully. He pulled up, switched the engine off and listened to the silence from the dead valley, a stillness broken only by the click-clicking of metal cooling beneath the hood.

In the slew of stuff on the back seat he found a crushed pork-pie hat with a daffodil-coloured band, and punched it back into shape and plonked it on his head. Just above the escarpment of the valley, a hawk picked his way through the heat, thinking about lunch. Joe checked the signal bars on his cell phone: zero. A man could die out here and no one might know for half a century, more.

Lost to civilisation, whatever that might be, Joe's thoughts turned to the men he'd been driven to kill, and the two women he had loved most truly: the woman who had died for him in Utah and the woman he'd killed for in the prison state. Katya was gone forever; Roxy was locked away, alive for all he knew, but dead to him, dead to the world, dead to the twenty-first century. That was also true of her two golden-haired boys.

What was Roxy doing right now, as he sat in his Beetle staring out at this barren land? Dusting the photographs of the two gods they'd had to worship – the one who was always smiling and the other one, who looked like a bad Elvis impersonator? Standing in a long line, waiting for her papers to be stamped, for permission to travel to the golden city? Or, most likely, staring into space, thinking about Romania, about Italy, about the life she could have led that was taken from her? He'd killed two men back there: one to save her and her boys; one to save himself. He could never go back, so what was the point of torturing himself by thinking about her?

Then his thoughts turned to Katya, and the melancholy that haunted him, that filled his soul, grew yet more intense. It always did when he had time on his hands, when he had little to do. That was why he worked so relentlessly. Not for money, but to not think about what he had lost. Katya had been dead for a year and a half, and he hated quiet, inactivity. He was still grieving, still hadn't come to terms with what had happened.

Heat baked the air, fuzzying substance. A lone cactus on a ridge wobbled so that it looked like a green man turning and turning again. *Best get on with this job*, thought Joe, whatever it was, wherever it would take him. The Beetle gurgled into life, and by and by Joe came across a closed gate, part of a metal fence that followed the contours of the land, two men high, on top of it three thin wires running through ceramic Os, murmuring a voltaic hum. Whoever needed an electric fence in this nowhere-land had secrets to keep and then some.

He got out of the Beetle and walked up to an intercom set on top of a short post. Joe leant on the talk button, lifted his hat out of respect and waited. In a stand of pine was a metal pole, camouflaged mottled green and brown, and on top of that a 360-degree CCTV camera looking him up and down. He had been living in Hollywood for nearly a year, and only now had he made it into the movies.

A woman's voice, tinny and robotic through the intercom, broke the silence: 'Hello?'

'My name is Mr Tiplady.' His voice was soft, and Irish as a sudden rain shower. 'I have an appointment.'

After a long moment, something whirred and the gate swung open – sorcery in the twenty-first century. The valley beyond narrowed into a gully, its cliffs crowding out the sky, the grade rising more steeply. After a couple more miles, the grade turned a sharp corner and everything was wet and lush and green, as if a giant had drained his fish tank.

Set against the western rock wall of the gully stood a faux-antebellum mansion with fake Doric columns. To the side was a small lake, or a big pond, fringed with weeping willows, and beyond that a meadow. From somewhere, a burst of electricity crackled, as if a bug had been fried, then the sound fell away. Joe had stumbled into a fake heaven.

Steps of white marble led to the front door, black but so glossy it served as a mirror. The figure in the looking glass was wearing a pork-pie hat, an expensive suit, pale cream and soft as silk, a dark-blue shirt decorated with little dolphins at play, no tie, no socks, and brown brogues that had never been polished. Joe had shaved his beard off the night Katya was shot dead in Utah. Around his neck, on a thin strip of leather, was the crescent moon she'd given him as a good luck charm. She was dead, he was alive, so it was working but not in a way he would ever have wanted. He hated wearing it, but not doing so felt somehow worse.

He knocked on the door and stuck a grin on his face to mask what was going on within.

The door opened magically before he got the chance to knock a second time. The contrast between the harsh white light outside and the cool gloom inside was so stark his eyes couldn't register detail. As his sight adjusted, he took in a hall, roughly square; at the back, two slender staircases arched up to a mezzanine floor; the walls were opaque, frosted glass, the effect like being inside a house full of bottled fog.

No one was about.

In the centre of the hall was an old mahogany table, exquisitely polished, and on it a lamp with a green shade; the light was focused on a document, a fountain pen with the top unscrewed next to it, the nib ready.

Joe stepped towards the table when a voice, feminine and elegant as invisible robots go, broke the silence: 'A non-disclosure agreement, Mr Tiplady. I'm sure you've signed many of these before.'

He leafed through some of the NDA in a bored, what-the-hell kind of way, then leafed through a lot more and flicked to the end.

'Forty-seven pages?' he asked the robot voice.

'Forty-seven pages,' it intoned.

'What's the job?'

'Sign the NDA and then we talk.'

Joe raised his head and stared around the room, void of humanity, knowing that he was being watched, spied on, taped, but he was not able to make out a single camera.

'I got a letter in the mail . . .' Joe started. No one answered back. 'It was out of the blue – not an email, not a phone call – inviting me to come to these map coordinates here, to the middle of nowhere on this day, at this time, for an appointment on a sensitive issue. The letter had no address and the signature was illegible. Now I'm being asked to sign the longest NDA I've ever seen and still have no indication what this is about.'

The robot repeated what it had just said.

Joe sighed, and signed.

One minute later, the sound of a woman's high heels click-clacked towards him.

'Mr Tiplady, I assume?' There was a twinkle in her voice but it had been pre-packed.

'No point in denying it,' he said.

'Oh, we do love a sense of humour.' Her voice was as smooth as honey and so, as his eyes adjusted, was the rest of her. She was in her late twenties or early thirties, darkish red hair or reddish dark hair tied up in a severe bun, wearing a starched white shirt buttoned high, the collar tapering into a slender neck, a black, ankle-length skirt and black flat shoes. What little of her skin he could see was the colour of bone china, so exquisitely pale he wanted to reach out and touch it, there and then, to see if she wasn't fashioned out of porcelain. Her eyes, liquid dark almonds, narrowed at the close attention Joe was paying her – not much, but enough.

'Nice hat,' she said conversationally.

'No, you're just being polite.' Joe took his pork-pie hat off and held it to his chest, as deferentially as he could. 'I didn't catch your name?'

'That's because I didn't tell you. Suffice to say I'm Dr Franklyn's attorney.'

'Dr Franklyn?'

'He's the Director.'

'You're an attorney and you work the tannoy? Ship ahoy, sign the NDA and all that?'

'Out here, multitasking comes as standard.'

Her accent was East Coast, old money.

'Uh-huh.' His accent was East Cork, no money.

'You really are Irish, aren't you?'

'Like a shamrock.' He paused, then said, 'So?'

'I'll take you to see him now.'

She led him upstairs towards a metal detector and, beyond that, a double airlock; beyond that was a large room, with a view through floor-to-ceiling windows of the big pond and the dead valley beyond. Someone had moved the Beetle. It must have lowered the tone.

The room could have been a library, only there were no books. To the far left was a long dining room table built of mahogany or another dark, hard wood, polished to a smooth gloss, around it a dozen upright chairs. To the far right, a sofa in the shape of a U. On the walls were fuzzy etchings of reptiles and amphibians, with and without tails. In the corner was a hatstand; on it hung a white US Navy cap boasting a fair amount of gold braid, and by the side of it a Victorian print of horses dancing around and lots of snaky things in the water. Dr Franklyn clearly had a thing about things that slither.

One of the opaque glass walls slid aside and a man walked towards Joe, the hand of executive friendship outstretched in pre-welcome mode. He was in his late fifties or early sixties, in superb shape, black hair thick and shiny, teeth white and gleaming, muscles lithe and pulsing. He was wearing a white smock and three-quarter sleeves, white trousers with a white corduroy belt, white socks and white sneakers: medical chic. He would have been quite the gallant doctor were it not for the fact that he was markedly short. Five foot two, if that. If he wanted to inspect Joe's mouth, he would have to stand on a chair.

'Mr Tiplady, I'm so glad that you could come.' It sounded as though he meant it – meant it very much. 'I'm Dr Franklyn, Dominic Franklyn. You've met Veronica?'

'I hadn't caught your attorney's name, Doctor.'

'Lawyers? Don't you hate 'em?'

Everyone laughed.

'Mr Tiplady has signed the NDA,' said Veronica smoothly.

'Oh no, did you make him do that? I'm so sorry, Mr Tiplady.'

'Call me Joe.'

'And call me Dominic. I'm so sorry, Joe. This country's getting so legalled up these days, you can't breathe.' Franklyn gestured for them all to sit down.

'So,' Joe said pleasantly, 'what's this about?'

Franklyn's face shifted from intense smiling to deep sorrow.

'My son . . .' His eyes fell to the floor while he paused for a beat. 'My beautiful seven-year-old boy, Ham, has been kidnapped. He has vanished off the face of the earth. Ham has been taken by his mother . . . She has, she has . . . mental health issues. I want you to find him and bring him back. This, I warn you, will not be easy. But money is not an issue. Joe, will you do this for me?'

Franklyn's eyes were light grey, flecked with obsidian.

'I'll need to know a little more,' Joe said.

Veronica reached into one of the manila folders she had with her and pulled out a colour photograph showing a boy, dark-haired with a light-brown complexion, wearing a kid's version of a business suit, starched white shirt and dark tie, standing on pricey teak or mahogany decking, the ocean lapping in the background, blue and mighty. He was laughing at someone else's joke. To Joe, he looked a sunny kind of kid.

'Ham?' Joe asked.

Franklyn nodded.

Veronica passed Joe another manila folder. 'Your copy, to be returned to us on completion.'

Joe opened it and saw a photograph that captured perhaps the most beautiful woman he had ever cast eyes on. Huge brown eyes lit up a laughing face of perfect symmetry, freckled lightly, framed by bubbling waves of long black curly hair. Clearly, Ham got his sense of humour from his mother, not his father.

The photo had been taken at night, the backdrop a bead of lights twinkling in the far distance. Maybe the shot had been taken from one of the Californian Channel Islands, at Avalon on Santa Catalina perhaps, looking back on LA. She was wearing a long black sleeveless dress with a black choker around her neck. Shining from her eyes was a vitality that leapt out of the photograph and kick-stepped around the bookless library, as gloriously out-of-place as a troop of cancan dancers in an old people's home.

'Jameela,' said Franklyn flatly. Veronica's eyes were locked on to nothing, far out in the parched wilderness. Joe got the impression that Veronica and Jameela were not bosom pals.

'She's beautiful,' Joe said.

'Jameela means exactly that in Arabic: beautiful,' said Franklyn. 'But she's also quite mad. Not only has she stolen my son, not only has she kidnapped him, but she has taken him to a place of great danger.'

'Why me?' asked Joe. 'I haven't had a private eye's licence for a full year. You don't know me from Adam.'

'But you have a track record in finding people who have gone off radar.'

'I've found a few people who had their own reasons not to be found, yes.'

'And you have glowing references from a former deputy director of the CIA?'

'I do.'

'And an Irish passport?'

'My passport's green.' It was a line from a Seamus Heaney poem.

'Then you're perfect. Veronica has done her due diligence.'

She beamed at Joe. So did Franklyn.

'Why haven't you gone to the FBI?' asked Joe, on the edge of petulance.

'The FBI?' Franklyn was incredulous. 'What good could they do? I believe this woman has taken my son out of the United States, back to her home country.'

'And that is where?'

'Syria.'

Far off, not quite smothered by acoustic proofing, the sound of a bark or a man crying out for something, once, twice, penetrated the stillness in the room. The bark or cry turned into a long, piercing scream, an animal howl. Then it stopped as suddenly as it had begun. Neither Franklyn nor Veronica registered it, which left Joe feeling as though he was treading on a step that had never, ever existed. He wrestled his mind back to what he had just been told.

'Syria? Where the war is – the war that's killed half a million people so far?'

'Yes,' said Franklyn.

'Ah,' said Joe. 'Why did she go back to Syria?'

'We don't know,' said Franklyn. 'We're worried that . . .' His voice tailed off.

'You're worried that what?'

'That she's joined ISIS.'

'ISIS? The so-called Islamic State, IS, ISIL, Daesh? The psychos who chop off people's heads in high-definition, broadcast quality?'

'Yes,' he replied. 'I don't understand it, but she became full of hatred: hatred of me, hatred of the United States, hatred of freedom. She seemed to be on a trajectory of anger. ISIS would have been the next logical step.'

'That's a fear. Not a fact.'

Veronica's eyes bored into Joe. 'We know this is difficult, but you will be properly paid. Here, two thousand dollars per diem; in Syria, twenty thousand dollars per diem; a success fee of two million dollars. Payment via bank account or in cash, however you please. A mentally ill woman has dragged this man's son to a war zone. We're asking you to do this for us, to get this little boy back to the United States. It's not about Dr Franklyn or our work here. It's about one little boy. Will you *try* to find him and bring him back?'

Then Franklyn spoke: 'Show him the video.'

Veronica opened up a tablet computer, flicked through a few folders, found the right file and handed it to Joe. He pressed play.

A moon rocket fallen to earth, a child's pink boot lying in the mud, a charred hand reaching upwards through a sea of cement dust, the light fuzzy, shot towards dusk. The camera zoomed in on the moon rocket, which was, at second glance, a felled minaret. Lying at an angle, you could make out the details of the minaret's top, normally hidden from the ground: three silvery moons, a lightning conductor, two loudspeakers. A starling took advantage of the temporary perch and hopped along from one moon to the next. Then a jump cut to a street, and five-storey blocks that had been knocked around by artillery fire. Suddenly, with a boom that shook the tablet, the images on the screen morphed into a mushroom cloud. Crazy camera angles, screams, yelps, then the mushroom melted away and what you saw was a half-memory of what had been there before. Whole blocks had become puddles of dust. Another jump cut showed a roundabout. On it, a ring of decorative iron spikes. On the spikes were four or five dozen severed heads, faces bluish and grey, eyelids closed. A laughing maniac stood in front of one, Kalashnikov on his shoulder, one finger upraised to a dark kind of paradise. One last jump cut, this time to brilliant daylight, the point of view swivelling around, starting with a child's bedroom, a Batman poster by the bed, bright-yellow wallpaper with laughing black whales on it, then shifting to where the front of the building should have been and you saw that much of it had gone, blown to smithereens, and the walls of the apartment were pockmarked with holes, concrete become Emmental, in front of it a telephone pole, still upright, just, but at a crazy angle, sprouting a thicket of wires that blocked the road.

Then the camera jerked once more and there they were, Jameela and Ham, mother and son, Jameela in a headscarf, holding her iPhone with an arm outstretched. Both were in black from head to toe, both standing in front of a large black flag with a white circle at its centre, on it lettering in Arabic, both raising a single index finger heavenwards.

Both were smiling; both wearing khaki suicide-bomb vests; behind them seven men, dressed in black, their faces masked by balaclavas, holding AKs to the sky. The selfie video stopped, dead.

'You're asking me,' said Joe, 'to reverse-kidnap a child from a mad woman who's become a jihadi fanatic, a member of the worst, most dangerous terrorist organisation in the world, from a country fighting the most pitiless war on the whole planet?'

'We're asking you to find my son,' said Franklyn. 'To find out where he is and, if you can, get him back to the United States.'

Franklyn's head sunk onto his chest, his fingers gripping his face, masking his features. 'For a grown woman to do this, to join ISIS – well, you can't stop someone like her. But for a mother to put a suicide vest on her only child . . .' He shuddered, and Joe, to his intense embarrassment, realised that the man was sobbing, softly to begin with, then becoming louder and louder. Veronica looked out at the desert, reacting to the Director's grief by turning to stone.

Clearly the doctor was a control freak. The games that morning with the map coordinates and the NDA were proof of that. But underneath the veneer was a father who was bereft not just at the thought of losing his son from his life, but of losing the life of his son.

Something deep inside Joe reawakened, an empathy that he'd thought had gone forever when Katya was murdered, and he reached over and grasped Franklyn's shoulder. Joe found himself saying over and over again: 'Don't worry, I'll get your boy back.'

After a time, Franklyn recovered his composure, wiped his eyes, lifted his head up and studied Joe closely.

'Joe, that crescent moon you've got around your neck? It's got some Arabic on it. What's it say?'

'May God protect you.'

'Who gave you that?'

'A friend of mine,' Joe said stiffly.

'You still together?'

'No,' Joe said in a tone suggesting the dead end of that particular line of enquiry.

The meeting resumed, weirdly, as if Franklyn's breakdown had never taken place.

Joe gestured to the tablet and asked Veronica: 'How did you get this?'

'By email,' she said.

'Any text with it?'

She retrieved a sheet of paper from a folder. On it, there was only one line printed: *Dominic, we're out of your life now. Forever. Don't try to find us.*

'Is this email account active?'

'No. It's only been used once, for this one email to Dr Franklyn. As far as we can tell, she sent this message from an Internet café somewhere in Syria, then she vanished off the face of the earth.'

'The Arabic on the flag? It's definitely ISIS?'

'Yes,' said Franklyn.

'The Jameela in the photograph in the black dress and the Jameela in the ISIS footage, they're the same woman?'

Franklyn told him yes, they were the same woman.

'So what happened? What went wrong?'

'Joe, you've probably gathered what we do here.'

'Not really.'

'Dr Franklyn,' Veronica said, 'is one of the world's most eminent practitioners of TMI.'

Joe put on his puzzled face.

'TMI – transcranial magnetic invasion. It's the very latest in elec-trotherapy,' she explained. 'Here at our facility we enable the ordinary to become extraordinary, the mentally troubled to attain some level of normality. We help high achievers who fear their full potential has not been attained and we treat those who have been rejected by or who have found no solace in conventional psychiatric centres. The mind-stabilising technologies Dr Franklyn has developed here are revolutionary. Don't take it from me. Some of our clients – well, they say that once they've been here, once they "plug in", they transform, and when they leave, they're on a higher plane of being.'

'*Plug in?*' Joe asked.

Franklyn gave a self-deprecating laugh. 'Veronica, you make us sound like miracle-healers. We simply do our best to help some people develop their full potential, and help others who may have been told, falsely, they have troubled minds.'

'Charitable?' Joe asked, perhaps too sharply.

'Charitable, often. Where clients have some access to resources, then we do reluctantly accept donations.'

'So you're a psychiatrist?'

'Not in the formal sense, no,' said Franklyn.

'But you're a doctor?'

'I'm a doctor of philosoph—'

'Mr Tiplady, you're not here to cross-examine Dr Franklyn about his qualifications,' Veronica cut in sharply. 'Suffice to say that you are sitting opposite a pioneer whose technologies will one day be recognised internationally as equal in power to discoveries like the double helix or quantum physics. Dr Franklyn is, in this very facility, unravelling the DNA of the mind's workings.'

'Very good,' Joe said. 'By the way, I didn't catch the name of this facility.'

'Fort Hargood,' said Veronica. Joe frowned a little. 'It was a military camp during the Second World War,' she explained.

'I see. And Jameela, she was a patient?'

'Not at all,' said Franklyn smoothly. 'The tragedy is, she was one of the most effective nurses we ever had. She understood the benefits of the technologies I was working on better than anyone. Her oneness with the technology was so complete – and I fear this sounds unprofessional – I fell in love with her.'

Joe chanced a look at Veronica's face. Again, her eyes were focused on the barren land beyond the fort's fake greenery.

Franklyn continued: 'We married, had our son Ham, short for Hamal. The name is Arabic for "lamb". Ham was our little lamb. It was a happy time.'

'So what happened to Jameela? What went wrong?'

Franklyn gestured to Veronica, who flipped open her tablet again and pressed play on a different video file. The Jameela of the candlelit photograph had gone. She was the same woman, but sickeningly different. A moronic emptiness in her pupils, staring, staring, staring into the camera, great black bags under her eyes, her once-gorgeous hair pinned back harshly, a hawkishness to her nose not to be seen in the candlelit photo. You couldn't make out where she was or what she was wearing because the framing of the image focused solely on her hating, hateful face, which was lit up in a pool of light, the background fuzzy and in shadow. In the Avalon photograph she had wriggled with loveliness and life; here the whole force of her being exuded something so dark it was beyond description. The image was video, but it was locked in stasis for thirty seconds or so, and then everything got so much worse. First, the whites of her eyes fluttered in their sockets, and then she started to scream, her face reddening all the while, her voice rising in pitch and tone. The sound grew in intensity until it became an ear-piercing shrieking: '*La! La! La!*', Arabic for 'No! No! No!' Beauty had turned to Monster, her eyes huge in the frame, twin pools of psychosis. And then her face buckled, the screaming stopped, all force gone, and she began to sob quietly, almost silently. Then the video ended.

'Quite mad,' said Franklyn.

'Mad,' echoed Veronica.

'When was that video shot?' asked Joe.

'Earlier this year,' said Franklyn.

'Where?'

'Here.'

Out of the window, high noon had passed and the shadows were, ever so slightly, beginning to lengthen. Joe gazed out at the greenery close by and the deadness beyond, the three images of Jameela haunting his mind's eye: the vivacious beauty; the wannabe suicide bomber; the woman as mad as mad can be.

'When did she leave with the boy?' he asked.

'One month ago.'

'July?'

The doctor nodded.

Something bleeped and Franklyn fiddled with a device clipped to his belt, then studied Joe. 'I'm being called away, I'm afraid. Is there anything else I can help you with?'

Joe couldn't think of anything, so said nothing.

The doctor's grey eyes bored into Joe as he took his right hand and clasped it in his own.

'Find my son, Joe. Find Ham and bring him home.'

'I'll do my best,' said Joe.

Franklyn smiled graciously, and then he was gone.

Joe asked Veronica for the video.

'I'll email it to you.'

'That would be foolish.'

'Why do you say that?'

'Ever heard of the NSA?'

She bit her lip. It was, perhaps, the first time he'd had the better of her.

'To send me an email with that video attached . . .' said Joe. 'Well, that would be a schoolboy error.'

Her whole being was a study in contrition.

'Load it up onto a clean flash drive.'

'I'll do that right now.' She disappeared, then reappeared with a USB stick and a piece of paper, on which was typed an address in downtown LA and a telephone number. She told Joe that, to communicate with her, he should write to her. No email. The telephone number was never to be used unless it was a life-threatening emergency. She added that on the flash drive was a file on Jameela, confidential, not to be shared. Joe nodded.

She led him back through the labyrinth of opaque glass, downstairs to the entrance hall, and opened the door. Out front, his Beetle had appeared, driven there by an enormous black man in a janitor's overalls, who got out and stood by the car, his eyes staring at the ground. He'd fixed the soft top.

'Thanks for fixing the top,' said Joe. 'And you are?'

'Samson, sir.'

'So, Samson, how did you start the car without the key?'

'Trick I learnt in East LA, sir, before I met Dr Franklyn, when I was baa-aad.' The way Samson said 'bad' made Joe wonder whether he ever regretted becoming good.

Veronica wished him luck. Joe smiled to himself, suspecting that he would need it, got in the Beetle and headed back down the track. The steel gate opened as he approached the silent, all-seeing eyes of the CCTV cameras watching over Fort Hargood. He may have been heading towards a world of trouble, but it felt good to get out of there.

Once through the gate, he gunned the Beetle. It burbled happily and he slammed in a tape – the car was so old it boasted a tape deck – of The Wolfe Tones, and sang along at the top of his voice:

*'Contentment of mind is not found in a city . . .*
*And though I have travelled the wild world all over*
*There's nowhere on earth that is dearer to me . . .*
*And fishermen's boats make their way by Dingle Bay.'*

A dip in the road by a wall of rock offered shade, some respite from the sun, but then the road ran uphill and he was staring directly into a hot orange ball. He was lowering the sun visor to shield his eyes when a huge black SUV came bowling straight at him. Joe swerved and the SUV missed him by half an inch, if that, but not before he got a long hard look at the man behind the wheel. He was staring beatifically into the distance, headphones plugged into his ears, his high cheekbones, thick bush of blond hair and extraordinarily fine teeth every bit as telegenic as when Joe had seen him in countless films. Luke McDonald, one of the most famous film stars on the planet, was going, fast, to Fort Hargood.

# TIRANA, ALBANIA

They sat around a conference table the shape of a coffin in the Ministry of Internal Affairs, a palazzo built in the time of King Zog, light and spacious on the higher floors, Ruritanian on the mezzanine and a cosh in the basement. Commander Ramiz Bejtullah of the State Intelligence Service was reading out his report in a flat monotone; the underlying message: nothing of interest here. Dressed in a Christian Dior suit of charcoal grey, a crisp white shirt and mauve tie, Bejtullah's jacket was hung over his shoulders, perhaps because, Agim mused, his arms were too grand to go through its sleeves. A smooth and elegant functionary of the secret state, Bejtullah had a future.

Agim was the past. They were all here to bury his investigation into the four corpses the shepherd had found at the top of the mountain: the one mutilated and burnt, the other three just burnt. Agim was the rustic from Tropojë, after all.

The ministry's officials were out in force, as were the police, represented by Agim, his boss, his boss's boss and his boss's boss's boss. Three goons from the secret police were there to lick Bejtullah's boots, as well as four Americans: some kind of military guy, chunkily built, dark hair in a crew cut; two clerks from the embassy who Agim had seen before; the fourth was old, the oldest man in the room. Slight, with a beard but no moustache and a gap between his teeth, he wore a black suit that had seen better days, a white shirt and dark-purple tie. He looked like a preacher down on his luck. When he smiled – which he did, often – he gave the impression of being simple, even perhaps an idiot.

Between the four Americans sat an interpreter from the foreign ministry – a man, bespectacled, with a high forehead and a forlorn expression, who gave the foreigners a running commentary in English and everybody else the impression that he was too talented for work of this nature.

'Four corpses were found in the high country, north-west of Tropojë' – Bejtullah droned on – 'in various stages of decay. Due to the passage of time and the effects of the immediate environment – high winds, rain storms, etc. – it has unfortunately not been possible to diagnose the exact cause of death . . .'

*Of course it hasn't*, thought Agim.

'In addition, the national police service has brought to our attention the deaths of three more men, found at the bottom of the mountain . . .'

Seven in all? This was bigger than Agim had imagined.

'The three bodies were so severely damaged in the fall that, again, it has unfortunately not been possible to establish the precise cause of death . . . The seven dead were of different nationalities: one Tunisian, one Moroccan, three Saudi Arabian, one Syrian and one Iraqi-American.'

*Aha*, thought Agim, *that's why the Americans have turned up: they have an issue of care in relation to their half-citizen.*

'We believe,' continued Bejtullah, 'that all seven were economic migrants seeking a new life in Europe, and they may well have fallen foul of the leader of the smuggling gang responsible for their illegal entry into Albania. This man has been apprehended and is currently refusing to cooperate with the authorities, claiming that he was not responsible and is not a smuggler.'

So Sotir the half-wolf was giving the intelligence people a hard time, thought Agim. They'd have a devil of a job understanding a word he had to say. Good for him, poor fellow. The idea that he was some smuggling boss, living up in the mountains with the eagles – that was just too stupid, even for the intelligence people.

'So, to summarise: the interior ministry of Albania and the special security police are grateful to Police Sergeant Agim Neza of Tropojë . . .'

*Sergeant? They've demoted me as well as staging this farce.*

'. . . for bringing our attention to this tragedy. The loss of life of economic migrants from the Middle East and sub-Saharan Africa in Europe is becoming a distressingly frequent reality. Now Albania, too, must shoulder this burden, though we note that the loss of seven lives, if compared to the loss of thousands crossing the Mediterranean, is small by comparison. One more observation: the loss of life has nothing whatsoever to do with the facility—'

'What facility?' Agim instantly regretted asking his question out loud.

Perhaps there was a flutter of suppressed anxiety on the Albanian side of the table, but the four Americans were impassive, in the dark, the translator not having conveyed what Agim had said. Bejtullah smiled smoothly at him and said in a personable way, 'This question is above your level of responsibility.'

'*Po, por kjo është një pyetje e drejtë,*' said someone in fluent Albanian. Agim was astonished to realise that the speaker was the American fool with the gap in his teeth, but not quite as astonished as the interpreter, who stared at the fool open-mouthed. Seeing as there was no response, the old man repeated himself in Albanian and then in English: 'Yes, but it is a good question.'

More silence. The American continued: '*A mund t'ju pyes, çfarë objekti nuk ka të bëjë me këto vdekje?*' And again he translated for the benefit of the other Americans: 'May I ask, what facility has nothing to do with these deaths?'

'Who is this guy?' hissed Bejtullah, in Albanian, to the official next to him.

'I don't know,' the official hissed back. 'He's not a regular at the embassy.'

Whoever this man was, thought Agim, he was not such a moron; in fact, not a moron at all.

'In fact' – the old fellow reverted to Albanian only – 'there are a number of issues I'd like to raise regarding your report, Mr Bejtullah, for which, much thanks.' His Albanian was extraordinarily good, as if he was born and bred in the back streets of Tirana.

'First of all, perhaps you can expand on your theory that the seven men were in some way economic migrants heading from the Middle East and North Africa to northern Europe. Why would any such person embark on a route that would take them via the highest mountains in northern Albania? There has been some people-trafficking through Albania but not much. The only conceivable through-route from these mountains would be into Kosovo and then across to Serbia or Montenegro, which are two of the most difficult and troubled border crossings in the whole of Europe. But even in that eventuality, the main road and mountain passes are at around one thousand feet high. Four of the dead men ended up on a mountain seven thousand feet high, and three at the bottom of the mountain, but still six thousand feet up. No one walks for days through mountains when they can go by road. So your theory that they were economic migrants is incredible. Which leads me on to the next point. You've arrested a shepherd on the basis of a theory that makes no sense. And in addition to the nonsensical motivation, why would the supposed killer report those killings to the police? You are confusing an innocent and helpful member of the public with the true killer out of administrative convenience.' The non-idiot smiled his strange, gap-toothed smile. 'Or out of laziness.'

Bejtullah visibly smarted at the suggestion.

'To reassure everybody around this table,' the old man said, still smiling, 'this mistake happens all too frequently in the United States of America.'

No one around the table felt reassured.

'In puzzling cases like these,' he continued, 'it's always best to go back to the primary evidence. Let's have another look at the photographs of the dead.'

Bejtullah turned to the official next to him and whispered something in his ear. The official, emboldened, said, 'Excuse me, sir, but with respect, some of these issues touch on matters of Albanian national security.'

'Likewise on American national security,' said the non-idiot, smiling once more.

'What's your locus in this?' snapped Bejtullah.

'Locus? I'm in Tirana,' the old man replied.

Agim cupped his mouth with his hand to hide his glee.

'If the national security of the United States is at issue,' said Bejtullah, 'you have to demonstrate your credentials. We were informed that you were an analyst from the embassy. Is that correct?'

'In a manner of speaking, yes.'

'Who are you?' Bejtullah rasped in English, his voice absent of all its previous oiliness.

'My name,' said the old man, replying in English, 'is Ezekiel Chandler, an—'

The American sitting next to him finished the sentence: 'And Zeke is with the Central Intelligence Agency.'

'Now that's cleared up,' said Zeke, returning to Albanian, 'I'd like to ask you to look again at the photographs.'

Opening a folder in front of him, Zeke took out seven colour photographs and pedantically organised them in front of him, one by one. 'Seven dead men. All have clearly been burnt – some so badly there is evidence of charring. Only one is burnt and mutilated; three, it would appear, have only been burnt; three have been burnt and have also sustained the tissue and skeletal damage you would expect from falling from a great height.'

Zeke stopped to extract an eighth photograph, taken by Agim, of the lookout post, standing high above the precipice with only one thin rail of metal separating whoever was on the post from the drop below.

'The lieutenant posits the three men were hit by lightning while standing on this lookout post, and fell backwards onto the mountain to be recovered by the shepherd.'

'This is nonsense,' said Bejtullah.

'Oh?' said Zeke, smiling.

Agim was beginning to wonder whether Zeke's smile wasn't a smile at all, but more like the click an automatic weapon makes when you switch the safety off.

'One can put forward a further hypothesis,' Zeke went on, 'that the three found by the police at the foot of the mountain died in exactly the same way, by lightning, but when electrocuted, their muscles went into spasm and they were projected forwards. They were all dead long before they hit the ground. Casual examination of this photograph of the lookout post allows for the possibility that anyone who was on it and hit by a bolt of lightning could fall either forwards or backwards. The literature says that people who are hit by bolts of lightning have been found up to several feet from where they were standing at the moment of impact.'

A fan in the ceiling flicked away at the air, as uselessly as it had done under King Zog, Mussolini, Enver Hoxha, and now democracy, sort of.

'So, we seem to be looking at six dead men, at least, who killed themselves by self-electrocution.'

'I repeat,' said Bejtullah, 'this is nonsense.'

'Oh,' said Zeke. 'So you have ruled out the Lichtenberg figures?'
He said the phrase 'Lichtenberg figures' with the same intonation that
someone else might say 'glass of milk'.

'What?' asked Bejtullah, incredulous.

'The Lichtenberg figures. You do know what a Lichtenberg figure is?'
The look on Bejtullah's face suggested that no, he did not.

'When lightning strikes a human being,' explained Zeke, 'it does
so at 220,000 miles per hour with an electric charge of up to one billion volts, generating temperatures up to 50,000 degrees Fahrenheit.
That's five times hotter than the surface of the sun. But the bolt lasts a
fraction of a millisecond and the human body, so much salty water in
a bag, isn't too bad at conducting electricity, so nine times out of ten,
people survive lightning bolts. Unless, that is, they're holding on to an
iPhone or a fishing rod or a golf club. That's why in America the state
with the most lightning fatalities is Florida – not because the weather's
freakish down there, it's simply a question of statistics. More people
are playing golf in Florida at any one time; golf clubs are metal and
so the person holding metal gets to sizzle. The lethality of a lightning
bolt increases exponentially if you're holding on to metal. If you're in a
metal box during an electrical storm, you're going to get electrocuted,
no question. Are you with me?'

Bejtullah scowled at Zeke, which he took as a yes.

'Lichtenberg was an eighteenth-century German scientist. A
hunchback, shrewd, witty, an Anglophile, an aphorist who came up
with "God, who winds up our sundials", an—'

Bejtullah coughed impatiently.

'. . . the father of plasma physics. While our Benjamin Franklin
was playing with kites in a storm, Lichtenberg went looking for the
victims of lightning bolts and repeatedly found the same phenomenon:
lightning-shaped marks – fractals, if you like – leaving a tracery of burnt
blood vessels on the skin. He then built his own electricity-generating

machine and reproduced the same fractals in other materials. Let's look, once more, at the photographs of our seven dead men . . .'

Zeke went through all seven. Each one had distinctive red tracery on his skin. Each time, Zeke pointed to the lightning mark and said, 'Lichtenberg figures,' and smiled at Bejtullah.

It was like watching someone's brain being salami-sliced, thought Agim. He almost felt sorry for Bejtullah.

'All seven, self-electrocuted by lightning. This theory,' Zeke continued, 'fits the known facts but begs the question: why do something so insane as to risk death during an electrical storm on a mountaintop in the middle of nowhere? And the seventh death is even more puzzling: the man has the telltale Lichtenberg figures but appears to have survived electrocution, only to stab himself in the face repeatedly with a sharp stone dagger. Why do that? We are looking for an anomaly, something unusual in the environment which might explain the behaviour of these men. But before we do that, we should ask ourselves a primary question: who are these men? I've done a little background data-checking and I'm confident that at least five of the seven are Islamic State operatives, senior players, hostile to the West and, I'm afraid, my country. That goes, in particular, for the dual citizen, the Iraqi-American.'

He paused, took a sip of water. He held the room, entirely.

'So, Mr Bejtullah, we return to the question you ruled out: what facility has the deaths of these men, at least five of whom were in ISIS, the most feared terrorist organisation in the world, got nothing to do with? Where is it and what happens inside it, what does it do and who does it?'

Bejtullah leant forward and said in English, 'Well, Mr CIA, it's your facility, isn't it? Why ask us all these questions?'

'Our facility?' asked Zeke. Now it was his turn to be incredulous.

A look of panic washed over Bejtullah's face and there was a sense that he had uttered something that should not have been communicated to this man. His wrist jerked in front of his face and he stared at his watch – not the room – as he said, 'This meeting has overrun and I am late for a conference with the minister. Thanks for your questions, Mr Chandler. One of my team will get back to you. Good day.' And then he got up and left in a hurry, his underlings standing up quickly and gathering in a huddle to block the exit so that Zeke couldn't pursue him any further.

———

Later that day, an encrypted call was made from Tirana to CIA headquarters at Langley in Virginia.

'The Angel Moroni is in town.'

'I heard.'

'He's been asking all the wrong questions.'

'Damn.'

'In Albanian.'

'He speaks Albanian?'

'Uh-huh.'

'Hot damn. Does he know about the facility?'

'Not yet, not the whole story. But the needle on his moral compass is troubling him. You know what he's like. If he's allowed to continue, the programme will be dead in the water. Get him off my back.'

'Understood. I'm on it.' And the call ended.

# WEST HOLLYWOOD, CALIFORNIA

Joe woke up and took his fool of a dog, a black whippet-poodle cross by the name of Reilly, for a long walk in Runyon Canyon. He climbed up and up, to a vantage point where he could see the Hollywood sign etched clear and bold against a bluff and, as he turned, the great dismal sprawl of LA stewing in the heat. It was only ten o'clock in the morning, yet already the sun was haloed by a dirty shade of bronze. He'd traded the overcast skies of Ireland, then London, for a sky of molten brown, and he scratched his head as to why that was the case. Reilly shot into some bushes, didn't like what was in there, and reversed out, tail between his legs, fear curled in muscle.

Truth was Joe was still running: running from the IRA, who still wanted to kill him; running from his time in North Korea, when he'd first realised in the act of killing a sociopath, their master in terrorism, that he'd been brainwashed into elevating his cause of a united Ireland into an excuse for spilling blood; running from the Russians who had tried to kill him because of their own stupid mistakes; running from the moment when their man inside the CIA had shot dead Joe's lover Katya in the mountains of northern Utah.

And so he'd ended up in LA, working as a private investigator, but one with a very unusual set of rules. No divorce, no corporate. That left him a pretty limited field. But his conscience did allow him to find people and, it turned out, he was exceptionally good at that. He could find people because he'd had to hide himself, first from the IRA, then the Russians. He knew the mistakes people made when they covered their tracks. Finding people in the digital age wasn't that hard. It was often more like following a burglar's footprints in the snow. Thing is, some people didn't want to be found. They had their own reasons to run. And as far as he could, within and without the law – Joe wasn't a huge respecter of lawyerly rubbish – he wouldn't give up people he found if they were running from darkness. His philosophy wasn't that sophisticated. Most people were a bit of a mess, true, but very, very few were genuinely evil. If you got that, you understood humanity.

So if someone had run from an aggressive or violent partner, then Joe wouldn't take the case or, if he had by mistake, their secret was safe with him. What he tried to do when the story was more complicated was ask the runner, when he'd tracked them down, for permission to tell his client that they were safe and, well, that they were OK. More often than not, the runners got that, said that was fine. The hardest bit of his new job was going back to the client and managing their expectations, telling them that though, maybe, they loved someone, the other person did not love them back. Sometimes, he didn't get paid. That didn't bother him too much. He was surviving. If he ran out of money, he could always get in touch with Zeke, who was forever asking him to meet in Virginia for breakfast, lunch, dinner, to chat about work. He loved Zeke, but he'd spent too much of his life in the shadows to want to work for the CIA.

Reilly had found a stick and was circling him at a bewilderingly fast pace, prancing, full of doggy joy. Joe smiled to himself. In Syria, he'd miss Reilly. But he would be in good hands while Joe was away. He'd found an old Navy vet, Alf, who'd been in the Second World War, who looked after Reilly when Joe was on his travels. The dog and the vet enjoyed each other's company so much that Joe sometimes felt like an interloper. Still, Reilly was his dog, the only living thing that truly loved him.

Joe could see it coming at him, a tsunami-style wall of melancholy at the memory of Katya. He did his best to sidestep it, thinking about the moment when Dominic had started to sob and Joe had given him a little hug. That was the truth of it: Joe could only survive if he felt he was doing some good. He would get Dominic's son back to him. That way, his own loss would feel less total.

He returned to his trailer, half-perched over a ravine, with a goodish view of the city offset by the possibility that it might collapse into said ravine any day now. Joe's strength as a tenant was that he didn't care, so he got a good imminent-death discount. It still cost him too much, but what the hell.

He started reading the file on the flash drive.

Jameela Abdiek had been born in Aleppo twenty-seven years ago, her father a colonel in the army, her mother a much-loved teacher. She became a star pupil at a *lycée* in Damascus and then, aged seventeen, made the move to California, prior to entering college to study English and American Literature. From the very moment of touchdown at LAX, she was no longer Jameela. She became Jam – or, more often, Jammy. Her family back home in Syria had enough money to make sure she lived the good life, renting a tiny but beautiful apartment three blocks from the Santa Monica Pier. It didn't say it in black and white, but Joe got a feeling that she'd ended up having way too much fun. There was a line or two on a few gossip websites, hinting at scandals that had been hushed up. One made some not-so-subtle hints at sex in a toilet at the Oscars with a Hollywood screenwriter on the make. Joe made a mental note to look up that particular sleaze merchant. Somehow it got through to her that when you go off the rails, you end up in a train wreck. Leastways, she got, not religion, but a conviction that TMI therapy was a force for good. She quit college and began working for Dr Dominic Franklyn. From that moment, the digital record didn't quite dry up but it got much, much drier. That first year in LA was brilliantly curated by the digi-snitches. But once she fell under the sway of Dominic, there was virtually nothing in the file about her life for the last seven years. She bore him a son, Ham, when she was twenty. And, seven years later, she and the boy vanished.

Joe closed the file and made himself a cup of tea. America was the greatest nation on earth, no question, but he still preferred tea to coffee. He went online to check his bank account and gave out a soft *woo*. The one thing you could say about Dominic Franklyn and his ice-maiden lawyer, Joe thought to himself, was that they didn't worry about money. The first tranche of cash had swished into Joe's account, two months' pay in advance, $120,000 in one fell swoosh and he hadn't even left West Hollywood.

The screenwriter was so easy to track down it made Joe laugh. His first name was Humfrey and his second was DeCrecy and there was only one of those online – or in the whole world – and he lived three blocks away. After another thirty minutes on the Internet, Joe figured out who he really was and what he did with some of his money and where he liked to go on holiday. Joe emailed him directly and DeCrecy agreed to have lunch on Joe, right there and then. Philip Marlowe, eat your heart out.

———

Marlene Dietrich blew a smoke ring at Joe while Frank Sinatra looked impossibly young in acne and a bow tie. The bar's theme was the Golden Age of Hollywood – the faces of stars from the 1920s to 1950s stared out from gilt frames, long-dead actors captured in repose, elegant for eternity. The stardust was wasted on the two customers drinking at noon on the dot, a morose Chinese man nursing a scotch, and Joe, sipping a pint of Guinness, Reilly slumbering by his feet, his snout on his paws. Unless he got a good run once a day – and he'd had that up in the canyon – he would turn into a cat. Unless, that is, he took a dislike to someone.

Humfrey DeCrecy entered the bar just like Peter O'Toole in *Lawrence of Arabia* had strode into the officers' mess to announce that he'd taken Aqaba. That is, he made his entrance with a theatricality bordering on farce, but it was very watchable. He had sandy blond hair in curly bubbles, slightly too long and not necessarily washed recently, bulging eyes, cornflower blue in colour, and finely chiselled cheekbones with the first flush of the burst little veins that mark an irredeemable drinker. He was tall, taller than Joe, built like a stick and dressed in a bile-pink shirt, white shorts and pink sneakers: a human flamingo.

'Hello, dudes!' he said. 'Surf's up!' His accent was West Coast, with a hint of something else, possibly the Deep South. He went up to the Chinese guy and asked, 'Mr Tiplady, I presume?' Joe corrected him before the other guy hit him and he joined Joe on the next bar stool along.

'My name is Humfrey Marmeduke DeCrecy. You can call me Mr DeCrecy.'

'That's a silly name,' said Joe. Humfrey growled, at which Reilly got up, nipped Humfrey on the back of the leg and then re-burrowed his snout in his paws.

'Ow!' whined Humfrey. 'Control that beast.'

'Don't criticise my dog,' said Joe, with an edge that brooked no argument. He ordered two pints of Guinness and, in hushed tones, called Humfrey a 'fecking idiot' in Gaelic.

Humfrey stopped dead, and his pop-eyes drank Joe in. 'So you really are Irish? Not just a plastic Paddy?' Joe told him to go play with himself, again in Gaelic, while keeping a mild but genuine amusement on his face. Humfrey was clearly a pain in the arse and funny, both at the same time. Joe liked him. It was kind of hard not to.

When his Guinness arrived, Humfrey downed it in one. He banged the empty pint on the bar, ordered a second, and closed his eyes and sat in a catatonic state for half a minute.

Then the pint appeared, and his eyes opened wide and he said, 'Paddy, people like you bombed London, didn't you? Naughty Paddy-dude.'

He shot Joe a look from the side of his eye that was somehow more knowing than Joe was comfortable with. There was, of course, no way that a Hollywood sybarite would know what Joe had done, or tried to do, during his years of useless idiocy. But Humfrey drained his second pint and was off again.

'What made you think of arranging to me meet here? Look at this place. Like so much else in La-La Land, we're worshipping at a shrine to falsehood. This one's shtick honours a past that didn't exist, or didn't exist the way they said it did. Look at these black-and-white photographs. Look at them! They give their subjects old-fashioned integrity, heh? Yeah? And the real people in those frames just weren't like that. The stars fucked the wrong people, punched waiters, snorted coke, befriended the mob and jacked up just like we do, dude, only the studios were much better at covering it up back then. Hollywood, then, was a lie factory. Still is now. The thing is, people, the people, they want the golden memories of a heroic age, not the tawdry reality of humdrum human failure. They want the lie. May I please' – he hiccoughed, unpleasantly loudly – 'have another one? Just the one. I presume Naughty Paddy-dude is paying, because I'm a little short at the moment.'

He shuddered, calmed down a little and sipped his third pint in the fashion of a normal drink, then looked at Joe out of the corner of his eye again, slightly bemused, and said, almost sheepishly, 'So, you wanted to talk to me?'

'It's about Jameela,' said Joe. 'I read something on the Internet, an old news story from eight, nine years ago, and I figured it might be yo—'

'Jammy!' He gave out a massive sigh. 'Oh no, is she OK? Tell her I'm so sorry. I feel so bad about it. The thing is, Paddy-dude, I really loved her. We both hit Hollywood at the very bang bang bang of the millennium, and she was such a hottie that I had to have her, and she found me amusing but we fought – oh my God! She had such a love of life. Such fun. The best sense of humour I've ever come across. And she could fight, she had a real temper on her. But she was, Paddy-dude, the most beautiful woman I've ever been to bed with. She had a body like a buttered angel. And in the morning she was so, so, so interested in words, in playing with the English language, in books, plays, poems. She loved Keats, could recite whole chunks of it. So romantic. The first night we' – his voice dipped an octave – '*made love*, I took her in the car and we drove off to the Pacific and watched the sun come up. It came up like thunder. I'm a Hollywood screenwriter and that's how the sun always comes up. Like thunder.'

He hiccoughed again. His eyes fluttered open and shut, then closed fully, then opened wide and he turned to Joe and said, 'She's not dead, is she?'

Joe shook his head. 'But she's gone missing. Good people want to know she's safe and well.'

'And who are you, anyway?' He'd gone quite cold.

'My name is Joe Tiplady and I'm a private detective.'

'Prove it.'

'Your real name is Dwayne Dunlop III, and you were born and raised in the Ozark Mountains, in Arkansas. Humfrey DeCrecy has been dead seven centuries. Your mother is English, from Essex, and you got the name from a crypt in a churchyard in Colchester when visiting family there. When you came to LA, you started out as an actor, but the stars weren't with you. You made three or four soft-porn films under the pseudonym Ronny Dymond. Then you made the switch to straight TV dramas. Your speciality is playing the man who gets murdered in the first five minutes. In the meantime, you turned screenwriter. You plagiarised your first screenplay, which was turned into a film, but you managed to get away with it, just. You've found a niche doctoring bad scripts for vanity projects but you think you're better than that and you might just be right. You affect to be a moronic hedonist but you anonymously give one thousand dollars a month to a leprosy charity, and you go to a leprosy centre in India once a year where you teach people with no fingers and rotting noses how to speak English. In the shallowest, most narcissistic, most self-obsessed town on earth, you are a fake. Deep down, you're a half-decent human being. Should I call you Dwayne or Ronny?'

'Humfrey; it's classier,' he said quickly. He studied Joe for a long beat, took a sip of his drink and then said, 'Clever Paddy. Is Jammy in trouble?'

'Big trouble.'

'I loved her. I let her down. I owe her one. So, what do you want to know?'

'How come that story about what happened at the Oscars leaked to the scandal sheets?'

Humfrey sighed into his beer and started to talk, this time in his real voice, a mongrel accent, mostly Ozark, a little La-La Land, a little Essex English. 'There's a private eye who works the low-life beat in Hollywood. His name is Rocky Montefiore and he's a snake. He used to be a gay-porn actor and he's set himself up as the guy to go to if you heard that some big hotshot hetero male lead is packing fudge.'

'So tasteful,' Joe chipped in.

'Yeah. Catch is, Rocky hoovers up the dirt, then sells it back to the star's lawyer or the studio's lawyer, or both, for double the money the *National Enquirer* will pay for it. Rocky picks up the gold and rats out the source to the lawyers, who close the story down.'

'So?'

'So, Paddy, I'm bi. Tommy Two-Ways.'

'Of course you are. You're Ronny Dymond.'

'Ronny Dymond only slept with women.'

'Fact?'

'Fact,' he said emphatically, sounding hurt on behalf of his porn pseudonym. 'A month before I had my fling with Jammy, I got down and dirty with . . .' And then he said the name of a Hollywood A-lister whose machismo was as bankable as a Goldman Sachs-backed IPO and then some.

'I was broke. Worse, I had the bailiffs on my tail. So, being a naïf in this town, I hear about Rocky – remember, I'd heard the good news about him, not the bad – go to him, tell him the story and he says, "Great, I'll get back to you." And then all hell breaks loose. The star's lawyer threatens to sue me back into the Stone Age. A big black van parks outside my condo, morning, noon and night. Jammy sees it, asks me about it. I tell her I don't know. It gives me the creeps, man. Every script I'm working on, the money phones me and says, "You're off the project." I'm dead in this town. Then my sister Sally comes up from the Ozarks for a few days with her little girl, Clara. My niece is the apple of my eye and, for some weird reason, little Clara thinks the world of Uncle Dwayne. We go to the beach, park the car thirty feet from the sea. It's a lovely day, not a cloud in the sky. I go to fetch ice cream. Sally is snoozing and Clara is running up and down in the waves. I can see them both but I'm around three hundred yards away. I've got three ice creams in my paws. Then, who bumps into me but Rocky. He says forget the story, it didn't happen, play nicely and then everything will be reset. I tell him to go play with himself and remind him that I told him the story and him alone, that it can only be him that's brought all this heat down on my head. "That so?" he says. "You sure you don't want to think this over?" He gestures down the beach and there's the black van, just by where Clara is playing in the sea. Side door opens and three men get out, the meanest mothers you ever did see. They start walking towards Clara, in step. Like they were synchronised, like robots. Clara's gone even further from Sally, who isn't aware of what's going on. So I say, "Stop this. Stop this now." Rocky says, "It didn't happen?" "It, didn't happen," I say. And he makes a call and the three mothers stop and go back to the van and it drives past us, real slow, and later that day I sign a document saying there wasn't a scintilla of truth in my sex story, blah blah blah, that I was led astray by the promise of money for falsehood, blah blah blah. But that's not enough. Rocky wants blood. He wants something from me, something that can get printed somewhere, which suggests that I'm a moral retard, so that if it were ever to happen that I had second thoughts about naming and shaming my fudge-packing star friend, then I have zilch reputation. The something, by the way, has to be true. And I give him the story about Jammy giving me head at the Oscars. It's not great for me. But it's the end of the world for her. And about that' – he turned to Joe and looked him directly in the eye – 'I am truly sorry.'

'And then?'

'And then she walked out of my life and I never saw her or heard of her since. I hope she's well and, if you see her, send her my most profound apologies.'

'Have you ever heard of a Dr Dominic Franklyn?'

'No.'

'TMI?'

'No.'

'Transcranial magnetic invasion?'

'No.'

'Plugging-in?'

'No.'

'Fort Hargood?'

'That would be a no, too. Do you want me to find out? To ask around?'

Joe told him that could be useful. Then he hesitated, thinking something through, before asking Humfrey the next question.

'Go on. Hit me with it. You can trust me.'

'I can trust a man who got into so much grief for ratting out his gay lover that he ratted out his girlfriend to make things better?'

'They threatened my niece.'

'You could have handled it differently. You could have gone to the police. You didn't have to drop Jameela in it.'

'True . . . But that was then. I'm a reformed character. I've been rebooted. You're looking at Humf DeCrecy 2.0.'

Joe laughed out loud. But he had to ask the guy the one question that was troubling him the most. It was the whole point of meeting him.

'When you knew Jammy, was she very religious?'

'You mean, Muslim-wise?'

'Yeah.'

Humfrey paused and thought about that for a beat, two.

'Well, she didn't eat pork. She drank – I mean, she drank alcohol – she snorted coke, she loved sex, she loved i—'

'Yeah, I don't want to know. Humfrey, I'm going to ask you a question and you're going to answer it honestly, and then you're going to forget I ever asked it and if anyone ever asks you about this part of the conversation, it didn't happen. Got me?'

'Got you.'

'Did Jammy ever strike you as someone who might join ISIS?'

'What?'

Joe repeated the question.

Humfrey was incredulous: 'You mean the psychos who kill people, anyone who doesn't agree with them?'

'Yes, them. ISIS.'

'No way.' He shook his head vehemently. Then he closed his eyes and held still for a mountain of time.

'So?' Joe asked.

'I don't believe it. I don't think she would do that. But she was, she could be, kind of crazy. I mean, she sucked me off in the john at the Oscars.'

'I don't want to know.'

'I'm answering your question, dude. It's a heavy question. I said no way immediately. But if I think about it hard, then, I gotta tell you, she got off on risk. She liked the extreme.'

Joe stared at him. 'So what's the answer to the question?'

'I don't think so. I really, really don't want to think so. But impossible? No. Jam in ISIS? It's possible. Where is she now?'

'Damascus, I think.'

'You going there?'

'Might be,' Joe said.

'Watch your head, Paddy-dude. Headless isn't a good look, even in La-La Land.'

Joe scowled at him to shut him down, and reminded him of what he had agreed to. Humfrey swore he would stay mum, they shook hands, and he said he would try to find out what he could about Dr Dominic Franklyn.

Outside, the sky had baked a faker shade of bronze. Joe breathed in the never-that-fresh air of La-La Land. His head hurt, and not just because it always did if he drank alcohol at lunchtime. It hurt extra because there were way too many dots and, much as he tried, none of them joined up in any meaningful way. He liked Humfrey and, in a funny way, he trusted him, but he'd worn what Katya used to call his stone-face for one moment in the conversation. The film star Humfrey had slept with? That would be Luke McDonald, who'd almost run Joe off the road the previous afternoon, hightailing it on the way to Fort Hargood.

———

A call from a payphone in downtown LA to a number in Langley, Virginia.

'You call too often. What do you want now?'

'There's an Irish PI working out of Hollywood, Joe Tiplady by name, who's been asked to go to Damascus to get back a kid from a Syrian woman, Jameela Abdiek. The party who's hired Tiplady is a Dr Dominic Franklyn. He's big in TMI, whatever that is. You interested?'

A pause.

'We'll look into it. Phone this number back in twenty minutes.'

The caller did so. The party in Langley was interested; very much so.

# TIRANA, ALBANIA

They never worked out how he did it. The muscle under contract – four of them, all ex-special forces, some ex-Delta, trained killers, hired by a front company and behind that another cut-out company and behind that the CIA – had a simple task. They had to look after one sixty-four-year-old man, slight, thin to the point of frailty, easily recognisable thanks to the gap in his teeth that made him look like a bit of an idiot, and an Abraham Lincoln beard hardly anyone else sported in the whole of Albania.

The cable summonsing Zeke back to Langley had been waiting for him the moment he returned from the meeting at the Albanian interior ministry. Zeke read it, sighed and found a seat in an empty briefing room overlooking the well-groomed yet morose shrubbery of the embassy garden.

The leader of the muscle was Francesco – Franco for short – 290 pounds of sinew turned to steel, crew-cut silver hair, originally from Hoboken, New Jersey.

After a time, Franco offered a polite cough and started speaking: 'We're here for your close personal protection, sir.' Polite as he tried to sound, his New Jersey twang gave him a flavour of the mobster trying to impress a judge.

'*Quis custodiet ipsos custodes?*' asked Zeke.

'Pardon me, sir?'

'That's Latin for "I'm like King Midas in reverse, here. Everything I touch turns to shit."'

Zeke's delivery of the line was pitch-perfect, reproducing the cadences of the vulnerable New Jersey psycho mafioso so closely that if you closed your eyes you would have thought Tony Soprano was in the room. The other grunts rippled with laughter. Zeke excused himself and went to the bathroom for rather a long time, returned and explained that he had stomach cramps.

Franco said that if they hurried to the airport, they could catch the only direct flight to JFK that day. Zeke countered that he had rather too much baggage, some of it bulky equipment that was classified and needed to be bagged up, and he would never get it through customs in the time they had available. (Later, they discovered that this was non-sense. Zeke always travelled light.) Franco gave way on that, so they had twenty-five and a half hours in Tirana to kill.

It was late afternoon, the sun sliding down towards a bank of gunmetal clouds blocking out the horizon. Zeke worked the room, enquiring politely where each of the grunts was from. Philippe – bald, unusually tall, sunglasses even though it was gloomy inside the briefing room – was from Vermilion Parish, Louisiana. The moment Philippe confided this, Zeke was off, chatting away in Cajun French to which Philippe replied, enraptured. Ordinarily a terse introvert, the man that Zeke's knowledge of Cajun had uncovered was a quite different human being. He signalled his transformation by taking off his sunglasses and referring to Zeke as '*Le Patron*' from then on.

Nahui was from El Paso, short, swarthy, always a smile play-ing on his face, his eyes and thick black hair clearly showing signs of Amerindian heritage. Spanish would have been an easy guess, but Zeke plunged straight into Quechua, the *lingua franca* of the indigenous peoples of the Andes. Nahui, stunned, struggled to return serve against Zeke's fluency in his grandparents' tongue.

Miller was enormously broad, blond, sullen, around fifty years of age and the toughest nut to crack. 'My ancestors spoke German, but I don't,' he said, closing down the old man's presumed approach.

Zeke's only request seemed hard to refuse. Zeke wanted to go to the main bookshop in Tirana and pick up a copy of *The General of the Dead Army* by Ismail Kadare. Franco said he would send one of the boys to pick it up.

Zeke smiled his simple smile and said, 'But Franco, I want to buy the Albanian edition, *Gjenerali i ushtrisë së vdekur.*'

'We can find that book for you, sir, no problem,' replied Franco. 'No reason for you to trouble yourself.'

'The problem is, Franco, I'm looking for the unabridged edition, which was published at the behest of Kadare's friend, Drago Siliqi, in 1963, during the Tirana thaw. Later editions of the book were heavily censored. They would be a waste of money.'

'What's the book about, sir?' asked Franco.

'It's abou—'

Zeke's cell phone trilled. 'Excuse me for a moment,' he said, and took a Nokia 1661, the lowest of low-budget phones, out of his jacket pocket. He hit answer and listened quietly and then, call done, he returned the phone to his pocket and continued where he had left off: 'It's about an Italian general who comes to Albania twenty years after the Second World War to try to find the graves of his countrymen slain here – the "dead army" of the title. He meets a German general doing pretty much the same job. It's a gentle yet melancholy satire, a disquisition on the tragic foolishness of blind militarism.'

This hit Franco, fifteen years a Navy SEAL, like the slap of an Atlantic cod across his face, and he fell silent. Philippe and Nuhai nodded; only Miller indicated with a slight shake of his head that he was against the trip to the bookshop. Franco sighed, intuiting somehow that he might be making a grave mistake, but he said, 'OK,' and the close-protection team and its subject threaded their way towards the vehicles.

The party consisted of a 'plain-clothes' embassy Humvee, driven by a team of out-of-uniform embassy Marines, and a black Chevrolet Suburban with armour-plated windows and an anti-car bomb, inner Kevlar shell. Inside the Suburban were the four contractors, all packing heat, with Philippe behind the wheel, Franco riding shotgun, Miller and Nahui in the back, and the package, Zeke, in the middle. The package was both protected and prisoner.

They set off towards downtown, in the general direction of Skanderbeg Square, named after a local version of George Washington. Skanderbeg hadn't defeated the British, but he had done something similar to the Ottoman Empire, for a while, in the fifteenth century. And so he'd ended up being the toast of a new, post-Versailles Treaty Albania and in time got his own statue, featuring a moustachioed brigand on his striding horsey. Back in the bad old days under Hoxha, you would have had no fear of being run over by traffic in Skanderbeg Square, because there wasn't any. You could have lain down in the middle of the square and fallen asleep, hearing only the *click-click*-heeled footsteps of the Sigurimi, Hoxha's secret police, coming to arrest you. On foot.

But that was then.

These days everybody who was anybody in Tirana got to prove that Hoxha had been an idiot by driving their own Mercedes or Fiat 500 from their house to the local coffee shop or launderette or office. The government was too busy lining its pockets to build a proper Metro or a tram network. Result: gridlock.

The Humvee and the Suburban inched forward through the constipated streets. Miller moaned, 'I hate everything about this country, but most of all I hate the traffic.' Zeke turned in his seat towards Miller, who was sitting diagonally behind him.

'Your accent? You're from Wisconsin?'

'Uh-huh,' replied Miller, as non-committally as he could without being overtly rude.

'Best Green Bay Packers team was back in '67, team that won the Ice Bowl. Coldest game ever played. Bart Starr suffered frostbite but won the game.'

'You son of a gun,' said Miller, his hard features now suffused with a smile. 'Bart Starr is my uncle.'

Later, much later, during the post-mortem, they agreed that Zeke had somehow unlocked something in every single one of them, but he had done so in such a disarming way that his psychological manipulation had gone unnoticed. And this against four men hand-picked by the most well-resourced intelligence agency in history to notice and react to exactly that kind of thing.

It was Zeke who suggested it first, that it might save everybody a whole bunch of time if they walked to the bookshop. Franco nodded and said, 'Miller, Nahui, come along.'

Leaving Philippe in the Suburban, and the other back-up crew in the Humvee glued in traffic, they were down to three close-protection officers and the package. The pavements were a little busy but not worryingly crowded. Zeke seemed happy to play his part, never leaving the centre of the loose triangle that Franco at the head and Nahui and Miller at the two base points created.

The bookshop was a piece of cake, or so it seemed at the time. Zeke spent a very long time chatting to a young female shop assistant, Ardita, at a desk at the back of the shop. She had close-cropped hair and blue glasses, and wore a sceptical frown that morphed into a beguiling sunniness when she was amused. Every now and then she would check the computer in front of her, clearly in response to Zeke's requests. One time she jotted down something on a notepad; shortly after that she picked up the store's phone, made a brief call, then put the phone down. The whole time, Miller stayed by the stack offering a view of the newest titles till he had them all committed to memory, and through the shop's window, a view of everybody approaching the entrance; Nahui lingered by the romantic fiction section and, it just so happened, a rear exit for staff members only; and Franco stood his ground in the middle of the shop, keeping an eye on the students and literary types mooching their lives away. Had the three spoken a word of Albanian, they would have been more concerned.

'*I sheh tre gorillat qe erdhen me mua?*' Zeke said, asking if she could see the three gorillas he'd walked in with.

Ardita dipped her head so subtly that none of the three watchers observed it. In Albanian, she replied, 'The big German-looking guy by the door, the giant in the middle and the South American one by Romantic Fiction?'

'That's them. They are my prison guards, in a kind of way. Without looking up or making a fuss, I need you to make a phone call in a minute. I want you to call a police officer. Write down his number. Tell him to meet me in one hour.'

'Where?'

Zeke told her the rendezvous.

'That's kind of a crazy place to meet,' she said. 'No one goes there anymore.'

'Let's just say I'm a crazy old man.'

Zeke whiled away the next fifty minutes making a microscopic search of the shelves, eventually buying a second-hand poetry book, then thanked Ardita for her help and walked over to Franco.

'All set, boss?'

'Yes sir,' replied Zeke.

'Get the book about the general of the dead you were looking for?'

'No, but I got an old book of poems, first published in 1927. *Poets of the Romantic Revival* by Geoffrey H. Crump.'

Franco shot him a look as if he was talking gibberish, but Zeke carried on talking, seemingly oblivious of his protection officer's response.

'I have got no idea how it ended up here, but it's one of my favourites. I lost my original copy years back, so today hasn't been a waste of time.'

Franco smiled blankly and led the way out of the shop. The vehicles hadn't made much progress, so they headed off down a wide boulevard called Bajram Curri to meet them. They hadn't got far when Zeke, at the centre of the triangle of escorts, stopped dead. To their right was an abandoned alien spaceship – or that was what it seemed – a low-slung pyramid, originally constructed in marble to commemorate the memory of Hoxha for evermore. But now his tomb was a memorial to a pharaoh everyone hated. The marble slabs had been stolen, the front entrance boarded up in a flimsy and half-hearted manner, the whole thing, close-up, coated in spirals of graffiti.

'Hoxha's mausoleum. This I must see.' He skipped towards the triangle and darted ahead. Franco, Miller and Nahui followed on behind, the strangeness of the building distracting them from the fact that the package was going off-track. For an old man well past his sixtieth birthday, Zeke moved surprisingly fast. The others did not want to be seen to chase him. He was, after all, a grown man. So they half walked, half trotted. But at that very moment, the Suburban, followed by the Humvee, zoomed towards them down the pedestrian path. The operatives looked behind them and clocked Philippe at the wheel, gesturing frantically that they should abort what they were doing and return to the vehicles. But that fresh distraction lost them three, four seconds. They turned to see Zeke sprinting to the pyramid. As he came up to the building, a stout wooden board swung inwards and then the pharaoh's tomb swallowed him up.

The muscle raced up to the board, which banged shut in their faces. Miller smashed into it, but it didn't budge. Then all three took turns to bash in the board using a series of karate kicks. On the ninth kick, the board's edge splintered open. They slipped inside and found themselves in a dark cavern, pools of water underfoot, a few random cones of daylight penetrating the gloom, tunnelling down where the roof slates had fallen in. Nahui produced a flashlight and its beam punched into the darkness. Nothing.

'Maybe we could track him through his phone?' suggested Miller. At that moment, something started to trill. Nahui trained his light on where the sound was coming from and illuminated Zeke's budget cell phone on the ground.

'Nope, we won't be tracking him by his mobile phone,' he said.

Zeke Chandler, of the CIA, had vanished off the face of the earth.

# BEIRUT, LEBANON

The plane landed at Beirut–Rafic Hariri sometime after dawn, the sky smoking, the air smelling of jet-engine kerosene and the heat to come. There are a handful of airports around the world named after victims of assassination – JFK, John Lennon – but, in terms of overkill, Beirut gets the palm. Joe knew his bombs, and he knew that the one that did for Hariri in 2005 was a big one, 2,000 lbs of TNT, leaving a crater in the road. The word was that the people who gained most from the bang were the Syrian secret police. So, not nice people.

Joe pushed through the taxi drivers thronging outside Arrivals until he found one with just an averagely dishonest manner, who agreed to take him direct to the Syrian embassy. Beirut was five thousand years old, they said, but it looked as though it had been built the decade before yesterday by a man with a concrete fetish. The defining feature was block after block, stacked up the slope from the Mediterranean like a ziggurat. That, and the heat. By nine o'clock in the morning, the sun had become a big fat psycho punching the earth and every living thing on its surface into submission. The fronds of the palm trees were a sickly grey; anything else that should have been green – pasture, lawns, little patches of grass – was dying or already dead.

The traffic was gloopy and the taxi driver ended up using a crazy but time-saving detour, or so he assured Joe by tapping at his watch, threading through the city's twin alternate universes. In West Beirut, men wore big beards and women wore black bin bags, so to speak. The Iranian embassy bristled with menace, watched over by a giant mural of an old guy with a beard sucking on a wasp. That would be Ayatollah Khomeini. In East Beirut, women wore miniskirts and men drank beer. Both sides, people sucked at hubble-bubble pipes and when they had a point to make, they jabbed a hand in the air, thumb high. Across the whole city, a host of people lingered on park benches and dead grass, loss in their eyes. They would be some of the million or so refugees from Syria, next door.

The taxi had to pull up two blocks away from the Syrian embassy thanks to cubes of concrete scattered on the road, as if someone had knocked over a giant sugar bowl. The cubes were there to prevent sui-cide truck bombs. Hanging around were a selection of heavies in green military fatigues and mirrored shades, toting sub-machine guns in a loving kind of way and giving anyone who lingered the thousand-mile stare. Beyond the heavies was a forest of razor wire, and beyond that was the embassy, which, once, had been a villa in the French style. It exuded a grandeur gone to pot, blended with fear.

By the time Joe had got to the front door, he was oozing with sweat. A heavy on the door patted him down, then he went through two metal detectors and finally he was shown a door marked *Visa Section* in English. Inside was a big ceiling fan that had lost the will to cool, and a small, fussy man with a light-brown slick of hair pasted over his skull and yellowing skin, who sat behind a desk too big for him. He wore a mustard suit likewise too big for him and sported General Jaruzelski sunglasses, shrouding his eyes. He scowled up at Joe nervously, and when Joe gave him his best East Cork smile he got back to wrestling with the nest of papers littering his desk. Above him, on the wall, were faded photographs of the two Zarifs, the Father and the Son. Joe looked around for Zarif the Holy Ghost but it must have been his day off. To the side was the Syrian regime's flag: three bands, of red, white and black, with two green stars on the white. The flag badly needed a dry-clean, like its government.

The waiting room wasn't that busy, boasting more chairs than occupants. In one corner was a biggish Middle Eastern man who seemed to be sobbing quietly to himself; waiting eagerly in the front row was a hefty man who was gargling Russian into a phone. The Russian gave the impression of being connected, but he wasn't that connected because, if he was, he wouldn't be murdering time in the visa section. The connected don't do the slow lane. But it was the third person in the room who held Joe's attention. In jeans, a psyche-delic Hawaiian shirt and flip-flops, riotously out of keeping with the embassy decor and decorum, was Humfrey DeCrecy – Hollywood screenwriter, libertine, screwball.

Joe sat down next to him and hissed in his ear: 'What are you doing here?'

Humfrey affected ignorance of Joe's presence, so Joe hissed again. Humfrey did a double-take and said, far too loudly for the hushed *amour propre* of the visa section, 'Paddy-dude! Surf's up?'

The clerk was fastidiously lifting one very important piece of paper from one very important pile and moving it to another equally impor-tant pile. He didn't look up; what he was doing was too important for that. But, mid-movement, he froze.

'Sssh!' Joe whispered to Humfrey.

'Such a small world, eh, Paddy-dude?'

Joe gripped his left wrist, hard.

'Ow!'

'Shut up.'

'Ow! You're hurting me, you big Irish brute.' His accent had morphed into soft-voiced posh girl, the captain of lacrosse at Cheltenham Ladies' College. He looked sharply at Joe, and then his free hand subtly indicated the clerk at his desk, his shifting paper still frozen in mid-air. It wasn't that difficult to decode the gesture: Humfrey would stalemate Joe, screw up his chance of getting a visa, unless Joe went along with his play. Defeated, Joe let go of his wrist.

'Listen, Paddy,' he whispered sufficiently quietly that the clerk unfroze and returned to shuffling his papers, 'I loved that woman and I let her down. I'm going to help you find her.'

'I don't need your help,' Joe said. 'Nor do I want it.'

'I'm coming with you. The alternative is that I screw you up here and every other step of the way. You do understand that I'm serious about this.'

His accent morphed again, this time into Ozarks hick. 'Tell me you get me and do that now, boy.'

'I get it.'

'Good Paddy-dude.' He was back to being La-La Land Humfrey now. 'You go first, then I follow.'

The visa clerk said his name was Mr Aziz, and he asked Joe the nature of his intended business in Syria and did he have a sponsor for his visit?

'I'm an art curator and I'm going to Damascus to pick up something, not of great monetary worth, but of poignant sentimental value, for a client who is now based in America. I plan to be in Damascus for a week, shorter if possible.' Joe handed Mr Aziz a fake business card he had had run up in LA, declaring Mr Joseph Tiplady to be a freelance art curator, and a fake letter from a fake business address in the dead centre of Damascus. Joe liked his cover story because it suggested that he could be a slightly crooked art dealer on the make, but no one the regime would worry about.

Mr Aziz twitched a little behind his big dark glasses and said, 'What is the object you're taking out of Damascus? Not something precious from our antiquity, I trust?'

'Not at all, Mr Aziz. It's a watercolour, done in the 1890s, a family portrait. It could have been couriered, but my client prefers that I retrieve the painting myself and bring it back to the States in person.'

'I see.'

Joe was pretty certain Mr Aziz didn't buy his cock and bull story, but nor was he that fussed about it to argue the toss. Joe filled in lots of forms and Mr Aziz took his passport and told Joe he could pick it up the next morning. He didn't mention the war that had killed half a million people and nor did Joe. That's diplomacy for you.

Joe returned to his seat to listen to Humfrey negotiating the chicanes of Syrian bureaucracy – and how good, or bad, his backstory might be.

'Nature of business?' asked the clerk.

'I'm a fancy-goods salesman,' said Humfrey, po-faced.

'*Fancy goods?*'

'Well, lingerie's my main line. Got to keep the morale of the troops up, you know.'

'Have you a sponsor in the Gulf?'

'Here.' He handed over his passport, in it a wad of hundred-dollar bills.

The clerk took the passport and placed it in his lap, palmed the dollars and magicked a visa stamp out of the drawer in one sweet fluid movement, exhibiting the most energy he had displayed the whole day. He returned the passport and made to usher both men out.

'It's all right, Paddy.' Humfrey smiled indulgently. 'I'll wait for you to get your visa in the morning.'

Joe ignored him and marched off, as fast as he could walk, and after turning back on himself a couple of times he felt pretty sure he'd lost him. By the time Joe had done that it was midday, and he was overheating and then some. He stumbled into a small Orthodox chapel, sunken into the ground, below pavement level. Joe had to crouch to get through the entrance, but once inside he gloried in the cool of the ancients. The chapel was gloomy, the only light coming from a handful of opaque barred windows and a small metal frame at the side of the altar bearing three rows of votive candles. The air in the chapel was still, holding a suggestion of incense. Joe slipped a few Lebanese pounds into a box, picked up a taper and lit a candle. The flame fluttered, then caught hold and began to burn firmly, and Joe knelt on a pew, crossing himself like the good altar boy he had once been, and said a prayer to the memory of his dead love, Katya, and a prayer for Roxy, locked up in the prison state. A heavily bearded Jesus with melancholy black eyes looked down at him from a gold-framed icon. Joe remembered a line he'd read in a newspaper: the journalist had said that in packed churches, he knew he was an atheist; in empty ones, he sometimes felt the presence of God.

Joe knelt there for some time. Nothing happened but he did no one wrong.

Seeking a low profile, Joe checked into a small, family-run hotel a few yards from the old Green Line, a long squiggle on the street map which divided Christian East Beirut and Muslim West Beirut in the civil war that had started in the seventies and trickled to a stop in 1990.

Joe dived into the shower and stuck it on cold, then dried himself off and had a snooze.

When he woke up, the sun was low in the sky. Time to do some work. Joe watched the footage of Jameela in the suicide vest again. Something about it troubled him – on top of the obvious, that here was a beautiful woman and a young boy showing their intent to kill themselves and others, oh so messily.

Joe was reflecting on the video, trying to tease out what Jameela might be up to, when there was a knock at the door. Not the ordinary, polite *tap-tap-tap* you get in hotels, but a theatrical drum roll. It could only be Humfrey.

Joe could have closed his computer and left Humfrey out of it completely, but for some reason he didn't. He opened the door, led Humfrey to the computer and pressed play, and it was his turn to see the video ending with the suicide vest selfie. Humfrey watched the footage in silence, scratched his curly locks, pressed play and watched it again. The video ended on the two of them, Jammy and Ham, facing the camera, mute, in their suicide vests, surrounded by seven warriors of the Islamic State.

'That's not her.'

'It's someone else?' Joe asked, puzzled.

'No, it's Jammy all right, but it's not her. She's not that kind of person. When I knew her she was alive and wild and crazy but she was *good*. She was a fine human being. That's her boy, right?'

Joe nodded.

'The Jammy I know, she was a bit crazy. But a suicide bomber? I don't think so.'

'For sure?'

'I can't say for certain. But I swear that she would never, ever, kill a child of her own or make him kill himself. There's something screwy about this.'

'What, exactly?'

'Good question. I don't know. Let's go for a walk, find an Irish pub, do some Riverdance.' And he jiggled his legs up and down to illustrate the art form, if art form it be.

They did go for a walk. The air carried a whiff of burnt rubbish and diesel fumes. The sun sank into the sea to the west, lighting the city a gloomy, darkening pink, then the colour of blood. At the end of the street, the prospect of the Med was made unlovely by a flyover choked with traffic; the deafening sound of car horns bleep-bleeping.

'By the way,' Joe said, 'a flight to Beirut, a trip to Damascus, that costs money. You said you were broke.'

'I was, very.'

'So?'

'Got myself some development money, Paddy-dude, development money.'

'Development money?'

'Breaking news: Hollywood has just heard there's a war on in Syria. Big money wants a Syria movie. Listen, Paddy-dude, it's Hollywood, it's just for show. They don't give a damn about the hajis chopping each other's heads off. They're really only interested in hottie teen archers saving fantasy worlds and cutie-pie robots tidying up the moon and saving Matt Damon from bad space aliens, but right now a Syrian movie tells the world the money's got a heart. It's a big fat lie but I'm happy to help them out, and, more to the point, help you find Jammy.'

Joe had a sense that this – going to Syria with the flakiest La-La Land fruitcake he'd ever met – was never going to be a good idea, but Humfrey was company and had money now and balls, and it was hard not to like the guy, infuriating as he was.

Around the corner stood the remains of a Roman temple of extraordinary beauty; they turned another corner and came face to face with a minaret of ethereal simplicity, one slim finger pointing to the reddening sky. Joe wondered about the men who had built this house of God so many centuries ago, when his ancestors were paddling about in peat bogs. Humfrey angled his long neck sideways at the minaret like the velociraptor in the kitchen scene in *Jurassic Park* and said, 'The concrete's wrong.'

'Explain to me the notion of right and wrong concrete.'

'We're not at home to Mr Grumpy, Paddy-dude. Jammy's suicide video is spliced, yeah? You can easily see that it's been put together using four separate clips. One, the downed minaret. Two, the city block morphing into dust. Three, the roundabout decorated with severed heads. Four, the selfie video of her, the kid and ISIS. You assume, don't you, that all four clips come from Syria?'

'Yeah. Where are you going with this?'

'Wait up. This here' – Humfrey pointed to the slender minaret – 'is the local build. Lebanon and Syria are states not even a century old, having been carved out of the old Ottoman Empire by the British and the French. This is the Levant, in Arabic al-Sham. The mosques in Beirut are the same as the ones in Damascus. The downed mosque in Jammy's video is all wrong. The concrete is different – greyer, coarser, newer – the minaret so much fatter. She's faking it. For some weird reason, Jammy's making out that Syria, the most screwed-up place on earth, is more screwed up than it really is. And that's odd.'

They hurried back to the hotel and went up to Joe's room, where he switched on his computer and they searched 'minarets dynamited'. To help clear his thoughts, Joe poured himself a hefty glass of Bushmills ten-year-old malt he'd brought with him. Humfrey gave him a sour look, so, with a proper show of reluctance, Joe poured him one, too. After a time Humfrey stumbled onto a page, and there was Jameela's fallen minaret.

Humfrey read the caption at the foot of the photograph.

'Bosnia, 1993. And the killers who toppled the minaret were not any kind of Muslims, but Croat Catholic extremists. Your religion.'

'I haven't been to confession for two decades.'

'Once a Catholic . . .'

'Shut up. Listen, Dwayne—'

'My name is Humfrey.'

'Your real name is Dwayne. But let's not fall out. You were right about the wrong concrete.'

Humfrey nodded, but Joe sensed he was holding something back, something secret.

'The Syrian movie you're working up,' Joe began. 'Who the hell is going to give you money to do the ultimate Damascus sob story?'

Humfrey started humming the theme tune from *The Lion King*.

'Mickey Mouse?' Joe asked, incredulous.

'Mickey Mouse. Swear to God.' Humfrey looked down the double barrel of his nostrils at Joe, taunting him to call him out as a liar.

Joe said nothing.

Humfrey smiled to himself and then announced: 'I need some hallucinogenic drugs.'

Joe told him that he was going to opt for a quiet night in. After Humfrey loped out of the room, Joe watched the video again and froze the frame showing Jameela and Ham in their suicide vests, then took out the photo of Jameela, bursting with bottled vitality, and held it by the side of the laptop and considered the two images, the playgirl and the wannabe suicide-homicide.

He poured himself one last long slug of Bushmills, breathed in its witches' brew of peat and dark Irishness, and, under his breath, asked the question that had been raging inside his head ever since Humfrey had worked out that the dynamited mosque had the wrong concrete: 'Jameela, why are you lying to me?'

Then Joe took another sip of Bushmills, then another, and another, but an answer to his question came there none.

Joe fell asleep soon enough, and dreamt of a little boy all in black running down a lane in County Cork in the rain. Joe shouted at him and he turned around and only then did he see it was Ham in his suicide vest, his thumb poised over the trigger.

# RAQQA, EASTERN SYRIA

Time wound back half a million days, or thirteen centuries. Under a molten sky, the black flag; under the black flag, they had tented over the sky. The canvas flapped in the hot noonday wind, carrying with it the smell of burning and the grit of war. The Euphrates glittered in the sun as it threaded its way through myriad muddy channels. In the city through which the shrunken river flowed, no radios burbled music, no TVs played Egyptian soaps, no one sang. Out in the open, the light burnt diamond-white; the shadows fell basalt-black.

In the main square, three small iron-barred cages faced each other, blasted by the furnace heat. In one crouched a man, still conscious – just – caged for one day by the Hisbah, the religious police, for smoking a cigarette. In the second, a man who had been caught with a Taylor Swift video on his phone; caged for three days, he had lost consciousness and, although on the final day of his sentence, he didn't have much longer to live. In the third cage was the torso of a man beheaded, left to rot for a week, the flies gorging on the bloodied meat of his neck. His crime had been selling SIM cards for cell phones.

Down a side street, a woman cloaked in black ran out of her house and grabbed her little girl who had wandered out. The little girl screamed, and the woman slapped her, viciously, because she was afraid that someone might notice that she had left the house unaccompanied by a male guardian, a *mahram*. She picked up her howling daughter and ran back into the house, almost tripping over the doorsill in her haste to vanish from public view.

Close by, in a shop, behind a curtain of beads, an old man, well beyond the fighting age, his beard far whiter than his grubby *dishdasha*, used a thick black pen to scratch over the face and hair of a blonde model on a dozen bottles of shampoo, whilst his young grandson, Haroun, looked on with a cold solemnity.

A lone motorcycle turned down the street, moving slowly, not much faster than walking pace. It idled past the side entrance to Raqqa's hospital, spun around and returned the way it had come, moving faster now. Ten minutes later it returned, followed by a second, then a third. The three motorcyclists came to a standstill, one hundred yards between each of them, in the middle of the tented-off street, as if they had the power to banish all traffic. Which they had.

Another ten minutes passed. In the distance, the rumble of artillery. An elderly green Renault Clio, its windscreen cracked, edged along, moving curiously slowly like the motorbikes, its progress hidden from the sky by the ceiling of canvas stretched from one side of the street to the other. The Clio wheeled by in first gear. The old man in the shop stopped his airbrushing of the blondes to observe its passing. Once it had gone, he spat twice on the ground at his feet. Haroun, nine years in age but his eyes glinting with a knowledge of inhumanity that made him appear immensely older, studied his grandfather steadily, and the old man closed his eyes and instantly regretted his act of reckless foolishness.

The Clio stopped directly outside the hospital's entrance, swaddled so heavily in canvas and plastic tarpaulins that the brilliant glare of day was replaced by a gloom, as if it were late evening. Beneath the awning, five people got out of the Clio and looked up, involuntarily, at the taped-off sky. Understanding that the Far Enemy's drones wouldn't pulverise the city but would target leaders' vehicles when they were on the move, Abu Bakr al-Baghdadi, the Prince of the Faithful, Caliph Ibrahim, had proclaimed a law that every home-dweller on pain of imprisonment should erect canvas tarpaulins twenty feet above all the main thoroughfares in the city. That way the Caliphate would render blind trillions of dollars' worth of eye-in-the-sky technology.

The Caliph's plan worked beautifully. His movements were all done quietly, with no pace and some subtlety; the point being that when the Caliph arrived anywhere, it should always be a surprise. Hidden within the people were spies – this way, neither the people nor the spies got any warning; none at all.

The Caliph's party: himself, overweight, heftily built, bespectacled, with a pronounced limp thanks to a bomb blast that almost did for him, his beard thick, streaked with grey, going white at the edges; Khalil, his bodyguard-cum-executioner, a moronic giant, powerfully muscled, dressed in black, his face cloaked by a black veil of muslin, carrying an immense scimitar; a guard, also in black, toting an American machine gun confiscated from the Iraqi army when they ran away at Mosul; Hadeed – an Iraqi, a former brigadier-general in the Amn, Saddam's intelligence service, now head of the most powerful of all the Caliphate's intelligence services, the *amniyat*, the Amn al-Dawla – dead-eyed, silver-haired, lean, showing a military bearing, his moustache noticeably and unfashionably thicker than his beard in homage to his former master; and a woman cloaked entirely in a black *hijab*, featureless, blotted out. Led by the Caliph, the party hurried in the hospital entrance.

Haroun followed them with his eyes, then his feet. As he left home, he gazed one last time at his grandfather, the old man's lower lip trembling, afraid of what might be to come, but the boy was off, darting out from the beads, running across the street to return to the factory where he worked and, more importantly, to follow the man held to be the closest to God.

As the Caliph swept inside, the hospital guards bowed their heads, caught unaware; women tending to their sick relatives hid behind their black *abayas*, scuttling to get out of his way. A child howled and his mother gave him a clout to shut him up, lest something bad happen; a surgeon in medical-green fatigues, grimy with dried blood, a devout Muslim, angry that his patients now lacked the simplest medicines, saw the commotion and wanted to challenge the Caliph about the shortages of antibiotics, blood plasma, bandages, but was blocked by his nurse. 'Don't be a fool,' he hissed, and the moment was gone.

Haroun caught up with the tail end of the Caliph's party as they threaded their way past beds full of civilians and soldiers – some amputees, some blinded, a few dying – turned right, and went down a set of stairs that led to the infant intensive care department. They were walking past a line of cots, from which wires led to bleeping machines, when the lights died. Someone swore, and then the Caliph's guard and Khalil the executioner produced flashlights, the beams criss-crossing, catching a breastfeeding mother nursing her malnourished infant in one direction, a black cloth over a cot in another. Lit by the flashlight beams, the party walked on through the darkness, reaching the end of the department, then down a second set of stairs, then down, down, down a circular stairwell carved in the rock until they came to a massive metal blast door. The guard rushed forward to knock on the door. It opened from within and then they were inside, Haroun darting ahead then merging into the crowd of man-children gathering around him.

This underground factory – brilliantly lit, powered by a set of petrol-engine generators different to those that powered the hospital – was a series of interlinked caves hacked out of the rock by the ancients, then vaulted by the Abbasid dynasty in the eighth century and improved upon by ISIS in the twenty-first. The Caliph stood on a raised section of rock overlooking the main space of the factory, one finger extended toward Paradise, Khalil by his side wielding his scimitar, its blade flashing in the electric lighting. Hadeed, the guard and the woman in black stood to one side, all eyes on the Caliph.

The workforce morphed into a congregation: one hundred and four boys, all below the fighting age of twelve; no girls, no women apart from the Caliph's concubine; ten men, mostly disabled in one way or another, lacking eyes, hands, legs. Only one man was whole; his name Timur al-Shishani, the master manufacturer: ginger, a delicate face, thinly bearded, skeletally thin, more spectre than man, his eyes carrying a glint of watchful, melancholic intelligence. He had the manner and appearance of the young Van Gogh. Timur stood at an angle to the Caliph, observing his child workers. All the boys seemed pale in the harsh light; the air was fetid, low in oxygen.

The Caliph started speaking in his softest voice, so quietly that everyone had to strain to catch his words, the boys spellbound, wide-eyed with excitement. The Caliph was the alpha and the omega of their existence.

'Lion cubs of the Caliphate,' he said. 'After our attacks causing the deaths and injuries of hundreds of the Crusaders, one would expect the cross-worshippers and democratic pagans of the West to pause and contemplate the reasons behind the animosity and enmity held by Muslims for Westerners, and even take heed and consider repentance by abandoning their infidelity. But the fever and delusion caused by sin, superstition and secularism have numbed what is left of their minds and senses. Their hedonistic addictions and heathenish doctrines have enslaved them to false gods, including their clergy, their legislatures and their lusts. As for worshipping the Creator alone and following His Final Messenger, then that is beyond their understanding. Rome' – his name for the West – 'wants a war of religion. They kill Muslims. They invade Muslim countries. So be it. We will conquer Rome, break their crosses, enslave their women by the permission of the Exalted One. When we are finished, they will weep for our mercy. We are few, for now. But already the whole world is afraid of us. The reason, my lion cubs, is simple: the management of savagery. There is nothing we will not do to defeat Rome. We are cruel to be pious. Focus is power. To build a true and pious Islamic State in Syria and al-Sham, we must hyper-focus on the management of savagery, as the scholar Abu Bakr Naji has written. We must be remorseless with our enemies. And our traitors, too.'

A murmur of consternation amongst the boys: *Traitors? What traitors?*

'The heart is another sign, linked heavily to the tongue,' the Caliph continued. 'Unlike other living beings, man is the most capable of eloquently conveying the content of his heart. He is even able to convey otherwise, by deceiving and betraying others, as is the character of hypocrites. To manufacture suicide vests in our factory here, quality control is most important. It's wrong to send a pious martyr, a *shaheed*, to his death, to Paradise, only for him to discover that his detonator or the explosive doesn't work, for him alone to die or, even worse, for him to be captured, turned around or exhibited as a prize fool because of a technical failure. Or, less bad than not working but still a major problem, premature ignition. What is the use of a suicide bomber if he blows up only himself? Rome will laugh at us. After a while it became obvious to the *shura'* – the high command of the Caliphate – 'that the quality of the vests from this, our most important factory, was poor, that one in ten, then one in three was not working. We are far fewer than the enemy. At Mosul, the second city of Iraq and the scene of our greatest victory, there were eighteen hundred of us and we defeated an Iraqi army of thirty thousand in the city, three hundred thousand in all of Iraq. The Americans had spent forty billion dollars on this army. The Iraqi army ran away from our most powerful weapon; the suicide bombs this factory produced. For the attack on Mosul we sent in twenty, thirty *shaheed* to attack army posts, and the enemy became so afraid of our fearlessness they stripped off their uniforms and fought with each other, the better to hide from our swords.'

Not too far off came the thud of explosions, the sound muffled by the rock but the shock waves still transmitted through it. The electric lights flickered momentarily and the Caliph paused to take a glass of heavily sugared mint tea from a boy servant. He took a sip and continued.

'They lost and we won because they have been seduced by the Satan of modernity. Our enemies are Rome and the moderns – Muslims who have turned from the true path to embrace the seductions of modernity. In this war, our savagery is our great shield. So if our suicide vests do not explode, our enemies will no longer fear us. And another factor we must reflect on is the cost. In the last twelve months, we exploded six hundred and fifteen car bombs. The explosives we use cost a great deal of money, around sixty million dollars a year . . .'

There was something not just actuarial but miserly about the way the Caliph spat out the figure – that he hated expense, he hated the monetary cost of jihad. Blood was to be spilt; treasure to be hoarded.

'At least there is no major problem with ignition failure in our car bombs. But here, in our most precious suicide bomb factory, there is, we now discover, a lurking serpent in our bosom.'

The boys looked at each other, wondering which of them might be the traitor.

'Faced with this slithering thing that crawls on its belly, hiding in our midst, pretending to be with jihad but actually working for the Crusader-Jews, working for Rome, we asked our dear brother Timur al-Shishani to investigate. He drew up a chart of successful detonations, premature ignitions and failed detonations. And only then did our error become obvious. Out of three hundred possible suicide-vest detonations, there were five premature ignitions. And eighty-six failed detonations. Someone in this factory is deliberately ruining active detonators.'

The lion cubs gasped in shock. Who was the traitor?

'Our brother al-Shishani studied you boys on the assembly line, all dutiful, all pious, all able to remember great lengths of the Quran, the

Hadiths. Al-Shishani is a great bomb-maker and he is cunning. He laid a trap for the traitor. He noisily discovered, then brandished, a faulty detonator which he had previously painted with an ultraviolet pen. He placed it in a box on his workbench, for everyone to see. Then he disappeared for a few days. On his return today, he discovered that the faulty detonator had been placed in a vest, the better to foil our jihad. But the creeping, crawling thing that did this was no match for our intelligence. Switch off all the lights.'

Instantly, all the lights died, apart from one candle, flickering at the Caliph's feet, held by the guard.

'In my hand is a UV light. Stand up, lion cubs, stand in line, and show me your hands. The innocent have nothing to fear. Those with guilt on their hands, they will be revealed.'

The Caliph stepped down from the raised pedestal of rock, followed by Khalil, his scimitar held vertical in his hands, its blade menacing in the candlelight. The lion cubs were in three rows, roughly thirty boys in each row, each boy holding out his hands. The culprit was in the middle of the second row. The moment the Caliph shone the UV light on him, his guilt was evident: on his hands, in his eyes. Khalil grabbed Haroun by the ear with one hand, causing him to sob with pain. Someone switched the lights back on as the Caliph walked back towards the pedestal of rock, Khalil following him, dragging Haroun along by his ear.

Haroun was, always had been, Timur's prime suspect: clever, aloof, the best and the most imaginative worker, but the most rebellious, an intricacy of trouble, through and through. Haroun dropped to his knees, watching, strangely cold-eyed, unfeeling.

'Has the traitor anything to say?' asked the Caliph, staring not at Haroun but into the crowd.

Haroun's high-pitched voice piped up as clearly as the *muezzin's* call at dawn: 'Sir, I was told to change the detonator by another boy. If I didn't, he told me he would kill me.'

The Caliph turned his gaze to Haroun, screaming at him: 'You lie!'

'No sir, it's the truth. I swear.' There was something so cold, so contained about Haroun's speech that it made it impossible to consider that he might be lying. If he was lying, then he was diabolically good at it.

'Which boy told you to switch the detonator?'

Haroun pointed his finger at the tallest, biggest boy in the room, more man than child. His name was Abdul, he was heavy-featured, sausage-fingered, thickset turning to fat, fully eleven and three-quarter years old.

'It was him, sir.'

'Is this true, boy?' The Caliph's full power concentrated on Abdul, his voice soft, almost caring.

Abdul mumbled something, but nothing comprehensible. He towered over Haroun. Hard to believe that the little one could bully an oaf like Abdul. What the smaller, younger boy was saying had the force of physical truth behind it.

'Is this true, boy?' repeated the Caliph, angry at Abdul's mulish incoherence.

Wide-eyed but stupid, Abdul's mouth fell agape but nothing came out.

'It's true, sir, everything I've said is true, sir.' Again the purest, clearest note from Haroun, his thick black eyelashes and liquid eyes the very picture of innocence.

'Boy? What have you to say, boy?' the Caliph demanded of Abdul.

Saying nothing, he sank to his knees, his neck lolling forward, head touching the ground in submission – a plea for mercy, not a denial of guilt. The Caliph nodded to Khalil, who let Haroun go and seized Abdul and yanked him up to the makeshift stage. Khalil ripped Abdul's shirt open, exposing his neck. Haroun, in the meantime, quietly walked down the steps to the factory floor and took his place amongst the boys below.

'This is God's justice,' cried the Caliph, and signalled that the execution be carried out. The woman in black turned her head towards Abdul and the powerful central light speared through her two veils, revealing her eyes to be of the brightest blue. She cried out something, incomprehensible to everyone present apart from Timur, who understood English.

'No, no, no, for Christ's sake, don't kill the boy!'

Hadeed punched her hidden face hard, twice. She took the full force of the blows, appeared to shrink physically, falling to the ground and curling up in the foetal position. But she had not finished.

'He's sick. Your Caliph, he's ill, mentally ill. There is nothing good about this place. It—'

'Shut the bitch up!' barked the Caliph.

Khalil raised the scimitar above her prone neck, but Timur, stepping out of his stupor, managed to place himself between the executioner's sword and the woman in black. None too gently, he picked her up in his arms and dragged her to his strongroom – the steel door was open – where he stored his explosives. He shoved her inside a cage, clanged it shut, locked it with a padlock and twisted around to exit the strongroom. She cried out once more, 'Don't kill him!' and then the great steel door closed behind him and her voice was silenced.

The Caliph spat out in Arabic that the sentence of death be carried out. Khalil raised the scimitar high above Abdul's neck. Understanding that speed was a kind of mercy, with a suddenness that startled everyone present, even the Caliph, he brought it down, slicing off Abdul's head. The blood from Abdul's severed carotid artery pumped so powerfully it hit the roof of the cave, then as the headless torso twitched this way and that, the jet of blood whiplashed around like a garden hose out of control. The Caliph, Khalil, Hadeed, Timur and all the boys by the front were covered with heavy splotches of blood. Abdul's head bounced once, twice, then fell off the pedestal to land at Haroun's feet. He kicked the head away as if it were a football.

'Behold, my lion cubs – the management of savagery. To be pious is to be cruel; to be cruel is to be pious. *'Allahu Akbar!'* – God is great – shouted the Caliph, and the lion cubs echoed him, their high-pitched voices fluting the phrase again and again, the intensity of it painful to the ear, the sound amplified in the close confines of the rock vault.

The Caliph raised one finger to heaven and then he and Hadeed were gone. Khalil, holding his bloodied scimitar aloft, studied Timur with an unpleasant stare, then he and the guard followed their master without a word. The lion cubs, many blood-spattered but curiously elated by the elimination of the traitor in their midst, returned to their work, chattering excitedly as they weighed the correct quantities of ball bearings and poured them into pockets in the vests and checked the wiring. When they grew just a couple of years older, they would become *shaheed* and enjoy the sweet glory of Paradise themselves, all one hundred and three of them.

# TIRANA, ALBANIA

As Zeke stepped inside the pyramid he was yanked off his feet and then pushed down into a hole in the floor to the right. He fell for a split second, only to be caught by a very fat man who stank of garlic. Zeke couldn't see clearly because his eyes hadn't adjusted to the gloom, but he could feel the girth of his saviour's belly. The fat man bounced him out of the way with his belly, only to catch the man who had pushed Zeke down. The fat man held on to the second man so that he could close the hatch above them. With the last of the natural light from above, Zeke realised that the second man was the Albanian detective, Agim Neza. The slight thud made by the closing of the hatch was masked by the racket created above on street level, as Zeke's American protection team karate-chopped the board at the entrance.

Zeke found himself in a thin tunnel, enormously long; at its end, some two, three hundred yards away, a single naked bulb. He mentally scolded himself, having not anticipated the tunnel. Tyrannies like secret tunnels, the same way that democracies like chat shows.

The party of three hurried towards the light without running, and, as it grew stronger, he could better make out his companions. Agim was wearing a leather jacket, his face wreathed with anxiety yet also sardonic, displaying a slight tinge of amusement that they might just be getting away with it; behind Zeke was the round tub of fat, wearing the cheapest suit he'd ever seen, face smothered by an enormous walrus moustache. Zeke became aware of a great snorting noise, only to realise that it was Mr Walrus, breathing hard, at the pace that Agim was forcing.

When they reached the light, the corridor hit a T-junction. To the left was a set of stairs, to the right more corridor. Agim fiddled with his smartphone and it let out a thin, piercing beam. As soon as that was done, Mr Walrus reached for a switch on the wall and killed the light from the bulb. The two men shook hands and Mr Walrus started leaving, to the right. Zeke had enough time to whisper *faleminderit* – thank you – and then the fat man was gone.

Agim led the way up the stairs, his phone punching out a narrow beam of light. A door at the top opened onto the basement car park of a shopping mall. The policeman led the way to a Fiat Punto with a crevice in the front bumper. Zeke studied it circumspectly. As Agim unlocked the car, he said, 'I am from Tropojë. We drive badly, but with courage.'

Zeke smiled to himself, then started to regret the chain of events he had started as Agim shot the Fiat out of the underground car park like Thunderbird Two taking off from its ramp on Tracy Island. No palm trees swung out of the way, however, for which Zeke gave thanks.

Agim didn't appear to like roads. He took a right down an alleyway, squeezed the Fiat up a kind of footpath, and turned left through someone's vegetable patch, only to emerge onto a main street, choked with traffic, from which there seemed to be no shortcut.

Agim examined the rear-view mirror, breathed an expansive sigh and announced, 'No one is following us.'

'They don't have to,' said Zeke.

'What?'

'You will be top of their list of suspects, as to which Albanian might have helped me do my Houdini act. We, er, they can track your phone.'

'It's switched off.'

'They can track your phone even though it's switched off. It makes it a little harder, that's all. In Washington, DC, they can hunt you down in ten minutes. Here, maybe we've got an hour before they lock on to it. Maybe less. Take this turn.'

Agim turned onto a side road and parked opposite a grim rectangle of concrete, subdivided into flats, the ground-floor apartments barred with rough wire to prevent burglars. Ahead was a café, twinkling neon, and outside it four or five cars and a few motorbikes. The Albanian picked up his phone, looked at it with disgust and rolled down his window.

'Should I throw it away?' he asked.

'Where are we heading?'

'Tropojë.'

'Why?

'You want to know about the CIA facility, don't you?'

'The facility that has nothing to do with the deaths of the seven fried ISIS men?'

'In the meeting you said five of the fried men had been in ISIS.'

'I was being conservative. Yes. I want to know about the CIA facility that no one at my level in the CIA knows about. What do you know?'

'Nothing. Only, whenever I hear rumours about it, people shut up. When I ask my bosses about it, they change the subject. Bejtullah' – and he switched to English here – 'Bejtullah, as you say, let the bag out of the cat.'

Zeke smiled to himself.

'My English is wrong?'

'Charmingly so. The correct expression is "let the cat out of the bag". But you've found something . . . ?'

'There is an old construction engineer who, under Hoxha, built many, many tunnels and bases in the mountains. He taught everyone in his line of business. He stays in touch with the young ones who do his old job these days, hears their gossip. He is my third cousin. If anyone knows the location of your secret facility, he will.'

'Agim, you married?'

'No.'

'Got kids anyway?'

'No.'

'OK. Tropojë's to the north-east, correct?'

'Yes.'

'Got any elderly relatives down south?'

'Yes, an aunt in Gjirokastër, not so far from the border with Greece.'

'How old is the aunt?'

'Eighty-nine.'

'Perfect. They won't give her a hard time. Go to that café, find a guy with a big powerful motorbike, and give him seriously good money to deliver your phone to your aunt, fast. Do that now.'

'So when they track my phone it will b—'

'Going at a hundred miles an hour in the wrong direction.'

Agim started to smile.

'We're fighting a trillion-dollar hunting machine with what's locally available. So hurry,' said Zeke.

Agim didn't hurry at all, but walked, a little half-heartedly, towards the café. Zeke liked that, liked the way he handled himself under pressure. The Albanian policeman reminded him of a much younger version of himself.

On his return, Agim fished in his jacket pocket and pulled out a lump of rock, knotted, gnarled, light in weight, like volcanic lava but somehow not like it.

'I forgot to give you this, a present. The shepherd who found the dead men on the mountain,' said Agim, 'he gave me this.'

'Fulgurite,' said Zeke in English. And then, in Albanian: 'My grasp on your language isn't good enough to say what this is, but in English we call it fulgurite. Rock that's been forged by lightning. Another name for it is "petrified lightning".'

'Mr Ezekie—'

'Call me Zeke, Agi—'

'Zeke, the way you speak Albanian is beautiful. The best.'

'Thank you. And thank you for arranging this. I'm worried that it might get you into trouble with your superiors.'

Agim started to laugh, his eyes closed. 'I am in so much trouble already, helping you is just the caking on the ice.'

Zeke grinned, but this time inwardly, only to himself, knowing that although the expression was new to the English language, he understood exactly what Agim meant.

'OK, so next, we've got to deal with the car.'

'It's an old car. Not mine.'

'It belongs to a cousin?'

'A second cousin.'

'They can dig that out in no time. They'll make a spider's web of your family, friends, colleagues, people you've slept with, loved, lost, met, helped, harmed, arrested – you're a policeman, after all – let go, prosecuted, freed. They're making that web right now, tracking all previous phone calls you've ever made, emails you've ever sent, websites you've ever watched. They don't do it in real time. They've had some clever folks from MIT, from Stanford, build a programme. They put your name in and out the data pops, billions of cunning searches in the time it takes to boil an egg. Less. Your second cousin ain't no secret anymore, Agim, and nor is his car. The registration number, they already know. If this was New York or London or Paris or Beijing or Tokyo, we would already be in grave trouble. But there aren't so many CCTV cameras in Tirana, so we have some time. We're going to have to walk away from the car, to lose it. The safest way to go to Tropojë . . .'

'Is how?'

'By bus.'

Agim's eyes widened in revolt.

'That will take seven hours.'

'Longer. We take local buses, we change, we go slow-slow.'

'That will take maybe two days.'

'Agim . . . I love my Agency. I love it what it stands for and I love who it defends – my people, the people of America, and beyond that the idea of democracy and the people of the world. Defends, more or less. Too often, right now, more less than more. We're in trouble, it's buckling out of shape, under pressure from ISIS, or more from our public's fear of ISIS, from us needing to be seen to do something, however batshit crazy that something might be. So you and I are on the track of something the Agency has gotten into, something secret and dark. We don't know exactly what the facility does, but we do know the results: folks, bad folks to be honest with you, but still human beings, end up electrocuting themselves in thunderstorms. The moment I got a whiff of this dark facility, I was ordered to head back to the States.

'I smell a rat. And so, my Albanian friend, do you. The solution we've got is to go see an old construction engineer in Tropojë. Now, I know my Agency. They're clever people, some of them the cleverest people on the whole planet. But they would never imagine that when one of their own executives goes rogue, he takes a slow bus. That ain't natural. They'll ask the Albanian interior ministry to put up roadblocks, but everyone will be looking for a deputy director gone rogue in a fancy car, not on a local bus. We want to do this right, we take the bus.'

And that is what they proceeded to do.

———

An encrypted cell call from Langley to Albania: 'You want the bad news or the very bad news?'

'Start with the bad.'

'We've got four contractors, seriously good operators. They have one job, to make sure the Angel Moroni behaves himself and goes straight back to Langley.'

'So?'

'They lost him.'

'Where?'

'Hoxha's mausoleum.'

'How?'

'He went down a bunny hole.'

'Like the White Rabbit in *Alice in Wonderland*?'

'Yeah.'

'And the very bad news?'

'They can't find him.'

'Tracked his phone?'

'Are you serious? 'Course we tracked his phone. He uses a caveman phone, out of the Jurassic.'

'So?'

'He dumped it in the mausoleum.'

'Any other leads?'

'We think he may have run away with an Albanian cop.'

'Can't you buy the cop? Cops here are cheap.'

'Word is he has moral objections. Anyways, he too has gone off the radar.'

'What about the cop's phone?'

'We tracked it to an old lady down south, Gjirokastër. She was gaga. My guess, we were being played by the Angel Moroni.'

'So?'

'We suspect he's heading your way. He's going to stick his weird Mormon nose into your facility.'

'He does that, he's dog meat.'

'We would not approve of that.'

'Bow-wow.'

'Not funny. We would not approve of that. Remember, soldier, we pay through the nose for your know-how. The bottom line? You do what you're told.'

'So Moroni sniffs the programme out, and there's jack shit that you're going to do about it, and I'm to do nothing?'

'You misunderstand me. I'm going to give you the telephone number of someone who, on occasion, can be useful. In our war against jihad, he is an ally. He has none of the Angel Moroni's scruples, to put it mildly.'

'Can't you text me the number?'

'No, that's potentially traceable. Encrypted phone calls like this one are much tougher to crack. You've got a pen and paper?'

The other party said that yes, he had. The number was read out.

'That's a Moscow number.'

'It is.'

'You in bed with the Russians?'

'The CIA is not now and never has been a soft-toy factory. You got trouble from the Angel Moroni, you call that number. You don't harm a hair on Ezekiel Chandler's head yourself, you understand me?'

'Got it. What's the name of the guy at the end of the line in Moscow?'

'Grozhov.'

'Can I call him now? Get him up to speed?'

'He's expecting your call.'

'Does this Grozhov know about the Angel Moroni?'

'Yes.'

'Does Grozhov like him?'

'On the contrary, Grozhov lost his favourite boy thanks to Zeke. Grozhov hates Moroni, hates him with a passion.'

'What about blowback – what if it goes wrong?'

'There won't be any blowback. It won't go wrong.'

'And our programme as a whole? It's black now, but if she wins the election, I'm hearing it's never going to get official sanction.'

'She won't win the election. He will.'

'Who told you that?'

'Grozhov.'

And then the line went dead.

# THE ROAD TO DAMASCUS

An elderly white Mercedes 300D taxi drove Joe and Humfrey out of the Beirut burbs, to the Bekaa, the great rift valley that cleaves the eastern flank of the Lebanon. Joe was wearing a suit and tie, sensing that when crossing borders you get a dividend from dressing like a bank manager. Humfrey sported a Hawaiian shirt of volcanic-lava red with blotches of vomit yellow, and salmon-pink trousers, sensing that behind outrageous dress you can hide in plain sight. Either one or the other ruse might have worked, but together, in the same car, they looked crazy. But their paperwork was good and the Lebanese had other, more important things on their minds, such as not losing the peace.

The road ran through small towns dominated by minarets, and passed vineyards and Crusader forts and monasteries and more minarets and then, it felt, the temperature dropped ten degrees or so as they encountered a long line of black flags with Arabic script scribbled on them.

'ISIS?' Humfrey asked the taxi driver. His name was George, and he had a black beard the size of a bush and was taciturn to the point of hostility.

'*ISIS?*' Humfrey repeated. George made no reply. Humfrey pressed him on who owned the black flags with a moronic insistence, pointing at them as the car whizzed by: '*ISIS? ISIS? ISIS?*'

'*La.*' No.

'If not ISIS – what?'

'Hezbollah.' And then George hid behind his beard.

Joe told Humfrey that Hezbollah was the Shia militia and, these days, a gallant ally of President Zarif – and, in an embarrassing kind of way, the West – in the war against ISIS. The West didn't like Zarif because he was a tyrant and tyrants were bad, but not as bad as ISIS, who preferred the seventh century to the twenty-first. Hezbollah hated the West, but ISIS were Sunni fanatics so extreme they thought the Shia were heretics and so they, the Shia, had little choice but to fight or die, and so they hated the West less than ISIS. Hezbollah soldiers were the grunts of the war in Syria and now, Joe explained, kind of the goodies – or, if not the goodies, no longer the baddest of the baddies. It wasn't the most sophisticated analysis of the current ebbs and flows of power in the Middle East, but it would do.

'You Hezbollah?' asked Humfrey.

'*La,*' said George.

'You Druze?'

'*La.*'

'Shia?'

'*La.*'

'So you're . . . ?'

'Sunni.'

'Why the big beard?'

George didn't answer the question.

They passed through a small town dominated by posters of a ferocious-looking cleric in dismal brown garb.

'Who's the dude in brown?' asked Humfrey.

'Sheikh Nasrallah,' said George.

'Who is he?'

'Hezbollah.'

Up towards the mountains ahead of them was a slurry of shacks, with tin roofs and plastic sheeting for walls: not-so-luxury accommodation for the refugees from the war on the other side of the border. After a spell, George slowed and they were at the frontier, situated on a lump of bare rock, Lebanon and the sea to the west, Syria to the east. Flags flapped in the stiffening breeze and, to the south, a murky red cloud boiled up a chunk of the sky.

Frontiers eat time. Border officials moved like sloths while Lebanese soldiers in American-style combat uniforms – with added Gallic shrugs – practised their nonchalance. They were good at that. On the other side of the razor wire, Syrian troops, in shades and Soviet battle fatigues, looked meaner. Joe and Humfrey chewed up an hour, and then another, standing on concrete waiting for stamps in passports, and then, after a meticulous search, they were in Syria.

The very first thing across the line was a roundabout: on it were two concrete plinths bearing posters of the two Zarifs, the old thug and the beanpole son, boasting his signature smudge moustache and giraffe neck in dark sunglasses and military fatigues. The colours had faded from too much sunlight, but the travellers got the point, that they were now locked inside and owed fealty to a colossal narcissism, one so monotonous and inelastic it could not change or evolve. It could only be broken, smashed to pieces by political violence; if that did not succeed, it would break anyone and everyone who questioned its right to rule.

Just down the flank of the hill, invisible from the Lebanese side, two tanks pointed their long snouts back towards the homeland.

The enemy was within.

The tanks weren't just for show. The grease on the soldiers' uniforms, the deep-black oil stains from the engine exhausts on the chassis, spoke to the fact that these tractors of war had been in battles and then some.

Hardly anyone had been trying to get into Syria. Tens of thousands, queuing patiently in the heat, were trying to get out. Twin photos of Team Zarif, father and son, were everywhere, but if the border queue was anything to go by, people were voting with their exit visas.

George switched on the car radio and a long torrent of Arabic splurged out, followed by the rhythmic chanting of the crowd: 'JayDee! JayDee! JayDee!' The American election campaign was news, everywhere.

'Switch that off,' said Joe, and the taxi driver did so. Humfrey had brought along some CDs, and he urged George to indulge him by slotting one into the Merc's audio system. So they took the road to Damascus to the soundtrack of The Beach Boys' 'California Girls'.

The land here was dying. Joe was reminded of the Californian desert on the track to Fort Hargood: parched scrub, yellow earth, grey-green stones under a relentless blue sky.

'Drought?' Joe asked George.

He nodded.

'Before the war?'

He nodded again.

'One year of drought?'

He shook his head and held up four fingers. So Syria, before the rebellion against Zarif broke out, had suffered four straight years of drought. A drought that long would have led to a whole army of peasant farmers being out of work, and armies never rest easy. The countryside didn't amount to much, apart from burnt scrub and boulders, populated by the odd flock of brown goats tended by Bedouin shepherds. George accelerated towards one such huddle that had drifted onto the road. The animals skittered out of the way just in time, but the Bedouin waved his crook at the Merc's exhaust and cursed them. A bad omen, Joe thought.

Every now and then they drove through hamlets of a few concrete houses, the Syrian flag prominent. Not being patriotic wasn't an option.

They learnt to read the subliminal signs of life in a war zone. Kids out on the street, lots of government flags, official checkpoints, buses and minibuses coming their way; traffic, people, busyness: the regime was strong.

Halfway to Damascus, George picked up speed to drive through a small town. There were no people about, no children on the streets. They hit a bump in the road, causing Humfrey to bang his head on the roof of the Mercedes.

'Hey, man, *shway-shway*,' said Humfrey, telling him to slow down.

'I didn't know you had some Arabic,' said Joe.

'I picked some up in Santa Barbara,' Humfrey replied delphically.

George didn't just ignore him, he sped up. Joe whispered to Humfrey, 'I guess this isn't a government strongpoint.'

The closer they got to Damascus, the more checkpoints they had to pass through. The soldiers registered surprise when they clocked George's passengers: a hippie drumming his fingers to 'Wouldn't It Be Nice', and a big European guy trying to ignore him. None of it was nasty, none of it quick. The soldiers checked their passports, chatted with George, opened the boot, walked around the Merc, then let them go, and they were off again, until the next checkpoint three or four klicks on. After one particularly painfully time-consuming check, Joe clocked George giving Humfrey the evil eye in his mirror. But nothing was said. It might have been Humfrey's choice of music.

Damascus stank of war. In a time of life and death, the ordinary things cities do in peace – picking up the garbage, cleaning the streets, sweeping the grit off the big roads, unblocking bunged-up drains – become unnecessary luxuries, the gilt of civilisation. So the city begins to rot, from within, from below. Piles of rubbish had banked up in the nooks and crannies of Damascus. Foul-smelling water seeped upwards from the sewers, the stink made worse by the pant of exhaust fumes in the afternoon heat.

George stopped to get his bearings. They got out of the Merc, stretched their legs, as a heavy-lift military helicopter clattered over the rooftops. Joe stared up and saw the side loading door was fully open, and made eye contact with the machine-gunner, hawk-nosed, brown-faced, boasting a long blue-black beard, who was staring down at him along the barrel of his weapon, as if to say: *Welcome to Damascus.*

The backwash of the chopper created a dust storm, scented with kerosene, forcing them into the taxi. George drove on, past a mural stencilled onto the side of a block of flats showing Zarif with stubble, staring out at the world from behind his shades. Joe hated PR men but he almost felt a pang of sympathy for whoever was spinning for the government of Syria. The iconic symbol of the regime? A giraffe in dark glasses.

War damage was surprisingly rare. Joe reflected that you wouldn't expect to see many ruins on the road from Beirut to Damascus, it being the main blood pump of the Zarif regime. Choke the road and the government would be dead. But it was grim enough: a shopfront blown in, on the road outside an axle, twisted, gnarled and red with rust, the memory of a truck bomb, nestling in a hole three feet deep, from which two boys, crazed with energy, took pretend potshots at the taxi with bits of wood carved to resemble Kalashnikovs. Shell splatters had left their telltale fans of shrapnel pitting on the road, on pavements, on the walls of buildings; windows were broken, patched up with wood or thick plastic but not replaced.

When they got to the hotel, they paid George. Joe gave him a bit more than the agreed price and then Humfrey chipped in with an extra fifty-dollar bill, thanking him for the 'interesting conversation'. George turned around in his seat and threw the bill back at Humfrey. 'Listen, you talk to foreigner, you talk to American, you must report it to Mukhabarat, secret police. So no one talks to foreigners.' And then he swore in English, very clearly, before Joe and Humfrey got out and the Merc left, tyres squealing.

The hotel was in the centre of town and upmarket. You could deduce that from the number of anti-truck-bomb concrete cubes dotted around its entrance. Within, it was rather fancy, or rather it had been fancy in 1983. It boasted pot plants that needed pruning, a water fountain supervised by an evil-looking cherub who had lost the will to trickle, a host of cheapskate Russian wheeler-dealers, none of whom looked as though they were engaged in selling anything to benefit the public good, a sprinkling of Arab businessmen and a blonde harpist tinkling her strings with an unforced melancholy.

The clerk on reception took an age to process their passports and hand out room keys. His brain appeared to be moving so slowly it was as if he was on benzos. When Joe finally got a key, it came with a piece of card entitling him to a free breakfast that had someone else's name on it. Joe was about to snap at the clerk when he looked closely at him. He had the eyes of a man who hadn't slept soundly in months. However fancy the hotel, the staff would never be that well paid, and some of them would be living on the east side of town, where the war was serious.

Joe said nothing and pocketed key and card. He turned around and his mind focused on something that he had been vaguely aware of earlier but hadn't quite registered. In the far corner of the hotel's atrium sat a fat little Buddha of a man, toying with a mint tea, holding a cell phone into his ear, staring into space.

The space he was staring into was occupied by Humfrey and Joe. But by the time they had dumped their bags and returned to the lobby, he'd gone.

———

The black tin sky creaked. Holed by a thousand stars, capturing Milky Ways of dust twisting and turning inside tunnels of saffron light, the roof of the Grand Souk fell quiet as the wind died. Joe swallowed his sticky tea and sucked once more on the apple-flavoured hubble-bubble pipe. The smoke was sweet-sour, harsh to the throat but somehow soothing.

In the souk, the war seemed so very far away. To Joe, it seemed he was in the oldest shopping mall on the planet. The tin roof had been added in the 1870s, but down the bazaar's narrow byways, choked with sacks of cinnamon, cedar, nutmeg, cardamom and turmeric, traders had been haggling with foreigners and getting the better end of the deal since before the time of Jesus. To the mix, these days, were added scimitars 'handmade' in factories in Guangzhou, and 'Persian' rugs woven in Shanghai. Prices were down because mass tourism had vanished with the war, but the knack for a commercial kill, that hadn't disappeared. Humfrey had gone off to explore the tat on sale, in search of a bargain. He had no chance against the home team, but it left Joe to zone out over tea and a hubble-bubble pipe, which was fine by him.

Joe let his eyes drift through a guidebook he'd picked up for a few dollars. Not far away was a museum of medicine, which told the story of Ibn al-Nafis, a thirteenth-century Arab physician who discovered the circulation of blood around the body three centuries before the Europeans did. Joe considered giving the museum a try, but knew he wouldn't. He liked knowing that there was culture to be had if he fancied it, but he seldom did.

*BOOM! BOOM! BOOM!*

The tin roof rattled and reams of dust, a century old, more, feathered down onto the floor of the Grand Souk. Two middle-aged European men in United Nations whites, who had been enjoying a hubble-bubble between them, jumped up and handed over their large-denomination Syrian pound notes to the tea shop owner. On their uniforms in small letters was stencilled *OPCW*, an international body tasked with a job from hell, the Organisation for the Prohibition of Chemical Weapons. Comedy fez on his head, the tea shop guy faffed around, trying, but failing, to find the correct change, judging his procrastination would in the end prove to his profit, which it did. As they fled from the souk, Joe caught him smile. He nodded at Joe, and Joe nodded back.

The exit of the two OPCW men had the effect of making visible someone who had been tucked out of sight, partly obscured by a hefty stone column: the squat little Buddha from the lobby, toying with a mint tea again, on his phone, again, and spending most of his time staring into space. But the space he was staring into just happened to be where Joe was sitting.

*BOOM! BOOM! BOOM! BOOM! BOOM!* The war was getting closer. Joe had lived through bigger, closer bangs in Belfast at the age of five, and he knew in his bones that, terrifying though the noise might be, it was two or three miles off. Figuring out incoming artillery is like riding a bike. You don't forget the knack.

Humfrey hadn't been brought up under the blue skies of Ulster during the Troubles, and so he hurried back and sat down, assembling and reassembling his limbs in the uncoordinated fashion of a freshly slaughtered lobster.

Humfrey's reaction to his very first experience of hearing shellfire was, to be fair to him, entirely in character: 'Got some hash, got some E.'

'Mickey Mouse will be so pleased his money is being spent on the best designer drugs in Damascus.'

Every now and then, Humfrey studied Joe with an expression of hurt. He did so now.

'Naughty Paddy-dude. We've got to print some stills from Jammy's video.'

'Why should we do that?' Joe asked sourly.

'We've been invited to a party tonight. We show the people the stills, they could tell us where they were filmed. We can block out the faces so that no one gets to see that it's Jammy and her boy.'

This seemed like a good idea but Joe couldn't bear to tell him so.

'Who invited us? Your dealer?'

Humfrey pulled a face, then started to laugh. 'Clever Paddy-dude.'

They returned to the hotel, used the business centre to print out two screengrabs of Jameela: one at Avalon; one in suicide vest, with Ham likewise attired, standing in front of the black flag of ISIS and the seven gunmen. Joe borrowed a thick pen and scrubbed out her face and Ham's.

At dusk, the streets of Damascus echoed with the *muezzins* calling the faithful to prayer, but mixed up in the sound was a lone church bell, tolling news of a different God. As night thickened, the streets became emptier, the traffic thinned. In the quietening, the soft thuds and gentle booms of distant artillery fire became more noticeable, less easy to dismiss.

The venue for the party was in a side alley off Straight Street, which gets a namecheck in the New Testament. The directions from the hotel concierge were simple enough: three hundred yards to Straight Street, then third on the right, then second left. It seemed pointless to hail a taxi, but a very good reason for doing so became obvious when, one hundred yards out, a power cut killed all electric lights and the city plunged into darkness. Every shadow became tinted with menace. Ahead of them, a silhouette lit a cigarette and Joe saw a man's face, fluttering in the sallow light of the match in his hand. He had a big emerald ring on the middle finger of his right hand, pitted skin, and cold, hooded eyes set deep in his skull. He studied Joe with contempt, then the match died and the gloom swallowed him up.

Petrol-fuelled generators fired up and soon the street was half-lit from shop-lights here and there, shadows dancing to and fro.

'Spooky,' said Humfrey.

Despondency for most Damascenes, but not for the in-crowd. Porsches, Mercs and SUVs lined the street on either side of the party venue, and from within came the melody of an Arabic soul singer, punched out through a sound system at a deafening volume. A side door opened onto a grand courtyard, with flaming torches illuminating a central fountain and palm trees disappearing up into the night sky. Waiters in tuxedos handed out flutes of champagne, while Bedouin in *dishdashas* stood guard, holding scimitars upright.

In Damascus, in LA, the same people flock to parties: the beautiful, the calculating, the drunk and the drunk-to-be. Humfrey was very much in the last camp. Joe was trying to sip – not gulp – a glass of champagne, when a shell thumped, dangerously near and terrifyingly loud. There were a few screams, then someone giggled, and that was picked up and soon waves of contemptuous laughter rippled out. These people had an urge to party, come what may.

Up above – three, four storeys high – people moved in shadow, their faces hidden by arches, looking down on the throng. A phosphorus shell arced across the sky, turning the night into brilliant day, penetrating the thick shadow of a second-storey archway overlooking Joe, and there was the squat little Buddha, on his phone, staring into space, Joe's space. The umbrella of light cast by the shell started to tighten as it fell to earth, and as it did so Joe glimpsed – or thought he did – two more figures standing in the darkest recess of the gloomy archway, that of a young woman and a boy.

Jameela and Ham? He couldn't be sure that what he'd seen weren't just blurrings on his retina imprinted there by the chemical brilliance of the phosphorus.

'Drink up, Paddy-dude. You never know, it could be your last,' said Humfrey.

'I dunno, but I think I just saw Jameela and Ham,' said Joe.

'Where?'

Joe gestured towards the archway above, now masked in darkness. Nothing could be seen.

'Your eyes are playing up, Paddy-dude. Drink up!'

Humfrey plucked three glasses from a waiter's tray, handed one to Joe and kept two for himself. Then he looked at him sidelong and said in his Ozark accent, 'In this game, Joe, you've got to remember the golden rule. Seeing is not believing.'

'What?'

'Enjoy the party, bro!' he said, and wandered off.

Joe walked towards the door on the ground floor, hidden in a recess, that led to the archways above – where, maybe, he'd seen the woman and boy. Only when he was in the recess did he see that, standing in deep shadow at the side of the door, there was a man in a suit, polite, bulky, not to be messed with. As Joe approached, the man pivoted on his feet and blocked the door. Joe mumbled an apology and tracked back into the thick of the throng.

For a city under the thumb of war, the party boasted an astonishing number of beautiful women wearing party frocks that would pass muster at an Oscars bash. And the men were no less fat and ugly than you would come across in Hollywood. Sex and genius is the dream; what you get is sex and money, which is not the same.

On the edge of the scrum were five or six young men in wheelchairs. They reminded Joe of his brother back in Donegal, crippled because of a stupid war. The grimness of that recollection made him slug his drink and stumble towards the next, and then the next.

Through a light haze of alcohol, he recognised some of the Russian wheeler-dealers from the hotel and, standing on her own, the melancholy harpist, in a black dress that hugged her figure from her neck to her ankles. She looked to be Russian or Ukrainian rather than Syrian. She saw Joe watching her and turned her back to him. It was a nice back.

Joe sidled up to her and remembered the sliver of Russian he had learnt from Katya: '*Kak dela?*' – how's it going?

'*Nichevo*' – nothing – she replied, as gloomy as gloomy could be. There was something so grimly miserable about her that, pig-headed Irishman that he was, he couldn't resist the challenge.

'*Toi naimet?*' he said, asking if she was a working girl.

'English asshole.'

She spoke good English, and now Joe had his opening, that of the mortally offended Irish patriot. 'I'm Irish. What you have just said, there is no bigger insult.'

'Irish asshole.'

'Thank you so much. *Irish* asshole makes all the difference. It matters to us, it really does. Has done since 1916. We are assholes in our own homeland.'

Seemingly against her own better judgement, she laughed.

In the centre of the courtyard, a belly dancer with a preposterous figure began gyrating, joined, seconds later, by Humfrey, who had somehow shrouded his psychedelic shirt in a gauze shift that he began playfully to unwrap to the rhythm of the music. The crowd whooped with joy, delighting in the dance-off between the official female entertainment and the American fruitcake walking on the wild side. Joe knew who he'd put his money on.

The harpist, Daria, originally from Donetsk, now caught up in Russia's frozen war with Ukraine, was on a contract to play her harp six nights a week at the hotel. She knew about Joe's connection with Humfrey, who was currently writhing, erotically for some, to Boney M's 'Rasputin' while the belly dancer looked irritated at the interloper.

'Are you two for real?' asked Daria. 'What are you really doing here? Are you an arms dealer? Is he?'

Joe shook his head and slurped his drink.

'Who is he? Who are you?' she said with a piercing directness.

'Humfrey is a lingerie salesman. I'm looking for someone.'

'Prove it, Irishman,' she said.

'My name's Joe.'

'Prove it, Joe.'

'Well, Humfrey is modelling some of his own lingerie right now. I can get you ten per cent off if you ask nicely.'

'No, idiot.' She pronounced 'idiot' wrong, making the last syllable rhyme with *yacht*, but not so wrong that Joe felt the need to correct her. 'If you are looking for someone,' she continued, 'who is it?'

Joe didn't know why, but there was a plainness about her manner that he trusted or that felt trustworthy. From his suit-jacket pocket he retrieved the printout of Jameela in her cocktail dress, full of life: the Avalon photograph.

For a fraction of a second, Daria's eyes opened wide, wider than they should have done had she not known the woman in the photo.

'No,' she said. 'No idea.'

'Sure?'

'I'm sure.' A pause, a stillness between them. 'She's very beautiful. Why are you looking for this woman?'

'I'm doing so on behalf of her family back in LA. They're worried sick about her and her boy, Ham.'

It was a credible line, and it had the virtue of being true – but not, of course, the whole truth.

'I'm not convince—' But Joe was interrupted by a commotion in the centre of the courtyard, as the belly dancer was throwing a tantrum at Humfrey's satire on her act. She slapped him hard on the jaw and the crowd went *woo!*, enjoying the comedy. Perhaps Humfrey did have a future in the movies, but not as a screenwriter. Jelly-legged, he staggered forwards then backwards, before slumping to the ground in front of her, playing dead. This performance infuriated the belly dancer even more. She started yelping something pretty toxic in Arabic, which only added to the merriment. Suddenly, the squat little man appeared by her side, said something soothing to her and courteously led her offstage. He returned, fast, to Humfrey, now back on his feet, and with a champagne flute in his hand the little man pretended to do a little belly dance of his own – cue mass hilarity – before proffering the glass. No harm done and the party continued on an even keel. Mr Buddha was quite the diplomat.

'Who's that?'

Daria explained that Mr Buddha was Adnan Qureshi of Qureshi Oil and Gas – billionaire, miracle worker, and host for the evening. She told Joe he managed to fund the Red Crescent across Syria, organised local ceasefires, and paid for a home for war orphans out of his own pocket. She stopped, sensing Joe didn't buy it.

'So he's the biggest philanthropist in the whole of Syria?' he asked.

She nodded.

'Philanthropy is what rich people do instead of paying their taxes.'

'Oh, he pays taxes. No question about that.' She smiled to herself. 'There are people in the regime who think he's a rich fat crook.'

'And you?'

'Well . . .'

'Well?'

'He's fat and he's rich and he's a crook. But he's not a bad man.'

'How can you be so sure?'

'He owns the hotel. He owns me.'

She caught Joe's sigh.

'He's not possessive. I can sleep with you, if he's not busy, if I want.'

'Do you want?'

'You can ask him' – which wasn't quite the answer to Joe's question – 'he's coming over now.'

And so he was, a great smile fixed on his lips.

'Mr Tiplady, I've heard all about you from your friend, the Ayatollah Princess.'

So Humfrey had traded up from 'Ronny Dymond'.

'My dear Daria,' Qureshi continued, 'I feel a trifle peckish. Could I ask you to find the chef and ask him to grill some shish kebab, fresh, for Mr Tiplady and I?'

'Of course, Mr Qureshi.' She skipped off, all melancholy gone. It was handled so gracefully that it took Joe a second to realise that what

Qureshi had done was get her out of the way so that the two of them could have a private conversation.

'What brings you to Damascus, Mr Tiplady, in our time of troubles?'

'I'm retrieving a work of art for a family back in the States.'

Qureshi's brown eyes studied Joe placidly.

'A work of art?'

'Nothing precious. A nineteenth-century family portrait that has sentimental value.'

'To be frank with you, Mr Tiplady, I don't believe you.' Qureshi surveyed the party genially and, just as genially, took a step closer. 'I'm afraid we don't have time to indulge in fantasies about an oil painting of sentimental value, Mr Tiplady. My enemies may come for me at any moment.' His hand gripped Joe's arm, holding him close. 'You're in Damascus to find Jameela Abdiek, are you not?'

'Jameela who?'

'We Syrians are killing each other in a stupid war, Mr Tiplady. But that does not mean that all of us are stupid. Stop insulting me. You and the dancing American used the business centre of my hotel to print a photograph of Jameela Abdiek in a suicide vest, and her little boy too, in front of an ISIS flag, with ISIS gunmen in the background. My chief of IT is loyal to me and brought this matter to my attention. His deputy works for me too, but also has acquaintances in the Mukhabarat, our secret police. Good acquaintances, you understand me? The possession of such a photograph here is no light matter. For the moment, my stock is low. I cannot protect you or your friend DeCrecy. Jameela Abdiek is not here. You are wasting your time. My strongest advice is that tomorrow morning, early, you go straight to Beirut. But before you go, you destroy this picture of Jameela and Ham and any memory stick carrying it. The Mukhabarat is a pitiless organisation, numb to human pain. They will already know about you and this picture. If they wish to, they will break you as they have broken so many others. You must leave Damascus first thing in the morning and forget about Jameela Abdiek.'

'So Jameela isn't here, is she? Because when that phosphorus shell burst, I could have sworn I saw her and Ham on that archway over there, standing next to you.'

Qureshi's brown eyes studied him for a time.

At length: 'She is not here now.'

'Where is she?'

'In Syria, the wrong word can kill. Forget about Jameela and get out of Syria. Fast.'

A waiter was coming towards them, bearing a silver platter laden with skewered meat, and behind him was Daria. Qureshi let go of Joe and clapped his hands above his head – 'Ah, food at last!' – and went back to being the all-smiling Buddha. Courteous as ever, he handed Joe a kebab skewer, then took one for himself. As he did so, a posse of unsmiling men in dark suits entered the courtyard. The way they held themselves signalled to all that they had the right, here, to do anything they wanted, whenever they wanted, however they wanted. Their leader was the man with pitted skin and sunken eyes who Joe had seen lit up by the flare of a match earlier in the evening. He looked no more pleasant on second acquaintance.

Qureshi said, *sotto voce*, 'That's Mr Mansour, from the Mukhabarat.'

'Friend of yours?' Joe asked.

'Not quite. A shame because the party was going so well.'

Qureshi turned to Daria and began a sentence in Arabic, then switched suddenly to English: 'This is bad. Tell her to warn Rashid. Tell her to get him out.'

Joe was trying to work out why Qureshi chose to say this in English when he realised that the waiter who had brought the kebabs was in earshot and was lingering near his boss. Daria nodded. Qureshi tilted his head slightly, a subtle gesture. Joe turned to follow his gaze and realised he was signalling that Daria might care to exit not via the courtyard entrance but the other way, through the kitchen. She disappeared without fuss. The moment she'd gone, Qureshi clapped his hands and announced that the party was over and thanked everyone for coming. People began to dribble past the Mukhabarat towards the courtyard door and then out into the main street. A number followed Daria inside, seeking the alternative exit. Humfrey, on the far side of the courtyard, had been deep in conversation with a young man in a wheelchair, but he looked up, sniffing out trouble, and started to make his way back towards the centre. Qureshi walked towards Mansour with a half-smile on his face and, shaded from the lights by a palm tree, entered a pool of darkness. Joe heard a soft metallic click. Someone killed the music but left the amplifiers on, so the courtyard echoed with the hiss of white noise.

Qureshi emerged back into the light, his hands cuffed behind his back. Mansour slapped him, hard across the face, once. Somewhere, a woman gasped. Qureshi, very much the older man and in no great physical shape, almost buckled to the ground but managed to stay upright, just. Mansour slapped him again, once on his left cheek, once on his right, then kneed him in the groin and slapped him so hard Qureshi fell to the ground. Mansour started kicking him in the head and neck as Qureshi tried to wriggle away from him, as lowly as an earthworm.

Joe's mouth had dried up. Mansour was in the Mukhabarat, so it was unsurprising that he tortured people or had people tortured. What was so sickening was the openness of it – that here, at Qureshi's own party, the Mukhabarat could hurt him and no one lifted a finger.

No one, that is, apart from Humfrey. He ran up to one of the fancy Bedouin guards, who was frozen to the spot, wrestled his scimitar from him and trotted towards Mansour, holding the sword high above him, its curved blade blood-orange, reflecting the light from a flaming torch nearby.

'Put the sword down,' Joe hissed. 'Stop this, Humfrey, stop it now.' But Humfrey ignored Joe and continued towards Mansour, more slowly than before.

Mansour kicked Qureshi twice more in the gut, causing him to cough up blood and vomit, all the while coolly observing Humfrey's advance.

'Humf,' Joe hissed once more. 'Stop it.'

The mad heroic bastard ignored Joe. Only when Humfrey was within striking distance did Mansour take out the gun from within his jacket and aim at Humfrey – and fire, once, directly at his chest. Humfrey's white shirt erupted into a mush of red and he staggered backwards, blood spurting from his wound, then slumped to the ground, the scimitar clattering on the stone as he fell. A woman screamed, piercingly, then shut up. Gun in hand, smoke curling from its muzzle, Mansour walked over to Humfrey and kicked him in the head. Humfrey's body moved with the kick, a pool of blood widening underneath. Mansour returned to Qureshi, kicked him once more in the face, then held his fingers aloft and clicked them.

Immediately, four of Mansour's goons swooped, two going to Humfrey's prone figure, one at the head, one taking care of the legs, trailing a slick of blood as they dragged him out. Two others got Qureshi to his feet and then he, too, was gone.

Mansour said something in Arabic and then in English: 'Mr Qureshi has been arrested.' His tone was conversational, smooth. 'Mr DeCrecy has been shot while resisting arrest.'

People started to drift away, avoiding the blood slick, most heading towards the kitchen. Joe's heart was pumping, his mouth bone dry. Silently, he joined the exodus.

'Mr Tiplady?'

Joe stopped, frozen, his back to Mansour.

'Excuse me, Mr Tiplady. We haven't had a proper opportunity to be introduced. My name is Mr Mansour.'

'I'm just leaving,' Joe said, not moving.

'We need to talk, Mr Tiplady,' said Mansour.

Joe didn't move. Joe didn't say a word. But he could feel the anger boiling inside him. If Mansour got much closer, he could jab an elbow in his face, knee him in the balls and go for the wrist of his gun hand, all at the same time. Mr Chong had taught him the move back in North Korea, and had him practise it so many times he was seriously good at it. But the rest of Mansour's posse? The other seven or eight of them? They would kill Joe in no time.

'Please don't ignore me, Mr Tiplady.' There was an oiliness to his voice that could grate on a man.

'Why don't we have a chat tomorrow?' Joe suggested, still with his back to him. 'I'll come to your office.'

'The protection of the state takes precedence over our traditional courtesy to guests, I'm afraid. Our work is more important than that. I suggest that you come with us now.'

Joe turned, a little, and then Mansour's phone rang. Whoever was calling had clout. Joe could see the deference ooze out of him into the phone. His cockiness had somehow dissolved. And that's when Joe started to run, run as fast as he ever had in his life, zig-zagging between the tables, curving around a palm tree and throwing himself through the kitchen entrance, where he was blocked by an unsmiling goon in a black suit holding a gun to his stomach. Joe backed out to see Mansour idling towards him.

Mansour slammed a balled fist into his stomach. Joe buckled, gasping, but made no attempt to fight back. Joe wanted to kill him, but if he tried, that would be the end of him.

'Duty calls, Mr Tiplady, duty calls. You stay here in Damascus. When we have time, we shall be talking to you.'

'Is that an order?' Joe asked.

'No. It's a polite request from the Syrian Mukhabarat.'

His smooth falsity, his affectation of politeness, was the thing that did it. Joe wasn't going to hit him, but he would be damned if he was going to play along with Mansour's psychosis dressed up as courtesy.

'You've murdered my friend. What are you really telling me? That I can't leave Damascus? Or that you're going to shoot me tomorrow, gun me down in cold blood as you did Humfrey? If you're going to kill me, do that now.'

'No,' said Mansour. 'You mistake me. You can leave Damascus whenever you wish. But . . .'

'But what?'

'You might not get very far. And these are dangerous times for Western travellers.' Mansour smiled bleakly. 'Goodnight. Go to your hotel. My men will escort you. We shall meet tomorrow. My advice: get a good night's sleep.'

No chance of that.

# NORTHERN ALBANIA

The old engineer, Ramiz, was extraordinarily frail, more skeleton than man, quite bald, in his late eighties or early nineties, sitting in a high-backed wooden chair with a blanket on his knees in front of a roaring log fire, his shrunken frame drinking in the heat. The house was high up on a bluff, twenty miles west of Tropojë, along a minor road that switchbacked through the mountains like a badly constructed amusement-park ride. It was late afternoon, the sky grey, overcast; summer on the plain by the coast, but up you here you could feel the threat of winter, hence the fire.

Ramiz's granddaughter, herself a woman in her forties, already silver-haired, meek to the point of offensiveness, showed them in, offered to make them coffee, withdrew. On the wall above the fireplace was a series of black-and-white photographs gone brown with age, of a much younger Ramiz, wiry, tall, curly-haired, authoritative in posture, standing with Enver Hoxha at the top of a hydroelectric dam; with Hoxha and Stalin – their fifth meeting – in 1951 in Moscow; with Hoxha and Mao in Beijing in 1956.

Zeke studied the details of the photographs while Agim watched him, fascinated, like a child would a magician, waiting to see how he might do his next trick. The old American had been right about the bus; arthritic as it was, it had been waved through nine out of twelve police checkpoints on the road between Tirana and Tropojë. The three times a police officer had bothered to board the bus, the smell of the huddled masses, their poverty, their hopelessness, had semaphored the pointlessness of the officer's task; he'd looked down the aisle, seen what he had expected to see, and got off before working out that hidden in plain sight in the third row was the CIA deputy director of counterterrorism everybody was hunting for.

Zeke tapped the sepia photographs of Hoxha, Stalin and Mao and asked, 'Great men?'

'Maybe, maybe not.' Ramiz's voice was a rasp, two dry sticks rubbing against each other.

'They're dead now, all of them. You can say how they really were.'

'In Albania, we have a saying: "No forest without pigs." Enver, Stalin, Mao, they were all pigs in their own forests. Mao was a pig, literally, a revolting human being, a pig in a silk dressing gown. Stalin was somehow worse. He smiled, was self-deprecating, told little jokes against himself, enquired about my health – and I was, to him, just a nobody. He'd studied for the priesthood and that smiling way he had, the physical expression of empathy, you felt it, you were warmed by it; in truth, he was a pitiless sociopath. I watched the people around him. They'd laugh at his jokes but their faces were green. People would disappear. Hoxha was different. Maybe not, he ended up the same, a snout with a crown. But to me, for me, to begin with, Hoxha had something – energy, authority, an intense self-belief, and a belief in Marxism–Leninism, that this new philosophy would make the world a much better place. He had passion. Over time, it – he – became more of a pig; paranoid, selfish, beyond stupid.' He shrugged. 'I served him willingly at the start; at the end, I served out of fear, lest he take the food from my mouth and give it to someone else.'

He fell silent; sap in the fire spat and crackled.

'I'm with the American embassy . . .' Zeke started.

'The CIA?'

'Yes.'

'And you want to know about the facility they've built?'

'Yes.'

'One of my old students designed it. Made no sense to him. Nor me. There's two nodes, ten miles apart. The first node is on the valley floor, set in the rock behind the turbine hall of one of my old hydroelectric power stations, something I built in the late sixties. The second node is all the way up one of the pipes, on top of a mountain.'

'I don't understand,' said Zeke.

'Nor does anyone else. In a dirt-poor country, with precious little oil or gas, they've taken a hydroelectric pipe out of action and put a secret train inside it. Down the bottom is a fancy laboratory. Up the top of the pipe is a prison, drilled into the rock. The prisoners, shackled prisoners, are shunted in the little train between their prison at the top and the lab down below. The logic is, it keeps the prisoners up top "sterile", away from the scientists in the lab until the scientists need them. And "sterile" from Albania. They cannot escape from the pipe. That was the deal with Tirana. Albania would host your facility so long as there was no possible chance of "contamination". As always happens, the people who dream this stuff up have no regard for humanity – that we need to breathe in oxygen and breathe out $CO_2$. The original prison up top generated too much $CO_2$. They had to build vents. The gossip is the prisoner—'

'Grandfather,' cut in the granddaughter, returning with a tray full of coffees, 'you'll bore these gentlemen with all your chat.'

But Zeke had heard enough to begin to put the pieces of the jigsaw together in his mind. He looked out of the window at the Toyota Yaris they had come in, a tiny car, two doors and a hatchback. Uncomfortable, yes, but the Agency would never imagine one of its own travelling around in something so tinny and unprepossessing. His adventure had been useful, no question, but now, having established some of the facts behind the black facility, his mind was turning to how best he could re-enter the world of the Agency; what was the most diplomatic way of him demonstrating the necessity for his vanishing act. He would need photographs of the pipeline; copies of the original design work for the train inside the pipe, the prison facility up high and the lab down below; testimony, witness statements from the guards. It was amazing that they had been able to keep such a facility secret from him for this long. It was, of course, a hi-tech, multibillion-dollar fingernail palace, hidden from proper scrutiny.

He had to return to Langley, the sooner the better, to hunt down who had signed off on this, how the black operation had been funded, who had lied to him. When he returned, he would raise merry hell.

The day was almost done, a miserable, forlorn sky becoming more grey by the minute. From within the Yaris a light flared. Behind the wheel, Jeton, one of Agim's cousins, thickset, useful in a fight, taciturn, the best possible man for such work as they were doing, had struck a match to light a cigarette. Zeke had left the Church of the Latter-day Saints because he'd realised that its founder, Joseph Smith, had been a confidence trickster. But he'd been a Mormon for the greatest part of his life and he couldn't abide cigarettes. He knew that the journey back to the mountain shack Agim had found for them as a temporary base would be torture. So be it. He turned back to Ramiz and started on his goodbyes. When on the run from the Agency, even for just a few days, it was never a good idea to stay in the same place for long.

———

After the rear lights of the Yaris had gone, Ramiz's granddaughter phoned her sister; the two of them loved a chat. They'd had two visitors, she said: a youngish Albanian in a black leather jacket and a much older man who spoke Albanian beautifully, maybe an exile or perhaps, a remote possibility, a foreigner. They kept on asking Ramiz, she said, about *'një trenit në një tub'* – some train in a pipe. Made no sense to her. She was worried that her grandfather might be going a little gaga.

To the west, some 4,800 miles away, a data vacuum sucked in the call, along with hundreds of thousands of others, and it flowed through a super-computer so powerful it could defeat every single chess grand-master since Alekhine, playing them all at once. The machine locked on to that phrase – *disa të trenit në një tub* – translated it, red-flagged it, and an email pinged to an analyst who made the connection and raised it to those high up his management tree.

A telephone call from Langley to northern Albania followed, giving exact coordinates for the location of the phone call and the likely route the party they were interested in would be taking right now. Then the line went dead. The time between the phone call from Ramiz's grand-daughter to her sister, and the call giving the coordinates?

Three minutes.

The party in Albania punched in the Moscow number he had been given.

The phone rang for five seconds, ten, then it was picked up.

'Grozhov.'

The caller spelt out the coordinates he had been given and the likely direction of travel.

Grozhov murmured that he had got it.

'You're going to do this thing?'

'It will be my pleasure.' Grozhov's voice was high-pitched, almost like that of a eunuch. But there was no concealing the excitement in it.

# DAMASCUS, SYRIA

*F**at spit-spit-spitting from a frying pan, dangerously hot, but for the life of me I can't turn the heat down because there are no control knobs on the hob. Qureshi told me to destroy the flash drive but it doesn't burn, yet the fat is getting hotter and hotter. The pan begins to spit not fat but bullets, then blood, then Katya appears, naked, terrified, running away from me, crying, 'Don't, don't, don't follow me,' and then the pan turns into a door and someone starts to knock on it but I can't open it because there is no door handle and the knocking gets more and more insisten—*

The god of dark dreams is good at this particular piece of devilry, calling on you to do a simple task, yet denying you the means to make it happen, so your mind plods around the same circle of cement like the mad polar bear at Berlin Zoo.

Joe, wide awake now but drenched in his own sweat, struggled to remain calm as memories of the night before crowded in: the crazy party, Jameela and Ham hiding on the balcony, Qureshi telling him to get out of Syria, Humfrey running at Mansour, scimitar aloft, then Mansour's gun snapping, the woman's scream and his friend dropping to the ground, blood oozing from his chest. Sweet Christ, it was no nightmare, it was all too real.

The knocking continued. Joe checked his watch. Three o'clock in the morning, the traditional time for a visit from the secret police. Clearly, Mansour had brought forward his appointment. Last night his men had escorted Joe back to the hotel through the silent, dark streets but left him in the lobby. The bad news was that Joe hadn't followed Qureshi's advice, and he still had the flash drive with the video of Jameela and Ham on him. It was in his suit pocket. There had been no sensible place to dump it. Joe had made up his mind to lose it first thing in the morning. They'd taken Qureshi, killed Humfrey and now they were coming for him.

The knocking continued while Joe pulled on his shorts. He considered brushing his teeth but that felt like he was pushing his luck too far. When he finally got round to opening the door, the person on the other side of it was not the party he had been expecting.

'Daria?'

She was dressed as before, in her full-length gown with the naked back, black high heels, her long blonde hair tightly braided down her back; Joe was naked apart from his shorts. The clash in their different styles of dress was unusual but, after all, there was a war on.

'Do you normally take this long to open your door?' she asked.

'I was expecting someone completely different,' said Joe. The surreality of the line unmanned him. Joe found himself smirking. That sense of the dread to come, that must have been getting to him.

The harpist studied Joe, half-amused, half-contemptuous.

'You're a hard man to find. The hotel has got you down in another room entirely. May I come in, Irishman?'

'Of course, I was forgetting my manners. Drink?'

She nodded. Joe found his precious bottle of Bushmills and went hunting in the bathroom for tooth mugs or whatever. To celebrate his happy mistake – that it had been Daria, not Mansour at the door – he poured her and then himself a generous portion of Ireland's greatest export.

'Peace?' she suggested as a toast.

'I'd rather drink to Humf. Did you hear what happened?'

'I did, yes. That's why I am here. Or mainly why I am here.'

They toasted Humfrey and sat in silence. Joe thought about the day he had first met him, in that tacky showbiz bar in Hollywood, how he had been both incredibly irritating and a force of nature, how he'd put on the front of being a callous, self-interested sybarite – which was true, but not the whole truth – and that he also gave time and money to the leper colony in India, that he had wanted to do his best to help find Jameela, that his life had been snuffed out in an act of heroism, that he and he alone could not stand the sight of a man being tortured in front of all of them. Humfrey had had a sister back in Arkansas. Joe promised himself he would track her down and tell her the grim news, when he left Syria. If he left Syria . . .

'I am sorry about your friend,' Daria said, breaking into Joe's reverie.

'Mad as a hatbox of frogs.' Joe shook his head. 'But an original.'

'And brave. I didn't see it, but people were talking about him running towards Mansour with a scimitar . . .'

'Brave and crazy,' he said. He poured two more drinks and she knocked hers back as if she didn't have long to live.

'If you sink my whiskey this fast,' Joe told her, 'we won't have anything left to drink.' She produced a slinky black handbag he hadn't noticed before and, with a magician's flourish, extracted from it a litre bottle of vodka.

'*Ochen horosho*,' he said, Russian for 'not bad, not bad at all', or something like that. She sat on the bed, prim and proper, very much the professional musician, and twisted open the screw cap of her bottle of vodka and poured a small bucket of the stuff into her tooth mug. Placing the bottle fastidiously on the floor, she drank her drink and studied Joe, still working on his second slug of Bushmills.

'Mansour's men, they're looking for me. I can't go home. Can I stay here the night?'

'What about Qureshi?' he asked.

'He's still a guest of Mansour.'

Joe shuddered, then said, 'They know I'm here in the hotel. There's some mistake with my hotel room number but they'll find me, and you, in the morning.'

'I have no choice. Just one night.'

'Well, of course,' Joe said in a slightly strangulated fashion, and sat down on a hard chair facing her. 'So?' he asked.

'So what, Irishman?'

'Give me some answers.'

'If I can. If my words don't hurt people I care about.'

Joe chewed that over and nodded his head. Maybe he was beginning to decode Syria. Maybe it was too late for that.

'Let's start with Jameela. Your eyes almost popped out of their sockets when I showed you her photograph. You know very well who Jameela is. So, where is she?'

She shook her head. 'Next question.'

'Come on. You've got to give me something.'

'Next question. If you don't want me to stay, I can go.'

'No, you can't.'

'Then next question.'

Joe's eyes dipped in submission. 'OK. Next question: why was it necessary for this sadist Mansour to beat the shit out of Qureshi and shoot Humfrey dead? Why do so in front of so many people? OK, he's the secret police. But aren't they supposed to kill in secret? Why turn killing into performance art?'

She poured herself another big drink but this time she didn't touch it. Instead, she stared at her mug in silence for a time, then took off her high heels and rubbed her ankles. Only then did she begin to speak: 'Mansour meant to humiliate Adnan, to show to everyone that he was finished. Humfrey was an accident. When he came to him with that sword high in the air, Mansour couldn't do anything but kill him.'

'Why was Mansour out to finish Adnan?'

'At the party you said that philanthropy was what rich people do instead of paying taxes, and I replied that Adnan paid taxes, no question. Think about my answer, Irishman.'

'I'm missing something here. You've got to help me.'

'Adnan is an oil man, yes?'

'Yes,' Joe said, as he finished the Bushmills in the mug and poured the last glug from his bottle.

'Syria's oil and gas,' she said. 'They're in the east of the country.'

'Wh . . . That's ISIS land.'

'*Da*,' she said, and her eyes swept the hotel room, a signal that they were entering dangerous territory.

'He pays taxes to ISIS?'

'*Da.*'

'So he's in bed with ISIS?'

'Not of his own choosing.'

'But he's an ISIS sympathiser?'

'Not at all.'

'How does it work?'

Still sitting on the bed, she leant towards Joe and explained the deal.

Adnan Qureshi's men ran the gas and oil refineries in eastern Syria. The regime got electricity and a third of the gas and oil; ISIS got two-thirds. Officially, Qureshi paid ISIS fifty thousand dollars a month to leave his refineries and pipelines un-sabotaged and his engineers un-dead.

'And what's the unofficial monthly number?'

'One million US.'

'Who delivers the money?'

'Qureshi has someone – Rashid. He is a surgeon, and because he is a surgeon he can cross the line, again and again. He saves lives in Damascus, he saves lives in Raqqa. Once Rashid told me that a dozen ISIS men came into his operating theatre because he was trying to save one of their commanders. If the commander died, they were going to shoot him and all the other doctors and nurses. Rashid ordered them to leave. He told them that it was his job to save lives and he didn't need the encouragement offered by their bullets. They left and the commander didn't die. So, even in Raqqa, he is respected. He is an extraordinary man, perhaps the bravest man I've ever met. Once a month he goes to Raqqa, saves lives, operates on ISIS fighters, children, anyone, pays tribute to the Caliph, hands over the dollars, talks to Adnan's engineers who are trapped there, who fix the pipework, who maintain Adnan's refineries. He negotiates with the Caliph in person. Every trip, he brings in medicines. If he can, he brings people out. Not big numbers, but he does his best in the worst of all places. ISIS make a great claim to be pious but they are corrupt beyond any imagining. Rashid pays them big dollars and buys lives.'

'Presumably Rashid gets well rewarded for playing the good shepherd?'

'Shut up, Irishman. No one in their right mind would dare to do what he does at all. Without him playing go-between, there would be no electricity in the whole of northern Syria. Without electricity, people in the hospitals would die. Without him, more people would be locked up there. During the French Revolution, there was the Scarlet Pimpernel, yes, saving people from the guillotine?'

'They seek him here; they seek him ther—'

'Well, Rashid is the Syrian Pimpernel. Believe me, Joe, Rashid is a hero. He saves lives on the operating table. He saves lives by keeping the power on. He saves lives by getting people out of there.'

There was something compelling about the ferocity of Daria's defence of Rashid that got through to Joe, cynical as he liked to pretend to be.

'When Rashid returns here – he is a calm man, but when he comes back from Raqqa, his hands tremble – he then has to deal with

Mansour, the palace, the torturers, all of them. He likes to listen to me play; he says the music of my harp soothes him.'

'You're his lover?'

'No.' She smiled at the thought of it – not altogether disagreeable by her reaction. 'He loves another. She is a good woman for him. Wild, crazy even, but she believes in him totally. They are deeply in love. Now that Adnan is in trouble, things will be bad for Rashid if he is in Raqqa.'

'Because the money tap has been switched off at the source?'

She nodded.

'So, officially,' said Joe, 'Zarif is at war with ISIS. And behind the scenes he lets Syria's oil billionaire Adnan Qureshi pay them off, to keep the lights on. The two blood enemies – the government and the most fanatical group of all the rebels – behind the scenes, in the dark, they do business together. That's a deal you keep hidden. But why would the regime want to screw up a deal that gets them oil and gas they wouldn't otherwise have?'

'The word is that the regime, or people in it, are still paying off ISIS. They just cut Adnan out. He looks rich but he isn't, or isn't as rich as he used to be.'

Her eyes focused on her drink. This time she considered it and took a careful sip, as if it was a new trick she'd just mastered. 'Adnan Qureshi throwing the party,' she continued, 'it was a big thing in this time of war. Maybe a show of wealth, maybe some kind of play, to show to the regime that he was still strong, carefree, still in control. Some people close to Zarif thought he was too greedy, that they could run the oil and gas just as well, that it was time someone taught Adnan a lesson in humility.'

'OK, that makes some kind of sense. But why Mansour?'

'Adnan has many enemies here, but Mansour is the most powerful of them all. He suspects . . .'

'Mansour suspects what?'

She leant even closer to Joe, so her lips were an inch from his ear. 'He suspects that Adnan is the treasurer of the FSA.'

'The Free Syrian Army?'

She leant away from Joe, then, very subtly, tilted her head up and down.

'Is he?'

She repeated her action.

'Christ,' Joe blurted out.

In the distance, a *pock-pock* of gunfire broke through the stillness of the night.

Joe downed his Bushmills in one and reached for her vodka bottle. He poured himself a big one and drank it.

'So now Adnan is out of the game, too,' Joe said. 'So no one knows about the oil deal.' She nodded, then touched her throat with her fingers.

'Well, just you and me left,' Joe added. 'No one important, anyway.'

Again, a slight tilt of her head.

'Zarif is across all this detail?' Joe asked.

'Yes . . . no . . . I don't know. He's both the leader of his gang, the Alawites, and its prisoner. Behind him are Hezbollah, the generals from Iran and now the Russians as well. Zarif's problem is he doesn't have enough people to hold Syria. The Alawites and the Shia and maybe some Christians – although there are not many of them left these days – are loyal to him. But three-quarters of the country is Sunni. He has to kill and torture to hold power. If he doesn't do what the gang around him want him to do, he won't live very long. Maybe he doesn't know what his men like Mansour do. No human being worthy of the name would want to know.'

'Why are you telling me all this?'

'Because I . . . Because I am Adnan Qureshi's woman and Ukrainian – worse, the worst kind of Ukrainian these days, a Russian Ukrainian.

So I am expendable. When Mansour finds me, I don't think it will be very nice for me.'

'Then get out.'

'Maybe I should. Mansour is pitiless.'

'Get out of Syria.'

'I can't. I am the last hope for what Adnan is trying to build, a Syria without Zarif and ISIS. He needs someone like me here. Adnan is extraordinarily resourceful. He plans for every eventuality.'

'Including being kicked in the head at his own party? Watching the one man crazy enough to stand up to his torturer being shot dead in front of his friends?'

'No, not that. But he would have planned for detention. So, I am waiting for his people to contact me, waiting for his connections to work.'

'From inside Mansour's fingernail palace?' Joe's words were freighted with such incredulity that she jolted as if he'd slapped her. A single tear welled up in her eye and slowly ran down her cheek. She stared at the carpet, not wiping it away. After a silence, Joe felt he had no choice but to continue.

'I'm sorry, but if Mansour can gun down an American citizen at a party in cold blood, in front of dozens of people, then I don't think you're being realistic. Where are you going to hide while you wait for Adnan's connections to deliver?'

'He still has some powerful friends in this city.' There was something mad, but madly impressive, about her belief in Qureshi. 'Here, you cannot move at night. The Mukhabarat own the darkness. In the morning, I can go somewhere, hide . . .'

She turned her head towards the pillows.

'So?' Joe asked.

'I'm going to bed. First, I shall take my clothes off. You can watch, if you like. Adnan used to like that.'

The thought of watching the lover of Mansour's prisoner undress unsettled him. Joe walked to the bathroom, had begun brushing his teeth when he saw her in the mirror, leaning against the doorframe behind him.

'Adnan liked watching me undress. But I liked it too. It made me feel alive.'

Her right hand reached up and untied the halter-neck, and she was half-naked when the marble of the hotel bathroom wobbled beneath their feet and the windows shook and only then came a great and deafening *BOOM!*

The hotel's power failed and they were cast into darkness. Joe tripped over to the window and pulled the curtain aside and then the dirty grey drape. Through the darkness, he could just make out a thicker darkness billowing towards him. Below, a car reversed at speed, its headlights catching people running this way and that, like ants who have had their nest poked by a stick – all of this manic activity happening to the soundtrack of car alarms bleep-bleeping. Growing up in Belfast in the Troubles as a small boy, Joe knew his explosions. That, and his later occupation.

'Car bomb,' Joe said. 'Big one – three hundred pounds of explosives, maybe more. Enough to make a crater a man deep.'

Daria edged past him and stood right by the window, staring out into the darkness, still half-naked. A ball of flame burnt a hole through the black smoke and its light tinged her with a red glow, as if she were on fire.

'Qureshi's villa lies in that direction, near Straight Street,' said Daria.

'So, another message from Mansour?'

'I think it might be, *da.*'

The fireball started to diminish, the red glow darkening to a crimson full of dread. He took a step towards her and kissed her on the nape of her neck, again and again. Neither of them had much of a future, it seemed. Very well then, let the present rule. Through the window they watched red tracer bullets loop across the sky. 'Fantasia', they call it, like the Disney film of old. Well, not quite . . .

———

In the morning, she'd gone.

The sun had long risen and Joe was lying on the bed, looking up at the smoke-stained ceiling of the hotel room, savouring Daria's smell, remembering Humfrey's extraordinary, foolish courage, and wondering, dispassionately, whether he would ever get out of Syria, when the whole room shook, but this time less violently than before. Another bomb, a big one, too, but this explosion was three, four miles away. He went to the window and to the east saw a pall of smoke climb up, blocking the risen sun. In the sky above him, pigeons ricocheted this way and that, bouncing off walls he could not see.

Joe took a shower, rubbed some wake-up-ness into his eyes and returned to the window. Something was wrong. The cloud of smoke hadn't faded. Rather, a dark shadow was enveloping the whole land-scape, diminishing the power of the sun. On the street, people had somewhere to get to and walked on. This, then, was how life was, in the centre of Damascus. The war was happening, no question, but for much of the time it was signalled by noises off-stage. People had a spasm of panic, then calm would return and, as best they could, they got on with the next hour of their lives. What you were left with was the slight but nevertheless very real threat of the next big bang killing you and, running along beneath that risk, not blaringly obvious but unremitting, a sense of fear in your gut that what might happen next would be worse, worse than before.

Joe felt no great hunger, but the human desire for stability, for routine, is strong, so it was down to the restaurant on the mezzanine floor for breakfast. It wasn't so busy: a few Syrians, the Russian wheeler-dealers he'd seen in the lobby and a score of officials in white uniforms with those letters, *OPCW*, printed on their uniforms. They kept themselves to themselves.

He headed off to an empty alcove by a window and listened out for more bombs, but everything was quiet. Outside, on the streets close to the hotel, Damascus seemed astonishingly normal. Too much traffic, too many concrete boxes for buildings, people hurrying this way and that, struggling with their work-life balance.

Yogurt, olives, stuffed aubergines: a banquet of a kind, while not so far away from him people were starving. He ordered tea, but nothing happened. He got up and tracked down the lone waiter, a grey-faced little man. The waiter apologised, wandered off, came back with a teapot and poured much of the hot water onto Joe's saucer and the breakfast table around his cup because his hands were shaking so much. After a time, he stared down at the puddle of hot water he'd created, unseeing.

His right eye twitched, once, twice.

Joe thanked him for the tea and he left. For the waiter, whatever he and his family had been through in the night, the war wasn't just a question of noises off.

Joe went downstairs and checked out the hotel lobby. A thin scattering of people, the water fountain still not trickling, an edge of nervous tension every time the revolving doors cycled into life. His eyes searched the room then settled, for a moment, on two men in cheap black suits sitting on a sofa by the hotel entrance.

He had company.

# RAQQA, EASTERN SYRIA

Two miles away, maybe three, a stick of barrel bombs fell on the city; the President's gifts to his unloving, unloved people. Deep below the surface, Timur al-Shishani was attuned to the particular vibration pattern of the barrel bombs, how the rock beneath his feet turned to jelly, wobbled, then returned to solidity so suddenly he could believe he had imagined the whole thing, were it not for a blessing of dust from the ceiling falling gently onto his desk. He looked across at the blue-eyed woman in the cage: she was asleep, or feigning it. The dust caught in his throat and he was seized by a coughing fit that somehow morphed into tears. Sitting with his back to the door of his strongroom, he wiped his eyes with his hands, then examined them. They were red-raw, from where he'd used the coarse wire brush to scrub them free of Abdul's blood. He'd forced himself to clean up the blood. Now he went to the little sink in the corner of the strongroom and washed his hands yet again.

'*A little water clears us of this deed.*'

Timur said it out loud, in English, and his slight frame was racked with tears of remorse, tears of shame, that he had done nothing to oppose the taking of an innocent life. He closed and opened his eyes, wiped the dust from his desk with a cloth, opened a drawer and retrieved the sturdy key for the antique, Parisian-built, walk-in safe that dominated his office. In the safe, he kept the dollars the Amn had given to him so he could buy explosives, ball bearings and detonators; that, and a few private possessions. He turned the key and the heavy door creaked open – he needed to oil it one of these days – and again the memory of what he had just done towered over him like a shadow on a cave wall. He'd watched the taking of an innocent life as if it were the swatting of a fly. The victim had been Abdul, a simple boy who had been guilty of being inarticulate; nothing more.

'*It will have blood; they say, blood will have blood.*'

Again, Timur said the phrase out loud, in English. Haroun had been the culprit, not Abdul. Of that, Timur had no doubt. So why had he gone along with Haroun's wicked pretence? A growing and yet necessarily secret detestation of his own function, his presence in Raqqa, his whole existence; a self-doubt so colossal that it had led to a moral inertia so locked in, so cemented, that he himself had watched the taking of an innocent child's life to protect a guilty one. Timur pinched his nose, the better to bring himself back from the depth of his remorse. Haroun was an orphan, but so had been Abdul; orphans were ten-a-penny in the bomb factory. Haroun's father and mother and three sisters had been killed by a Zarif bomb – but he, his grandfather and his older brother, Farzin, had all survived. Haroun had more family than most.

The smiling boy had been so clever, so alert to and so interested in the chemistry of explosives, willing, eager to learn from Timur; that is, until his older brother had been called on to be a *shaheed*, to be a suicide bomber. Farzin had driven a truck bomb towards a Syrian army checkpoint, but the soldiers inside had shot at him and, regrettably, he swerved in the opposite direction, blowing up a mosque and a line of children queuing for water at the water pipe. A holy act had led to a most unholy consequence. From that moment on, Haroun had become cold, driven, pitilessly selfish. His elder brother had died in heroic futuity; Haroun was resolved never to make such a mistake.

Making suicide bombs was a bleak occupation but, occasionally, the boys would generate some fun; the others never involved Haroun in this. They had grown to fear him. Only Haroun would have dared to sabotage the bomb-making process. And he had done so not out of hatred of ISIS, the organisation that had led to the death of his brother, but out of perversity. He wanted to wreck the bomb factory's work simply because he could. Timur had suspected him for a long time. And now his trap had sprung, but Abdul, a dull-witted but fundamentally sweet-natured boy, had been beheaded in his stead.

Timur returned to his desk and sat down, his face lit up in a cone of light from a lamp, the rest of the strongroom in shadow. He became aware of a sensation of being observed. Instinctively, he swivelled in his chair to see the woman in black sitting upright, her head clearly turned to him.

'Please may I have some water?' she asked in English. The sound of a woman's voice was unknown in the bomb factory and, stunned by it, Timur did not move. She repeated her request, her voice softer than before. Timur stood up, fetched her a bottle of water and walked quickly over to the cage where she was held. It wasn't the standard ISIS cage for prisoners, so small that they had to crouch within, but a largish space where she could lie full length on the floor if she chose. He passed the bottle to her through the bars of the cage and she thanked him with a dip of the head, then unscrewed the bottle lid and automatically lifted up the veil, exposing her face, blue eyes and much of her blonde hair. She drank urgently, all the while watching him stare at her. Her thirst sated, her hand moved as if to bring her veil down, to blank out her femininity, but instead she pulled it back even further. Timur's Adam's apple bobbed twice but he said nothing; nor did he move from his position, just on the other side of the bars.

'What is your name?' she asked in English.

'Timur,' he said.

The blue eyes bored into him, intensely.

'Free me, Timur. Let me go.'

'I cannot do such a thing,' he said.

'Why not?'

'I cannot.'

Her right hand undid her *abaya*, revealing a white blouse buttoned to her neck. Her fingers went to the neck of her blouse and she unbuttoned the first button, then a second.

A bomb exploded not so far away. The dust fell slowly, specks coiling in the cone of light by Timur's desk. When the tremors and the sound of the bomb had died away, the tension in the room grew. They both knew that for the Caliph's concubine to expose her face and hair to another man, it was *haram*.

'Let me go,' she said, her fingers undoing the third button.

'Please don't do that,' said Timur, turning his back on her.

'Why not?' she said. 'Why can I not have power over my own body?'

'Because if you do show me your body, the Caliph will have me castrated.'

She absorbed that and knew that he spoke the truth, and her hand moved away from the neck of her blouse. She started speaking, talking softly, as if to herself: 'If you do not let me go, Timur, then I will surely be killed. If you will not free me, you must remember me. My name is Beth. Remember this. I am a Christian, a woman of the Book. Remember this. I am an aid worker, and three years ago I came to Syria to help children. I came here to prevent the spread of polio, so that innocent children would not end up crippled because of the stupid superstitions of the ignorant. I came to fight darkness with the light of medical science. I tried to do good. And look at me now. I have been sold as a slave in a sex market, sold to the highest bidder. I have been raped, time and again. And now here I am, locked in a cage in a children's suicide-bomb factory. I am sure I am to be killed. If, when I die,

I want my family – they live in Oregon, by the Pacific – to know that I love them very much. Remember this.'

'If it is in my power and God is willing, then I shall tell your family this message.'

'That boy, the one they talked about executing. I know they often play games, stage mock executions. They have done this to me, time and again. What happened to him?'

Timur hesitated and then said, 'He was beheaded.'

There was a long silence, disturbed only by the faintest of trembling underfoot: bombs falling in the far distance. Eventually, he heard her sigh and say, 'I shall pray for you.'

'And I will remember you and pray for you, Beth.' In that place, at that time, the very utterance of her name had the intimacy of a love poem.

'You were quoting Shakespeare,' she said. '*It will have blood; they say, blood will have blood.*'

'I was. Something from my past, before . . .'

'Before ISIS?'

'Yes.'

Suddenly, they were both aware of a sound, a creak, a third presence. 'A rat?' she asked tentatively.

The door of the strongroom swung open to reveal the shadow of a slight figure cast against the wall. Timur had thought the door closed but, in his distraction over the execution, he had not shut it securely. The shadow grew bigger on the wall. Beth pulled her veil over her head, her fingers working quickly to hide any trace of her blonde hair from view.

'What's that you're saying, Master?' Haroun, cold-eyed as always, emerged into the light. The boy spotted a flash of movement and turned to the cage in which Beth was covering up the last strands of her hair – but not fast enough. The boy's face lit up with a smile of the purest sadism.

'The woman has been pleasing you, Master?'

Before his talent as a bomb-maker had led to his current occupation, Timur had been a fearless fighter, especially during the jihad against the Russians in his native Chechnya. But when he considered the boy who, only an hour or two before had faced the near-certainty of execution, something within him felt afraid.

'No,' Timur said.

'I am so sorry, I was mistaken,' said Haroun.

The cold eyes, as black as anthracite, examined Timur.

'What is it, Haroun?'

'I have a confession, Master.'

'What is that, Haroun?'

'It is about my grandfather. When the Caliph passed our shop in his car, he spat twice on the ground. He was not just disrespectful of the Caliph in that one moment, sir. There have been other times.' His voice lowered an octave: 'He . . .'

'Go on,' said Timur.

'I suspect that he might be an agent for the Jew-Crusaders.'

In Raqqa – in any city, town, village or hole in the ground held by the Islamic State of Iraq and al-Sham – such an allegation, of itself, was tantamount to a death sentence. Haroun stared up at his master, presenting an indelible image of childish purity and innocence, though Timur knew, now, that he was anything but.

'I think you must be mistaken, little Haroun. I know your grandfather to be a good and pious man and to be a true and devoted servant of the Caliph. He must have had a cough.'

'Very well, Master.' Timur waited for Haroun to leave but instead those cold eyes flickered this way and that, taking in the details of strongroom: the woman now masked behind her *niqab* in the cage; the door of Timur's safe open, and its specially constructed wooden shelves, pigeonholes for his precious detonators; on his desk a laptop with a dongle so that he could connect to the Internet – he was one of a tiny number of senior officers in the Caliphate who had authority to communicate with the world, so that he could know the latest prices for explosives; a long shelf of books, his battered Quran, books on Islamic law and jurisprudence in Arabic, and several technical volumes in English on chemistry and explosives. But none of those held Haroun's attention for long.

In the safe were stacks of hundred-dollar bills, six unusually delicate detonators and a paperback, on its front cover a picture of a woman with dark-red hair, exposed for all to see, in a dark-green dress with naked arms, holding high a crown of gold. In ISIS-land, ownership of such a book was an act of wilful pornography, punishable by death.

Timur followed Haroun's eyes and, despite himself, answered the unspoken question: 'It's a book about a bad king.'

Haroun tilted his head a trifle, made to leave, then turned back and asked, 'And the name of this king?'

'Macbeth,' said Timur.

'Is the bad king like our Caliph?' And the look of shock on Timur's face made the boy's eyes glitter with amusement. From not far off, footsteps could be heard.

Timur closed the safe and turned the key in the lock. As he was doing so, Hadeed entered the room followed by three members of the Hisbah, the ISIS religious police – young, long-bearded, dressed in white blousons and trousers cut off at the calves and black waistcoats. The Iraqi man nodded towards the cage where Beth was being held and said, 'Take her out to the car.'

Timur unlocked the cage and Beth stepped out, and as she brushed past him she whispered, 'God be with you.' The Hisbah dragged her out of the room, Timur looking down at his feet, the child Haroun grinning at some inner amusement.

The Iraqi sensed something untoward and looked at the master bomb-maker.

'What did she say?' Hadeed asked Timur.

'Nothing,' said Timur.

Timur and the woman had a secret between them. Hadeed, the intelligence officer, could smell it. He had risen from a home so poor it had been little more than a mud hut on the outskirts of Tikrit, by means of a mixture of ferocious loyalty to his distant kinsman, Saddam, and a gift, an intuition, for discovering people's silent terrors and then calibrating the exact amount of cruelty to get them to talk. In the Amn he had risen to become the chief inquisitor for the whole of northern Iraq. When the Americans invaded, they had ranked him on their set of cards of Saddam's most trusted lieutenants as the five of clubs, a lowly designation that had insulted him. He'd slipped away into the desert, faked his own death and ended up in Damascus. Zarif's Mukhabarat had kept him in prison but not duly uncomfortably so, and had waited for their moment. When the Arab Spring was at its height and the days of the Zarif regime looked numbered, they released him and hundreds of other undesirables and he joined ISIS. He wasn't remotely religious – far from it, he craved whisky and Cuban cigars, like in the happy times under Saddam – but he did seek vengeance against the Americans for what they had done to his country and for having destroyed his own place in it. For the moment, he would serve the Caliphate, not out of piety but out of something, to him, purer: hatred.

Hadeed knew that, eventually, he could dig out the secret from Timur and the woman, but that it would take time. She was an American pagan harlot, nothing better than a slave. She had first pleased then infuriated his master and now the Caliph wanted her out of the way. He'd grown sick of her. She knew too much to be kept alive but the Caliph hadn't quite made up his mind that she had to be executed. Timur had extraordinary gifts and had been a dutiful, pious and some-times brilliant servant of the Caliphate, but lately Hadeed had detected in him something new – what? An absence of zeal, perhaps, a lack of belief in their holy mission.

Haroun was sitting at Timur's feet, smiling in that unsettling way he had. Hadeed reflected that he was a strange one – a man-child, years older in manner and tone than his age and innocent looks would suggest. It had seemed pretty clear to Hadeed that Haroun had been the culprit, the saboteur, but he admired the way the little terrier had foisted the blame onto the big oaf.

The Iraqi put all of this to one side. Timur, the gifted engineer, was needed for a supremely important task.

Hadeed ordered Haroun out of the strongroom and cuffed him about the ears as he ducked out of the way. Then he turned his head a trifle, gesturing to the retreating boy.

'Smart, that one,' said Hadeed. 'I'm glad he didn't die today. He may prove useful to us elsewhere.'

'Oh,' said Timur blankly. His eyes did not look at Hadeed but were focused on the ground beneath him, an intimation of fake humility that riled the former brigadier.

'Berlin. London. Washington. No one in the West would suspect such a small boy.'

Timur remained still, his head down, his eyes on a square of concrete just in front of his feet, saying nothing.

'Timur, I am not just here to take the woman off your hands. We need your engineer's brain.'

'Why is that, Hadeed?'

'Our men have found something hidden in a tunnel.'

'What something?'

'Something left by Zarif's men in a great hurry.'

'What could it be?'

'Chemicals, Timur, chemicals.' And Hadeed smiled thinly, as if someone had told a joke but not a funny one.

# DAMASCUS, SYRIA

In the freezing canteen, dinner had been served, watched over by the two fat gods, the big one with the Doris Day teeth and the little one, the bad Elvis impersonator. Their breaths ballooned in the frozen air and their stomachs rumbled as the two cooks, the fatter, jollier one and the sad, pitifully thin beauty, both with the regime-ordained pudding-bowl haircuts, ladled out the only serious meal of the day: kimchi, rotting cabbage in brine, and sometimes, if the six of them were lucky, gristle with claws still attached. They ate it because they were so hungry, more hungry than they had ever been in their lives. Their teacher, Mr Chong, a sadistic sociopath, liked to call the meat 'chicken', but one of the guards who had a smattering of humanity said different. Joe asked the not-so-inhuman guard what food they were eating. He grunted towards a murder of crows. So that was their chicken.

Tired beyond all understanding by the day's exertions on the pretend battlefield, practising the killing of hyena-faced American and British bastards by rote, eating dinner was not the end of the day. Lessons continued through to nine o'clock at night as they sat on hard chairs, trying to stay conscious. Mr Chong took them through the theory and practice of Jucheism or Kimilsungism, the philosophy of the state religion. Even now, Joe could hear his dry voice intone:

'*The Leader is the supreme brain of a living body, the Party is the nerve of that living body, and the masses are only endowed with life when they offer their absolute loyalty.*'

Joe had hated every word of it. But not all the lessons were a sickening tribute to tyranny, not every moment was a waste of time. Mr Chong had also told them how to stay strong under torture and how to evade capture. And embers of memory from that last lesson fired up in Joe's brain as the two goons by the hotel entrance noted that he was gawking at them.

Mr Chong would have failed him on the spot. '*Never let the enemy know that you are conscious of them,*' was one of his favourite sayings. Had he seen Joe oh-so-obviously clock the Mukhabarat goons in the hotel in Damascus, he would have had him spend the whole day in the pit, a shiveringly cold open-air dungeon of mind and body. It was Mr Chong threatening to send Donnelly, their brigade commander, to the pit – effectively, for him, a sentence of death – that had forced Joe to act that day in the way that he did, to kill Chong. But all of that was a long time ago, and Joe had become a different human being. Or so he liked to tell himself.

The goons, as one, as if by remote control, stood up and began to make a move towards Joe. One was immoderately tall, pimply, more of a youth than a man, with a smudge of a moustache running along his upper lip and a bulge showing through his jacket. He either boasted a heart too big for his ribcage or he was packing heat. He made to go for his gun but the other guy gestured for him to put it away. Killing Humfrey in a private residence was one thing but the government had to keep up a bit of an appearance, and having a shoot-out in the fanciest hotel in Damascus would not look too good. Besides, Joe had a sense that killing him outright, immediately, was off the table. Mansour had wanted to talk to him. He wanted information. And that being the case, his minions needed to serve Joe up to Mansour alive, not dead. Knowing – or rather suspecting – that gave Joe a slight edge.

The second goon was no advertisement for the regime. In late middle age, he was short but had a thick, powerful torso, an oiled quiff of black hair that was so dark Joe suspected that it was dyed, and a face that was somehow blistered or bubbled with acne. The disfigurement made you want to feel sorry for him, to rise up against cheap and petty prejudice, but there was something about his posture, the way he carried himself, an innate and irredeemable violence about him, that let you understand he would never, ever let you. Nature had insulted him, and his whole existence was directed at making sure that no one else would ever repeat that mistake.

The non-trickling fountain and the stagnant, be-weeded pond it fed stood roughly midway between Joe and them. The youth headed for the north side, Mr Hideous the south.

Joe had picked up quite a few tricks in North Korea. One of them was simple: when cornered, and capture was unacceptable, go mad. He ran straight into the pond, seventeen stone of Irishman plunging in with all the grace of an elephant seal. It was deeper than it looked, soaking his suit trousers. He almost tripped up but staggered on and out, dripping water and leaving a trail of pond weed through the lobby; running, heading for two swing doors the staff came in and out of. Behind him there were shouts in Arabic, fast and vitriolic, but he cannoned through the doors. In front of him was a narrow passageway leading straight ahead. He zipped along it and pivoted hard, running up a set of stairs. Above him, the staff-entrance door clattered open; his pursuers were only three or four seconds behind.

At the top of the stairs, you could go two ways: to the left, the wallpaper was grubby and old-fashioned; to the right, newly applied, executive. He ducked right, running some way before coming across a door, unlocked, which opened onto a room full of private cubicles, a little like at a swimming pool or health club, but on a central table were objects you would find in neither: bulletproof vests, gas masks, biochemical warfare suits, and military helmets in blue neatly laid out, each one labelled *OPCW*. He picked up the nearest suit and opened a cubicle, got in and locked it. Seconds later, two things happened, from the sound of things: the goons entered from the staff-door side, but Joe could tell from the louder shouts that the chemical weapons team had come in from the hotel side and were outraged to discover two Mukhabarat poking about in their changing room.

'Get out, get out, get out!' cried an American voice with an unmistakably New Jersey accent. 'Or so help me God I'm going up to the Presidential Palace this minute and I will happily cancel this mission.'

A door slammed. Joe couldn't see anything, but his guess was that the goons had backed off. Joe began to strip off his soaking-wet trousers and donned the OPCW suit. The cubicle next to him opened, then slammed shut, and he heard a second voice, speaking in English with a slight Spanish accent: 'Hey, Marty? What's on the menu today?'

'We've asked to go to the site' – it was the same New Jersey accent; the speaker had to be Marty – 'for the twentieth time, where they deny using sarin. Mehmet has prepared all the paperwork.'

'If Mehmet has prepared all the paperwork . . .' said one voice.

'Then we're screwed,' said another.

'We have satellite intelligence,' continued Marty, 'that the site is safely in regime-controlled territory and has been for the last six months. The regime says, "You're welcome." We suit and boot up and get within five klicks of the site and someone, almost certainly the Mukhabarat, lets off a round of Kalashnikov fire. And then our hosts tell us – surprise, surprise – "We can't guarantee your safety," and we have to go back all the way we've come without doing diddly-squat, and another day in paradise is wasted.'

'Is that a fact?' said a French-accented voice.

'No, Laurent, it's a prediction.'

'I bet you one bottle of St Emilion that your prediction will come true today.'

'Listen, Laurent, you're going to win the bet. But I like drinking St Emilion so I accept your wager.'

More doors opened and closed. A new voice, British English, asked, 'What's Team Zarif saying about how many sites he's got?'

'Nineteen,' said Marty.

'And how many does our intel say he's got?'

'Forty-five,' said Marty. 'It's like Albania in 2002, when they told us they had no chemical capability whatsoever and – oops! – they found sixteen tons of sarin and VX precursors in rusting hulks on the side of the mountain, and they'd forgotten about it all. Difference is, there's a war going on and ISIS have a habit of rolling up and taking over territory, and – oops! – the government's forgotten about that little ol' chemical facility. So ISIS are gassing people with sarin, and we ask Zarif's people where they got it from and they say, "We dunno, maybe they made it themselves."'

'Bullshit,' said Laurent.

'Marty? Where's my suit? Marty, where's my kit?'

'Check your room, Teodor, maybe Supplies left it in your room.'

Joe moved his valuables – wallet, passport, flash drive, printouts of Jameela and Ham – out of his suit into a white OPCW holdall and pulled a gas mask over his face. The urge to rip it off again immediately was strong. Not so long ago, Reikhman, Katya's psychotic ex, had placed a gas mask on Joe and tortured him. Joe's fear of having his breathing constricted was real. But there was no way he was going to get out of the hotel unless he was disguised, and the gas mask was the only thing to hand.

Tentatively, he opened the cubicle door and stepped out.

'You the new guy?'

Ten men and two women were in varying states of dress around the room. Joe was the only one wearing a gas mask.

'Kazumi from Tokyo, right? You got in late last night?'

Joe nodded.

'I'm Marty, the team leader.' Marty turned out to be a big, thickset man with crew-cut ginger hair and a sardonic smile. 'We don't normally mask up in the hotel, Kazumi. It's kind of taking the chemical weapons security protocol a little too far.' Joe sensed a ripple of amusement in the ranks.

Joe attempted a Japanese accent while hoping the gas mask would make his voice sound less obviously Irish: 'It new suit and I want stress-test. Better find out it works here in Damascus, rather than on-site. Makes sense, Marty?'

'Yeah, sure,' he said. Joe's sigh of relief was short-lived, however. 'You've got a great Irish accent for a Japanese,' said Marty. He edged closer and stared directly at Joe through the mask. Joe's eyes, close up, didn't look the slightest bit Japanese.

'I'm half-Japanese, half-Irish. My da's from Tokyo, my ma is from Tipperary. She's an O'Grady.'

'Japanese-Irish? That's an unusual combination,' said Marty.

'But one allowed under the Universal Declaration of Human Rights, I believe.'

That sandbagged him.

'Heh, Kazumi, no offence. It's great to have you on the team.'

'Thank you, Marty. And one more thing: I bet you a bottle of Japanese whisky that the Syrian side will find a reason to block us today.'

'I'm hoping you're wrong there, Kazumi.'

The OPCW team trooped out of the changing room, picking up four UN security men and a phalanx of Mukhabarat in the hotel lobby. By the reception desk, Joe saw the two goons – the ugly one was on his cell phone, the young one was staring, listlessly, in their direction. A small coach was parked directly outside. Joe hurried ahead, got on first and walked down the aisle, and yes, there it was, a second exit door at the back of the coach, on the opposite side to the hotel. Joe muttered something to the others behind him, wrenched open the door, went down the steps, pulled off the gas mask and hurried towards a taxi. Joe got in the back, fished out a hundred-dollar bill and said, 'Beirut.'

The cab driver studied Joe in the rear-view mirror coolly, put the taxi into gear and drove off, taking a sharp left, then a sharp right, driving smoothly but fast.

The two goons darted out into the street, just in front of the coach, staring in the wrong direction, then spun round, but by that time the taxi and, in it, a man in a bio suit from the Organisation for the Prohibition of Chemical Weapons, had vanished down a side street.

'Beirut,' Joe repeated.

'No Beirut,' said the taxi driver flatly.

Joe was still looking out of the rear window, to check that they weren't being followed. Not even ten o'clock, but the sky was red, redder than before, the sun a blur of smoky bronze towards the east.

'Why no Beirut?' Joe asked.

'Beirut checkpoints, Mr Chemical' – in the rear-view mirror he studied his fare – 'no go checkpoint.'

The driver was right, of course. It was just plain crazy to try to get to Beirut looking like someone from a chemical-hazard horror movie.

They traded names: the taxi driver was called Hussein, but not, he added drily, Saddam Hussein. Driving a big Peugeot estate, Hussein was in his late twenties, thin, balding, wearing a fading but snazzy Union Jack T-shirt.

'Mr Chemical go tailor?' suggested Hussein.

'Mr Chemical go tailor,' Joe agreed, and the car slipped through a myriad of backstreets to an address not far from Straight Street. Outside the Peugeot, the air swirled with grit and it made Joe cough.

The tailor's shop window boasted mannequins in mock-Savile Row suits and, for visitors from the Gulf and western tourists, *dishdashas*, the ankle-length Arab robes, complete with *keffiyeh*, white headdresses that, when necessary, double-up as scarves.

'Mr Chemical go Mr Dishdasha?' suggested Hussein.

'Mr Chemical go Mr Dishdasha,' Joe agreed.

Joe paid the tailor, a dapper, pale-faced guy called Mohammed, exactly what he asked him, and then gave him a hundred dollars extra. Mohammed edged close to Joe, so that the rest of his staff could not overhear: 'Sir, will you be taking the clothes you were wearing with you?'

'No,' Joe said. 'You keep them.'

'Sir, too many people would have seen you enter the shop. The taxi driver, maybe, tells the Mukhabarat.'

Through the window Joe glanced at Hussein, sitting behind the wheel of his Peugeot, scowling at the world.

'*La*,' Joe said.

'Then maybe someone on my staff. No one can be trusted these days. Everyone tells the Mukhabarat. So, to protect ourselves, I'm afraid I'm going to have to call them.'

'Can you give me twenty minutes?'

'No, five. Please, go now.'

In the short walk from the tailor's door to Hussein's Peugeot, Joe inhaled so much grit he fell into a spasm of coughing. Now the sun was wholly occluded by a browning of the sky. He got in the car, cleared his throat and said, 'Beirut.'

'Beirut,' echoed Hussein, and the car slipped into the treacly traffic. Eyeing the *dishdasha* through the rear-view mirror, Hussein said, 'Nice.'

'What's wrong with the sky?' Joe asked.

'Sandstorm.'

And there was Joe thinking it must be the end of days. 'How long will it last?'

'Three, four days.' And then, after a pause, Hussein asked, 'Checkpoints, passport, no problem?'

Good question. Joe had specifically been told by Mansour not to leave Damascus. Worse, Joe was some kind of associate of Qureshi – or at least he would have to explain why he had been a guest at his party.

And worst, he had fled Qureshi's hotel in a stolen bio suit. The very first roadblock Joe came to, he would be stopped. His *dishdasha* looked local but his Irish nose didn't. Nor did his passport. If by some crazy luck Joe made it to the border, the moment his passport was examined there he would be held. So he had to think again. He could go to the Irish embassy or consulate, the Swiss or Swedish, whatever, and get some diplomatic protection. But Joe had a feeling that if Mansour were happy to kill Humfrey in cold blood, he wouldn't be that fussed about diplomatic niceties.

Joe was trapped. If he tried to flee Damascus, Mansour would track him down. If he stayed, he was dog meat. He could go back to the hotel and sit in his room and go bonkers staring at the wallpaper, waiting for the knock on the door. Only, next time, it wouldn't be Daria.

Or he could do his job, do what he had come to do in Damascus in the first place. Joe could locate the block of flats where Jameela had filmed her ISIS video. Why not?

As the Peugeot hit the main road parallel to the tailor's shop, three police cars zoomed towards it. Joe slid down in his seat and waited. When the police had passed, he sat up and produced a crumpled screen-shot printout of the ruined street where Jameela and Ham had posed with the ISIS flag and gunmen, the telephone pole at a tilt.

Joe showed the photograph to Hussein: 'Know that place?'

Hussein scowled at him, then nodded. 'Ghouta,' he said. Joe produced a hundred-dollar bill, then a second, a third.

'Ghouta, a thousand dollar,' said Hussein.

Joe nodded. This morning was proving rather expensive for Dr Franklyn. On the dashboard he saw, for the first time, a tiny photo frame in the shape of two hearts, in the hearts were two little girls.

'You sure?' Joe asked.

In the rear-view mirror, Hussein's scowl turned even more ugly. He wasn't an idiot; if he said yes, it meant yes.

'I born Ghouta,' Hussein said, now almost the chatterbox. In the middle of a wide boulevard, he executed a 360-degree turn that made him no friends, and headed south-east. Joe could work that out from the position of what had used to be the sun and now was a fuzzy ball of brownish-reddish light.

'Is it safe now?'

Hussein shook his head.

'Who owns Ghouta? Zarif or ISIS?'

He jabbed at the photo of the street. 'In the day, Zarif, perhaps. In the night, ISIS.'

'Does anyone live there anymore?'

'Sure.'

'I want to go there to ask a few questions. Not long.'

'How long?'

'Say, twenty minutes.'

'Make it ten.'

Joe had a deal. As it turned out, even ten minutes was too long, too long by half.

————

The storm was forcing people off the streets, into their homes. The further south and east they drove, the emptier Damascus became. The sand started to seep in through the Peugeot's air vents, and soon it was as if someone had put up a brown net curtain between Hussein at the wheel and Joe in the back seat. Hussein suffered a coughing fit so severe he stopped at a kiosk, got out and bought them both bottles of water. But even the brief opening of his door, twice, let in a settling of sand, fine-grained, on the seats, on the floor mats, on Joe's hands, on every surface where it could land. Outside, sky, roads, trees, earth, buildings, ruins – all brown. No great noise came with the sandstorm but the silence made it all the more ominous. Claustrophobia gripped Joe, as if he were tied down, helpless, while a giant emptied an hourglass down his throat.

The distance in space from peace – well, a kind of peace – to war zone was extraordinarily short, four miles if that. But in time it was far longer, because Hussein drove like a bumblebee, switching direction again and again, left, left, right, left, right, right, zig-zagging down brown alleys, the springs of the Peugeot crunching in protest at every pothole. Every now and then, a Syrian army roadblock would emerge through the sand-fuzz and Hussein would grunt a single-syllable curse in Arabic, brake sharply, and reverse, fast, before the soldiers could do anything about it.

The brown-out made the desolation all the more surreal. Now they were driving through a Somme-scape, re-versioned for the twenty-first century. Instead of blasted trees, there was chewed-up concrete. City blocks held their shape, a memory of before, but the ruin was in the detail: window frames intact, windows gone; shopfronts pockmarked, flats shredded by bullets, walls pitted with shrapnel scars. The half-ruins afforded a sick, voyeur's pleasure in seeing other people's tastes in wallpaper, bathroom suites, clothes.

Hussein took a right and they almost collided with an army patrol, three jeeps with anti-aircraft guns, coming their way. He reversed as if without looking, and fishtailed the Peugeot down a street, left, then right.

'Sand bad,' said Hussein.

'You can say that again.'

'Sand make night. Sand make ISIS strong.'

The longer their journey took, the browner, the darker the sky became, until their way was blocked by a telephone pole at a crazy angle like a felled tree, bringing with it a cat's cradle of wires, so thickly entwined they blocked the road. Hussein pulled up.

'This,' he said.

He handed Joe the photo and, even through the mist of sand, Joe could see that every detail in the video shot on a clear, sunny day chimed with what was in front of them.

They got out of the car.

Joe pressed his *keffiyeh* against his mouth to try to block out the sand. That's what it had been designed for. The wind was picking up now, a soft susurration much of the time, every now and then rising in power and causing the telephone wires to sob eerily. From the middle of the street you could see inside people's old flats. Hussein studied the screenshot showing the innards of the flat Jameela and Ham had stood in wearing their suicide vests, realigned himself, walked some distance backwards, went too far, came forward, looked up, stopped. He pointed to the first floor and you could clearly see, even in the darkening storm, a Batman poster by a bed, bright-yellow wallpaper with laughing black whales on it.

Joe whipped out his phone and concentrated on getting the zoom right. In the sandstorm, that simple task was beyond fiddly, so fiddly he ignored Hussein's warning shout. He hit the button and took a fast series of photographs of the wallpaper and the Batman poster, and was examining the phone's screen to see the results when Hussein rugby-tackled him to the ground, knocking him flat.

'What the hell!' Joe shouted, fearful that Hussein was about to kidnap him. Then a rocket-propelled grenade socked into the Peugeot, igniting the petrol tank and sending a flash of heat rolling towards them that singed his skin. Hussein grunted at Joe and gestured with a nod of his head towards the far end of the street, about three, perhaps four hundred yards away. Through the flames from the ruin of the Peugeot, Joe could make out six or seven men in black, wielding Kalashnikovs, walking steadily towards them, shouting '*Allahu Akbar!*'

But the figures vanished, momentarily, as the sandstorm gathered force and a hail of grit rained down, reducing visibility to twenty yards, if that. Under cover of this fresh flurry, Hussein, far slighter than Joe but with the strength of a madman, grabbed hold of Joe's arm and got him on his feet, and they ran into the block of flats where Jameela and Ham had once been. Running now, running for their lives, they climbed a blackened stairwell, up two, three, four, five flights of stairs, before coming out on the roof. The cries of '*Allahu Akbar!*' were getting closer and closer.

On the roof, they had two choices, neither of them good. One way led back in the direction the ISIS fighters were coming from; the other way was good for thirty yards, then there was a steep cliff of concrete, maybe twenty feet high, and beyond that a tower block offering the possibility of shelter. Hussein darted towards the concrete cliff.

'Wh . . .' Joe shouted but his voice was lost in the roar of the sandstorm, now a monster, a raging torrent of dust and grit in the sky, clogging mouth, nose, ears. Joe's eyes smarted so much he couldn't see. He had to stop to wipe them, almost tripped on a bare sprig of wire emerging from a lump of cooked concrete. Looking ahead, he realised that Hussein had a plan after all. At the very edge of the roof, overlooking a drop of fifty feet, was a spindly frame bolted onto the smooth wall of the tower block, supporting an array of four or five satellite dishes, one on top of another. Hussein zipped up the dish framework like a chimpanzee climbing a gnarled tree at the zoo, standing on the tip of the highest dish and then throwing a hand up to a lip of the top of the tower block. He wiggled his legs, kicked one over the lip and was out of sight.

But would the frame support Joe's weight? More shouts of '*Allahu Akbar!*' rose above the racket from the storm, giving Joe no choice but to try. He almost made it. He was shinning up the framework, his hands on the top dish, when the whole thing sheared from the cliff, bolts popping like flying bullets, and he flew through the air, hugging his satellite dish, legs wrapped around the framework as it arced 180 degrees and came to a sickening halt with him dangling in mid-air, upside down, thirty feet from the ground. The base still held, so the framework, though horribly buckled on itself, was sound for the moment, but to what end? Death had been delayed for a few seconds, that was all. If Joe let go, he would break his neck. If he stayed where he was, soon ISIS would be on the roof. They could shoot him. Or, if they chose, rescue him, so that he would star in a video kneeling in the sand in an orange jumpsuit, a man in black with a scimitar in his hand standing over him.

The sandstorm intensified again, but within it there was something new, a mechanical clatter, like a tractor, from above, from the sky. And then came the end of the world.

# TROPOJË, NORTHERN ALBANIA

To the west, the light blurred scarlet, but just before the invisible sun dipped completely below the horizon, the cloud cover broke and a long thin letterbox of brilliant red illuminated the mountains. Jeton drove the Yaris; Agim sat in the passenger seat with Zeke behind the driver.

'This country is beyond beautiful,' said Zeke, and that was when the first bullet punched through the windscreen and drilled a hole in Jeton's forehead, killing him instantly. The car lurched out of control off the road, its left-side wheels sinking into soft mud and sliding, sideways, towards a steep gully, down which a river flowed furiously.

Slowly, inexorably, the Yaris tilted side-on into the river. Water ran past the windows, spurting through the ventilation ducts so that the footwells on the left were soon awash. The water level was rising by the moment. A second bullet clanged into the engine, while Agim scrabbled over his dead cousin and fought hard and pointlessly to open the driver's side door. It wouldn't open, the door had somehow jammed in the crash; to open the passenger door would be to invite more attention from the sniper. To pick off a man climbing up out of the car would be like shooting fish in a barrel.

'Best open the window,' said Zeke as conversationally as he could, bearing in mind he was trapped behind a dead man, in the back seat of a two-door car filling up with water while someone was shooting at it. The moment Agim did so, water from the stream rushed in, so cold it took his breath away. Agim tried to move Jeton but he was pinned to his seat.

'Best unbuckle his seat belt,' said Zeke in that calm, matter-of-fact voice of his.

Cursing at his own foolishness, Agim hit the release button for Jeton's seat belt and tried to shove the dead man out of the window. The corpse tilted down, half out of the window, but an ankle had jammed underneath the accelerator, trapping it, trapping them. Agim sucked in some air, put his head below the rising waterline, felt his hands find the dead man's foot, shifted it so it was free and then he came back, snorting hungrily for air. There was two feet of water in the car; maybe more.

Agim thrust the dead man through the window, and followed him out. The corpse got snagged almost instantly, and for a moment the force of the current pressed Agim against the dead man before he wriggled free and the river's blind energy took him in its grip, bashing him against rocks and knocking the wind out of him until he surfaced, gasping for air, his feet finding a gravel bed where he could get some kind of purchase. A high bank protected him from the sniper. He scuttled towards the safety of a concrete culvert a few yards ahead. Once tucked in that, he looked back to see Zeke sliding over the rear seat. As he did so, the car slithered further down, almost to the stream bed, ruining the sniper's third shot, which whistled a good inch above Zeke's head. Zeke disappeared from Agim's view only to surface in front of the car, and he, too, crawled into the safety of the culvert.

'OK?' asked Agim.

'Never felt better,' replied Zeke.

Their situation was not good. If they went forwards through the culvert, some twenty yards of it, they would expose themselves head first to the sniper, presuming that he was playing nice and staying exactly in the spot from where he'd fired the first shots. If they went backwards, back the way they had come, towards the river, they faced the same problem, though his field of vision was more circumscribed that way.

The fiery envelope of light to the west was dying. Soon it would be pitch-black. They were both gasping for breath from their exertions, and from the coldness of the water they were crouched in.

'Shall we wait here until it's fully dark and then run for it?' asked Agim.

'He'll have a star-scope on that weapon of his. Picks up starlight and magnifies it to the power of ten, so night becomes day. We wait till it gets fully dark, he'll pick us off, sure as eggs are eggs. Funnily enough, we have a better chance now in this weak light. It messes with the optics a little.'

'Forwards or backwards?'

Zeke looked up at the cone of red sky ahead, framed by the culvert's entrance.

'Backwards. Then we track downhill, fast. He'll be expecting us to go up to the mountains. Let's not oblige him by doing the obvious. We go down, we lose him, then we go high when it's safe, when he's gone. You go first.'

Agim didn't question the older man's judgement. Later, on reflection, he realised that although the risk for the first person backing out of the culvert to the car was slight, the risk for the second person following the same track was much higher.

Disaster almost did for Agim the moment he started. Cold, colder than he realised, his legs were stiff and slow and pushing against the current was hard work. Very soon he slipped and fell awkwardly, banging his head on a submerged rock. Bloodied, still in plain sight, halfway between the culvert and the car, he struggled to get moving, to shift himself the next few yards so that he was at least covered by the car. Only then did it occur to him that he wasn't – he had never been – the assassin's target.

The gap between the bottom of the Yaris and the riverbed seemed horribly narrow, but he dived down back into the stream, pulling himself along by grasping on to rocks, struggling to squeeze through the newly created funnel before coming head to head with his dead cousin, his hefty body still snagged, blocking the route to safety. He twisted around and used his feet to stamp on the corpse's head, furiously, desperately, until suddenly the dead man was freed and floated out from underneath the car. Agim pushed himself down, under the car and beyond it, and resurfaced, his lungs burning with pain, desperate for air.

He scrambled along the riverbed, using the high bank to shield himself from the sniper. One hundred yards on, he found a hollow in the bank where he could hide and rest. He looked back to see whether Zeke had been able to follow him.

No sign of the American.

Agim, shivering, screwed up his eyes and thought he could make out something inside the culvert: a darker shade of concrete, or the shadow of the old man? Then Agim heard the unmistakable clatter of a tractor, coming along the road behind them. His experience as a policeman was that snipers didn't like company. All they had to do was hunker down and wait, and when the tractor came along, hitch a ride on it.

What he didn't expect was a hail of sub-machine-gun fire from the tractor, spraying the car, the stream and the surrounding countryside with bullets. Agim pressed himself into his hiding place and stayed there for an hour until the light was dead. Then he fell back into the stream, slithering along it, head down, for two hundred yards. He forced himself upright, climbed out of the bank and started to run, hitting a slope of loose scree and sliding down it so fast that he almost went head over tail. Eventually he came to a stop, panting, shivering with the cold because he was soaked to the skin from the stream, his breath forming balloons of vapour in the cold air. But he was alive. And that somehow felt wrong, and he began to wonder how that could possibly be.

Of Zeke, there was no sign; none at all.

# RAQQA, EASTERN SYRIA

The bus from Damascus toiled through the barren land, an emptiness broken only by telephone poles every two hundred yards, linking dead lines to eternity. In silence, the passengers stared out through dirty windows, at multistorey villas pancaked flat, burnt-out shops, and bridges bombed to shards of concrete, strands of steel wire and thin air. The people on the bus had little to say because they were lost in their own troubles, thinking of what the future might hold and what had been taken from them by the past. The men were heavily bearded, the women garbed in black *abayas*, the girls the same, the boys dressed in *dishdashas* or plain T-shirts because any symbol of Western culture, however tatty or faded, would be an invitation for unwelcome attention once they crossed over to territory under the control of ISIS, from the Hisbah, their vice squad. All that is, except one, a bright-faced, sunny-looking boy with dark-brown eyes in a Batman T-shirt.

Ham gripped his mother's hand and started counting out loud: 'One and one is two and one and two is three . . .'

He was doing one of his most favourite things, adding up Fibonacci numbers – a curious mathematical sequence that is found in nature in tree branches, on leaves, ferns, pineapples, artichokes and the family tree of honeybees. But Ham was speaking loudly in English and that, on this bus, considering its ultimate destination, was not good.

'. . . and two and three is five and . . .'

Karim, one of Qureshi's men who had been prevailed upon to act as Jameela's *mahram*, turned around in his seat in front of them and punched Ham in the head with his fist, causing the boy to shriek in pain.

'Woman, tell the kid to shut his mouth or I stop the bus here and get off and you go there on your own.' Karim was a thin, agitated man, with long wisps of hair fussily plastered over his baldness. His nervousness at the prospect of going to Raqqa was written in his every gesture, an anxiety that transmitted through to everyone on the bus. Karim was the only member of Qureshi's security team who had been willing to take the big risk of going to Raqqa at this time, because he had a sister there, whom he was hoping to get out. But the closer they got to the ISIS capital, the more jittery he became. Had Qureshi still been at liberty, Jameela would have appealed to the oil baron to send a replacement *mahram*. But Qureshi had been arrested by the Mukhabarat and his whole operation had gone silent.

Jameela had no option but to submit. No woman could go to Raqqa on her own. She shushed Ham as best she could and told him that he could play his game, only he had to count in Arabic.

'One and one is two . . .' Ham said slowly in Arabic, mutinously loud. Karim scowled at him but kept his fists by his sides and the bus trundled on. Overhead, a trio of Russian jets streaked by, part of Zoba's fraternal solidarity with the people – or rather, the government – of Syria. There was a distinction between the two that the Kremlin seemed unaware of.

At the last government-controlled town before they entered ISIS-land, soldiers entered the bus and went through the passengers' bags, ripping open thin plastic holdalls with their bayonets at the slightest delay, surly – no, angry – that people were daring to cross to the other side.

A sergeant stopped by Karim. Jameela buried her head; Ham looked out of the window, silent.

'Why are you going there? To make jihad?'

'No boss, no way,' said Karim. 'Our mother's in Raqqa and she's dying. We've got no choice but to go.'

Ham jolted in his seat – he hated lies of any sort – but said nothing.

'I'm sorry to hear that.'

Karim, soothed by the tone of the sergeant's voice, did not anticipate the knife at his throat.

'If she's dying, she doesn't need any money, does she?'

The sergeant tweaked the blade so that it caressed Karim's Adam's apple. Karim handed over two hundred dollars in dirty twenty-dollar bills he'd stashed down a sock. Every other man on the bus did the same.

The 'security check' done, a soldier with an iPhone went through the bus and took photographs of everyone on board. Jameela did her best to look away, to thwart the shot. The sergeant, standing behind the photographer-soldier, told her, 'It's fine if you don't want us to take your photo. But if you insist on that, you don't go to Raqqa.'

She hugged Ham and grinned at the iPhone camera; the soldier took the shot. Every face recorded, the government troops got off the bus, counting their dollars. As the bus chugged forever eastwards, out of the last regime-held town each and every woman dived into her handbag and got out a pair of black gloves and two black veils, one on top of the other, so that not a trace of their femininity was visible. So on the bus, as throughout ISIS-land, womanhood, as a visible entity – as a spectacle – ceased to exist.

The first checkpoint was signposted by black flags fluttering in the wind and manned by men in black, their beards ferociously long, their chests garlanded with ammunition belts. The bus was waved through;

the ISIS security and modesty check took place at the second check-point. There, everybody was ordered to get off the bus and stand by their bags. Three men from the Hisbah went through every possession with a fastidiousness that bordered – no, that crossed the line into – a kind of madness. Hairbrushes, bras, razors, an electric toothbrush – all were thrown aside, *haram*, forbidden. But no money was stolen. The regime were gangsters; the other side fanatics. There was nothing left in the middle.

Karim and Jameela had heard tell of the search process, and had deliberately packed nothing that the men of the Caliphate might object to. But Jameela had overlooked Ham's Batman T-shirt, his pride and joy, because he always wore Batman gear. The youngest of the Hisbah, a wispily bearded youth not more than twenty years of age, if that, grabbed hold of Ham's shirt and barked, '*Haram.*'

'Sir, I'm so sorry,' said Jameela, 'but his grandmother is dying and this is his favourite T-shirt.'

'*Haram*,' he repeated.

Karim snapped at Ham to take off the T-shirt, which he did, and reversed it so the bat emblem was hidden when the boy put it back on again. The Hisbah man looked at Ham irritatedly, but half-nakedness, even for a boy, was more *haram* than a hidden Western logo, so he moved on. Jameela, suppressing a smile, gripped his hand and squeezed it.

'He reminded me of the Joker,' whispered Ham in English. The hissing sound they heard was Karim, hating the boy's cheek but afraid to take out his anger lest it bring back the Hisbah.

The bus pulled to a stop on the edge of Raqqa and the passengers hurried off into the tented streets, looking up at the sky for fear of bombs. They passed a TV reporter doing a piece to camera in front of a bombed-out building; the man was gaunt but well dressed, speaking confidently in English. He stooped down, scooped up some dust from the bomb site, then let it fall through the fingers of his hand. In the background, a mini traffic jam of white saloon cars waited for the lights to change; beyond them was a small crowd of men going about their business, moving diagonally to and fro, and through that crowd a youth carried what appeared to be a small child in a white sheet soaked in blood.

'Again,' shouted a man in Arabic, his moustache noticeably bigger than his beard.

The white cars reversed in sequence, the crowd of men walked backwards to their starting positions, and the youth laid the child-doll down on the ground and adjusted his underpants. The TV reporter wiped the dust from the palm of his hand.

'This time, more passion,' said Hadeed, and the reporter nodded quickly and the scene repeated itself, every fabricated detail – the traffic jam of cars, the politely criss-crossing crowd, the youth running in the background with a small child in a white sheet soaked in blood – choreographed for the greater glory of the Caliphate, every deceit rehearsed to the nth degree.

Jameela found what she had been looking for, what she had feared, just past the film set. In the main square, in the dead centre of town, sat five metal cages, in them five men dressed in orange jumpsuits, the latest captives of the Caliphate. The light was harsh, brilliantly white, but even so Jameela could make out Rashid's big frame in the confines of the second cage along.

Karim started walking away. 'Please, Karim, don't go,' begged Jameela, knowing that if she was caught without a *mahram* it would be the end, not just for her but for any hope of saving Rashid. Karim ignored her, pivoted on the spot, and ran down an alley and vanished.

Jameela held back in the shadows, trying to make herself as invisible as she could. The heat pulsed, causing the men in the cages to shimmer, as if they were dancing. As a woman, she dared not move in a public place of her own volition. She couldn't walk a step on her own without fear of arrest. But Ham was a boy. Ham could move freely without drawing attention to himself. Jameela fetched a water bottle out of her bag, opened the lid and gave it to Ham.

'See Rashid's cage? You see his hands are tied behind his back?'

Ham nodded.

'Run to his cage and pour the water on his head. If you can reach his mouth, that would be wonderful. Run there and run back.'

Ham nodded again and lolloped across the open space to the cages. On the far side of the square, deep in the shade, sat five Hisbah. When Ham got to the cage, Rashid looked up at him and his throat, raw and parched through dehydration, managed to croak one word: 'Run.'

But Ham would not do so – he did what he had been told to do by his mother, dutifully aiming the water from the bottle directly over Rashid's head and onto his tongue, slowly, almost drop by drop, the perfectionist in him to the fore.

'Boy! Leave the prisoner. Get out of there,' yelled one of the Hisbah.

Ham ignored him; his concentration was total.

Two Hisbah got up and ran towards the cages, yelling their anger at this grotesque insult to the management of savagery. Ham, intent on his task, did not hear them. Every drop he poured found its mark.

'Run,' Rashid repeated.

In the shadows, Jameela put a hand to her mouth and whispered through it, 'Run, Ham, run.'

The last drop fell from the bottle. And then the leading Hisbah knocked Ham flying with the back of his hand. Ham fell over, and wriggled up only to be hit once more. But the policeman was slow, and in a sudden movement that took him completely by surprise, Ham lunged forward and bit him on the hand and kept on biting.

Now the second Hisbah started kicking Ham, the two men laying into the boy, beating and punching him till blood gushed from his mouth. Hadeed looked up from the film shoot, puzzled by the commotion, to see a woman in black running on her own to one of the cages in the square, by which two Hisbah were wrestling with a boy.

In Raqqa, women dare not run.

The woman kicked the first man; the second clubbed her on the side of her face with his fist.

'Stop!' said Hadeed to the film crew. Motioning to the TV reporter, he said, 'Put him back in his cage.'

Hadeed took out his revolver and fired one shot into the air. One shot would be enough.

# DAMASCUS, SYRIA

The al-Hayat prison: it sounded like the hotel chain, but it wasn't like the hotel chain. Joe had come to in a basement cell, with frosted windows casting some sense of daylight on the gloom within. The cell was a big rectangle that would comfortably hold fifty men. But it was home to three hundred, so tightly packed together that at night, if one man wished to change his sleeping position, ten others had to do so, too. The constant traffic of humanity killed sleep. You couldn't rest, couldn't zone out, because every few minutes or so you had to make room for someone passing. Some prisoners were incontinent, moving to the stink-hole at the back of the cell to piss or shit; others wrestled with demons in their half-sleep; a few fought to get to the bars at the front, intending to beg for release, only falling into stillness when they got close; and some returned from amiable snitching with the guards to murderous hostility once back in the cell. The prisoners who had been tortured, they were easy to tell. The favoured method of interrogation was to cuff men's hands behind their backs and then hoist them up on hooks, so that their own weight killed their shoulder nerves. After suspension for hours, sometimes days, all a man could do with his arms was flap them, helplessly, like a newborn chick.

Joe was in no great shape himself. He couldn't quite work out exactly what was wrong with him, but a shortlist would include a concussion, a broken or possibly just severely bruised right arm, a broken or severely bruised jaw, stitched lower lip, broken or twisted ankle, burnt left hand and loss of sight in his left eye, permanent or temporary he did not know. That made him one of the fittest men in the cell, and so he ended up helping to shift the dead. In his *dishdasha*, with three or four days' stubble and his dark hair, he passed as a local.

Nobody had taken his name when he arrived at the prison because he had been unconscious, in a semi-coma. By the time he had re-entered the land of the living, the guards – never enough of them – seemed to have forgotten all about him. In the cell, nobody had engaged him in conversation for long. If they did, he made a point of turning his back on them, playing deaf-mute, very occasionally grunting or mouthing words that made no sense. His size meant he was left alone.

Every night, someone would die, nearly always one of the zombies whose torture had gone on for too long, or whose hold on life was too feeble. In the morning, the dead would become obvious. Most of the time they would be found close to the stinking hole at the back of the cell that passed as a toilet. If you had an ounce of life left in you, you fought to get away from the hole.

Joe's stint as the corpse-man started on his second morning in al-Hayat. At the back of the cell, next to the wall but some distance from the stink-hole, a man in a grey *dishdasha* lay on his belly. It was obvious from the space around him that he was dead, but none of the prisoners close to him cared to move him. One of the guards, whose face was as grey as the prisoners he watched over, pointed unambiguously at Joe, gestured to the corpse, and beckoned for him to shift it. Joe picked his way through the men lying on the ground to the back of the cell. Tentatively, he turned the dead man over to discover a knife blade lodged in his right eyeball. Joe removed the blade from the eye, placed it in a pocket of his own *dishdasha* in full view of everyone, guard included, then dragged the corpse with his good arm, limping across the cell to the door. The guard unlocked the cell door to allow Joe and his cargo through, then locked it while Joe placed the body on a gurney. The guard then led Joe, pushing the gurney, down a corridor to a much bigger room, half-open to the sky, that had become a kind of morgue. It stank of some kind of bleachy chemical, which did something but not enough to mask the honey-shit stink of the dead. There were ten or twelve corpses in the room, all of them naked, watched over by two photographs high up on the wall of Zarif the Father and Zarif the Son. Shortly, a pitifully thin, nervous-looking man with bloodshot eyes entered the morgue, and took a camera and flashgun out of a shoulder bag. The man with the camera started methodically taking photographs of the dead.

Keen to make himself useful, Joe helped the photographer pose the bodies for the best possible shot. The guard watched the two of them work for a time, then sat down on a chair and lit a cigarette and gazed at the dead, lost in quiet contemplation.

The photographer was, Joe thought to begin with, a silly fusspot. He insisted on taking several shots of each corpse: the face, in close-up; belly up and belly down; and he would concentrate on any scars or wounds. Some of the dead were pocked with cigarette burns or vile bruises, which could only possibly have been the result of torture. Happy to be doing something, however morbid, away from the crush of the cell, Joe assisted the photographer as best he could. He was on the fifth corpse when it suddenly struck him what the photographer was really doing. He wasn't just logging the dead, but collecting evidence of how they had come to die.

The sixth corpse was a young man with a fine physique. He looked untouched, but his groin was covered by underpants. Joe looked at the photographer. His eyes floated towards the grey-faced guard, still staring into space, but not their space. Joe knelt down beside the corpse and pulled the underpants down. The man had been castrated. The photographer did what he had to do and when he was finished, Joe pulled the underwear back up. The photographer smiled grimly at him, and Joe returned the smile. Horrible as it was, they were doing something good.

When the work was done, the guard escorted Joe back to the cell. Touched by death, his fellow prisoners made room for Joe. And so his prison routine began.

On the fifth morning, the grey-faced guard started yelling at Joe, furiously, in Arabic. Joe didn't understand a word of it, but he was the sole focus of attention in the cell. Three hundred pairs of eyes were on him when Mansour, dressed nattily as ever in a charcoal suit, cream shirt and saffron tie, appeared from behind the guard and said, 'Ah, Mr Tiplady, so this is where you've been hiding from us. How clever of you.'

It didn't feel like good news and it wasn't.

# PALMYRA, SYRIA

Before dawn they prayed, then rode away from the rising sun. Seven in their party, on three motorbikes: three guards, experienced motorcyclists, at the handlebars; Hadeed riding pillion on the first bike; Timur on the second; the executioner, Khalil, and the child, Haroun, on the third. As they drove out through Raqqa, Timur noticed that there was a sole prisoner in the line of cages in the main square: Haroun's grandfather.

They travelled in the same direction along the same road, but separately, each bike two, three miles apart. The warriors of Islamic State had learnt from experience that the enemy's drones would target convoys of any size, but that lone cars or motorbikes were, in general, left be. The safest option was to travel with a child – hence Khalil, the most beloved by the Caliph of them all, enjoyed the effective protection of Haroun. Whether Haroun's companionship provided Khalil with other benefits, Timur did not know.

For Timur, for far too long shackled to the bomb factory, trapped below ground in fetid air, the idea of a trip away from Raqqa had seemed something of a liberation. Everywhere they went, the black flag of ISIS flew tall but, Timur observed, men were pitifully thin in number on the ground, the tanks they had stolen from the Iraqi army well camouflaged, hidden from the skies.

They passed through a landscape deformed by war: burnt-out villages, windows socketed by soot, roof beams turned to spider's webs of charred wood, cement pitted by shrapnel, craters wider than the road, tank tracks ribbing the asphalt so that their motorbikes juddered for miles on end. Aside from the physical damage were the holes hollowed out of people's souls.

Twenty miles out of Raqqa, Timur and his driver came across a family trudging along the road: a father with a club foot, wheeling a pushchair, in it his infant daughter; a boy, around ten years old, walking along the road; his mother behind him, and bringing up the rear, the grandmother. The family stopped dead at the sight of the two men in black riding towards them, knowing that it was against the law, as ordained by the Caliph, for any family to flee Raqqa. Struck by the family's frozen tableau, Timur realised that they feared he was from the Hisbah or the Amn, coming to order them back. When Timur's bike passed the family, their faces were wreathed with anxiety, but the men in black had somewhere to get to and rode smoothly on. Timur noted that the man with the club foot stared at him intently, as if memorising the features of the men from ISIS, as if, powerless as he was, he would do harm to them if he were ever given the chance.

In the heat of the afternoon, Timur and the others rode into an old caravanserai, stopping for tea and fuel. They were together for the first time since leaving Raqqa: Khalil, Hadeed and him. Unbidden, his mind's eye suggested the midnight hags of Macbeth, recast for twenty-first-century Syria: *Double, double, toil and trouble* . . .

The ancient inn had been popular before the war with tourists from the West, but now the place was empty, its corners dank, strewn with rubbish, smelling of piss and shit. A three-legged dog sat in the shade, eyeing the visitors morosely. They ordered tea but it didn't come; the boy serving seemed both fearful of them and inattentive. No adults were visible, perhaps because the men in black were not welcome here. Khalil barked at the boy fiercely, to no effective end. Hadeed vanished into the kitchens and came back, to announce: 'They've run out of gas so they're having to make tea by burning wood. We will have it soon.' Hadeed's mirrored shades hid a practical sense, rare in ISIS.

Khalil muttered something under his breath. Hadeed challenged him to say what he had on his mind out loud.

'I said that you always find an excuse for everything.' The executioner enunciated every glottal stop with vehemence. 'That blue-eyed American bitch, she's a threat to us, but you always interfere, begging the Caliph to spare her.'

In silence, Hadeed took off his sunglasses and stared at Timur and Haroun, then returned his gaze to the executioner. The implication was clear: Khalil had spoken about something not to be discussed in front of a technician like Timur and a child such as Haroun. Khalil, a huge man, seemed to shrink in size, and said not a word more until the boy came out with the tea.

They set off separately again, at thirteen-minute intervals, taking a higgledy-piggledy route away from the main roads, approaching Palmyra from the south through the desert. Their path took them through a landscape of extraordinarily austere beauty, past wave upon wave of immense dunes, suggesting an inland sea made up, not from droplets of water, but grains of sand. The shadows of the dunes lengthened in the evening sunlight, turning the burnt land from ochre to charcoal.

At dusk, they rode underneath a transmission tower, painted red and white, high on a bluff, and then into Queen Zenobia's oasis capital, Palmyra. She had been a pagan enemy of Rome in the third century, her god Bel, her ancient city of colonnades and bathhouses an affront to the pure of the Caliphate. Palmyra's famous arch had been dynamited by ISIS warriors in an act of pious desecration.

The men on motorcycles turned away from the town and rode through the Valley of the Tombs, past towers of stone – ancient at the time of Jesus – and little hillocks of rubble marking entrances to hypogea, underground chambers, pretty much every single one looted by grave robbers. In a deep cleft between two ridges was a cliff-hang, and underneath that a tunnel had been carved into the rock. Hadeed arrived before the others and waited by his motorbike, one hundred yards inside the tunnel and so invisible to the drones of the Far Enemy; next to the bike was a truck, covered with a white tarpaulin. Then Timur arrived and they waited in silence, engines off, for Khalil and Haroun.

Swifts flew in and out, emitting swooshing sounds as they gunned across the darkening half-moon of sky framed by the tunnel entrance. Timur stretched his legs and marvelled at the beauty of the birds, luxuriating in their speed, when he heard a fresh sound. He turned slightly and realised that it came from what was hidden underneath the truck's tarpaulin: a soft, low whimper, as if from a wounded animal. He looked across to Hadeed who, he realised, had observed him registering the sound and was studying him closely.

Khalil the executioner was a beast, Timur reflected, a moron armed with full powers to hurt, maim and kill, but somehow Hadeed was worse, a civilised and intelligent man who out of cynical calculation had ended up one of the Caliph's most trusted lieutenants. A few minutes later, Khalil and Haroun joined them and all three bikes switched on their lights – the truck, too, driven by one of the Hisbah – and together they drove deep into the tunnel, their engines extraordinarily loud, reverberating monstrously in the confined space. They drove into the rock for maybe a mile, the tunnel not straight but curving through the rock, until they came to a stop in front of a wall made of steel, three men high, and the engines were killed. Cylinders of dust turned in the bike headlights. Someone coughed and spat; the cough and spit echoing and re-echoing down the tunnel; that whimpering sound was heard again, softly echoed and re-echoed. Backlit by the headlights, Hadeed walked towards a door embedded in the steel wall and produced a key to unlock a padlock. He opened the door, disappeared from view for a second, and the sound of a generator filled the tunnel. Light poured in through the far side of the door, and Hadeed reappeared and gestured for the others to follow him.

Through the steel door, a vast space receded into gloom, beyond the reach of the electric lights. Immediately to the right was a small portacabin, its door open. Timur glanced inside and saw two portraits, side by side: one of a smiling Asian man with gleaming teeth; the second, on its left, another Asian man, pouty, rather sulky, with an air of petulance about him. Ahead of them was a wire fence and, behind that, long rows of stainless-steel cylindrical drums, each one featuring a skull and crossbones and something written in a script Timur had never seen before: not Cyrillic, not Roman, not Chinese ideograms, but curling squares and squarish circles.

Hadeed studied Timur, whose powers of deduction were famous throughout the whole of Islamic State.

'So, Timur, what do you make of this?'

Timur made no reply, but walked past the cylindrical drums, counting under his breath, then found two small prefabricated sheds. He opened the door to the first, and discovered it was packed with cardboard boxes, again featuring this alien scribble. He opened a box at random and found three chemical warfare suits; a second box contained three gas masks.

'Bio suits, gas masks, chemicals hidden from the sky, far underground,' said Timur. He was aware he was being played by Hadeed; the more literal his observations, he sensed, the less danger for him. But he was becoming sick of the pretence, and he let some measure of his true feelings show directly: 'So, why this game, Hadeed – why bring me to this hole in the ground? I have work to do for the Caliphate.'

'Your work is now here. So, Timur, what have we found?' Again the challenge from Hadeed, taunting him, putting him on his mettle.

'I will need to take photographs and check on the Internet, but this looks to me like a consignment of chemical weapons – sarin, VX gas, something like this. The writing I don't recognise, but from the two photographs in the office, I suspect this was a gift to Zarif from the people of North Korea.'

'Excellent,' said Hadeed. 'We've seized a lot of paperwork, but much of it is written in foreign gibberish.'

'Korean,' said Timur.

'Foreign gibberish,' repeated Hadeed. 'A few words are in English, which can be read. The gas is sarin, so you guessed correctly.'

Timur inclined his head, then said warily, 'What is it that you wish me to do?'

'Your immediate task is to stay here in this place and master the ways of this gas, so that we can manufacture chemical suicide bombs. But first let's see whether this devil's gas works.'

Khalil turned towards the clever Chechen engineer. His mouth smiling but his eyes not, he gestured to Timur to follow him. He walked back through the door over to the truck, and pulled off the white tarpaulin, revealing what was hidden: seven cages, a metre square; crouched within were five men in orange jumpsuits, a woman in a black *abaya*, her face covered by two veils, and a boy of around seven years old. Each prisoner was handcuffed with his arms behind his back, though the lack of space, the confinement, would be torture enough, Timur thought to himself. Six were silent, their eyes watchful, impassive; one of the men was whimpering, his mind gone.

Khalil clicked his fingers, and gestured for Timur and the others to take the cages off the truck and through the door in the metal wall to just outside the second hut. The cages were heavy and could only be manhandled one by one. The men had a wooden stick inserted underneath their armpits, further immobilising them. One or two did their

167

best to struggle, but the others accepted what was to happen next as if their will to fight for survival had been extinguished.

Khalil went to a control panel on the outside of the hut and pulled a switch. A light clicked on, revealing that it was lined within with stainless steel and had a small observation window, like a porthole, on one side. Khalil operated another switch, and the hut's heavy metal door with rubber lining started to swing open. One of the men in the cages – not the whimperer – started to scream obscenities, damning the Caliph to hell, mocking Islamic State as 'Daesh'.

Hadeed yelled at him: 'Shut your mouth, Rashid! Your time has come.'

But Rashid, clearly a brave man, was having none of it. 'You call yourselves Muslims but you are committing crimes against Islam. Daesh is filth! Daesh is filth! Daesh is filth!'

The other men who were still in control of their faculties took up the chant. For the first time, Timur noticed that the woman and the boy had tape over their mouths so they couldn't talk.

Hadeed said something to Khalil, who took off his backpack, and from it produced a strange chunky pistol, coloured black and yellow, that Timur had never seen before. He switched it on and an electric-blue spark of fifty thousand volts flashed brilliantly against the cave's shadows. The other caged men fell silent, but Rashid carried on with his heretical chant: 'Daesh is filth!'

Khalil passed the electric gun to Haroun, whose black eyes lit up when he pressed the trigger, making the sparks leap. The boy went up to Rashid's cage and plunged the Taser down through the bars, zapping the man within. The chant died, to be replaced by the heavy clunking sounds of a man's head, limbs and torso jerking uncontrollably against metal bars in electric spasm.

The spark died, and in the time it took to rebuild a charge Rashid said his chant again – 'Daesh is filth!' – but this time far more feebly, almost on the edge of hearing. Haroun waited for the recharging cycle to complete, then carefully aimed the Taser directly at Rashid's face. His eyeballs spun white as the blue sparks made contact, and Rashid's agonising scream was something that Timur would never forget. Rashid passed out, unconscious, quite possibly dead. Haroun, reluctantly, returned the Taser to Khalil. The eyes of the other prisoners, even the whimperer, never left the Taser until Khalil put it away in his backpack.

'The woman, the child, the noisy one whom Haroun has shut up with that electric gun,' said Timur, 'let's keep them for another day.'

Hadeed shook his head. 'They must all die.'

'No. I cannot experiment on corpses. I cannot calculate the required dose of gas for chemical suicide bombs unless I have living specimens to work with. Give me these three, or what you ask of me is impossible and I shall have to inform the Caliph of that.'

Hadeed gave way. He saw the common sense in Timur's position and he didn't want him to go complaining to the Caliph. Quietly, the four cages containing the condemned men were lifted into the hut and the heavy metal door was closed, then sealed with eight butterfly locks tightly screwed down. Hadeed, Khalil and Haroun – and Timur, despite himself – gathered at the observation window to see what would happen next. Inside the hut, eight eyes swivelled this way and that, mutely watching what fate had in store for them.

Hadeed turned a valve that opened a tap on the inside of the hut, then took out his phone and switched the camera to video mode. The men in the cages reacted within ten, fifteen seconds: their arms and legs flailed within their confines, their eyes fluttered in their sockets, strawberry-pink foam started oozing from their mouths, noses, ears and eyes; their faces went pale, then paler still until they were all a ghostly white and all four were dead. It had taken two minutes, if that. Haroun clapped with joy, his applause echoing inside the confined space. Khalil disappeared and reappeared with a gas mask, which the boy eagerly put over his face. Raising one finger to Paradise, Haroun posed for a photograph – behind him, just visible through the porthole, four corpses, deathly white. There was something bewildering and dark about the contrast between the childishness of Haroun's physique and the plastic exoskeleton clamped to his face.

In Timur's mind, the line jumped up, unbidden: *Something wicked this way comes.* Outwardly, he did not speak.

'Well?' asked Hadeed.

Timur looked at Hadeed, then his eyes turned to the four white ghosts locked in their cages in the hut, Haroun prancing in front of it, his gas mask wobbling, too big for his face. Still, Timur made no reply.

'What do you think of this gas that we have found, Timur?'

Timur said, softly, '*Allahu Akbar*' – God is great.

This was a pious answer, but Hadeed sensed that Timur, yet again, was holding something back from him.

'*Allahu Akbar*,' Hadeed echoed, then clicked his fingers, ordering the others to leave. He barked at Haroun, still capering around in the gas mask, to take it off, and told them all that what they had seen was a secret, not to be whispered about. Then Hadeed, Khalil and Haroun exited the main chamber and returned to the tunnel. They mounted their motorbikes, and the tunnel shook with the roar of their engines, headlights spearing the dark, and soon all that Timur could see were brake lights dwindling to red dots. Then they, too, died – and the last murmur of the machines faded to stillness. He stood in the dark, not moving, and at length turned and headed back towards the barrels of poison and the three human beings in iron cages, gifts for him to experiment on.

# NORTHERN ALBANIA

Solemn as a high priest, the boy was as thin as a stick, around ten years of age, walnut-brown. How he found the stone shack belonging to Sotir, the half-wolf shepherd, high up in the mountains where Agim had gone to ground, they never discovered. He knocked twice on the wooden door, and when Sotir opened it the boy said nothing but reached into his pocket, brought out a strange lump of rock and held it in the flat of his palm.

Sotir, puzzled, took the rock, thanked the boy, closed the door behind him and showed it to Agim who, while still full of aches and pains, was on the mend. The detective took one look at the lump of rock and knew that, in the age of the cell phone, of texting and email, Zeke, who did not dare communicate with him by any of those marvels of twenty-first-century digital technology, was letting him know by this gift of fulgurite that he was alive. He could not help but suppress a smile. Once again, the American idiot had proved himself to be no idiot at all.

———

The half-wolf had been gone for hours. Agim nursed a cup of cold tea and added an unnecessary fresh pine log to the wood-burning stove that super-heated the shack. The wind soughed its melancholy song outside. He shivered, despite the warmth. Where were they? What had gone wrong this time? The snow-capped mountains above turned pink and then a darker shade of red, and only then did he hear it, the sound of a badly maintained sewing machine. He pressed his face against the small, grimy window and made out two figures on an ancient, underpowered motorbike, the half-wolf at the handlebars, behind him a passenger wrapped in a sheepskin coat. Agim swung open the door, and half-ran to the motorbike to get Zeke into the warmth of the shack as quickly as possible. To say the CIA man was in a bad way was an understatement: his face was as grey as a wet newspaper, his breathing erratic, not just his nose but his lips and lower face a darkening blue. As Sotir and Agim gently laid him down on the rough bed inside the shack, a dry rattle came from his throat, his eyes rolled in their sockets and he lost consciousness.

Agim looked searchingly at the half-wolf, and the shepherd's eyes looked down. Nothing needed to be said.

# PALMYRA, SYRIA

The North Koreans were beyond strange, their regime ungodly, but their technicians were not fools, Timur reflected. He'd read that they'd exploded three nuclear bombs, buying the know-how from a rogue Pakistani scientist. They'd managed to launch a rocket across the Sea of Japan and for it to fall in the north Pacific. So they knew what they were doing. To build a chemical-weapon testing facility inside a rock vault with no egress, no way to purge the facility, was foolish, and that was not like them.

Reflecting on this problem, his ears pricked up as he heard a muted cry come from the direction of the three cages holding Rashid, the woman and the boy. Ignoring that, he examined the exterior of the hut where the four bodies of the dead men remained, untouched, their faces almost imperceptibly turned from deathly white to the palest of greens. The hut was placed against the wall of the cavern. Using a flashlight, he saw what he was looking for: an extraction funnel sitting just below the roof of the hut's sealed chamber. Lining the wall beyond the hut were boxes and boxes of chemical warfare suits and gas masks, all marked in Korean. Manically, he pulled away box after box, letting them fall higgledy-piggledy until he exposed a small circular steel plate set into the wall, flush with the ground.

He worked through the boxes, examining the markings on the side, ripped one open, took out a chemical suit and tried it on, but it was too short, even for him. Again he trawled through the boxes, found one that would fit him, and then donned it and a gas mask. Fully fitted out, he unscrewed the bolts fastening the small steel door and opened it.

In front of him was a ladder. Crouching down, he wriggled his way through the hole and started climbing. Two hundred and seventy-three steps later – he'd counted every one – he came to a small platform, and above that a second cylindrical plate, identical to the one far below. The plate was easily unscrewed, and it opened on a hinge to reveal a bowl of stars.

Timur climbed up, sat on a rock overlooking a dark mass of mountains and – in the near distance – the dim lights of Palmyra, and breathed deeply of the warm night air. It should have been a moment of calm and rest, but his mind churned with guilt. He'd watched, immobile, as they had beheaded an innocent child in front of his eyes – and then, when a woman of the Book, who'd only come to Syria to help fight sickness, asked for his mercy, he'd done nothing to help her.

'*All the perfumes of Arabia will not sweeten this little hand.*'

Timur had read a book arguing that – although it was possible to allow one's mind to submit to a sacralised determinism; for one's soul to be taken over and constricted by a new vocabulary, restricting feeling and thought; to live inside a policed reality – what someone had experienced and known in the time before submission would, occasionally, break the mental surface, puncturing their subjected, quiescent mental state. Every time a line or an image from *Macbeth*, a play that had been read aloud to him when he was a child, pinged inside his head, it weakened the thought control exercised by Islamic State.

He repeated the line from *Macbeth* and made his decision.

---

Everything alive crawled into shade, away from the unbearable heat. In direct sunlight, it was 45 degrees Celsius. Even in shadow, the sun's brilliant glare hurt the eyes. Khalid and Haroun were playing chess in a tea shop in Palmyra, surrounded by tourist bric-a-brac – stuffed toy camels, mini pyramids containing different layers of coloured sand, plastic scimitars, all of them covered in a fine film of sand – for which there were no customers, or to be more accurate, not the right kind of customers. The executioner towered over Haroun, his forearms almost as thick as the boy's torso, but in front of the chessboard his forehead was knitted in a comic display of concentration.

Overhead, a trio of Russian fighter jets ripped up grooves of sound in the blue sky, delivering presents from Zoba. The bombs fell close – three, four miles away. They saw the smoke first, then almost immediately they felt the earth quiver under their feet, birds flapped and car alarms squawked and only then did they hear the explosions.

The boy moved his knight, said 'checkmate' and smiled, coolly, at the loser. Khalid, taken entirely by surprise, swept the board with an enormous paw and cried out, 'This is the work of Satan!' then made to strike the boy. Hadeed, sipping tea at a separate table with Timur, lifted one hand upwards and said, 'Khalil, *la*.' No.

The executioner stood up and barrelled out of the teashop, his muscle and mass no competition for the authority of Hadeed. They had been waiting for a reply from the Caliph for more than a week now, waiting for his permission to use the devil's gas, and were beginning to tire of each other's company.

To ask the Caliph for his religious judgement about whether or not they could fight jihad with the chemical weapons they had found, the simplest thing would have been for Hadeed to have used his cell phone to call the Caliph or his office. But that was forbidden. Instead,

Hadeed had written out a letter in longhand and copied the video of the gassing of the four men onto a second phone, and given the letter and phone to one of the guards, who got on his motorbike to make the trip back to Raqqa. The problem, they intuited, was that the guard, not so very high in the pecking order, was clearly finding it difficult to locate the Caliph – or, if he had done so, to compete with all the other petitioners to enter his presence, to capture ten seconds of his time, so that he could show him Hadeed's letter and the video. The goal of Islamic State was to turn back the clock to the seventh century. In terms of speed of communication, they were doing rather too well.

The logic of no phone calls to and from Caliph Ibrahim was sound enough. ISIS were fully aware of what had happened to the Chechen warlord Dzhokhar Dudayev back in the nineties. Dudayev had been beyond the reach of Russian spies, living with the goats high up in the Pankisi Gorge, part of the Caucasus mountain range and halfway to Georgia, when the Russians sent two cruise missiles whistling down onto Dudayev's satellite-phone signal. For a movement that used suicide as a weapon – very much part of its philosophy of the management of savagery – the delicacy surrounding the security of the Caliph himself was extraordinary. Still, they all understood the importance, the centrality, of submission to his God-given authority.

Haroun wandered off somewhere. Hadeed looked at his watch, stifled a yawn and moved over to pick up the chess pieces and align them on the board. When he was done, he suggested a game to Timur. The Chechen engineer nodded politely, but soon they had thrown diffidence to one side and were hard at battle: Hadeed was white, advancing his knights in daring adventures; Timur constructed a prickly defence of pawns in depth, castling queenside, then sending three pawns up on the king's side, setting up a relentless momentum of sacrifice that looked unsophisticated at first glance but wasn't at all.

The Iraqi mulled the board, sipped his tea, then spoke: 'The prisoners, Timur, what did you do with the prisoners – Rashid, the woman and the child?'

'For the moment, nothing. They are secure in the vault.'

'So you say,' mused Hadeed.

'And I say the truth. God knows it.'

'Of course, to a traitor to our cause, a pretence of piety would be the perfect way to mask his inner feelings.'

'That would indeed be most cunning,' replied Timur, before taking a bishop for the loss of a pawn. Hadeed made a sour face, moved his queen forwards.

'The traitor,' said Hadeed, warming to his theme, 'would have to be most ingenious, seeming to be a dutiful, pious servant of the Caliphate. But in reality he would be planning a trap.'

'Such a plan as you suggest, it is beyond imagining,' replied Timur.

'But if there were two traitors, one who had cleverly constructed the fantastic scheme of piety, and the second, a mere opportunist, who saw through it but was ready for betrayal for his own personal reasons, what then?'

Timur stared at Hadeed, then moved a knight, catching the Iraqi off guard.

'Checkmate,' said Timur.

At that precise moment, there was a slight, childish cough, then Haroun emerged from behind an antique Persian carpet – on sale, so its price tag said, for three thousand dollars.

———

They came for Timur at the traditional time, in the small hours of the morning, as he knew they would: Hadeed, Khalil, three Hisbah. Timur made no protest but simply smiled weakly.

'Do you not ask why?' asked Hadeed, as Khalil bound Timur's wrists with the plastic handcuffs donated so generously to ISIS by the American taxpayer – via the mechanism of the Iraqi army running away from Mosul.

'Clearly,' said Timur, 'I have been most unwise.'

'Rashid, the woman and the boy, they were moderns' – the dismissive term the servants of the Caliphate used for those who did not submit to their own dark interpretation of the Quran – 'fit only for death. They have vanished. There were guards at the entrance to the tunnel. They saw you leave once in the truck.'

'The guards searched the truck and found nothing but four corpses. I was taking the dead away to bury them. That is no crime.'

Khalil slammed him down on a chair and slapped him on the face, three times.

'Your crime is treason,' said Hadeed.

'So you say,' replied Timur. It was enough to inspire more blows from Khalil, most to the head, some to the stomach, winding him.

'Timur, you think your little ploy of leaving the hatch on top of the rock open worked? We found the barber and he talked, didn't he, Khalil?'

The executioner stood behind Timur, massaging his neck, his cheekbones, then lightly caressing his eyeballs. Timur breathed in hard, saying nothing.

'The barber came to our attention. Before rogues and pagans flee from the saintly state we have created, he would clip their beards. People talked and we seized him. Under interrogation he told us that a thin man with a Chechen accent six days ago had come to him and bought the clippings of a beard for five dollars – too good a price, too generous a deal. You smuggled Rashid, the woman and boy out underneath the dead, and you bought the beard from the barber so the woman could disguise herself as a man. Very ingenious. But treason.'

'So you say,' said Timur.

The pressure on his eyeballs grew.

# THE MEDITERRANEAN SEA

Huddled in the cold, they sat in the ruins of an Orthodox church, listening to the sea lap against the shingle a few yards away. Darkness cloaked the land; out to sea, to the west, the phosphorescence of the surf gave way to blackness, then, seven miles away, the brilliant lights of Kos lured them to a different world. Seated in the nave of the church, they could take in the stars because it was roofless, abandoned in 1922 when a new and powerful Turkey banished the Greek Christian citizens who had lived and died on these shores for a thousand years. A sense of wars, lost and won, of ordinary people crushed underfoot by forces more powerful than them, of the innocent seeking refuge, lingered in its old, comfortless stones.

Jameela's hair was cut short, like a man's. She was wearing a black sweater over a white T-shirt and blue jeans; warm enough for Syria, but far too cold on the edge of the great inland sea in the bleak hours before dawn. The breeze strengthened and the masses in the church and the hillside beyond shivered afresh. Five hundred people, all of them running from war. Ham was physically puffed up because of the life jacket he was wearing, but the boy within was shivering. Still, he was the same old Ham.

'Mom,' he piped up in English, 'you promised me *Pirates of the Caribbean*. Not this pile of crap.'

Jameela, worried sick as she was about the sea-crossing ahead of them, could not help but laugh. A thin man with cropped silver hair, the head of a large family, hissed in Arabic, 'Tell your boy to cease his chatter. He'll bring the police down on us and then we will never get to Germany.'

'Mom, please,' Ham mock-whined, 'tell that asshole the killer whales in Sea World get treated better than this.'

The thin man didn't speak English, or at least not well enough to work out that Ham was being far from polite about him. But there was real anger in his voice now: 'Listen, woman, the people-smugglers will hear your brat show off in English and they'll order us off the beach, and all of us will lose thousands of dollars because of him.'

The thin man had a point. She had paid the smugglers $2,400 for two tickets for herself and Ham; there was no way they could afford to lose that money.

'If he doesn't shut up,' the thin man hissed, 'I'll take my belt to his backside.'

The colonel's daughter in Jameela came out of nowhere: 'You touch a hair on my boy's head and I will slit your throat,' she replied in the guttural Arabic of the backstreets of her home town of Aleppo. The man held his tongue. In ISIS-land she would never have dared to say such a thing to a man. But now that she was on the edge of Europe, she felt free to speak her mind – and that was a kind of liberation. Nevertheless, she turned to her son and hugged him tightly and whispered into his ear, 'Ham, you've got to pretend that this is the *Pirates of the Caribbean*, for real. The baddies are after us, so we've got to be very, very quiet.'

'I'll be Jack Sparrow,' Ham said. 'Where is the Black Pearl?'

'It's coming, honey, it's coming.'

Ham fell silent at that, and put his hand in his mother's. Soon they could make out the sound of an engine. The hillside stiffened. Was this the Turkish police? But there was something about the slow, unhurried build-up of sound that didn't suggest the agents of law and order on the move. By the light of the stars, they could just make out a truck, using its sidelights only, coming around a bend. It trundled along a track that dipped below the church and came to a stop a few yards from the beach. Ghostly shapes got out and started unloading big boxes, dumping them close by the waves.

As if to mock the refugees' anxiety about making too much noise, the sound of the smugglers ripping open the cardboard boxes could be heard for miles. Someone flashed a light, and then they heard a petrol-driven compressor start up, its clatter further assaulting the quiet of the night. A flashlight beam cut through the darkness, illuminating a pump forcing air into a large grey tube, two feet around, which morphed into a U-shaped inflatable, thirty feet by seven. The smugglers placed the flattened-out cardboard boxes on its bottom, to give it a semblance of a keel.

The people on the hillside started gathering up their belongings and slowly, then more hurriedly, making their way down to the beach. The smugglers knew their business. Soon, seven inflatables lay half-in, half-out of the water. A few of the refugees tried to get on board but the smugglers snapped at them in Turkish to stay back. One by one, the inflatables were taken into the sea and a smuggler would go to the truck and return with a small electric outboard motor.

The first inflatable was ready. A couple of smugglers held it steady while fifty, sixty, seventy people crowded on, then one smuggler sitting at the stern opened up the electric outboard and with the softest of buzzing, barely audible, the inflatable slipped into the darkness, towards the bright lights of Kos. What the rest of the people waiting on the beach didn't see was that one hundred yards out, the smuggler at the outboard stood up, nudged a young Syrian sitting next to him, pointed his arm straight out directly towards Kos, then suddenly backflipped into the sea and started swimming powerfully back to the beach.

Stunned, the young Syrian had no choice but to grip the outboard's tiller and head west for Europe. The process repeated itself: each set of refugees thought the smuggler would guide them the whole way across; each smuggler jumped overboard some yards out, leaving the refugees to fend for themselves. It was, of course, good business: five hundred people paying $1,200 a head meant $600,000 for a night's work. The inflatables were around $500 each; paying off the Turkish police and coastguard was the most expensive cost – around $50,000 to look the other way. But, still, more than half a million dollars for one night's work: there was more money in shifting people than shifting heroin.

Once out in the Kos channel, the refugees were on their own. The wind grew stronger. Practised sailors would have checked the weather forecast and seen that a storm was forecast. The refugees were not practised sailors.

The thin man and his family were at the head of the queue for the second boat, and Jameela and Ham thought it smarter to let them go ahead. But that meant they lost their place in the line. Not only that, but every subsequent boat they waited for seemed dangerously crowded. In the end, they realised they had been too choosy, because the last and seventh boat was more overcrowded than all the others. It seemed cursed from the moment they stepped aboard: water was lapping over the sides into the bottom, making the cardboard soggy. Already an old lady had vomited into the bilges, someone was crying, a man was loudly intoning his prayers. Someone's phone rang, and broken fragments of a surreal conversation could be heard in Arabic: 'No, I swear to God . . . I'm on a boat . . . Hear that? That's the sound of the waves.'

Jameela hugged Ham as closely as she could, trusting that their life jackets would save them if the worst came to the worst. She was wrong about that: the jackets were packed with the cheapest foam the smugglers could buy. If you relied upon them to help you swim, you'd end up sinking.

Around her neck she had a plastic purse, in it three thousand dollars, given to her by Rashid, wrapped in cling film to prevent the cash from getting soaked.

The sky had become less black, was now a dark purple. Jameela and Ham waded towards the boat and clambered over to the stern of the inflatable, squeezing themselves in to find a perch on the very end of the port tube, just by the transom where the outboard was fixed. Their position on the boat was precarious, but it meant they got a better indication of the next disaster. Less than thirty yards out, the smuggler at the helm of the outboard backflipped into the sea and there was a great splash. Rudderless, the inflatable bounced around in the waves until a hapless Afghan took over the motor. The Taliban had burnt his village down because it was thought to be too friendly with the Americans. Reason enough to flee his homeland, but his country was landlocked. He'd never in his life been in a boat before, never mind made a sea journey. Panicking at the wholly unexpected responsibility of playing skipper, he turned the outboard's tiller hard to steer the inflatable back to land, back the way they had come. A man sitting next to him, from Iraq, yelled at him in Arabic: 'Listen, idiot, we lose our money if we don't head to Greece.' The Afghan didn't understand a word – Arabic and Pashto are as alike as English and Finnish – and in the watery darkness, with sea spray flying this way and that, the two men fought over control of the motor. The inflatable beat a crazy path, first heading to Greece, then racing back to Turkey. Each time it turned side on to the waves, seawater spilled over the inflatable's sides until it became more and more waterlogged, slowing its progress. Finally, the Iraqi punched the Afghan hard, took full control and, once again, they headed towards the lights of Kos. The wind's force grew, the sea tossing the boat around, causing the people to murmur, then cry out loud. The fear of making a noise and being caught by the Turkish police and coastguard had been replaced by a much bigger terror: that they might never make the sea-crossing alive.

A big wave sideswiped the inflatable, drenching everyone. Some people swore in Arabic, then in English, using phrases that would make gang members in Chicago's South Side blush – while others prayed out loud, the mix of cries all-too-accurately reflecting the dysfunction of religious and secular Syria. Jameela hated the mess her country had become. Her father had been a colonel in Zarif Senior's air force, but he and especially her mother had never been blind to the nature of the regime: corrupt but not grotesquely uncomfortable if you rolled along with it; a closed fist if you opposed it. But now Syria had become a byword for a religious fanaticism that had sucked in the dross of the world to kill in the name of a perverted and sick abomination of Islam.

She thought of Timur, the jihadi fanatic who'd grown sick of killing. God knows how he had gone back to being a human being again. He had been extraordinarily brave, releasing Rashid, her and Ham from their cages. Rashid had been in a bad way, his muscles palsied after days inside the cage; his arms, legs, face and neck horribly bruised after he went in spasm while under attack from the Taser. Timur had given them water, some bread to eat, showed Rashid some stretching exercises so that he could begin to recover some power in his muscles. Then Timur had hidden them under the four dead men in the truck, so they would not be gassed.

———

After their escape from the mountain, Timur left the three of them in an ancient catacomb in the Valley of the Tombs for several hours, returning in the dark on a motorbike. He brought with him scissors, glue, a vast beard shaved off some other poor soul fleeing ISIS, and all the accoutrements of a Hisbah: white tunic, calf-length trousers, black waistcoat, Kalashnikov. He was so fastidious about making her look exactly right. They were going to have to cross the battlefront and no woman, as a woman, could do that. Worse, not only could Rashid not walk on his own, but his arm muscles had become so atrophied he couldn't even hold a teacup to his mouth unaided. There was no way he could drive a motorbike at speed across the front line. So Jameela had to look like a man, and she had to drive the bike with Rashid, helpless, in the middle, and Ham on the back making sure he didn't fall off.

The moon came out, basking the city of the dead in a ghostly, silvery luminescence. Timur cut her hair so that she became a young Hisbah, not too long but not too short; he'd spent further time snipping and shaping the beard to her face so that by the end she looked so utterly convincing that Rashid pretended he was afraid of the Hisbah – of him/her. Timur said that he would glue the beard on two hours before sunrise, when they planned to cross the line.

Meanwhile Rashid lay flat on his back on a gravestone, luxuriating in twiddling his toes and patiently explaining the night sky to Ham, mapping out Mars, Venus and the pole star. Soon Ham fell asleep and Timur laid a blanket over him, and the fake Hisbad guided the invalid Rashid along the avenue of ancient tombs. As ever, Rashid and Jameela bickered, gently; as ever, the arguments helped them dance around the depth of the love they held for each other.

'You're a fool, Rashid,' she said, loving more than anything to goad him. 'Fancy thinking you're such a big shot that you could have got away with negotiating with ISIS. You're nothing more than a jumped-up butcher, not a diplomat.'

'So I'm the fool? I'm not the one who came running to Raqqa to save a foolish doctor.'

'Ah,' she said. 'I didn't come to Raqqa to try to help you.'

'You didn't? Then I am crushed.'

The moon suddenly hid behind a cloud and the night darkened, and just as suddenly the cloud passed and its light seemed even more powerful and surreal as the tombs cast long shadows. In the distance, a dog howled. They were walking arm in arm, him limping badly. If she let him go, he would fall down. She found the reversal of their normal physical dynamics – because he was much bigger and far stronger than her – strangely exciting.

'So why did you come to Raqqa?' he teased.

'For the shopping,' she said, deadpan.

'The shopping?' repeated Rashid, relishing the absurdity.

'I was misinformed,' she said.

'You are the maddest woman I have ever met, ever. You were mad when I first met you in Aleppo, back in high school. Mad then. Mad now.'

'But that's why you love me.' The naked truth of her statement stunned him for a second, and then he turned and tried to grip her face in her hands, but he was too weak to do so and so she smiled and helped him lie down on a flat tomb and they kissed, hungrily, passionately, with the intensity that only doomed lovers can enjoy. Afterwards, they lay staring up at the moon, Jameela nuzzling his hands with her mouth.

'If we make it across the front line and get to the free side' – the patchwork of land held by the Kurds and the rebels, neither Zarif nor ISIS – 'alive . . .'

'That's a big if . . .'

'What shall become of us?' asked Jameela.

'You are taking Ham to Germany and you will wait there for me.'

'And you?'

'I'm a surgeon. I'm needed in Aleppo. I have to go home, to help, to do my job.'

'I hate you.'

'I hate you back.'

'Why can't we ever be together?'

'I'm not the one who left Aleppo and ran off to Los Angeles and had a kid with some rich American doctor.'

'Dominic is not a doctor.'

'You call him a doctor.'

'He is not a doctor like you.'

'How do you mean?'

'You save people's lives.'

'Not always. These days, hardly at all. In fact, I think it was the jihadi who saved our lives.'

'Stop changing the subject.'

'Jameela, I love you but I have got to go to Aleppo, to go home, to help as best I can. If I sit this thing out, I will have to watch our people rip each other apart and do nothing to help. I will have failed, as a doctor, as a human being, as a man.'

'So you are a stupid man.'

'And you are a mad lady.'

After a time, they walked back to where Timur was watching over Ham, still fast asleep. The moon sank below the horizon and soon it was time to cross the line.

They looked the part, no question: the Hisbah gripping the handlebars of the motorbike, surprisingly thickly bearded for one so young; the big man in the middle, a Kalashnikov on a belt hanging off his shoulders; the kid on the back, one hand steadying the big man, the other behind him, locked on to the bike. They saluted Timur, who bowed from the waist, and then Jameela gunned the bike and it clattered off, into the desert.

Timur had drawn them a map of how to drive north-north-west out of Palmyra, avoiding the ISIS checkpoints he knew about. He told her that twenty, twenty-five miles beyond Palmyra was the front line with the Kurdish forces, but it was fuzzy and porous and it shifted.

They almost didn't make it. She didn't use the headlights – that would have made them a sitting duck – but drove slowly, using the starlight and the murmur of brightness to the east to work out where was asphalt, where was desert. A twist in the road caused Jameela to slow down, almost to walking pace, and suddenly she saw the checkpoint, the black flags of ISIS drooping in the predawn calm. A man shouted, a Kalashnikov started to bark, and she twisted the throttle and gunned the bike and surged ahead, sparks flying to left and right as bullets missed their target again and again.

After running the ISIS checkpoint, a long, lonely ride began through an empty, reddening no man's land, every shadow hiding a threat. In the distance, she made out the Kurdish checkpoint, a riot of flags, smoke rising from a chimney, some donkeys chewing grass to the side. She slowed the bike and it crawled towards the Kurdish Peshmerga, their baggy trousers flapping in the dawn breeze. Five Kurds – three men and two women – trained their rifles on them, their faces uneasy, cautious not to get too close lest this be another suicide bomb.

What happened next was the talk of the Kurdish battalion for weeks to come. Jameela rested the bike on its stand and ripped her false beard off with pained relish; the big man in the middle fell, like an oak tree, plumb in the middle of the road, landing in a guffawing heap on the tarmac, while the little boy got off the bike and did a step-perfect impression of Michael Jackson doing his moonwalk.

No one had ever crossed the line like that, ever.

———

'Mom, I'm freezing,' moaned Ham, bringing her back to the wretched here and now.

'Shh, darling, shh,' said Jameela. 'We won't be long.' But she said that through chattering teeth. The level of the scummy water in the bottom of the inflatable was rising, fast. When she had first stepped in the boat, it had covered her toes, now it was washing around her ankles; sometimes when the inflatable hit a deep trough, around her knees.

They were halfway across the channel dividing Turkey from Europe when the electric motor cut out.

# TROPOJË, NORTHERN ALBANIA

A phone call, encrypted, from Langley to northern Albania: 'Any news of the Angel Moroni?'

'No. The Russian said they found the corpse of the driver, but not him and not the Albanian cop, either.'

'Yeah, I heard that too. So he's gone AWOL in northern Albania. You can't find him; the Russians can't find him. But being who he is, he's going to find your facility, isn't he?'

'That's not a fact.'

'You know what I'm going to say next, don't you?'

'That would be an overreaction. We have no idea where Zeke Chand—'

'Don't say his name.'

'This call is encrypted, isn't it?'

'I'm superstitious. Anyway, we're closing it down.'

'No.'

'We're closing it down. Effective immediately.'

'And the patients?'

There was a pause on the line.

'What are you going to do with the patients?'

'We're sending a ship. We're thinking North Africa.'

'Listen, you're overreacti—'

'No, you listen to me. Our adversary is the most brilliant linguist in the Agency's history. He's not someone who runs away from this kind of intellectual puzzle. He lives and breathes to solve them. We don't want to appear on the front page of the *New York Times* and nor do you. So, we close this facility down and we move elsewhere. You carry on doing what you're doing. We just move. So start packing.'

———

The half-wolf sat on the bed looking down at Zeke, lying on his side, his breathing growing weaker by the second. His nose and lips were dark blue, his chest looked odd, unequal, as if one lung was bigger than the other, the veins on his neck bulging. Sotir lifted his head, his eyes to the side. The wind rose outside, spoiling the intensity of his concentration. Agim coughed and Sotir raised a hand, matted with hair, calling for absolute quiet. The wind softened and Sotir closed his eyes. Then he reached down to his belt and brought out a knife and slashed Zeke's shirt in two. The left side of his chest was covered by a bandage, bloodied, covering some kind of entry wound. It was very small, not big enough to have been made by a bullet; more like a piece of shrapnel from the road or concrete from the culvert had pierced his chest. Gently, Sotir turned Zeke so that he lay on his belly. The exit hole was easily missed, no bigger than a musket ball, out of it bubbling a pink broth of blood and air.

Sotir went to a metal strongbox by the bed, opened it and took out a sheet of plastic and some sticky tape. He cut the plastic with his knife so that it covered the wound, and taped it up so that it was sealed at the bottom and on the two sides but not at the top. It allowed excess air to escape, but not to enter.

The moment the patch was on, Zeke's breathing seemed less troubled. Within five minutes, his nose became a lighter shade of blue;

within ten it was grey; within twenty, pink. After an hour had passed, both the veins on his neck and the shape of his chest had returned to normal.

Agim examined the half-wolf with wonder and said, 'Doctor Sotir, I presume.'

The shepherd said something in the mountain dialect that Agim did not understand, and went over to the pot where a lamb stew was bubbling. A minute later, Agim looked over at him again and saw that he was smiling. That was, Agim reflected, the strange thing about people, not just in Albania but everywhere. This man looked like a savage, his body and face covered with hair, he could barely grunt, and yet somehow he had learnt some proper medicine. He had saved Zeke's life, and that wasn't just strange, it was amazing.

In the morning, Zeke woke – hungry, thirsty but very much alive, the gap in his teeth and his wide-open smile offering the false impression that he was simple, but his eyes glistening with that piercing intelligence that left Agim not just in awe but sometimes a little frightened. Sitting up in bed, drinking a cupful of the lamb broth, Zeke started a conversation with Sotir in a language that Agim had no knowledge of. Astonished that his patient could understand him, Sotir gabbled away, twenty words to the dozen. Zeke shushed him to make him slow down, and then the two conversed for five minutes, ten.

Eventually Zeke turned to Agim and explained: 'He's a Vlach, the ancient people of southern Europe. His mother abandoned him and he was adopted by a nurse at the hospital. She taught him the essentials of first aid.'

'He fixed the wound on your back, the one that was leaking air out of your lung.'

'Yes, he told me. He also said that your security people beat him up. They were trying to get him to say that he had killed the men who stood out in the thunderstorms and got hit by lightning. He knows where the prison is. They drilled holes in the mountain to give them air and the men, they escaped out of the holes. He told me he had no idea what they did to these men, but to see them afterwards, electrocuted by lightning, it must be the devil's work.'

'So what now?' asked Agim.

'I know a little about the facility,' Zeke replied. 'Not enough but, given time, I can work out the rest. I'm going home.'

'It's a long way to the United States from here by bus.'

'Where is the nearest phone?'

'You told me not to use one.'

'It should be all right now.'

Zeke jotted down a name and a telephone number on a piece of paper.

'You trust this man?' asked Agim.

'Yeah, he's the head of tactical operations, CIA. I appointed him. He won't let me down. My guess is in the other direction, that he might just go a little over the top.'

Zeke guessed right. Within two hours of Agim returning from the farmer's hut, where he had called the number, the sky over the shepherd's shack was full of heavy metal, the air trembling with chopper blades: two Apache gunships to keep the peace, two Chinooks packed with special forces muscle, and a fifth machine that was more flying clinic than helicopter. The last thing Agim and Sotir saw was Zeke being loaded on a stretcher up the medevac's ramp, a medic fussing over him, and Zeke waving at them, grinning his simple smile.

Then the ramp was raised, and Zeke vanished in a storm of dust.

# PALMYRA, SYRIA

They left him handcuffed in his room in the hotel, returning shortly after dawn. Under the canvas awnings to blind the spies in the sky, they led him towards a tractor pulling a trailer, its cargo masked by a grey sheet of plastic. Khalil lifted the plastic aside: underneath were three cages, one occupied by a man in an orange jumpsuit, another by a woman in a black *abaya*. Khalil opened the roof of the third cage and manhandled Timur in, none too gently, and then closed the cage, locking it in place with a thick padlock, and pulled the plastic sheet back in place. The tractor's engine chugged into life and they rode off, at fifteen miles an hour, the true nature of the load hidden from the enemy.

Timur's cage was at the back of the trailer and he had been placed in it facing the rear, so he couldn't communicate with the others; nor would it have been wise. He did his best to make himself as comfortable as was humanly possible with his arms handcuffed behind his back, in a cage less than a metre cubed. The journey was horrible – every bump and hollow in the road was transmitted directly up through Timur's spine – but it was not, mercifully, a long one.

The coolness of the tunnel gave away their destination – that and the echoing racket the tractor made as it chugged into the side of the mountain. After a short spell of time, they pulled up with a jerk. Each cage was lifted from the trailer and carried through the steel door into the facility, where they were dropped, gently, onto the concrete floor. As the cages were shifted, Timur was able to make out his fellow prisoners. One was Beth, the woman with the blue eyes who had condemned Abdul's execution. The other occupant was no less exotic: Korean, and not from the south.

A Hisbah slouched towards them. Timur contracted in his cage, remembering Rashid flinching from Haroun's use of that evil electric stick, but it was a false alarm: the Hisbah emptied a bottle of water over his head and some of it landed on his tongue. Then the Hisbah performed the same act of mercy two more times and they heard his steps retreat, the lights were killed, the steel door slammed shut. Beyond, they could make out the sound of the tractor starting up. Only when its last echo had receded and the silence was total did they dare speak.

The Asian man said something in a language Timur did not understand. His tone, though, was entirely readable: the wheedling of a doomed man.

'Timur, it's you, isn't it?'

'Yes, Beth, it is me.'

'How did you end up in a cage?'

'I made a miscalculation,' he said drily. 'How are you?'

She paused, and then came the reply: 'It's wonderful to know you're here.'

'Beth,' he replied, 'sometimes I wonder whether you are who you say you are. No native English-speaker could possibly call this situation wonderful.'

Her laughter, when it came, was delicious. Her voice lowered an octave as she continued: 'Timur, I have a question for you. Just before the lights were switched off I saw a big stack of drums, stainless-steel drums. They had death's heads on them.'

'You did.'

'What's in them?'

'Sarin,' said Timur.

'What is sarin?'

'Sarin is an organophosphorus neurotoxin,' said Timur dispassionately, reciting from his prodigious memory. 'Twenty times as lethal as cyanide. It tastes of nothing and is a clear liquid with no colour. It works by blocking the enzyme that causes nerve cells to stop firing. The effect is that sarin jams every nerve switch "on" so that the heart and lung muscles go into spasm. The actual cause of death is asphyxiation.'

'How did it end up here?'

'Our friend in orange is a gentleman from the north of Korea, I believe. His government has twice been caught shipping chemical suits to the government of Syria. It makes no sense for Zarif to buy chemical suits but not the gas. This is it. When ISIS overran Palmyra, they discovered this place. All the other North Korean technicians managed to run away. This one got left behind.'

'So why have they left us here?'

Timur said nothing.

'It's not good news, is it, Timur?' Somehow Beth forced laughter into her voice, the laughter of the brave. 'They're going to gas us with this sarin, aren't they?'

Timur held his tongue.

'How many people could ISIS kill with this amount of sarin?'

'Hundreds, thousands. Too many.'

'Promise me, Timur, that if you ever get out of here, you will find someone, someone good, and you will tell them about this place so that it can be destroyed.'

Timur remained silent.

'Timur,' Beth said quietly, 'I came to Syria to help, to save lives, to prevent children from being paralysed, from being crippled for life by an entirely preventable disease. Because of bad luck and maybe naivety on my part, and pure evil on theirs, I am to end my life being gassed in a cage. I have been traded at a slave market, raped, again and again, and have been used horribly by this pig you call the Caliph. So my entire life has ended up some ghastly, cosmic joke, and every single thing I believe in and cherish – the power of human goodness, the necessity to behave honourably, to honour other people's faiths and customs while doing one's best to help people, to help children – that has ended in this – this darkness.'

No sound at all in the cavern, apart from the light murmur of their breathing.

'But my life will not be a joke,' she continued. 'It will not be in vain if somehow we can prevent this horrible gas from being used against ordinary people. So this is the last request of a woman who is to die: will you, Timur, promise me that, if you survive, you will tell someone good, someone with the power to prevent this gas from being used? Will you, Timur?'

In the distance, the clatter of motorbikes became louder and louder in the tunnel.

'Will you, Timur?' she repeated.

Over the sound of the fast-approaching motorbikes, now deafening, came Timur's voice, loud and strong: 'I will, Beth, I promise.'

The bike engines stopped and the door to the cavern swung open. One headlight's full beam remained switched on. Timur watched as the shadow of a thickset figure limped across the light. The Caliph himself had come to see the devil's work with his own eyes. The Caliph's shadow was holding hands with a much smaller shadow: Haroun.

The lights came on with a clang, and Timur noted the arrival of Khalil and – last to enter – Hadeed. With a dryness in his throat, Timur noted that Haroun had brought his electric gun with him.

The boy rushed over to the three cages, smiled his iciest smile and plunged the Taser into the back of the neck of the Korean, the electric-blue sparks creating a spider's web against the iron bars of the cage.

The prisoner convulsed in agony and gibbered something pitiable in his own language.

'Where is this *kaffir* from?' asked the Caliph.

'He was left behind,' said Hadeed, 'the only one we caught when the other North Koreans ran away. He speaks no English; he is useless to us.'

Again, Haroun prodded the Korean with his Taser. He screamed and this time broke into Russian, a long, soulful sentence expressing his regrets for any wrongs he had committed. The prisoner's skull, arms and legs stopped their banging and crashing against the cage, and into the sudden quiet Timur found himself replying in Russian: 'Hush, soon you will be with God.'

'Timur, what did you say?' hissed the Caliph.

Timur twisted inside his cage, as much as he was able, to turn to face the Caliph. 'I told this man that soon he will be with God.'

'What tongue?' asked the Caliph.

'I spoke in Russian, sir.'

'So you can communicate with him? I was told this man was useless to us.'

'Russian is my second language, sir, after Chechen.'

'Ask him a technical question,' said the Caliph. 'Ask him how many people one canister of this gas can kill.'

Timur translated the question into Russian. The Korean's answer was complicated and long.

'Well, what does he say?' demanded the Caliph.

'He says that is a difficult question to answer, because it depends on a number of factors, including the delivery system and the nature of the target, in particular the density of the population. So, if one were able to release the gas at a controlled rate in a closed room, like a concert hall, with no easy access to fresh air, then you could kill hundreds in one go. Technically, if you administer the smallest dose of gas to the maximum number of people – and this is an impossibility – then each canister could kill one hundred thousand people.'

The Caliph clapped his hands with joy.

'What is his name?'

Timur discovered that his name was Mr Zhang.

'Release him.'

The guards cut the plastic handcuffs and unlocked the padlock holding the cage door in place. Zhang was so stiff they had to lift him out. He tried to stand up and fell over and stayed down, gripping his thighs, trying to squeeze some life into muscles that had gone dead through lack of use. Meanwhile, the Caliph inspected the stack of sarin drums, the chemical suits and the gas masks with a look of satisfaction. He barked a series of commands in Arabic, and the guards picked up the cages holding Beth and Timur and began carrying them into the gassing hut.

'Sir,' said Hadeed, 'if we spare the Korean but execute Timur, we won't be able to communicate with him. Timur is the only one of us who speaks Russian and Arabic fluently, and he is a capable engineer.'

'But Timur is a traitor, sir,' Haroun piped up. 'He freed the three moderns.'

When the Caliph spoke, his voice was so soft it could have been a girl's: 'Haroun, my boy, we have a traitor on our hands whose voice could be useful to us. What would you do?'

'The traitor must be punished for his crimes against us,' said Haroun, his face suffused with piety. 'Timur's voice is useful to us, yes, but not his eyes. Let him be blinded.'

'Khalil,' barked the Caliph. 'Deliver our mercy to the prisoner and let all our judgements be as wise as this one.'

Child's play for a man of Khalil's strength to blind a prisoner trussed up in a cage. Timur did his best to make no sound, but the moment his second eyeball was mashed to a useless pulp he let out a shudder of pain. Haroun clapped, excited.

The Caliph barked an order, and Khalil went over to Beth's cage to carry it into the gassing hut. As it was lifted, Beth started to sing:

'*Amazing grace, how sweet the sound*
*That saved a wretch like me . . .*'

Khalil placed the cage in the hut facing the observation window, but there was a problem sealing the door. Timur would have solved the problem in an instant, but he was sightless. So Hadeed and Khalil had to fuss over the locking bolts while still she sang, her voice not wavering once, a thing of beauty, echoing in the cavern.

'*I once was lost but now am found*
*Was blind but now I see . . .*'

Timur sat in his cage, his hands still cuffed behind his back, his muscles locked in the agony of enforced stasis, his eyeballs gone, blood and jelly dribbling down his chest, but his heart beat with pride that he had known this Beth, who could go to her death with such raw courage. The door was closed, shutting off her song.

Beth would have died like the others: her muscles jerking in violent, incoherent spasms, pink foam bubbling out of her eyes, nose, mouth and ears, then her face falling deathly white.

The Caliph watched in silence, then his face lit up with a wintry smile. 'This is a most excellent weapon.'

Unbidden, inside Timur's head, came the lines:

> *I am in blood*
> *Stepp'd in so far that, should I wade no more,*
> *Returning were as tedious as go o'er.*

'Timur,' asked the Caliph, 'what was she singing?'

'A song of forgiveness, sir. A Christian song.'

The Caliph walked through the steel door out to the tunnel proper in absolute silence. The Caliph's motorbike was a Harley, taken from the home of an Iraqi general in Mosul. The Hisbah who drove it opened the box above the rear wheel and took out a black *abaya*, black gloves and a black facemask. The Caliph donned them and sat on the back of the Harley, with Haroun sitting in the middle. The guard switched on the engine and the Harley roared along through the tunnel and out into the light of day.

To anyone watching from a mountaintop or a video feed seven thousand miles away in Colorado, they would only make out a motor-bike, a rider, a child and a woman. They could only be an innocent family on the road.

# DAMASCUS, SYRIA

It stopped, as suddenly as it had begun.

Once you've heard the distorted sobs and squawk-box yelps and popped howls of a man being tortured through a malfunctioning public address system until they stop or he's dead or his vocal cords give way, your life changes. The sounds of agony are imprinted on your mind, forever.

Joe sat with his back against the wall, the cell so deep below ground he could feel the air pressure suck and pop in his inner ear. It was as if he were in a tomb. The only light was a dagger's slash under the door from the corridor beyond. To smother the sound of a fellow human being subjected to monstrous agony, Joe had his hands over his ears, but the noise – piercing, intense, ethereal – got through. That was, of course, their purpose. Joe didn't know how long the victim lasted before he stopped making any sound. It was probably ten minutes. It felt like ten centuries.

Time slipped in the tomb. Joe had no idea how long he had spent in the darkness. He feared that if he spent much longer without seeing daylight, he would go mad.

The white noise of the loudspeakers was killed with a loud click, and the tomb fell into silence. This, something Joe had begged for, when it came, bore down on him more horribly than the screaming. Physical pain is one thing, but the agony one's own mind invents, the agony of what might be to come, is fiendishly worse. And the heft of the silence intensified his fear.

The cell was very deep underground. No natural light, no rays of the sun penetrated it; no sounds from the outside world, no car engines, no car horns, no dogs barking, no children playing. What sounds you could just make out were muffled, gagged, suppressed: a soft *thunk* might be a cell door slamming in the distance; a *tick-tack, tack-tick*, footsteps coming towards his cell, then receding into stillness. Only the screams could be heard at full volume.

His mind's ear still echoed to the sound of the man in endless agony. The fear that they might do to Joe what they had done to the screaming man was so strong he felt he could eat it.

Coming down the corridor, the *click-clack* step of a guard, but alongside that the soft shuffle of a prisoner, barefoot. Joe craved company, the solace of another human soul. Would they walk past his cell, as they had done so many times before? His dislocation from humanity was nigh on complete. No one had spoken to him. Every now and then, the guard – Joe had baptised him Mr Click-Clack – and a second person, a man, some kind of doctor or medic, would arrive at the cell door. Mr Click-Clack would throw a blindfold at him, which he would put on. Then, in Arabic, the guard would command Joe to lie on his belly with his hands behind his back. Only then would they enter. The medic would cut his bandages, dab his wounds with sour-smelling and extremely painful antiseptic wipes and then re-bandage him. Then they would leave. At the start, Joe had asked questions: *Where am I? What is the charge against me? When can I see a lawyer?* Neither man had said a word. If Joe became too insistent, Mr Click-Clack would bring down a cosh on his arms or legs. Once, with Joe not getting the message, the guard smashed the cosh against the base of Joe's spine with such force he feared he would never walk again. From then on, he asked no questions.

The silence was eating up his sanity. They were passing Joe's door . . . *Oh God, how wonderful.* The door was unlocked and in they came. Joe heard the prisoner being pushed forward, the door slamming then locked, then Mr Click-Clack clack-clicking away until his steps dissolved into quiet. In the distance, Joe made out, or thought he made out, the suggestion of a door slamming shut, of someone weeping, in another direction, of a sneeze.

The newcomer began to shiver uncontrollably, and then he started to moan to himself. In near total darkness, one's other senses – touch, hearing, smell – explode into a capacity you would never have thought possible. The new man stank, of shit and piss and blood and cooked meat, like kebab, so much so Joe could feel himself gagging. The smell was too disgusting, and Joe found himself vomiting, his stomach muscles in spasm. Eventually, the retching stopped and Joe cleaned himself up with a damp, smelly rag.

'Good morning,' Joe whispered.

Nothing.

'Or should I have said good evening?'

Still nothing.

Then a light, soft murmuring in Arabic, verses of the Quran. Joe cursed silently to himself. He had had enough of religion to last him a dozen Paradises and then some.

At the core of the Troubles were two nationalisms entwined with two religions, fighting each other. After his father was shot dead in Belfast when he was seven, his mother had taken him and his older brother south, to the relative calm of the Republic. They'd ended up in Cork. On Joe's first day at his new school, he'd written in his new diary: *We had a god but then we put it in the attic.* The teacher, a Christian Brother – though not much of either – read his blasphemy out loud and gave him the strap, a short strip of leather that, correctly applied, left a stinging pain on the palm of your hand. Worse than that was the class's mockery of the new boy, with his weird Belfast accent. Their new parish priest had come round to the house that very evening to enquire what devilry these new people from the north, the Tipladys, were up to. When Joe's mother heard his question, she laughed out loud, the first time he'd seen that happen since his father's murder.

'We had a crucifix, Father,' she'd said. 'And I decided I didn't want it on the wall of the living room in our new home so I put it in the attic.'

The priest was on the doorstep, his mother at the front door, Joe was eavesdropping from behind the living room door, his brother Seamus was out playing football.

'Go easy on us, Father,' his mother continued. 'The Rah shot my man. Now Seamus and Little Joe have got no da. Your God may be able to explain that to two little boys but mine can't. So we're not going to have a crucifix on the wall and we're not going to Mass anymore. We'll go to hell our own sweet way.'

The priest swore. His mother swore back and slammed the door and braced her back against it and laughed so much that tears of joy trickled down her cheeks.

But Joe had been to the world's purely atheist state, too, and that wasn't so wonderful. Though, of course, you could say that North Korea has a religion, that the ruler is some kind of god.

And now this man, Joe's cellmate, he took solace in God, his God, in this place. Well then, who was Joe to hold that against him? He stopped praying and Joe sighed, more to himself than the other man, and said, 'I'd love to hear some English, just a phrase in English. Anything . . .'

Silence, then a light cough, then from out of the gloom:

*Tomorrow, and tomorrow, and tomorrow,*
*Creeps in this petty pace from day to day,*
*To the last syllable of recorded time;*
*And all our yesterdays have lighted fools*
*The way to dusty death. Out, out, brief candle!*
*Life's but a walking shadow, a poor player,*

*That struts and frets his hour upon the stage,*
*And then is heard no more. It is a tale*
*Told by an idiot, full of sound and fury . . .*

'*Signifying nothing.*' Joe completed the verse from *Macbeth*. To him, to hear those words in that darkness, it was unbearably moving. Tears ran down his face, tears he could not stop.

'Thank you, that was beautiful,' Joe whispered.

'It was nothing.'

'The screaming just now?' Joe asked. 'That was you?'

'I'm embarrassed to say it was. They amplify it, you know, to accentuate the effect.'

'I noticed. But the loudspeakers distort it, kind of makes it worse.'

'Of course. It's their version of' – the man hesitated – 'Justin Bieber.'

'That's a bit harsh,' Joe said, and together they colluded in the quietest of chuckles. But in that place of hate and fear, even the softest laughter was an act of sedition.

'Perhaps. Perhaps not.' His English had a strong accent, but the grammar was good, his voice suggesting someone younger than Joe but cracked, if not yet broken, beyond exhaustion, on the edge of life. Yet there was a quality that shone through his words, something that placed him, if not out of reach of his torturers, then at least aside from them – a sardonic intelligence that glittered in the dark, that was irrepressible.

'The strange thing is I was telling our . . .' He paused to search for the right word. 'Our *hosts* the truth, the absolute truth, and they knew it. But for them, the truth is dangerous. Better hear what they want to hear. This request, I found it difficult to oblige. Hence my misfortune.'

'I'm so sorry I vomited. It was the smell of burnt skin.'

'Shh. It's over now. Let's not talk of these dull things.'

Joe paused, wanting to know more but afraid to press him. Only then did he remember his manners.

'Is there anything I can do for you?'

'My wounds, perhaps they need a wash.'

'There's a jug of water somewhere here,' Joe said. 'And one of my bandages is not too dirty.'

'Your accent is not quite British?'

'I'm Irish.'

'Oh . . .' He said it long, as if he'd worked out who Joe was, or who Joe might be.

'*Oh* means what?'

'Nothing.'

Joe shuffled on his bottom to the back of the cell, away from the door, and put his fingers out tentatively so that he grasped the water jug – not to be confused with the foul-smelling pisspot that was in danger of becoming full. He brought the jug back to his usual place and asked his cellmate to move as close as possible to the knife-slash of light. What Joe saw made his hands shake so much, he almost dropped the jug.

'Holy Mother of God,' he cried out. Joe could swear like a trooper when he stubbed his toe. For something like this, he had to go back to when he was six years old, when he'd been an altar boy, when blasphemy meant something. The man before him had been blinded in both eyes, his nose broken, his chest peppered with cigarette burns, but worst of all was the stench of burnt flesh from his groin.

'How did they do this to you?' he asked in a whisper.

'Blowtorch.'

Joe gagged again, but this time, thank heaven, he didn't vomit. He dabbed his used bandage on his cellmate's useless eyes, his nose, then handed it to him to clean up his groin, as far as that was possible. The other man inhaled sharply; when Joe was done, the bandage was black with blood.

As Joe moved, his moon necklace rattled slightly. His cellmate's fingers moved to Joe's chest and scrabbled around before locating the necklace, running his fingers around it in a way Joe found overly intimate.

'This moon, a gift?' he asked.

'Yes,' Joe said, 'from a friend.'

He shuffled out of the light and Joe returned to his usual place, with his back to the wall, his arms on his knees.

'My name is Joe Tiplady. And you?'

The darkness ensured Joe couldn't see him but Joe sensed, though it sounded strange, that he was smiling.

'I have so many names that I forget them all. Forgive me, Mr Tiplady—'

'Call me Joe . . .'

'In this place, Joe, the less you know about me, the better. Suffice to say, you can call me Aladdin. My hosts here think of me as a thing of darkness. So call me Aladdin. It amuses me.'

'Aladdin, like in the movie?'

'Aladdin, like in the pantomime. I had an aunt who lived in London for a time. Auntie Natasha went to see *Aladdin* at the Drury Lane theatre. Her description of this pantomime was glorious. Aladdin wasn't a man at all but a woman dressed up as a man. The wicked uncle was played by a man in a fez called . . .' He hesitated, dredging his memory and failing. 'Alas, my memory is going. A magician, but so bad at magic. I was a boy when the Russians were bombing Grozny and I had already lost most of my family. I used to tremble with fear, and to get my mind off the bombs, my aunt would describe this man in a fez trying to turn a handkerchief into a white rabbit and failing, and failing, and failing . . .' He started to laugh softly, almost on the edge of hearing, a sweet, infectious giggle that reminded Joe of someone in his past.

'The worst magician in the world? I saw him in a show in Cork when I was but a boy. His name was Tommy Cooper.'

'Ah yes,' he said. 'Tommy Cooper – how wonderful to rediscover that in this place.' Joe joined Aladdin in laughter, just a gentle giggle at first. Tommy Cooper had been a big working-class man with a drinker's nose – something silly, not quite right about him in fez and tuxedo. Something melancholy, too, about his doomed attempts to bring off magic tricks, a puncturing of magic's pretension; about all human endeavour, perhaps. In this dark place, which had been echoing with screams only minutes before, laughter was a weapon. Joe's mind's eye pictured the clown-magician trying and failing to procure a white rabbit, and it got funnier and funnier until his ribs started to hurt.

'Shh,' the stranger warned. 'They must not hear us laugh because they might think we are laughing not at the magician, but at them. And that would not do.'

Joe bit his lip and the cell returned to quiet.

For a while Aladdin said nothing, then he sniffed. 'Forgive me, Joe, I smell antiseptic cream. It's quite unusual for our hosts to treat you here for the injuries they themselves have created. Are you injured?'

'Before I arrived here.'

'How?'

'I fell off a roof.'

'Forgive me, Joe, but that was clumsy of you, and I do not think you are a clumsy man.'

The hairs on the back of Joe's neck stood up. There was something alarming about this man's intelligence, the power of his insight.

'I found myself in Ghouta during the sandstorm.'

'Ghouta is not at all safe for a European.'

'It was a big mistake. We were almost captured by ISIS. Running from them, we got to the roof, and then I climbed onto a satellite-dish frame which buckled, and then a helicopter came and barrel-bombed ISIS. I was protected from the full force of the blast by being shielded by the building. The army must have picked me up. First they brought me to an ordinary prison, then I ended up here. By rights I should be dead.'

'Thanks be to God that you are not. And how nice of them to treat you. No torture?'

'The guard has hit me with a cosh a fair few times, once on my spine. But no, nothing like what you've been through.'

'So you are here but not being tortured, a most unusual paradox, Joe. You must be an honoured guest of the government.'

'I hadn't quite thought of it like that.'

'We are guests of air force intelligence, if I am not mistaken. Seven floors below ground. Here, they keep the most interesting guests in all of Syria.'

'Is this the worst place in Syria?'

'If you're assuming that only Zarif tortures, then I'm afraid I cannot say yes. This is the worst place the regime has that is, er, mapped. There are other places – villas in Damascus, villas in the countryside, towards the sea – where the Alawites are strong, where people can be forgotten about. They may be worse. I have no personal knowledge of this. There are places under the control of ISIS that are differently appointed but no better. But this place is not at all good. I know of many people who have been through here, and more who have left here dead, and you are the very first to be treated in this most special way. That changes things.'

'How so?' Joe asked.

The man paused to gather his thoughts. 'If they have made a decision not to torture you, and I think that best fits the facts, then I can tell you some things I would like to be communicated. I do not, I think, have so long to live. At the moment, what I have to say has been falling on deaf ears. But I think you are a good listener, Joe, and I trust you.'

'Why would you trust me?'

'Because my sister did.'

In the distance, a cell door closed with a soft thud.

# THE MEDITERRANEAN SEA

The inflatable lost all forward motion and began to slop around crazily in the sea, which was getting wilder by the second. Without power, the inflatable's lack of a proper V-shaped hull reduced it to a part-deflated grey balloon, not just bouncing around in the dark but wallowing within its own length, generating its own caterpillar motion. In the bow, the old lady who had already thrown up in the bilges vomited profusely over a fat man who, outraged for his dignity and fearful for his life, slapped her hard across the face; the old lady's son punched the fat man on the jaw, knocking him overboard. The fat man's wife let out a piercing scream. His son, a twelve-year-old boy, reached out his hand to rescue his father; the fat man, heavier than his boy, dragged him into the sea with him. The screaming woman followed her son, her cry extinguished by a throat full of brine.

Three young men in the starboard middle stood up to remonstrate with the hapless Iraqi who had been piloting the inflatable, yelling at him to restart the outboard – but the truth, unknown to the people on the boat, was that the smugglers had not bothered to recharge the electric motor properly, giving it only enough juice to get the refugees a mile or two away from the beach and out of their hands. The Iraqi shouted back, gesturing by dumbshow that the outboard would not start, but as he did so the boat tipped heavily down the biggest trough yet and two of the young men standing, gesticulating with fury, fell backwards into the sea. For so many of the people on the boat who were suffering the delusion that their life jackets might save them, the screams from the men in the water, turning to gurgling as they sank, proved them wrong. Their friends leant over to bring them back but, as they did so, the middle of the starboard side of the rib deflated some more, allowing in yet more gallons of seawater. The rescuers abandoned their attempt, and the men at sea gibbered in terror. The water level inside rose remorselessly, and more and more people started to scream, to stand up, making the boat more unstable, allowing more water in. There was no true captain, no legitimate authority; in its absence, in the predawn murk, there was chaos and frenzy and inhumanity.

The wind strengthened, the waves reaching two metres, and the inflatable started to sink, bow first. The smooth plastic offered no hand-holds, no traction, so that people who, with immense self-discipline, had spent the crossing sitting down, now were awash and floated off into the sea helplessly. Soon thirty, forty people were bobbing about in the waves, some trying to cling on to the grey plastic, others splashing around desperately in the choppy water, half in and half out. As luck would have it, by being amongst the last to board, Jameela and Ham at the stern of the inflatable were in the safest, or least risky, place. She clung on to the wooden transom to which the outboard was fixed with one hand, and to Ham with the other. But soon, they both knew, the stern would become so waterlogged that it would lose buoyancy and they would go under.

'Mom,' said Ham, 'I love you.'

Jameela kissed him, hating every fibre of her being. She had fought for so long for them to be free from fear – and now, by her own actions, by her own reckless stupidity, they were both going to die.

Some already had. As the sun came up, Jameela saw seven, eight, nine corpses float past them, face up and face down, men, women, children. In the slop at her feet, inside the three-quarters-sunk inflatable, was an infant, barely two, bobbing up and down in the water, its face white with death.

# DAMASCUS, SYRIA

Wolf Eyes – Joe's dead love – had been Chechen. Katya had told him about her little brother, Timur: how he had been radicalised after the Russians had tortured him, how he had joined ISIS and had been, for a time, lost to the world, and her.

'You're Timur, aren't you? Katya's little brother?'

'Call me Aladdin, Joe.'

'That wasn't a negative.'

'And you're the Irishman Katya fell in love with, after she ran away from the Russian. We were able to communicate, a little, in that time, and she told me about this man called Tiplady. I suspected it might be you, but it was only when my fingers were able to touch the moon necklace that I knew for sure. I gave it to her. So, here we are.'

'I miss her, every day of my life,' Joe said.

'Before you die, you cannot get enough of breathing.'

'What's that?'

'A saying that Auntie Natasha liked.' He said nothing for a time, then: 'May I ask, how did Katya die?'

For a time Joe was lost, the memory of that dusk in Utah; his love, lifeless in his arms.

'A killer, a CIA man turned traitor, working for the Russians, held an old woman hostage. Katya challenged him to shoot her instead. She was extraordinarily brave.'

'The killer?'

'I shot him.'

'She was buried according to our tradition?'

'No, I am sorry, according to mine.'

'And what is your religion?'

'I'm a lapsed Catholic.'

'What does a lapsed Catholic believe in?'

'That God is a drunk, I suppose. I had Katya cremated and then I took her ashes to an island off Donegal in my country. The Atlantic rolls in, big surf, seabirds, seals, no humans in sight, a small chapel, abandoned. It's a place . . . It's a wilderness of savage beauty. You could call it holy. It is . . . it was for us. Before, we had a few days together there, in hiding. It was, for Katya and for me, the best of times.'

'Perhaps I can go there someday,' Timur said.

'Perhaps,' Joe agreed, but the uncertainty in his voice gave the game away.

'Perhaps, but not so likely.' There was something wry about the way Timur spoke, acknowledging the reality that they were both locked in a tomb, deep below the ground.

'This . . .' said Joe. 'Our meeting in this place is too much of a coincidence.'

'In here, there is no such thing as a coincidence.'

'So this is part of a game? They've deliberately put the two of us here together?'

'Tyranny is cruel, but it is not stupid. If it were stupid, too often it would fail. They may have a reason. Or they know that you don't speak Arabic but they don't know that I can speak some English. I haven't told them. The logic may well be to frighten you, to get you to talk. It's a smart idea to put you in a cell with a man who has been badly treated. You did vomit when I first came into the cell, so their logic has some force.'

Joe fell silent for a moment to give Timur's argument some thought. Then something else occurred to him: 'Another question I should have asked earlier . . . Are we safe to talk here?'

'I think so,' Timur said. 'I don't know if Katya told you, but I have some technical abilities . . .'

'She said you were a genius at radios, computers.'

'She was always kind about me, my sister. I have a genuine gift for anything involving numbers, for mathematics, for engineering. I hacked Zarif's computers, read the minds of our enemies. I became, for a time, useful to the head of one of ISIS's intelligence arms. The Caliph, Abu Bakr al-Baghdadi, sits at the centre like an octopus hiding in a sea cave, wafting his tentacles in the currents to sniff out what is happening. He is a deeply intelligent and sensitive man, and a psychopath, both at the same time. This combination he has, of subtlety and savagery, is extraordinary. He speaks so softly you can barely hear him. This is a problem for some of our bravest fighters because they have been deafened by enemy bombs. With this soft voice, he can order a man to be burnt alive. For a time I enjoyed his blessing. And then I began to understand his true nature, and the true nature of ISIS, and he and his men turned against me. It felt like the sun dying—'

The air pressure in the tomb changed suddenly, causing an intense pain in Joe's ears. 'Sweet Jesus, my ears!' Joe cried out.

'Yes, the barometric atmosphere here is no friend of the prisoner. It was an accident, a consequence of poor design, not deliberate, I understand. Zarif's Mukhabarat blunders more often than everyone in Syria realises. We hate the changes in air pressure. The air is not good, too thick with carbon dioxide. This makes it stuffy, gives you headaches, bad dreams sometimes, and if they do not open the door for days, hallucinations. Bad for the prisoners but bad also for the guards. As a result, they have a real problem keeping people. I hacked into the main server for the Mukhabarat. Like any bureaucracy, they groan and grumble all the time: the air pressure here, the lack of money to do things, not enough staff. The regime's single biggest challenge is that Zarif can truly rely upon only a tenth of the Syrian population and even his people, the Alawites, don't love him. But to answer your question, there is no recording equipment in the cells in this place. If there had been, I would have read the transcripts. We are safe to talk but, Joe, remember the use of particular words or phrases that can become habit-forming, that can become dangerous.'

'So you ended up ISIS's intelligence chief?'

'No, never that. I was one of the Caliph's technicians. My task was not to spy but something else.'

'And that was?'

'Making bombs.'

'I did that too, once.'

'This is a joke, no?'

'This is the truth. I was a bomb-maker for the Irish Republican Army. And then one day I realised that I was brainwashed to kill people who – I might not like them, I might not agree with them, how they ruled the north of my country, but they weren't intrinsically bad. Stupid, wrong sometimes, but not bad, like Zarif, like al-Baghdadi. It – my moment of awakening – happened in a terrorist training camp in North Korea. I realised that the North Koreans were brainwashed into believing their rulers were gods. And if they were brainwashed, then so was I. From then on killing people on the orders of my IRA masters seemed senseless to me. So I made no more bombs, only duds.'

'So we are two bomb-makers in prison, but we don't have a single detonator between us.' Joe could hear the smile in his voice, the savouring of irony.

'Tell me, how come you ended up here?' Joe asked.

'*Promyvaniye mozgov* in Russian, *ghasil damagh* in Arabic.'

'Which is?'

'Joe, you have already used the word: brainwashing. The Russians brainwashed me into hating them. They killed my father, then my mother, then my two older sisters were burnt to a crisp. I hated them so much I joined the jihad. My brainwashing was not immediate or instant, but slow. After our two older sisters were killed, Katya and I were taken in by a Russian woman, our Auntie Natasha, the one who saw the pantomime in London. She was a good woman. But goodness was not the essential quality for surviving in Chechnya then. Our aunt was killed, Katya became a whore for the Russians and I became a killer and a fanatic. It seemed the logical, necessary thing to do.'

'How did they brainwash you?'

'Sometimes I think I did it to myself, but that's not the whole truth. You need two things to become brainwashed – the first that a wrong has been done to you. I was fourteen and tortured – everyone I loved had been killed, apart from my sister who became a whore.'

'Katya wasn't—'

'A whore is better than a killer. What I became was worse than what Katya did, but I don't want to bend reality. It's too distorted already.'

'And the second condition?'

'Someone to brainwash you, who is themselves brainwashed, who believes in the brainwashing totally and absolutely. First I became a Chechen jihadi, then a follower of Osama bin Laden, working for al-Qaeda, then I joined Islamic State, ISIS. I was brainwashed into hating everyone. I became, I thought, a warrior for Islam. They cut me off from the world I knew. They controlled more and more of my life. The words I could use, the vocabulary, how I saw the world, how I thought, all of that was reduced, restricted, throttled. I followed the Prophet, I venerated the Quran, the Hadiths, but simply repeating them doesn't make you a better Muslim. I lost my capacity to reflect, to calculate, to calibrate whether what I was being told made sense, whether I was truly honouring the Prophet or something else. After a time, the brainwashing turned me into a robot. I obeyed my masters and only them.

But there was a strange joy in this submission. The surrender of self to the cause, the greater good, to God – that is joyful. I abandoned responsibility for my actions and I submitted. The US Marine Corps, the Jesuits, they do something similar, I believe?'

'And the Rah,' Joe whispered, almost under his breath.

'To make a bomb, that is one thing,' Timur continued. 'In Iraq, then Syria, I ran a production line. Soon I was in charge of the biggest bomb factory for the whole Caliphate. My bombs were not ordinary bombs. I had a team of one hundred boys. When they were not at the ISIS *madrasahs*, they worked for me below ground making suicide vests. I don't know how many people have died because of me. Hundreds, maybe thousands . . .'

'When did you wake up?'

'It took a long time, a very long time. I had learnt to unlearn. To un-think. Logic, experience, facts, I took only what was useful for the cause; the other evidence in front of me I ignored. My un-thinking began among the Russians on their torture train. In Chechnya they kept a secret-police train in a siding, where they would electrocute us, half-choke us to death, leave us shackled, naked – minus twenty degrees outside. It was there that I welcomed the idea of jihad; I submitted to it. And yet I also knew that my Russian aunt Natasha was a good woman, she had cared for Katya and I, and the things she loved when she went to London, the things she taught us about as the Russian bombs fell – the pantomime, Tommy Cooper, *Top of the Pops* – I knew they were good things. She saw *Macbeth* at the Old Vic. I have her copy of the play – or I used to. I loved this play. And yet when I was with ISIS, the ISIS part of my mind hated her and her "paganism". You unlearn doubts, you block out those moments when you remember something before the brainwashing took control. But the whole time I was a fanatic, a part of me – a dim, shadowy, suppressed part of me – knew that what I was doing was wrong, some species of lie.'

'What changed?'

'The Internet. Access to the Internet was extremely difficult for most of us fighters in ISIS – first in Iraq, then in Syria. But when I became not just the principal bomb-maker but also the main suicide vest manufacturer, I had to source supplies, I had to have good Internet. I also had – I gave myself – a wider brief. I wanted to understand what Rome was doing to defeat us.'

'Rome?'

'Rome is our word for the Crusader enemy.'

'It sounds so medieval.'

'It isn't. ISIS is of our time. Their ideology – or their narrow interpretation of the words of the Prophet – harks back to the seventh century, but they use the very latest American weapons technology captured from the Iraqi army: Abrams tanks, M16s and M4 rifles, night sights. They use the Internet. They use your humanity against you. To understand Rome, I went online obsessively. I am an obsessive man. It was, if you like, my university. In the process of trying to understand you – the West, the Western mind – to defeat you, I forgot my unlearning. I began to learn. Of course, I wasn't aware of this as it was happening. To begin with, I just wanted to understand how the American military studied ISIS, how it thought about us. They said we were a death cult, that we were brainwashed. So what is a "cult"? What is "brainwashing"? I read many papers on this, written at Quantico, the US Marine headquarters, written by American military psychiatrists, and finally I came across Dr Robert Lifton. Do you know of his work?'

The tone of his voice was eager, hopeful. Joe let him down gently.

'This man is a genius,' Timur continued. 'An American military psychiatrist. He treated GIs captured and brainwashed by the Chinese Communists during the Korean War. He wrote a book about it, *Thought Reform*. An American journalist took the ideas behind it and came up with a novel, *The Manchurian Candidate*. It became a film with Frank Sinatra. The singer of "My Way".'

'I know who Frank Sinatra is.'

'Of course,' he said. Again, in a world without light, that smile in his voice shone through. 'Brainwashing has happened down the ages. The Inquisition, the Reign of Terror during the French Revolution, Stalin's Great Terror, what Koestler wrote about in *Darkness at Noon* – all brainwashing without being defined as such. But the term was first coined by Chinese victims of Mao's regime: "wash brain", they called it. To supply a musical analogy, ISIS brainwashing is just a new cover of an old song.'

'So how did you un-brainwash?'

'In Raqqa I came across Lifton's book online, and slowly I began to realise that I was truly brainwashed. Emotionally, my eyes were opened by three separate evils. The first, a mass killing. One day we, in ISIS, captured a big patrol of the Syrian army, fifty-five men in all. That night we worked hard, watched over by the Caliph, and we beheaded all fifty-five, so their heads could be placed on a roundabout in Raqqa the next morning. What is this Caliphate if, at the heart of our citadel, is a roundabout full of severed heads? When you kill so many people in the same place, the ground seeps with blood. I could not sleep, could not function properly afterwards. I decided that to save Islamic State we needed to get rid of the Caliph. I got in touch with my sister to suggest that I had information on "Picasso". No one in the West seemed to be interested, so I did nothing, and then Katya was killed.'

He fell silent for a time.

'The second event was a single killing. In Raqqa, these days, one death is barely noticed. But this one mattered to me.'

'Who died?'

'An innocent boy called Abdul. He died in the place of another boy, Haroun.'

'Haroun was a good boy?'

'No, on the contrary. He was to be executed, but he managed to blame Abdul and I went along with it, knowing that it was a lie. I watched the beheading of an innocent boy and I will never forget this, my crime of omission. I had become a monster. Why? Because of "wash brain".'

'Timur, you were a servant of the Caliph. He's responsible, not you.'

'But I went along with him. In the old, pre-brainwashed part of my mind I knew the Caliph was cruel, that he had a taste for killing, as a pleasure in itself. The two parts of my mind would fight each other in the middle of the night. I went on the Internet to clear my brain, to try to banish these heresies. There, I read the official story about Mao in Yan'an in the wilderness years – how after the Long March he held himself apart from the other Chinese Communists, that he was reserved, theoretical, quiet, just like the Caliph, that he gave his life over to contemplation of how to achieve power, how to better the lives of the masses. Then I read in an unofficial book about Mao, *The Unknown Story,* that Mao was a liar, that the Long March was a lie, that famous battles were in reality a fiction, that Mao, rather than heroically walking the whole way was carried in a litter like the landlords of old and, most damning of all, that far from spending time in contemplation, that "Mao liked killing". This hit a chord with me. The Caliph, in his dealings with the people, affects a modesty, a piety. But I have seen him close up, I know him better. I have seen a dark, dark side to him. Like Mao, the Caliph enjoys killing. So while manufacturing suicide vests, I began to ask myself a great yet terrible question: am I a servant of Allah or of a death cult?'

'And the answer?'

'Lifton set out three tests for a cult: one, it has a messianic leader. Abu Bakr al-Baghdadi has charisma; he tells people he is directly related to the Prophet. He's messianic, no question. Two: a cult brainwashes. How could I stand by and watch them execute an innocent boy, unless I was brainwashed? Three: it does harm. ISIS does a lot of harm. It is a cult of death.'

'What made you get out?'

The air pressure curled itself up into a ball and banged itself against Joe's inner ears, causing him to gasp out loud. Timur paused. Joe held his nose and blew, his ears popping.

'The hard shell of my brainwashing,' Timur continued, 'began to crack from within. In a cult, they control information: how you think, the words you use to formulate ideas, thoughts. But they can't control your memories; they do not have power over your previous life. I balanced the harshness of the Caliph, the beheading of Abdul, with my memory of the time before. I remembered the happy times in Grozny, before the war, when our family was together; and even when we were bombed with Auntie Natasha, she told us these amazing stories of her life in London, of the failing magician, of going to see the play *Macbeth*, of the London Underground – "the Tube", they call it – a whole city under the street. There, your ears pop like they do in here.'

'The Victoria Line. I knew this place reminded me of somewhere,' Joe said, laughing out loud.

'Shh. We don't want them to think we're laughing at them. But the final hammer blow was the chemicals. When ISIS took Palmyra, our fighters discovered a secret base, in a tunnel in the mountains nearby. They sent me there. In the tunnel there are hundreds of stainless-steel barrels with skulls and crossbones on them, and next to them a series of boxes – in them chemical suits, gas masks. The barrels are sarin, nerve gas, which Zarif's men hid from the chemical weapons investigators. On the barrels was a script my brothers could not read.'

'Korean,' Joe said. 'The North Koreans sent chemical suits to Zarif. No point doing that unless you've sent the chemicals, too.'

'How did you know that?'

'I spent some time in North Korea. We saw things.'

And then, in his mind, Joe was back there in the dark state, walking zombie-like through the woods, following his comrades, the air freezing, mist swirling on the surface of the lake behind them. Mr Chong led them into a hut, inside it nine chairs. That was a puzzle because there were only ever eight of them, at the maximum: six from the brigade in West Belfast and their senior instructor, Mr Chong, and the junior instructor, Mr Zhou. Beneath each chair were a gas mask and a chemical suit.

Chong disappeared and reappeared with a prisoner, an old man, silver-haired, head bowed but something distinguished about him; he'd held power, of a sort, once. Chong arranged the ninth chair to face them, and handcuffed the man's arms behind his back and sat him down on the chair. Chong and Zhou then locked the door and they both produced flashlights from their packs and left them on their chairs, pointing towards the prisoner, the play of light beams on him suggesting, a little, the 20th Century Fox logo. They did without the drum roll.

Chong and Zhou taped up the door and windows with black plastic and then they stripped down to their underwear and donned their suits, putting their masks on top of their heads, at the ready. The Irishmen sat on their chairs, wondering how the show would end. Chong stared at them, daring them to question his authority. Joe and his comrades stared back at him, as per usual, in numbed silence. Then Chong spoke: 'Strip off your clothes, put on the suits and masks. You have five minutes. If you are lazy and slow, Irish, you die.' He blew a whistle and then the game began.

Joe would never forget the neurotic frenzy as the six of them, all brave warriors for the cause of Irish freedom, ripped off their clothes and donned the suits and masks. Faithful to the idiocy of the training programme, none of them had the wit to run out of the hut. In North Korea, there is nowhere for a foreigner to hide. The prisoner eyed them arrogantly at first, but when the full majesty of Chong's sadism dawned on him, his eyes began to show panic.

Five minutes up, Chong blew his whistle a second time, then the two instructors pulled down their masks so that they were clamped over their faces, checked each other's so the seals were secure, and then Chong produced a canister. By the light of the two flashlights shining in the dark, Joe watched the instructor as he snapped the lid off the canister and pressed a red button. Perhaps Joe heard a hiss of gas; perhaps his mind suggested it. But there was no perhaps about what happened to the prisoner. The old man started to jerk, his legs and arms flapping dementedly, then snot, then blood bubbled from his mouth and nose. Then his face lost all colour and became a ghastly white. Slowly, his head collapsed awkwardly against his chest, and the dead object in front of them lost its balance and fell, chair and all, onto the floor. Chong and Zhou stood up and, without looking back at the prisoner, burst open the door. The others followed them, walking out of the hut around the edge of the lake in the suits for half an hour, sweating despite the cold, until they were confident that all remnants of the gas had gone.

That had been Joe's lesson in chemical weapons warfare, North Korea-style.

Timur's narrative gained renewed energy: 'To show the excellence of the sarin, they first executed four prisoners. Then they were going to gas three prisoners, a woman called Beth – she spoke English – a North Korean called Zhang, and myself.'

'What had you done to upset them?'

'I cannot tell you. If I reveal what I did, it might endanger the lives of some innocent people who deserve a chance to live in peace.'

'So you were about to be gassed?'

'At the last minute, Zhang said something in Russian, which I speak, naturally. The Caliph had thought Zhang only spoke Korean and so was of no use to ISIS, but the fact that I could communicate with him spared him and I. Beth went to her death, handcuffed, in a cage, singing "Amazing Grace". It was the most beautiful, the bravest song I've ever heard.'

'She was American?'

'Yes. She came to Syria to help fight polio, but she was kidnapped and ended up a concubine of the Caliph. She never lost her humanity.'

'You couldn't have saved her.'

'I wish that were true. In fact, there was a moment, perhaps, when I could have freed her. I did not. And for this mistake I shall never forgive myself.'

They sat, thinking about what it must be like to go to your death, handcuffed, crouched in a cage, waiting for the nerve gas.

After a time, Joe broke the silence: 'How many barrels of sarin were there?'

'If I tell you this, someone may torture you for this information. So, as your friend, I shall not tell you.'

'And the location?'

'The same difficulty applies.'

Joe heard him shift a little, arranging his bones so that they were less uncomfortable.

'How did you end up here?'

'The Hisbah are like policemen everywhere. Some are dutiful, some tick the boxes, some are – how do you say it? – bent. I had stashed a lot of money in various places. I found a Hisbah who was greedy and wanted to get out of ISIS and he helped me escape.'

'And that cost?'

'Seventy thousand dollars, in two packets, the second to be released given safe delivery in Damascus. By this time I had been blinded for my crimes, and it's amazing how easy it is for a man with no eyes to pass through checkpoints. The corrupt Hisbah man did not betray me but got me directly to my destination, a Western hotel in the very centre of Damascus where the OPCW – the Organisation for the Prohibition of Chemical Weapons – was based. I made it and got an appointment to see the mission secretary, a Turk called Mehmet. We met in a private meeting room at the hotel, just the two of us. I told him everything I knew, how ISIS had discovered a secret tunnel not so far from Palmyra, where stainless-steel vessels containing sarin were hidden. I told him that that the sarin had been supplied by the North Koreans to the Zarif regime, and that now that Palmyra had been overrun by ISIS, the

Caliphate planned to use them to make nerve-gas suicide bombs. He wrote everything I said down, asking me questions about this and that. After listening for two, three hours, Mehmet apologised to me and said he needed to make a quick phone call. He was gone ten, fifteen minutes. I began to get nervous, to suspect that something was not right. I had been blinded so could not move without help. On reflection, I should have acted on my impulses, but I did not.'

'So what happened?'

'Suddenly the door to the hotel conference room opened and in walked some men. They were Zarif's Mukhabarat. The Turk had betrayed me.'

In the unnatural quiet, the sound of an elevator descending.

'Zarif's intelligence people greeted you with open arms?'

'They did, in a manner of speaking. It was as if this news about the chemical weapons – their chemicals, before Palmyra fell to ISIS – was not so welcome. But I have more bad news for you, Joe. Had I been willing, ISIS could make these chemical suicide bombs within one month, maybe two. It will take longer, but they need this Zhang, the North Korean I saved. He can help them. They will find someone who speaks Russian or even Korean.'

'Timur, you've got to tell me where the sarin is. Give me the coordinates.'

'This information is deadly. I will not.'

'Please, there's more than just our lives at stake.'

They sat in silence, listening to time creak by.

'Timur, you said earlier that nothing down here is recorded.'

'Joe that is true. I also told you of my conjecture, that it is strikingly unusual that you have ended up here and you have not, thus far, been tortured by our hosts. But my conjecture is not a fact, not a guarantee. And this information, the precise location of the sarin – if you know it, you will die.'

'I've got that.'

Silence.

'Please.'

'Very well. What is your address?'

'You mean here? Hole in the ground, Syria.'

'No. In the United States.'

For some reason Joe didn't give his own address, but that of Alf, the old Navy vet who was looking after Reilly back in LA. The very articulation in the tomb of '1452 Blossom Drive, West Hollywood, California, USA' sounded absurd. Timur repeated it, twice. Joe couldn't stop himself from blurting out the question burning inside him: 'What use is a postal address in here?'

'It may take a while – weeks, months. But, God willing, you will get a letter.'

'Why can't you tell me now?'

'No.'

'Get an email sent?'

'No. The United States Postal Service is so much more secure. Trust me, I used to be ISIS's best hacker. If a letter can be sent, most likely I shall be dead when you get it. Katya said that you had a friend named after a Hebrew prophet who is in the CIA.'

'Zeke?'

'Not exactly.'

'Ezekiel?'

'Him. Ezekiel may find my letter interesting, about the chemicals, about other matters.'

'Why are you doing this, Timur? What's the point of telling me these puzzles, these half-facts?'

Timur laughed apologetically. 'Joe, do not be so dismissive of my puzzles and half-facts. *Inshallah*, they may yet protect you. This hole in the ground they've put us in, it is deep but it is rotten. Zarif is rotten. ISIS is rotten. Before, I believed in ISIS. I believed even though my own intelligence – and, better, the wisdom of Dr Lifton – told me that I was in a cult. I believed even though I saw them sever the head of a young boy who was innocent. It was Beth who, in particular, woke me from my sleep. Before, I had thought that ISIS and Zarif were two big dogs in a pit, fighting for survival against many other dogs. After the chemicals, I realised that ISIS and Zarif were' – he paused, trying to find the right words – 'one dog, two heads. This knowledge, I wish to share with the world. And you, Irishman, are my only hope. So that is why I am not going to burden you with information, right now, at this instant, that may yet kill you. You must wait.'

'The people you can't talk about? Can you tell me something, anything, about them?'

'Shh,' he said. *Clack-click, click-clack* sounded in the corridor outside.

# THE MEDITERRANEAN SEA

The wind blew over the savage waters, waves sweeping along the length of the inflatable, now all but submerged. Jameela and Ham had fought hard to grip the transom at the stern, but their strength was ebbing away; soon they would have to let go and the waters would close above their heads. A huge wave rumbled towards them, spume flying from its top; at the same moment a fresh, enormously strong gust of wind came running down from the Peloponnese mountains, flipping the inflatable.

Suddenly, far from being whipped by the wind and the raging sea, Jameela and Ham were encased in a plastic tomb, the bottom of the inflatable grazing their heads. They couldn't see but they could feel that there was just enough buoyancy for the boat to stand proud of the sea, so that they could breathe air and be protected from the storm. It was something of a respite, but again the smooth plastic afforded them no handholds, no traction. Jameela used her fingers and bare toes to search for something, anything, to grip on to. Eventually, she found what she was looking for. It wasn't much and it wasn't strong, just a coil of plastic connecting the input air valve to the boat. But she could wedge a finger in that and grip her toes against the transom, and hold Ham close to her, his mouth facing up.

Her fingers went to her neck, to check that her plastic purse with the money was still safe. It was gone. But that was not worth worrying about while their lives were in the balance.

'One and one is two,' said Ham.

His face was blue with cold.

'And one and two is three,' said Jameela.

He had – what? – another ten, twenty minutes of life left in him, if that.

'And two and three is five.'

The Fibonacci sequence, his favourite game. Once he was gone, she thought, matter-of-factly, then she would go, too.

'And three and five is eight.'

No point in life without him; no point at all.

'And five and eight is thirteen.'

They had got to 144, with Jameela making several mistakes on the way and Ham not a single one, when the blast of a horn aroused her from a kind of stupor. Her mind was foggy and she didn't get it, didn't get where the noise was coming from, didn't think what this might be. Then she looked up at the grey plastic ceiling and remembered that in the upturned prison they'd ended up in, the air pocket had no way of being freshly replenished with oxygen. She would be suffering from $CO_2$ poisoning, as would Ham.

'Eighty-nine and one hundred and forty-four is . . .' Ham didn't finish his arithmetic.

With a raw courage she didn't know she had possessed until then, she gripped his pitiful excuse for a life jacket and said, 'Come on Ham,' then dragged him out from underneath the inflatable using the power of her legs to kick away from the transom. They surfaced, gasping, and he yelled, 'Two hundred and thirty-three!'

The brilliance of the light and the darkness of the shade was astonishing. Her eyes, red-raw from the seawater, couldn't make out what the wall of shade in front of her might be. Slowly they adjusted, and she realised that she was staring at a vessel of the Italian coastguard.

The sailors had been staring down at a scene of utmost melancholy: an upturned inflatable, the sea littered with corpses, when suddenly one of them shouted in Italian, 'There's a survivor!'

Without hesitation, he leapt into the sea, resurfaced, then speed-crawled over towards Jameela. She pushed Ham into her rescuer's arms and then started to sink, fast. But the Italian, while holding on to Ham, gripped her by the hair and pulled her back, and she broke surface and gasped for air. Soon, two more men dive-bombed into the sea, and mother and boy were not just safe, but surrounded by a trio of laughing Italians, delighted that, in the midst of such sorrow, they had been able to save two human beings. This had been their very first morning's watch on the station and it had been grim beyond the saying of it – more than seventy corpses floating in the sea – but the saving of two lives, well, that was something to tell Grandma.

———

The Italian captain was sitting on Jameela's bunk, looking down at her holding her son in her arms. She had no idea how long she had slept, but the sea was no longer rocking and sunlight was streaming through an open porthole. Ham was still asleep, breathing sweetly.

'Welcome to Europe,' the captain said in heavily accented English, a slight smile playing on his lips. He was a big man, six-foot-two, heavy, bald, with stubble on his face, a broken nose. Behind him were the three sailors who had rescued them, all grinning from ear to ear. Then her eyes refocused on the captain and she realised that in his hands was something very incongruous, a wicker basket.

'We see that you have nothing, no passport, no money. The crew are so sad to pick up the dead from the sea. This was our first day here.

But today we helped to save you and your boy. So we have made a present.' He handed her the basket: in it was a bottle of prosecco, a cured ham, some biscotti, a small jar of truffle jam, some hard cheese, a bottle of Frangelico, chocolates and, in an envelope she opened later, five hundred euros.

'Thank you,' she replied in English, and to his astonishment and to the giggling delight of the sailors present, she sat bolt upright and kissed the captain on the lips, the first and last female Syrian refugee ever to do so.

———

In the morning, Jameela and Ham woke up in their tent, inherited from a previous family of refugees, just outside the ancient stone fortress of Kos. Watched by gawking tourists from all around Europe, they left the camp, known as Little Syria, and set off on the short walk to the police station, past the harbour full of one-hundred-foot wooden yachts, their masts towering into the sky, the scene telling the story of decadent Europe and wretched Middle East in one simple image. It promised to be a fine day, the sun already strong, the storm a memory. Jameela looked across the silvery-blue waters of the channel – deceptively, sickeningly calm – to where the white houses of Bodrum stood; to the south, green wooded slopes ran down to the sea. Somewhere among those trees stood the abandoned church from where so many of them, now lost forever, had left for Kos only two nights before.

Jameela, wanting to adopt the lowest of profiles to fit in with her fellow refugees, dived into a clothes shop and bought a cheap, dark-brown headscarf, which she wrapped around her closely cropped hair. By the time they arrived at the police station, it was already thronged with several hundred refugees, some of whom had been waiting for permission to leave for two weeks or more. Seven out of ten were from

Syria, smaller numbers from Iraq and Afghanistan; others were fleeing the paranoid and neurotic regime in Eritrea; and there were economic migrants from Pakistan, Ghana, Ivory Coast, Congo – all the places where poverty overwhelmed hope. Frustrated, depressed, fearful that their journey north had been stymied on just the second or third rung of the ladder, they were milling around, voices becoming angrier by the second. A thin line of Greek riot police, stone-faced, stood facing the crowd.

Outside the station was a long wooden board covered in sheaves of paper, and on each sheaf was a typewritten list of names written in English, in no alphabetical order. Every morning, around ten o'clock but never exactly at that time – sometimes later, sometimes earlier, sometimes not at all – a Greek police officer would stick up a fresh list of people who had been given the authorisation to leave Kos and take the ferry to the mainland. The result was that every head of every family crowded around the police station, every morning, to see if they were lucky or not.

The refugees were given three days' grace to leave Greece after they got their authorisation to leave Kos. If they did not succeed in those seventy-two hours, they could either claim for asylum – something none of them wanted to do in the poorest country in the European Union – or face deportation. The sense of jeopardy – that they might be sent back to where they came from or blocked in Greece, never to be allowed to go north – consumed them. They were locked within a desperate stasis, and the key to unlock the stasis was held by people with no true understanding of what they were running from. People with passports, people who could prove their Syrian identity, were fast-tracked. With no passports and no papers, Jameela and Ham were very much in the slow lane.

On the seventh day, Jameela's false name, Maryam Khashoggi, came up, and they were on the move. With some of the euros the Italians had given her, she bought two ferry tickets, one adult and one child, to Piraeus. The wind came up and a fresh storm raged, but the ferry was the size of a block of flats and she and Ham slept through it.

# DAMASCUS, SYRIA

Conditioned to behave like one of Pavlov's dogs, lest Mr Click-Clack cosh him on the base of his spine again, Joe scrabbled over to his side of the cell and lay there, belly down, his hands clasped together behind his back, his heart racing. The door opened and the brilliance of the lights from the corridor burnt into his eyes. Mr Click-Clack fixed a pair of handcuffs on Joe's wrists and chains on his ankles, then dragged him upright. As Joe shuffled out of the cell, he took a glance at Timur. He was a slight man, like Katya, less than five foot six inches, pitifully thin in his grey prison garb, his ginger hair cut short, his beard no more than a week's stubble, his eye sockets empty, his feet a sodden mess of blood and bone.

Mr Click-Clack locked the cell door and placed a black bag over his head. He then led Joe along, the ankle chains forcing him to take three steps for every one of his jailer's. At the end of the corridor, they paused while he selected a new key from his belt. This turned in the lock, the door opened and then slammed shut behind them, and they hurried along the new corridor before coming to a halt at a second door. He opened and closed that, and then they were in a bigger space. Something pinged, doors opened and the guard shoved Joe forwards. Looking down at his feet, Joe could just make out the floor of an elevator. He heard the doors close and felt it move up, not that fast, so Joe could count the floors: seven in all. At the top, Joe was led along a corridor, smoother under his bare feet than before, and into a room, its flooring some kind of white linoleum. Looking down, he could make out reflected light on the lino. Not electric light but the real thing: daylight. Joe half-shuddered with relief, that the known world was not all dark.

In the distance, car doors slammed shut and an engine revved, then its sound grew weaker. Mr Click-Clack sat him down on a hard, wooden chair.

And then they waited.

After a time, the door opened behind Joe. There was the sound of a man walking in and then something else, something strange, a different sound – rubber wheels, a high-pitched whine . . . an electric wheelchair. It came to a stop with a click. One of the new arrivals smelt – no, stank – of lavender.

'Mr Tiplady, tell us, please' – Mansour's voice, suave, elegant – 'pray tell us, what do you know about a consignment of nerve gas in Palmyra?'

The question caught Joe quite cold. He had been expecting to be taken to task for being found, concussed and bruised, in Ghouta, for running out of the big hotel in Damascus in a suit belonging to chemical weapons inspectors, for being some kind of associate of Qureshi. But never had he anticipated that they would start with a question about the Palmyra sarin. Not knowing what to say, Joe gave no answer.

'Mr Tiplady, you haven't answered my question. Please answer my question. Tell me about the sarin.'

'What are you talking about?'

'Wrong answer, Mr Tiplady.'

A phone chirruped. It was answered, listened to, and then a different voice, not Mansour's, said, '*Nichevo.*' This voice sounded like the high notes of a flute, querulous. Joe had spent enough time with Katya when she was at her most nihilistic to know that *nichevo* was Russian for 'nothing'.

'Mr Tiplady, when did you become a CIA asset?' asked Mansour.

Joe laughed out loud.

Mansour repeated the question. This time Joe replied, 'Listen, Mansour, I am not now, nor have I ever been, nor will I ever be a CIA asset.'

'Very good, Mr Tiplady, very good. That resolves a puzzle for us. We are most grateful. Taahid?'

So that was Mr Click-Clack's name. A lighter snapped on, and then there was the unmistakable, forced hiss of a blowtorch igniting. Although still mummified by the bag on his head, Joe felt a wave of heat wash over his upper body. Then the focus of the heat shifted to behind him, and the hair on the back of his cuffed hands began to singe.

'Our concern was, Mr Tiplady, that the Agency is quite vengeful and, therefore, we have established certain modus operandi. We do not torture CIA assets, and they do not whisk our people off to Poland, Romania or the middle of the Pacific for what they like to pretend are Enhanced Interrogation Techniques. These rules of thumb are respected by both sides. But as you freely admit that you have nothing to do with the CIA, then you are, as they say, fair game.'

The heat was becoming painful; his hands felt as though they were on fire. Joe shuffle-scraped the chair away from the heat. The heat followed him. Joe shifted some more until, blind, he hit a wall. The heat washed over to his right; he shuffled to the left until he realised he had been boxed into a corner. Joe started backing out when, to his relief, he heard the blowtorch going out. The blow to the side of his head, when it came, was utterly unexpected. It poleaxed him, chair and all, to the floor, his skull making an unhealthy crack as it connected with the floor. A few beats, then the lighter snapped on again and the blowtorch was reignited. Joe could hear it burn but the heat stayed away from his skin.

'You see, Mr Tiplady, we don't quite believe you. You are something of a mystery to us. An Irish national, you turn up in Damascus, affecting to be an art dealer. The address you give for your sponsor does not exist. He is a fiction. You consort with the treasurer of the so-called Free Syrian Army, Adnan Qureshi, and his Ukrainian mistress. On your very first night in Damascus, you attend a party thrown by Qureshi, a man known to us as a supplier of the nerve gas sarin to ISIS. And then – and at this point the puzzle becomes all the more problematic – you pop up in Ghouta, where no CIA operative would dare go.'

'Perhaps you are a tourist,' suggested Flute-man, this time not in Russian but in fluent English, 'with an interest in antiquities of the ancient world, regime change and nerve gas, who somehow lost his way? But unusually for such a tourist, we have a record of a man with your name entering Pyongyang some years ago.'

That Flute-man knew about Joe's time in North Korea was not good. He'd placed, or so it felt, an icicle in Joe's bowels.

'So' – Mansour again – 'our hypothesis is that you work for the CIA, that you are here to cement the false Western narrative that the government of the Syrian Arab Republic has hoarded nerve gas, and to build ties with Qureshi's circle to foment regime change.'

'That's just rubbish.'

'Rubbish, you say? But Qureshi's whore confirmed our hypothesis. Are you suggesting that she is a liar?'

Joe grunted non-committally. A slap to the side of his face, stinging, then blood trickling into his mouth. Joe remembered that the only time he'd met Mansour he was wearing a big emerald ring on his middle finger. Now it was fulfilling its function.

'She liked you, you know. She tried to protect you. It took Taahid some time to persuade her to confess the facts. I fear Taahid may have enjoyed himself too much, but . . .' His voice was a soft caress, whimsical even. 'But eventually, confess she did.'

The inside of Joe's mouth felt horribly dry at the thought of what Taahid might have done to Daria to make her talk.

'So, do you still deny that you're in the CIA? Or, to be more precise, that you're a CIA asset? That you work for them?'

'I deny it.'

This time the heat grew closer, more intense than ever before, burning the small of his back where it was exposed until the stink of it reminded him of kebab, of Timur. Someone screamed, a piercing cry. And then Joe realised the scream was coming from his own mouth.

'You're confident in your denial?' asked Mansour.

The heat reversed away from the base of his spine a few inches, then a foot, more. Then the cold of a knife against his belly, his trousers and underwear ripped to shreds, pulled away, exposing his penis and testicles to the air.

'So, Mr Tiplady, once more for the record. Do you deny that you are an asset for the CIA?'

The heat found his groin.

'Aaaaaargh!'

And then a cell phone rang.

'*Kak dela?*'

'Aaargh! I'm in the CIA,' Joe screamed. 'I'm not an asset, I'm an agent. Pyongyang, Damascus, Syria, all for the CIA.' The blowtorch died. The torture was put on hold while the call lasted. Joe forced himself to suppress his fear and listen. His Russian wasn't good enough to follow the conversation, but he did hear, over the racket of his breathing – heavy, erratic, inhaling great gasps of oxygen – Flute-man say, 'Pennsylvania, Ohio, Michigan, Wisconsin.'

A pause, then more Russian, but he made out two phrases: 'the White House' and '*Kompromat*'.

After a time, the conversation ended.

'Perhaps it was not a good idea to take that call, Grozhov,' said Mansour, the irritation clear in his voice. 'You cannot assume that others will not be listening.'

'It was Zoba's personal aide-de-camp,' said Grozhov.

'So?' said Mansour.

'Syria is a sideshow. Interesting, yes, but we have more essential work elsewhere,' replied Grozhov. 'I must return to our embassy, to make an important call on a secure line. Continue giving heat to this Irish. I believe he killed a loyal servant of Russia, Reikhman, in cold blood. In my personal experience, only when a person screams at the highest possible pitch for some time is their mind genuinely open to the truth. Do not spare him. Ask him everything he may have found out about the sarin. Understand?'

Mansour grunted his agreement.

'Ask him about Reikhman. Ask him about what he did and didn't do in Pyongyang. Whatever happens,' said Grozhov, 'I wasn't here and Russia knows nothing about him or the nerve agent. Understand?'

The tone was of master unto servant. Joe didn't know Mansour very well but he knew him well enough to know that he would not like that.

'Of course,' Mansour replied, with a fluency, almost a graciousness, that Joe had not expected.

An electric whine sounded. Grozhov was leaving. And then a whir, as if the wheelchair had reversed.

A pause.

'Mansour, one other thing. I asked for a package. Nothing has been delivered to my hotel.'

'Mr Grozhov, the Syrian Arab Republic is your host here. But there are some things which we do not provide. You can find your own . . . packages.'

'I see,' said Grozhov softly. 'On another matter, Qureshi's oilfields—'

'Are now the property of the Syrian state,' said Mansour with a proprietary air.

'Pity. They've been selected as a priority target by our ministry of defence.'

'No, no,' said Mansour, 'that's precipitate. The trade gives us useful leverage with ISIS. You must reconsider.'

'It's out of my hands,' said Grozhov flatly.

'Then, Grozhov, put it in your hands.'

The electric whine got nearer. 'Mansour' – Grozhov's voice was as close to a cobra's hiss as Joe had ever heard – 'I'm beginning to wonder whether we've overestimated you. It seems the most striking thing about you as an intelligence operative is your choice of tailor. The facts are that you and the giraffe-cum-ophthalmologist in the palace on the hill are in danger of losing control of this state. Out of fraternal solidarity, we are coming to your rescue. We abhor colonialism in all its forms. Syria is, of course, not a Russian colony.'

'Of course not,' echoed Mansour.

'But, for the time being, it's probably more time-effective for all concerned that you think of it as being something like that. We suggest. You concur. When we act, don't waste time questioning our decisions. The bombing of Qureshi's oilfields started ten minutes ago. Had you been in any way a competent head of military intelligence, you would already know that.'

The electric whine began again, the chair moving off. Then, one more whir and click. 'Oh, Mansour, the Irish. We need an answer to every question I wish answered. If he dies, we will not mind. The next time we meet, try telling me something I don't already know. The novelty of that might prove stimulating. Surprise me.'

The electric whine receded. Far off, Joe heard car doors slam and the sound of a powerful engine picking up speed. Someone, Joe assumed Mansour, spat on the ground, close to him, then walked out of the room, and Taahid returned Joe to his cell in the tomb, his shoes click-clacking all the while. When the guard closed the door behind him, Joe realised that Timur had gone, been taken somewhere else. Joe sat on his haunches against the wall in near total darkness and listened to muffled thunks and slams as his ears popped with the changes in air pressure, and he wondered, in some crazy delirium, whether he had imagined meeting Timur, ISIS's heretical bomb-maker-in-chief. But on the concrete floor, close to the dagger-slash of light, lay Joe's bandage, blackened with blood.

Then the light outside Joe's cell door, the light from the corridor, died, and he was plunged into blackness so complete it was terrifying beyond the utterance. Deep below the surface of the earth, he was locked inside a tomb that his jailers could no longer power nor light.

# PIRAEUS, GREECE

The ferry landed in Piraeus just after dawn and, as soon as its huge door opened, the throng of Syrians ran frantically for the bus stop in the docks, to queue for the buses that would take them to the train station. Jameela realised that there was a kind of gold-rush psychosis about this movement, a species of collective madness. And yet, if you were inside it, it was extraordinarily difficult not to be consumed by it.

At Athens railway station, a posse of Golden Dawn fascists, with skinhead haircuts, black T-shirts and black-and-white camouflage trousers, strutted up and down, waving red flags with a black rune on them, suggesting a variant of the swastika. One of them, a big lout with a fat belly, peeled off from the main group and came nose to nose with Jameela, evidently a Muslim in her headscarf, and yelled '*Allahu Akbar!*' deafeningly in her ear. She ignored him but Ham, sensing that the man was being obnoxious to his mother, bit him on the hand. The skinhead howled in pain and was about to knock Ham flat when a Greek police officer armed with a sub-machine gun danced between the two of them. The officer smiled, unsmilingly, at the Golden Dawn man until he rejoined his group, nursing his fat paw all the while. The officer watched over Jameela and Ham as they bought their train tickets, and waited with them until they boarded their train and it started clanking away, heading north. As Jameela gazed at Ham waving goodbye to their guardian-angel police officer through the train window, she reflected that Greece's finances might be broken but not its heart. Safe, for a time at least, Jameela scolded Ham: 'You shouldn't go round biting people.'

'Mom, I was hungry. I wanted a Big Mac and all I got was a fat finger.'

She shook her head and reflected that maybe Europe had something to be afraid of in this particular Syrian – well, half-Syrian – child refugee.

———

Midnight and a fresh shower of rain fell on a mudslide made of people, making the wretched of the earth yet more miserable. You could sense the mass of humanity stuck on the wrong side of the border. Every now and then the car headlights of aid workers or visiting journalists would flick across the field and capture thousands and thousands shivering in the muck. The lucky ones had tents but most sheltered from the incessant rain under blankets. The Macedonians to the north had closed their border with Greece but the pipeline of humanity kept on flowing, so the numbers and the pressure grew and grew.

Jameela and Ham, exhausted after a grim three-mile trek through the rain from the last train station on the Greek side, were bewildered by the scene. You couldn't make out much in the headlights: just the rain and a great field, as far as the eye could see, sheeted by wet plastic. To bed down for the night, she chose asphalt over mud. She chose the side of the road.

'Darling,' said Jameela, 'we shall soon be safe in Germany, love. Maybe two, three more nights, but then we will be in Berlin.'

Together, they lay down on the asphalt, Ham on the side closest to the field, her with her back to the road. She draped the blanket a Sikh aid worker from Coventry had given them and – wet, miserable and afraid for what the future might hold for them – they tried to sleep.

'One and one is two,' started Ham.

'Oh, baby . . .'

'Go on,' said Ham.

'One and two is three.'

'Two and three is five . . .'

But exhaustion is the best anaesthetic, and soon Ham had forgotten about the Fibonacci sequence and was asleep. Jameela tried to stay awake, to protect them from danger, but she, too, succumbed. In the night, Ham, always a restless sleeper, managed to wriggle out of his mother's arms and upend himself so his head was facing the road – and that was how, at five o'clock in the morning, a green Volkswagen van driven by a party of journalists from Belgium reversed into him, smashing into his jaw.

# DAMASCUS, SYRIA

*Seven, ten, twelve, fourteen feet high, ten times seventy, no twelve times seventy, no twelve times seven, no, eighty-four plus fourteen, ninety-eight a tomb one hundred feet below the ground the pit there Chong put me in the pit it was March and the land was still rimed with frost and the cold, the cold ate your bones and I killed Chang I broke his back so that he would never put us in the pit again but this this is worse, once our fishing boat off County Mayo flipped in the Atlantic swell and for ten, fifteen seconds we were all upside down drowning in dark but then slowly the old fool of a boat righted itself but this isn't happening the darkness weighs deep on the boat the engine screamed the sea sloshed and gurgled as it found its dark way into our warm cabin but this blackness is silent the rumble rumble rumbling of machinery that might have been the lifts working in the lift shaft falls silent still power cut, power cut blood pumping in my ears breathe breathe breathe they built stairs down to my level yes no I don't don't don't no know no probably, yes but I can't shut the possibility out of my mind that I am absolutely trapped, deep below ground, with no one on earth knowing where I am, Katya no shoot me no no no Katya no run away and I pull the trigger and he dies but she is dead and I scatter her ashes in the cold cold Atlantic but this this this forgive me Katya oh sweet Christ . . .*

Joe pounded the door of his cell until his knuckles cracked with blood and the salt from the tears in his eyes fell on the broken flesh and made him smart with pain. Later, he suspected it must have been the intensity of his fear, the fear of being locked in the dark for eternity, that drove him to act in the way he did. The only explanation he could offer was simple and bleak – that, for a time, far longer than he had thought possible, he'd lost the balance of his mind.

Joe remembered ripping off all his clothes. He remembered daubing the walls of his cell with his own shit. He remembered howling like a wolf, for hours on end, until his voice cracked and he could only croak.

Then the light in the corridor outside came back on.

Taahid took him down the corridor to the elevator shaft and then up seven storeys, and he was allowed a shower and was given a new set of clothes: a black tracksuit, underwear and a white T-shirt.

Then Zeke walking towards him, his trademark, gormless grim in place, shaking his hand: 'Hello, Joe. You look pale. Not been getting enough sunshine?' Joe started to cry and Zeke hugged him, then turning to Taahid and saying something in Arabic and Taahid was frowning, not liking what Zeke was saying, and Mansour bowing at Zeke and Zeke smiling but not meaning it, not meaning it at all, so Mansour pulled a face and disappeared, and then they were outside in fresh air and into a convoy, three big SUVs, driving fast, men in shades, with guns, driving west, towards Lebanon.

Zeke didn't ask Joe anything on the journey to Beirut. He just gazed out of the window most of the time, watching the arid land go by. Once or twice Joe caught Zeke studying him, a worried look in those shrewd eyes of his, and then he smiled blankly at Joe, nodded to the security men sitting in the front seats, suggesting that they couldn't talk until they were alone, and looked out of the window some more.

At the American embassy in Beirut it was 'Open Sesame' the whole way, every single gate parting wide as they reached it until their convoy ducked down into the basement garage.

Zeke said, 'Follow me,' and Joe traipsed after him. In turn, they were followed by four grunts, all of them armed, through a door and out into the embassy gardens. As dusk approached, the light over the Mediterranean began fading from ochre towards blood. Zeke led Joe towards the shade of a giant, ancient cedar tree, and they sat down on a handmade wooden bench that circled its base.

'Joe, this is a private conversation,' said Zeke. 'If such a thing exists in this world anymore.'

'You sure?'

'Sure.'

Joe smiled. It was beyond wonderful to be in safe hands again – and with Zeke, he couldn't have felt safer – and to breathe free air, to observe the dance of light made by the leaves of the cedar tree filtering the reddening sun. Back in the tomb, Joe had given up all hope of rescue. He had accepted that he would die, forgotten, deep beneath the surface of the earth.

'Joe, listen up. I've got to be in Langley in no time. So that you know, I'm back in the game, but not at the centre. Not so long ago, in Albania, I got shot—'

'You OK, Zeke?' asked Joe, alarmed.

'Fit as a fiddle.'

Joe considered that and pulled a sceptical face. The old man looked tired, pale.

Zeke laughed gently and continued: 'To get you out of Zarif's fingernail palace, I did a trade. Zarif got some of the fruit of one trillion dollars' worth of Uncle Sam's investment in rockets and satellite imaging, and I got one Irishman.'

Joe looked Zeke squarely in the eye and said, 'Thank you.'

'That's worth a dollar. For the rest of the trillion, I'd be grateful for any useful information you picked up back there.' Zeke paused and studied Joe shrewdly. 'Did you come across a fat Russian in an electric wheelchair with a squeaky voice, name of Grozhov?'

'I did. They started using a blowtorch on me. Then his phone rang. He took the call. He was talking in Russian, but I heard him say "Pennsylvania, Ohio, Michigan, Wisconsin", then he mentioned the White House and another word, "Kompromat".'

'Repeat what he said, word for word,' said Zeke.

'I can't because it was in Russian. I can clearly recall he named those four states and talked about the White House and *Kompromat*. What's that Zeke?'

'*Kompromat* is Russian short-form for "compromising material". We'd call it blackmail.' Zeke wiped his lips with the back of his hand and stared into space for a long time. Then the focus in his eyes returned and he asked Joe to tell his story from A to Z.

Joe started not at the beginning, but with Timur's information about the drums of sarin hidden in the tunnel somewhere near Palmyra.

'How much sarin?' asked Zeke.

'He wouldn't tell me. A lot.'

Zeke's expression gave way to a frown.

'Where, exactly?'

'Again, he wouldn't tell me, in case they tortured it out of me. He asked for my address in Hollywood. I gave him the address of my dog minder.'

'Good.'

'He said he was going to write me a letter.'

Zeke smiled to himself. 'That's kind of smart. And very typical of the ISIS mindset. Whatever else this guy is, Timur is genuine, of that I have no doubt. Against the Soviets in Afghanistan, Cuba, Congo, when we got a lead about something like this, we would deploy our intelligence firepower, send in agents, sweep radio traffic, phone calls – what the young people these days call data mining. Against ISIS, nothing doing. They write letters and post them. If they can't post them, they give them to a guy on a motorbike. If they can't find a guy on a motorbike, they walk all the way to the letterbox. To folks in the NSA, that's kind of cheating. To old-timers like me, well, it's just smart.'

Only then did Joe start at the beginning, the drive to Fort Hargood and meeting Dr Dominic Franklyn. Zeke interrupted him almost immediately: 'I don't know the man, but it's on file that Franklyn's helped the Agency out in the past, I do believe.'

Joe absorbed that and continued, explaining Franklyn's request for him to find Jameela.

'She walked out on him, took the boy with her to Syria and defected to ISIS?' asked Zeke.

'That's what Franklyn said. I met no one who told me different.'

'Uh-huh. Carry on.'

But Joe couldn't, because at that moment they were interrupted by a fleshy, red-faced man in a dirty cream suit walking heavily towards them, followed by eight grunts, carrying sub-machine pistols. Zeke's grunts looked meaner, but the old man held out his palm, flat, gesturing that his men take no action.

'Mr Crone, what a pleasant surprise,' said Zeke, grinning his moronic, gap-toothed smile. Joe knew him well enough to realise that that was his equivalent of a cobra puffing up its hood.

'You're out of line, Zeke, way out of line.' Crone's accent was from the Deep South, and it was clear from the timbre of his voice that he did not like Zeke. 'You vanish in Albania. You get shot up by some bandits. You call in the Sixth Cavalry. And then you sidetrack to Damascus to hand over gold-star intel to Zarif. You're beyond the outer limits, Zeke. You needed executive approval for this fool's errand and you had none. Rinder's authorised me to take over the debrief, and these gentlemen here are to escort you back to Langley immediately. You've got an interview with the Inspector General the moment you step off the G-5.'

'The Inspector General? Young Phil Lansing?'

Crone nodded, his natural frown intensifying a fraction.

'It would be good to catch up with him,' said Zeke nostalgically. 'I gave him his first mission back in—'

'We're not here to indulge your appetite to wander down memory lane, Zeke. You handed over to the Syrians satellite images they should never have had. You did so without permission or authority, in return for a non-American citizen.'

'Joe's not a piece of meat, Jed.' Zeke's tone changed, his voice less hillbilly, more that of an acute intellect trying to explain complexity to someone less gifted. 'He's got intelligence of strategic interest to the United States and I believe that I am the intelligence officer best placed to receive and analyse it.'

'You're wasting air, Zeke. Here's the order from Rinder.' Crone flourished a sheet of paper with *Director, CIA* on the letterhead. Zeke read it, scratched his temples, returned it to Crone and went over to Joe.

'Joe, there's been a miscommunication. I need to go back to Langley, now. Mr Crone is going to take over the debrief. You're in good hands.' And he smiled his gap-toothed smile and Joe knew he didn't mean a word of his last sentence.

Zeke stepped towards Joe and Joe hugged him. Joe didn't want to add to the old man's difficulties, but he couldn't not say what he wanted to say: 'Listen, Mr Crone, I trust Zeke like no other man on earth. More than my own brother. Can't you tell Langley that I'd rather talk to him?'

'No,' said Crone. 'That request does not fit with my orders.'

Zeke was already walking away as four of Crone's men gathered round him – a protective cocoon, or a guard detail to the gallows.

'Take care, Zeke,' Joe cried out to the old man's retreating back. Zeke stopped, turned round, and looked at him and said, 'No, Joe, you got it wrong. *You* take care.'

Then Zeke turned again and walked up towards the embassy building and disappeared behind a wall.

With Zeke gone, Jed Crone came over and sat next to Joe.

'They give you a hard time back there?'

'Uh-huh,' Joe said, as uncommunicative as could be.

'You're with friends now.' Crone gestured to the embassy building. 'Zeke overstretched himself. He did not have the authority to do what he did for you.'

Joe hunkered forward, leaning, saying nothing.

'I heard you're working for Dr Franklyn,' Crone said.

Joe held his tongue.

'Dr Franklyn has done some great service for our country. You get his kid back, it might help Zeke out. Langley might look less severely on his transgressions.'

'You know a lot about me, Mr Crone.'

'I'm an intelligence officer, Mr Tiplady. It's what I do for a living.'

'Jameela, she's gone over to ISIS, no question?'

'That's the way it looks, yes. Mr Tiplady, here's my advice: get Franklyn's kid back. That might just save Zeke from our version of the electric chair. Then stay out of Agency business. I gotta go. We'll talk more in the morning.'

Crone's four remaining grunts took Joe into the embassy. Joe had a nice room, with an en-suite bathroom and a small kitchen, the fridge fully stocked with all the good things in American life: coffee, Coke, Oreos. He tried the door. It was locked. He tried to open the balcony window to get some fresh air, which, after the tomb, he craved; worse, the denial of it made him tremble with anxiety. It, too, was locked. Conditions in the embassy lockdown were better than the tomb, but the basic principle – that he did not have access to fresh air, was not free to leave, was not in control of his own destiny – that was the same.

He slept fitfully, waking up in the middle of the night from a nightmare in which he was locked in a cage, hands tied behind his back. Anointed with sweat, it took several long moments before he realised where he was: in safety, in a room at the American embassy in Beirut.

And then he remembered what the Russian who stank of lavender, Grozhov, and Mansour had seemed most insistent to know – the extent of his knowledge about the nerve gas in Palmyra. Although Zeke had been taken out of the equation, he must tell the new team that is what the Russians and Zarif's Mukhabarat were most worried about.

In the morning, he was taken to a debriefing room, windowless, antiseptic, somewhere in the bowels of the embassy. Two of Crone's grunts stood behind Joe, chewing gum. He sat on a hard chair, facing an empty chair across the empty table.

Joe asked for coffee – milk, one sugar. One of the grunts, the most solicitous, obliged. Joe asked when the debrief would begin. The grunt told him soon. Three, four hours passed. Joe had no watch. Just before lunchtime, Joe spoke: 'Inside Zarif's prison, I met a man who had been an ISIS bomb-maker. He told me—'

'Listen, sir,' said the friendlier grunt, 'we're just the protection team. We don't do the debrief.'

'You need to tell someone high up that the Russians and Zarif's people want to bury any mention of a tunnel full of sarin—'

'Sir, are you deaf? You're wasting air.'

'Write what I'm saying down,' urged Joe. 'Write it down. Please.'

The grunt folded his arms; the other grunt examined the ceiling.

At lunchtime, Joe was escorted back to his room and told to take a rest. Again, the door was locked behind him. In the room was a Big Mac, going cold. He ate it gloomily.

Two hours later, the grunts took him back down to the debriefing room. This time Joe waited six, seven hours. No Crone. They took him back to his room, and in the morning the non-briefing cycle continued. The morning session, no show from Crone; lunch, a return to his room, a Big Mac going cold; the afternoon session, no show from Crone. On the third day, early, he was blindfolded and handcuffed, with plastic ties, not steel links, and taken into the embassy garden and told to wait.

Joe could hear the *thwack-thwack* of a helicopter landing and he was bundled on board. It lifted off and after an hour of flight, maybe less, it landed. He was manhandled, quite gently, and someone led him away from the landing zone, then he heard the chopper's rotors kick in and from the wash of air and the ramp in engine noise he realised that the helicopter was taking off. Then a new sound hit him: the *whoosh-whoosh* of jet planes revving up to taxi.

It wasn't hard to deduce that they were in an airbase and Joe assumed, obviously, that it was an American one, until he heard someone bark something in Russian and then somebody else reply in Russian and he began to worry. An hour's helicopter ride, maybe less, from Beirut, to land in a spot where Russian was the language of choice? Uncle Sam had dropped him at a Russian airbase back in Syria.

Still blindfolded, he was hurried into a building, banging his head on a low ceiling, and through a series of doors until he sensed he was in a room that was not quite sound-proofed, but in which the roar of the jets seemed softer than before. His guards sat him down on a chair, and he felt a length of rope securing his arms and legs to the chair and another length of rope coming to rest gently around his neck, and then that started to tighten, just a tad, but enough to signal that he was by no stretch of the imagination in good hands. Grozhov couldn't be far away.

And then the guards left him.

# THE LONG ROAD

In the rainswept darkness, Jameela carried Ham, his jaw bleeding profusely, towards the lights at the edge of the field. She felt physically sick that her boy had been badly hurt, but her sense of remorse and panic was countered by the necessity of him getting urgent medical attention.

In a first-aid clinic, a medic dressed Ham's wound and gave them both hot soup – their first hot drink, their first proper food, since lunchtime. The medic advised that they should go to hospital for an X-ray.

'In Macedonia,' said Jameela.

The medic pulled a face, but didn't demur. Ham was stoic in pain, and his injury meant a big jump in their living conditions. From shivering underneath a soggy blanket out in the rain, they ended up in a palatial Médecins Sans Frontières tent with dry blankets, which was so wonderfully comfortable and safe that neither mother nor son wanted to stir. But stir they did. Ham was given some painkillers, a fresh smear of antiseptic cream and then they were back on the long road.

Crossing the border from Greece into Macedonia – the first of the fragments of old Yugoslavia they had to pass through – was constipated. Everything was arranged for the convenience of the bureaucracy, not the refugees, which meant long lines of people in the heat, then registration, and only then air-conditioned tents constructed by the UN Refugee Agency, offering a bit of shelter and food. The medics inspected Ham's jaw and recommended that he go to hospital in Belgrade.

Once through the system, Jameela and Ham were put on a train, which chuntered through the flattish countryside, speckled by corn-fields, for three hours until it came to a stop in the middle of some-where, nowhere, a few miles from the border with Serbia. Ahead of them was the same rigmarole, with border officials in slightly different uniforms, all over again.

The crossing into Serbia wasn't much, just a walk down to a gate in a barbed-wire fence. But the refugees faced arrest and deportation back to Greece if they were not registered in Serbia, and to do that, Jameela and Ham had a long walk ahead of them – five miles, more, in the eve-ning heat. The slim fingers of minarets dotted here and there amongst the cornfields were a reminder that not so long ago in human history, this land had been part of the Ottoman Empire.

To lessen the pain of the long walk to the Serbian registration centre, some taxi drivers ripped off the richer Syrians. Stories buzzed around that refugee families would pay one thousand euros for the fare all the way to Vienna, only to get dumped in the Serbian countryside, and if they complained – well, they hadn't registered with the police. But it wasn't all grim. Locals provided free coffee and water to those they could. The locals watched the refugees stumble along with some sympathy. Here, war and fleeing from war were in their bones – and not so long ago. The last fighting in this part of the world had been between Orthodox Serbs and Albanian Muslims in 1999.

The last mile or two was an endless, miserable, dispiriting trudge in the heat. The queue seemed without end. Ham, who hated the lack of precision as much as the press of people, howled his head off and, luckily, his cry was heard by a Serbian social worker. She examined the wound on Ham's jaw, now going septic, and admonished Jameela, who bowed her head but whispered, 'What could I do?' Soon, the social worker was leading Ham and Jameela through a back entrance into the registration tent. First the number, then treatment. Registration was the same deal as in Greece and Macedonia: the refugees had seventy-two hours to get through Serbia and into Hungary. Any longer meant trouble.

A set of army medics efficiently dressed Ham's jaw with antiseptic cream, but his wound was going puffy, and bruising was showing on his cheekbones, as if he'd been beaten up. The medics helped them, showing the way to where a series of coaches were running the refugees, for a price, to Belgrade. Mother and son slumped in their seats and soon fell fast asleep. Their luck was holding, for a time.

––––––

The waiting room, the whole hospital, stank of a heavy-duty disinfectant that pricked Jameela's exhausted eyes. The room was decorated in a functional style, with stolid furniture left over, Jameela suspected, from the days when the old Yugoslavia was Eastern Europe's most prosperous – or least backward – nation state. That was before the war in 1991 when – galvanised by the local strong man, Slobodan Milošević – neighbour turned on neighbour.

She stood up and pulled back the heavy net curtains that obscured a view of the Belgrade railway station's goods yard. She sat down and made a cursory examination of the reading matter: a scattering of Serbian popular magazines, full of short, breathless stories illustrated by badly taken, badly framed paparazzi photographs. She couldn't read a word of them because they were in the Cyrillic alphabet, but from the look of them, nor did she want to. She hadn't been this long apart from Ham since before the flight from California and she hated it.

Jameela stood bolt upright as soon as Dr Ludmila Jelić marched into the waiting room. The doctor swept a hand through her thick black hair, sighed and took off her glasses and let them hang from their chain on her matronly bosom, squinting at the patient's mother. There were times when dealing with difficult cases, it was – how to put it – less disagreeable to be a little myopic. It put off the moment when she realised that people were crying.

'Please sit down,' said Dr Jelić in English.

Jameela did so and the doctor followed suit, sitting opposite her. In a subtle way, the age-old hierarchy between doctor and patient was established. 'Is he OK?' asked Jameela.

'Yes. We've given him a series of injections, primarily antibiotics. He's as good as can be expected.'

'What does that mean?'

'The X-ray shows that his jaw is broken. It's become badly infected and we will need to keep him here under observation for several days.'

'But we've only got a total of seventy-two hours in Serbia.'

'We will need to keep him here under observation for several days.'

'Can I see him now?' asked Jameela meekly.

'No, I'm afraid not.'

A look of bewilderment crossed Jameela's features. This was the *worst*.

'What?'

'I've called the police and they will be arriving shortly. There is something we need to sort out.'

Jameela almost collapsed from shock as she registered the horror of what the doctor had just said: *I've called the police . . .* They had come all this way, suffered so much, escaped from ISIS, almost drowned, only to face arrest here in Serbia. And then what would follow? Discovery was inevitable. And that would mean the end of all hope.

Struggling to keep herself under control, she said softly, 'What on earth is wrong? There was a car accident. It wasn't my fault.'

'What's your name? Your real name?'

'My name is Maryam Khashoggi and my son is Ham Khashoggi and' – Jameela dipped into the bag she'd bought on Kos, and scrabbled in it to find the paperwork from three separate countries, Greece, Macedonia and Serbia, saying exactly that – 'this proves it.'

'It does no such thing. Where is your passport?'

'It was lost in a storm when we crossed from Turkey to Kos. Seventy people were drowned; we were the only survivors.'

'A likely story.'

'*What?*' Jameela was not just incredulous, but angry that her word was not trusted. '*What did you say?*'

'You haven't answered my question,' said the doctor. 'What is your real name?'

'My name is Marya—'

'Your son is a very intelligent boy. He can calculate the value of pi to a hundred places. He says that is a lie. He says that your real name is Jameela Abdiek and his is Ham Franklyn. So why are you lying to me?'

Jameela collapsed, crumpling to the floor, and started to sob uncontrollably. Dr Jelić left the waiting room to fetch a nurse to look after her, locking the door with a key so that the mystery woman could go nowhere.

———

The moment she was out in the corridor, Dr Jelić's pager bleeped: another refugee child had arrived in Emergency, this one a suspected case of typhus. It turned out to be a false alarm – the child, a six-year-old girl from Afghanistan, was just badly dehydrated – but by the time she had attended that case, the police had arrived. The two men looked gloomy, as they always did when faced with child protection cases. Dr Jelić took them up three flights of stairs to the waiting room where she had left the Syrian woman. But when she unlocked the door, she found herself looking at an open window, the grimy net curtains flapping in the breeze. She hurried back down the three flights, followed by the two police officers, and stormed into the paediatric ward and all but ran towards the bed where the boy was being kept. The bed was empty.

Dr Jelić found a nurse who told her: 'The new Arabic translator came to take the boy, who had been booked for some eye tests. She said she would be back in ten minutes.'

Dr Jelić doubted that, she doubted that very much indeed.

# WESTERN SYRIA

Night had fallen. Joe was still blindfolded, but he could discern the darkening of the light coming through, or not coming through, the edge of his vision. No one had returned. Time to check out. He listened hard to the rhythm of the fighter jets taking off and landing. The take-offs were loudest, but the roars came in three stages: the first big one as the throttle was opened up, to move the jet from stasis; the second as it taxied down the runway; and the third, the loudest of them all, was take-off itself.

The first roar started the clock; the second roar normally came about fifty seconds later and the third – it was a long runway – about ninety seconds after that. After the first roar, Joe started counting. When he got to 135, he started rocking the chair he was tied to with all his strength, swinging back and forth like a maniac. Bang on 140, the chair crashed over and he was on his side. Panting, he strained his ears to detect whether anyone had heard him.

Nothing.

Like some poorly developed precursor of the hermit crab from the Jurassic period, he side-shuffled across the room, dragging his chair-shell along with him, hunting for something he could use to free himself. He bumped his head against the legs of the table. They were too smooth to be of any use, but whoever had bolted the table together hadn't done a proper job and the edge of a screw stuck out a few millimetres beyond the trim – enough for him to try to break the plastic ties of his handcuffs. Every time he tried, he wrenched his shoulders and the skin of his wrists where the cuffs bit got chafed some more. The pain grew more intense with every attempt, and the only thing that drove him on was the absolute likelihood of pain to come. The thought of what Grozhov and Mansour might do to him once they arrived – safe in the knowledge that he definitely wasn't someone the CIA prized, because why dump him at a Russian airbase? – kept him at it. Eventually, the plastic tie snapped and his hands were free to loosen, then untie the ropes that bound him to the chair as well as the rope around his neck.

Once free, Joe ripped off his blindfold and lifted his head to the window. He was in one of a row of huts lying along the base of a long runway – its lights twinkled away to a near eternity. What lay on the other side of the hut was impossible to work out because there were no windows on that side. He was still wearing the tracksuit and white vest he had been given by the Syrians. On the floor of the hut he found a blue-and-white stripy T-shirt, the kind worn by Russian marines. It smelt so strongly it cried out for a wash, but he thought it might just help him camouflage himself so he suppressed his squeamishness, took off his shirt and donned the smelly Russian one.

He listened for two, three minutes. He could make out occasional traffic from a road, not so far away, the *chug-chug* of power generators and a bit of chit-chat in Russian, not Arabic, further off. He opened the door – it wasn't locked – and stepped out with a flourish. When you're up to no good, moving confidently, without a care in the world, is the way to do it. Which was lucky, because he was immediately challenged in Russian.

'*Kak dela?*'

Joe couldn't make out the whereabouts of the sentry. In front of him was a jumble of merchandise, cases, large trucks, a couple more huts, and in the distance an arc light shining from the airport perimeter that effectively blinded him.

'*Nichego.*' 'Nothing' was pretty much the only response he knew; that and 'very good' and 'two beers' and 'I love you'. Joe was quite the linguist when he thought about it.

The sentry gave a kind of muffled laugh. Clearly, the moment he heard a bit of Russian, he could go back to zoning out. Joe carried on moving to the right, along the line of huts, not too slow, not too fast.

The night was clear, chillier than he had expected, the skies above pockmarked with stars. If he looked up, away from the airport perimeter lights, the stars seemed extraordinarily bright thanks to the lack of light pollution you get when the electricity dies. In the distance, a dog howled twice; closer to, insects chirruped gossip to the invertebrate night watch. It felt like it was the first clear night that he had been free – or free-ish – since he'd left LA. But to go home, he had to get away from this Russian airbase. The difficulty was that the perimeter fence lay a good two or three hundred yards off. To run towards that would clearly mark him out. But to stay was to invite the certainty of arrest and torture the moment the new day started.

And then someone fired up a phosphorus shell, turning sleepy night into Benzedrine day. As the shell reached its zenith, the base was bathed momentarily in a chemical brilliance, light and shade etched as unforgivingly as high noon. He cursed his luck, but if it hadn't been for the phosphorus he would never have spotted the bicycle, leaning against the side of a hut. It was a black Mary Poppins lady's bike, with a wicket basket hanging from the handlebars. He got the feeling it didn't quite belong to a Russian airman, that someone had pinched it. Morally, it didn't feel that naughty to steal it himself – *Father, it has been two decades since my last confession* – and the bike would be down towards the bottom of a long list of sins, starting with killing.

The shell was falling now, the light beginning to fade to chemical dusk. He wobbled onto the runway and then a second phosphorus shell lit up the night, and again the sentry shouted something in Russian at him, this time more forcefully than before. Joe guessed the sentry was asking him to stop.

His mind froze, then unfroze. After Weaver had shot Katya dead in Utah, there had been a long, horrible wait while the authorities ummed and ahhed before they freed her body for cremation. Zeke had done his best to chivvy them along, but Joe had spent about three weeks as the old man's guest, mourning the loss of the woman he loved. Pretty soon Zeke, a teetotaller his entire life apart from one night of madness, worked out that only Irish whiskey would see Joe through his grief, so he drove off and came back with bottles of Bushmills, Jameson and something called Writers Tears. Where the old ex-Mormon had got that stuff in Utah's mountain country, Joe didn't know, but he had.

Being an Irishman, when drunk he sang. Zeke's wife, Mary-Lou, had a fine voice, and regaled them with songs like 'Green Grow the Rushes, O', but eventually they got a song off Zeke – the Soviet national anthem, the Stalin version. Joe had got to know every word:

*Soiuz nerushimyj respublik svobodnykh*
*Splotila naveki Velikaia Rus.*
*Da zdravstvuet sozdannyj volej narodov*
*Edinyj, moguchij Sovetskij Soiuz!*

And so that's what he sung when the sentry called out. He roared the anthem Zeke had taught him at the top of his voice while peddling hard for the dead centre of the runway. Once at the centre, he somehow forgot to balance properly and crashed onto the concrete.

Not just the sentry but the whole airbase – everyone who was still up – seemed to find that extraordinarily funny. In the full glow of the shell-light, his shadow etched huge against the runway concrete, Joe got up, bowed to his audience, brushed the blood from his knees, and sang the lines he knew all over again. Jubilant at the madness of it all, his watchers joined in. They saw a drunken Russian marine singing Stalin's anthem. That was fine by Joe.

At the end of the first verse, he remounted his bike and headed off down the runway, weaving in and out of the airport lights and singing the anthem over and over again until a dip in the earth cast the runway into shadow and he knew they could no longer see him. To the left, the land sloped away, the darkness widened. He turned the bike that way and soon enough he came across the perimeter fence. He leant the bike against it, climbed up and jumped over the razor wire. Next he took off his tracksuit trousers, fed them through holes in the wire fence and knotted them around the bike frame and then, bit by bit, pulled it up, over the razor wire. It toppled onto his face, giving him a black eye. Fair enough.

The land was dry and rough underfoot, but he dragged the bike over it until he came across a road. It was, he guessed, three or four o'clock in the morning. He mounted the bike and turned away from the airbase. The moon sank quickly but there was just enough light from the stars above to make out the blacker asphalt against the darkness. He'd spent enough time at sea to read the stars so he looked up and headed north, to Turkey. Alone in a silent dark world, afraid and exultant, he hummed quietly the songs he truly knew, those he really loved: The Saw Doctors' 'N17', The Wolfe Tones' 'Dingle Bay', The Dubliners' 'Dirty Old Town'.

A few miles on from the base, the road curved up and down through the hills. One tight bend, the sound of rushing water led him to a small waterfall, and he dropped the bike with a clatter and gulped down the freezing cold water, as fresh as he'd ever drunk in his whole life. Thirst quenched but hungry, he rode on through the darkness that comes before dawn. When the road was open to the sky, he could navigate by the stars. When the road was confined – or worse, the sky blocked by overhanging trees – he stood a good chance of crashing. Soon his knees, elbows and the backs of his hands were bloodied. It hurt, but not so much as to make him slow down. The more miles he could put between the airbase and him before daybreak, the better.

The airbase, he guessed, was in the Alawite heartland, ultra-loyal to Zarif, and close to the coast. In this area, as someone who could be mistaken for a Russian he wouldn't be treated with immediate suspicion, but it made sense to lie low once the sun came up. To the east, the sky was fading from midnight black to imperial purple to postbox red. Pretty soon the road began tilting downhill and he could make out, through the aroma of lemon trees and olive groves, the smell of the sea. He cycled through a small hamlet, past a few houses and a small mosque, running the gauntlet of a variety of yapping dogs that tried to nip his ankles. Once the world was awake, the make-believe Russian marine wouldn't get so far.

Then he heard them: two or three vehicles, behind and above him, twisting and taking the U-bends at speed. They could be passing traffic; they could be part of a manhunt under orders to capture the missing prisoner without delay. To the left, through a thickness of pine, he could make out a steep, almost-vertical drop to a black cove illuminated by waves breaking against rock. At his feet, only just visible in the reddening gloom, was a miserable path, probably more often used by animals than people, pointing downhill. He took the path, the bike forcing its way through the undergrowth by sheer force of gravity. He was moving dangerously fast when he saw headlight beams flash past above his head. They hadn't seen him.

Like an idiot, he kept on going downhill, too fast. A bird shot out of the undergrowth and brushed against his face and, startled, he closed his eyes – only to open them to realise that he was staring down at the sea, seventy feet below. He slid off the bike and rolled towards the cliff edge, grabbing onto a gnarled root with both hands. The bike fell first, making a splash far below. Joe's feet were dancing in thin air, and now the root he was clinging onto – slowly, inexorably – started to come free.

Now he was falling. He closed his eyes, fully expecting to crash onto the rocks below: dead outright, if he was lucky; broken and paralysed, a slow, miserable ending, if he wasn't.

The water that swallowed him up was cold and shocking, but he was alive.

Gasping for air, he surfaced, looking around the cove for some kind of beach or rocks that would allow him to get back on dry land. Nothing doing on the main shoreline, but in the distance was a sliver of white sand. He swam towards it and clambered onto the sand, panting. Further along he saw the entrance to a shallow cave. Inside the cave he found a very old skiff, its paint cracked and peeling. Two oars, weathered with age. With a fair wind and a bit of luck, it might – just – get him out of this corner of Syria. But would it float?

He dragged the skiff out onto the beach and into the sea. It bobbed around, satisfactorily enough. Hungry and thirsty as he was, it made no sense for him to row to Turkey in broad daylight. The Russians would be scouring the coast for him. They knew he couldn't have gone far.

Getting to Turkey was going to be slow work. He rowed over to the cliff he'd fallen down, and there was the bike, clearly visible in the crystalline water at the bottom. He threw the skiff's anchor over the side, took a great gulp of air and dived, using the anchor rope to pull himself down to the seabed. It was some time before he lifted the bike into the back of the skiff. He rowed back to the cave and hid everything, then he lay on the sand and closed his eyes.

The sun was low in the sky by the time he woke up. He waited another hour, then tied the bike to the back of the skiff, sat in the front with his face to the stern and started to row. Navigation was simple enough. However dark it got, he kept the black hulk of land to the east and rowed north, the oars dipping and rising, through a silvery sea. It was a still night, and in the distance he could make out an artillery duel, guns barking at each other.

———

Not too much to the Syria–Turkey border at sunset: a long, rickety fence topped by a coil of elderly barbed wire, wooden watchtowers every mile or so. Where the land was flat, the border would be tricky to cross, and so Joe cycled west for a dozen miles until the terrain grew more lumpy, creating blind spots for the soldiers in the watchtowers.

As the light in the sky to the west died, Joe hunkered down in a small copse of trees and fell asleep. He woke up in darkness and realised that a light, gentle rain was falling. Thunder rumbled, close by, and a flash of lightning lit up the night sky, illuminating a towering cliff of black clouds coming his way. He'd come to depend on his bike so much that he hated the thought of leaving it in Syria. So Joe shifted it onto his shoulders and carried it, stumbling every now and then, through the rough country towards the border fence.

A great fork of lightning ignited the darkness. Its electric clarity defined the world in front of him: the fence and, at his feet, a narrow asphalt road; some yards away a tall, spindly watchtower, on guard a soldier, the outline of his face, rifle and upper body etched against the lightning. Then the clouds broke and it started to rain, big fat droplets. Joe set off in the opposite direction to the sentry, and when the road dipped down into a cleft in the hills, he mounted the bike and started to pedal, as fast as he dared in the darkness.

A series of lightning flashes lit them up: four figures, walking. A short, stocky man with a kind face, a thick moustache and a club foot. He was hobbling along, wheeling a pushchair piled high with blankets and plastic bags; from within came an infant's cries. With the man was a boy, dark-haired, wet through, crying half-heartedly; behind them a woman, her hair dyed blonde; on her arm, an old lady in a headscarf and black clothes, limping. A sorrier sight would be hard to imagine.

Joe got off the bike, and as the lightning flashed he mimed a soldier holding a rifle and pointed in the direction the family were heading. The man with the club foot understood and shrugged – *what to do?* Joe pointed at the wire fence in front of them.

Joe kneeled down by the fence and scrabbled away at the earth with his hands. The soil was loose, not hard rock. The man joined Joe and the two of them worked hard, scooping out the soil. During a break, he pointed at himself and said, 'Mustafa.' Joe did the same: 'Joe.' Soon the hole was deep enough for them to crawl under the fence. A puddle of water had formed in the bottom of the hole and Joe looked a mudlark when he got to the other side, but Mustafa gave him a huge grin.

Joe looked back at the pushchair. They could never get it through the hole. The women seemed to read his mind. The old lady took out the baby and comforted it, while the blonde woman emptied the pushchair, draping blankets, clothes and shawls over the old lady. The pushchair was dismantled, and Joe got down on his belly and pulled it through the hole under the fence. Eventually the whole family had crawled under, muddy but undefeated. The bike was the most difficult to manoeuvre, but with Mustafa pushing and Joe pulling, it was done. Then they all scurried away from the fence to another road, this time on the Turkish side. Joe lifted the boy onto the bike, and Mustafa and the whole family beamed at him.

'*Shukran*' – thank you – said Mustafa.

They were out of Syria.

Together, they started walking slowly west, as an edge of light rippled behind them.

———

Sunrise: the rain had stopped, leaving streaks of mist lying in the bottom of the valley, turning from pink to gold. In the far distance, they could still make out the sounds of war, the rumble of artillery, but the longer they walked, the fainter it became. By mid-morning they entered a small town. There was a mosque and a square dominated by a statue of Ataturk, the founder of the modern Turkish state, and also a small bureau de change and a kebab shop, the signature beehive of lamb gently roasting in the window. The sight of it made Joe's tummy rumble.

Next door to the kebab shop was an Internet café. Joe had buckets of money sitting in a bank in Hollywood, but no passport, no ID papers. Mustafa had a Syrian passport, but only a few hundred dollars.

After a lot of sign language, Mustafa and Joe had a deal. Joe borrowed a few Turkish lira from Mustafa, went into the Internet café and wired him five thousand dollars. Then they waited. After a time, Mustafa popped in to the bureau de change and returned with a thick wad of dollars, which he handed to Joe.

Joe walked into the kebab shop and ordered ten kebabs.

'My ancestors half-starved,' said Joe. 'I'm not going to make the same mistake, if I can help it, and nor are my friends.'

Mustafa may not have grasped the exact meaning, but the family ate with the hunger of wolves. After Joe had devoured three kebabs himself, he palmed one thousand dollars to the grandmother – suspecting that Mustafa would never accept that kind of money from him. He walked out of the kebab shop, turned to wave goodbye and began hurrying to the nearby taxi rank.

A few seconds later Mustafa came out of the shop, waving the dollars Joe had given to the grandmother, and started hobbling towards him. Laughing, Joe waved and got in the first taxi at the rank. 'Istanbul,' he said, and the taxi sped by Mustafa and his family.

It was the first good deed Joe had done for what seemed like a very, very long time, and the taxi driver, eyeing his new fare through the rear-view mirror, was surprised to see the big man crying his eyes out.

———

When he got to Istanbul, Joe spent some cash on clean clothes and a fancy hotel. The sheets felt as though they were woven from silk. The moment his head touched the pillow, he fell into a profound sleep. He dreamt of a stranger in black carrying a posy of orange and red flowers, who was chasing him through a cemetery back home in Cork. In the dream, Joe slipped on the marble-smooth surface of a grave and fell, and the man caught up with him and offered him the flowers but at that very moment they turned into a blowtorch.

Joe jerked bolt upright, his neck locked in tension, his body drenched in sweat, the madness of his nightmare still with him. He closed his eyes and absorbed the soft hum of air conditioning, the noise of traffic and the sound of a dog barking on the street outside. He opened his eyes and took in the red diode lights of the hotel's digital alarm clock: *03:10*. He lifted the sheets off him and walked to the door, naked, and flung it open to make absolutely sure that this was no prison – to the astonishment of a hen party returning from a bachelorette night on the town. They cackled at seeing a naked man; he shut the door instantly, stammering an apology, locked it behind him and slid down with his back against it, coming to a rest in a crouch, sobbing his heart out. Physically, he'd lost almost two stone in weight but, despite everything he had been through, he wasn't in terrible shape; mentally, he was broken. But he had a job to do, and that was the only thing that gave shape and meaning to his life, so he determined to get on with it.

In the morning, Joe dialled the LA area number Veronica – Dr Franklyn's attorney – had given him for a crash contact. She picked up on the second ring – it must be connected to her cell phone, Joe reasoned – and in the frostiest voice imaginable she told him that Jameela and Ham had left Syria. Joe told her that he'd heard that, too.

'Where did you pick that up?' she asked.

'Damascus.'

'How was it there?'

'Grim.'

'You will, of course, be properly remunerated.'

'It was grimmer than anything money can make up for. But you don't want to know the details, do you?' asked Joe, testing her.

'Not now. Time is pressing.'

She told him that Jameela and the boy were travelling without passports using the fake names of Maryam and Ham Khashoggi, but there had been a possible identification on the Greek island of Kos. And better for the hunt, but not good news, Ham had been involved in a car accident somewhere along the road, in northern Greece or Macedonia. They had gone to hospital in Belgrade where the doctors had X-rayed him and found that his jaw was broken. They had also become aware that something was wrong and the police were called, but due to a misunderstanding Jameela and Ham had managed to escape. They were now believed to be somewhere in northern Serbia, and were heading to Hungary and, from there, on to Austria, then Germany.

'Find them. Arrangements will be easier to make in Serbia and Hungary, less so in Austria or Germany.'

'Arrangements?'

'Getting Ham back to the States without too much paperwork. We want to avoid unnecessary court cases. The fact that she took a severely injured child out of hospital speaks for itself. She is not just a terrorist but also dangerously mentally ill, of that there is no doubt.'

Joe had nothing to add to that. He explained that he had to pick up a fresh passport in Istanbul. Veronica, startled, said, 'How on earth did you mislay your passport in the first place?'

'I lost it in Damascus, but we've already agreed that you don't want to know about that, haven't we?'

The phone line crackled, and through the transatlantic static Joe became aware of another sound, a third party, breathing heavily.

'Who's this?' asked Joe.

'It's Dominic here, phoning in from Luxembourg. Find them.' And then the line went dead.

# SERBIA–HUNGARY BORDER

Exhausted beyond all endurance, Jameela and Ham walked sleeper by sleeper along a never-ending single train track carved through the flat countryside where northern Serbia became southern Hungary. The border zone was featureless because all of this domain had been Habsburg land, part of the Holy Roman Empire, until men with absurd moustaches sat round a map table at Versailles and sketched imaginary lines where Hungary should stop and the then-new Yugoslavia should start.

The day was ending, the shadows lengthening, as Jameela and Ham, his jaw still wrapped in a bandage, trudged past a family huddled in the shade of a tree, past a mound of blankets thrown away by people too tired to carry any extra weight, however useful a blanket might be that very night, always heading north. They traipsed underneath a Cold War watchtower, its ironwork as rusty as its purpose. It had been erected in the aftermath of the Second World War, when Stalin broke with Tito and bemoaned to his diary: 'I trust no one, not even myself.'

Beyond the shadow of the moribund watchtower, dozens of workmen were hurrying to build a new border fence. Not yet complete, it glinted like an array of sharp knives in the sunlight. In Hungarian, the phrase *Welcome to Europe* was written in razor wire. They walked through a narrow gap in the fence and they were in Hungary, but their sense of relief, that one more country had been entered, was short-lived.

Ahead of them was chaos. Hundreds of refugees were roiling around, confronted by dozens of Hungarian riot police, some in black helmets but many in red berets, their faces grim, etched with – to put it most diplomatically – distaste that they were having to deal with so many Muslim refugees. The police were seeking to shepherd the refugees onto buses to take them to internment camps for a registration process far more bureaucratic and time-consuming than anything they had experienced further south. Warned by calls or text messages from relatives who had found themselves locked away in the Hungarian camps, a sliver of refugees ran back the way they had come, through the gap in the border fence, seeking another route, through Croatia and Slovakia, to go north, always north. But the majority of the refugees thrashed in restless stasis, fish captured in a net, knowing they were trapped, fearing that this could be the end.

Jameela and Ham walked closer to the edge of the crowd, and from their position on a low rise of ground they were able to see a group of refugees getting on a bus. The driver closed the doors, unaware that his action had caused a family group to be split up. A woman in a black *abaya* pressed her face against the inside of the glass door of the bus, a still image of horror and despair every bit as powerful as Edvard Munch's *The Scream* – worse because it was real. The driver and the police did not yield, the door did not open, but an infant, the mother's child, was carried over the heads of the knot of people next to the vehicle. A man wrenched open a window on the bus, stiff from lack of use, and the infant was delivered to her mother; then the bus drove off.

That night, Jameela and Ham found themselves in a green-tented camp, surrounded by a razor-wire fence. Beyond the fence was a sterile zone, and beyond that a second razor-wire fence, and beyond that the Hungarian army, toting sub-machine guns. They were the first true soldiers the people had seen since Syria. Jameela felt like she was trapped inside some dreadful category mistake. The people were running from a war, but here they were treated like toxins, like war-bearing bacteria.

Around two o'clock in the morning, someone outside yelled '*Allahu Akbar!*' in mock-Arabic, a second man howled like a wolf, a third roared with malicious laughter and then a shot was fired. In the stillness of the night, the sound of the gunshot echoed and re-echoed amongst the hills, setting the farmyard dogs barking. Inside the camp, in the darkness, you could eat the fear with a fork. Ham grabbed Jameela's hand and she said, 'Don't worry baby, it's going to be OK' and then he said, 'One and one is two and two and one is three,' and out of desperation she said, 'One hundred and forty-four,' and to her immense joy she heard him laugh out loud.

In the morning, things seemed less bad. The food was strange, a curious kind of soup, but the bread was fresh and the water was plentiful. Some of the people giving the food out wore armbands saying *Hungarian Red Cross* and seemed to go out of their way to be pleasant to the refugees, as if to say, *The razor wire and the guns, these are not the only expressions in our language, these are not the only things Hungarians have to say.*

Around eleven o'clock in the morning, Ham was sitting out in the sun, examining the grass and shrubs inside the camp to see if he could find any Fibonacci sequences, when Jameela heard a strange buzzing noise. She looked up into the sky and saw a white plastic object, not that much bigger than a tea tray, hanging in the sky only twenty feet above their heads, bearing a simple black video camera, its lens unblinking. Without thinking, she ran to pick up Ham, solid as he was, and half-running, half-stumbling, pushed him back into the deep shade of the tent.

———

The drone buzzed off, to return to its master, parked two miles away by the side of some woods. It landed and he inserted a cable into the camera and downloaded his catch onto his computer. Then he uploaded the images he had of Jameela and Ham and ran the feed at high speed against the face recognition program, and within two seconds it pinged: the image of the boy's face, absorbed in examining the leaf of a fern, was a poor match, not clear, not definitive, but the image of his mother, looking directly into camera as she hurried to hide him from the drone, that was nigh on perfect. She'd cut her hair.

For the Hungarian authorities, Jameela had prepared Ham, had made him swear that, if asked, he would say his name was Ham Khashoggi and Jameela was Maryam Khashoggi. In the end, when the Hungarian registration process was carried out, it wasn't that painful: a few simple lies and then their papers, such as they were, were stamped with the Hungarian state coat of arms. Ham examined the stamp carefully and said, 'The crown's wonky,' which it was.

Their paperwork was completed, but they were not free to leave. The Hungarian government had a point to make, that it did not want or welcome Muslim refugees or refugees who happened to be Muslim, and the more everyone understood that, the better. So the process was made far longer than it needed to be. In the end, they were released on the seventh day of their enforced captivity. Summer was over and autumn had arrived with a jolt: instead of the bright, garish sunlight they were used to in Syria, and before that California, they were wrapped in a cocoon of fog. You could barely see your hand in front of your face.

Along with the other refugees from the camp, they were loaded onto a special bus provided by the authorities. They were taken not to the Austrian border but to a point on a map someone in the interior ministry in Budapest had designated as the offload point, two miles' trudge from the frontier. They walked in silence through apple groves and oak trees, the fog thinning on the hilltops, but still deep in the valleys. The road went downhill, quite steeply, and they found themselves wrapped in murk. Ham, in his beloved Batman T-shirt and jeans, skipped ahead, enjoying the freedom to run that the camp had denied him for too long.

'The border's only three hundred metres away,' one of the refugees said in Arabic, encouraging them all onwards.

Jameela hurried into the fog, calling out Ham's name, again and again, but answer came there none.

# LANGLEY, VIRGINIA

The sunlight outside never punctured the citadel within. Antiseptic light beamed down on white floors, grey walls, grey rooms that were lined with grey filing cabinets because, as the Agency feared being hacked, more and more of its vast treasure-hoard of secrets was being transferred back onto paper, to be archived in cardboard folders in locked stainless-steel cabinets. In the twenty-first century, the most advanced intelligence-gathering machine the world had ever known was hurrying back to the time before digitalism.

Zeke had been at the Agency so long that his personal file, all thirty-two separate volumes of it, was wheeled in on a trolley. The three-strong committee called together to adjudicate on his fate were grim-faced. But it took quite a while for the files to be offloaded from the trolley onto the desk in front of them, testimony in paper and ink to Zeke's service to the organisation.

Paperwork duly in place, the assault began. Phil Lansing, the Agency's Inspector General, began to cite paragraph 12, subsection C, reminding intelligence officers of the necessity to be mindful of the Agency's broad goals and not just to be concerned 'with the narrow confine—'

'. . . of the specific operation in hand.'

Zeke completed the subsection for him from memory. The two other executives, sitting either side of Lansing, registered surprise. Zeke smiled his idiot smile and explained: 'If you're going to throw the book at me, be it noted that I wrote the aforesaid. Or at least updated it, some seventeen years ago. If you'd all care to check page three of the hard copy of the Guidance for Intelligence Officers manual, you'll see the evidence for my assertion. No pressure, gentlemen.'

'Mr Chandl—'

'Call me Zeke, Phil.'

'The protocol of this personnel inquiry into your actions and inactions vis-à-vis the integrity of this Agency requires that I use your surname, Mr Chandler.'

'I didn't write that rule,' said Zeke, mildly affronted.

'No, you did not.'

The case against him proceeded. Sure, he'd taken a risk leaving his security detail in Tirana, but he had begun to suspect that they were there to stop him from investigating the possibility of a CIA black ops facility in northern Albania. Him being an intelligence officer and all, it had seemed the right thing to do at the time.

'This foolish adventure' was how Lansing termed it.

'We must agree to disagree—' chipped in Zeke.

'This caused a great deal of anxiety to your colleagues. You were seriously injured and it was only the prompt medevac by Agency personnel that—'

'Yadda yadda . . .'

'Excuse m—'

'Some shrapnel pierced my lung. A shepherd fixed me up. I was right as rain by the time you folks wandered b—'

'The second error is of a far graver magnitude to the Agency. You traded satellite images with the Zarif regime for a non-American subject.'

'A man called Joe Tiplady,' replied Zeke. 'It was not just morally the right thing to do, it may yet deliver significant HUMINT on Syria at a time when the Agency's technology-driven obsession with SIGINT is delivering precious little product. The catch from the Agency's HUMINT trawl against ISIS is pitiful. ISIS, leastways some of the people in ISIS, are smart. Sure, German intelligence has done well by picking up a flash drive containing the résumés of thousands of recruits, but they're low-level grunts. The Agency's SIGINT penetration of ISIS's high-level command – for example, anyone who has physical proximity to the Caliph – is negligible, *de nada*. So a HUMINT operation which might yet bear fruit is worth a few snaps from space. Or maybe I'm wrong about that. Got any others?'

'No fruit as yet; not even a seed,' said Lansing.

'Intelligence against a SIGINT-aware organisation like ISIS requires time,' said Zeke. 'If the Agency runs its operations with the patience of a duck, it will be found quacking.'

Zeke scored high on languages and subjective analysis, but these were Palaeolithic skills in the digital age.

'The truth is,' said Lansing, 'you traded satellite imagery of immense value to this Agency, for a foreign national whose loyalty to the United States is very much an open question.'

'Immense value? I doubt that.'

'The charge is that you're trading Agency gold for a pinch of tobacco and a shard of glass, Mr Chandler.'

Zeke eased back in his chair, almost languidly, and smiled his open-mouthed smile and said, 'This is all a smokescreen, isn't it? What you're really worried about is me stumbling on your black operation in Albania, isn't it? The secret facility in the mountains near Tropojë, near where I got shot for poking my nose in things which weren't my business.'

Lansing stared at him, cold-eyed. 'I do not know what you are talking about.'

'You don't?'

'No.'

'Oh, I need a break,' said Zeke. 'Please, excuse me.'

Zeke realised the mood music for his future was all wrong. He was heading, fast, out of the door, no question; he would lose all his security clearances; they were not above taking his pension off him. He found the nearest bathroom, finished his business, and was on his way back to the hearing room when he bumped into Mike Rinder, the Agency's Director.

'Zeke,' said Rinder, 'how's it going?'

'Not good, Mike, not good.'

'I heard that, too. The specifics aren't great, Zeke. You shouldn't have traded satellite imagery for that Irishman.'

'I believe I did have authority to do that.'

'I can't stop this process, I'm afraid.'

Zeke said nothing.

'Why don't you vanish for six months or so?' said Rinder. 'Come back after the election, when things are clearer, when people are less sore at you?'

'This isn't about me, is it? It's about the black facility in Tropojë, isn't it?'

'Why don't you vanish for six months or so?' repeated Rinder, the expression on his face glacial.

'Surely, the logical response to my strange question ought to have been: "What black facility is that, Zeke?"'

'Whatever it was, it no longer exists.'

'My, my . . . So you've closed it down.'

'I haven't closed anything down.'

'But it no longer exists?'

'You've won that battle, Zeke. But don't let your victory be Pyrrhic. In my judgement, you are a great asset to this Agency. But your enemies here in this very building think that you're making the war on terror unnecessarily harder. They want your head on a plate, and at this moment in time you've given them a nice wooden chopping block and a lovely sharp axe.'

'I didn't create a black facility. Why am I in trouble for asking questions about something that should never have existed in the first place?'

'Good question. But that's not the question the Inspector General is asking right now. He's asking why the Agency should spend a trillion dollars on satellite technology so that you can go around handing out its product to dictators in return for favours. So, if I were you, I would lie low right now.'

'And walk out on an internal affairs investigation?'

'So you will be a naughty boy, for a while. But it's better that you go and then we can sort this out when you get back. Deal?'

'No deal. I did not join this Agency to turn my back on the American constitution. We serve our democracy. We uphold the rule of law, Mike, and the law says no black ops.'

Rinder looked over Zeke's shoulder, double-checked that the corridor remained empty.

'Power's draining from me, Zeke. I haven't got the juice. The word is soon I'll be out. I can't defend you anymore.'

'If she wins, you'll get another term in office, surely?'

'She's not going to win.'

'Do we prejudge the American people their right to a fair and free election these days?'

'That's not going to happen.'

'So who gets your job?'

'You're my choice. If she wins, you could take the chair. But she isn't going to win. If he wins, Crone will be the new Director. He has no time for the human rights stuff that gets you all het up.'

'The Irishman I got out told me that when he was being tortured, Grozhov was in the room, and then Grozhov's phone rang and the

Irishman heard him say, "Pennsylvania, Ohio, Michigan, Wisconsin." Grozhov talked about the White House and *Kompromat*.'

'Straight up?'

Zeke nodded.

'The Russians seem to have a skin in our election,' said Rinder. 'I'll talk to the FBI, but they're only interested in her emails. Meanwhile, I can't save you, Zeke. Get out of here. They can't rip you apart if you're not in the building.'

'Understood.'

'Attaboy,' said Rinder. His smartphone bleeped a message. By the time he'd read it, Zeke was no longer there.

# SOUTHERN HUNGARY

It had been all so easy. Having established which registration camp in Hungary Jameela and Ham were housed in by using the drone and the face recognition program on his computer, he'd paid off a guard, established their release date, and then tailed them discreetly to just short of the border, always the place of maximum chaos. The fog had been an unexpected bonus, making everything that bit easier. He'd waited until Ham had run ahead of his mother into the fog where it lay at its thickest, picked him off his feet, knocked him out with a carefully calibrated dose of chloroform and then hurried off – the child, to anyone who might have given them half a glance, asleep in his father's arms.

Ham's jaw was still swollen, puffy, but he seemed fine enough. As Joe climbed towards his car, he heard Jameela's increasingly frantic cries: 'Ham! Ham!'

Joe felt a stab of remorse and then remembered that she had played with this boy's life; she had made him join an ISIS suicide cell. Taking a boy from a mother this crazy was, in reality, an act of mercy.

Joe had parked his car half a mile away, on a quiet road at a diagonal to the main refugee track. No one saw him lay the sleeping boy on the back seat; no one saw him drive off. The airport was close by – small, ex-military, boasting a couple of civilian flights a day. At the far end of the single runway, away from the terminal, the G-5 jet sat next to an aircraft hangar, a wide, open door revealing something of the cavern within. Dominic Franklyn was standing at the bottom of the jet's steps talking to Veronica, the lawyer, who was dressed in a white nurse's uniform.

Joe parked the car a short distance from the executive jet and opened the rear door. He scooped up Ham, and walked towards the jet. The fog was beginning to burn off. But it was still chilly, and the sudden drop in temperature was enough to stir Ham from his sleep. Joe could feel him wriggle a little and then his eyes opened. He closed them, opened them again, refocused them and spat out, 'Who are you?'

Joe was within twenty yards of the jet.

'Mission accomplished,' said Franklyn, beaming a smile as bright as Pacific Ocean surf. 'We'll take him now.'

'Who are you?' Ham repeated, no friendlier than before.

'I'm a friend of your father,' replied Joe.

And that's when everything started to go wrong. Joe would never have imagined that a seven-year-old boy could headbutt him that powerfully. Momentarily stunned, his nose bleeding, Joe felt Ham rocket out from his arms and start running, extraordinarily fast, away from the jet, towards the hangar.

'Ham!' roared Franklyn. 'Come here, Ham, come here!' Franklyn shot past Joe, who was still reeling from the headbutt, and ran into the hangar. Joe wiped the blood from his nose with his shirt sleeve and trotted on behind.

The hangar housed three small aircraft and the machines to service them: compressors, fuel pumps, baggage-handling trucks, tow trucks. It was big and gloomy and there was no sound nor sign of Ham. Franklyn was walking deep into it, Joe behind him to the right, Veronica to the left. They were a posse hunting down an outlaw; this wasn't exactly how Joe had imagined the reunion of father and son.

'Ham, come on out,' said Franklyn, an edge of desperation creeping into his voice. 'Game's over, Ham. It's been fun, but now it's time to go.'

Silence, apart from the soft footfalls of the three adults slowly walking forward. The jet pilot, young, fresh-faced, earnest, jogged into the hanger and called out, 'Dr Franklyn, I'm afraid we need to take off in the next ten minutes. Sir, we've got to take off. Please return to your seat, sir. Otherwise I'll be in breach of my flying-hours limit.'

Franklyn made no reply and continued to walk forward slowly. He was almost at the far end of the hangar. There was still no sign of Ham.

'Dr Franklyn,' the pilot followed up, his tone more insistent than before. 'If we don't take off in the next few minutes, sir, I can't fly the jet. You're going to have to take off now or book another pilot.'

Still there was no reply from Franklyn.

'Sir, did you hear me? We take off now or you get another pilot. And that might take many hours.' The pain in his voice was almost comical; he did not want to irritate his boss; he did not want to lose his pilot's licence.

Franklyn pivoted on a sixpence and walked towards the pilot, who was tall, gangly, pink-faced. It was a long walk. Joe kept an eye open for Ham, but he turned to make sure he did not miss what happened next.

Franklyn got within a foot of the pilot and said quietly, 'What did you say?'

'Sir, I said we must take off now. Or, sir, because of the laws limiting flying hours, I can't fly.'

'Really?' asked Franklyn.

'Yes sir.'

'Come here, boy.'

The pilot leant his face towards Franklyn, puzzled. The doctor's first punch was to the pilot's temple, knocking off his hat; the second and third to the side of his face, bringing him down. The split second he was on the ground, Franklyn started kicking him in the gut, repeatedly.

'Dominic, no!' cried Veronica.

At that very moment Ham broke from cover, darting from behind a baggage truck to bolt for the open runway. It just so happened that he started his escape while Joe was standing in the shadow of the tail fin of one of the aircraft. It was the easiest thing in the world for Joe to grab hold of the boy. Having been headbutted by Ham, this time Joe was taking no chances. He grabbed Ham's arms and pinned them behind his back. Ham kicked backwards, trying for Joe's groin, but Joe sidestepped him, his captive safe in his hands.

'OK, we fly, we fly now,' said Franklyn coolly. He reached out to the pilot with his arm and pulled him upright. 'Come on, soldier, we've got to move.'

The pilot stood up, rubbing his temple where Franklyn had hit him. He had a moment to make his choice: fly the client who had just hit him or swallow his pride. Given more time, he may well have made a different decision. But he shook his head to clear it and started to walk, fast, to the jet, calling out behind him: 'OK, let's go.'

On reflection Joe, too, may well have behaved differently. But the necessity of getting the jet airborne, the take-off deadline ticking by, made him move fast. Only later did he think hard about what he had seen with his own eyes: a boy running from his father, and the same father violently attacking an employee – one critical to his own and other people's safety at that – for no good reason.

As it was, Joe, moving slower than the others because he was pushing a reluctant Ham towards the jet, was last up the steps. Veronica welcomed Ham with a frozen smile and the needle of a syringe that she jabbed into his arm. Rendered unconscious almost immediately, Ham folded into her arms. Joe stood awkwardly, halfway up the steps, while Veronica disappeared then reappeared.

'You're not coming.' The finality in her voice brooked no reply. 'Dominic's very grateful. We'll send a banker's cheque to your account the moment we're airborne. Thank you.'

Joe stepped down onto the tarmac. The moment he did so, she hit a button inside the plane and the steps flipped up and folded themselves back into the fuselage; the plane door closed with a thump; the engines started to whine. Joe jogged over to his car, switched on the ignition and began to pull away. Quick as he was, the car was still buffeted by the backwash of the jet's engines. Within thirty seconds, the jet was barrelling down the runway; within a minute it was becoming an ever-smaller dot in the sky.

Joe had returned a boy who had been kidnapped by an ISIS sympathiser to his father. He'd done the right thing and had been paid more than two million bucks into the bargain. But, looking up at the sky, it didn't feel like that. It didn't feel like that at all.

# CARACAS, VENEZUELA

The eyes of Hugo Chávez – brown, seductive, watchful – gazed down on the barrio from the mural on top of the decrepit tower block. A heavily tattooed Chavista in a red T-shirt was exhorting the masses through a loudspeaker on top of his minivan: 'We are fighting the economic crisis the people are facing, but all through the Bolivarian Revolution we have been attacked unceasingly.'

The clouds stacking above the eastward hook of the Andes hung heavy in the air. Caracas sweated at the bottom of a bowl of hills, the humidity made more unbearable by pollution from too many elderly cars running on too-cheap fuel. The air was slimy and gaseous. The rain, when it came, would be a blessing.

The man of the new-old faith in the minivan had the voice of a crow and his sound system had seen better days. Passionate, pious, the crow warmed to his theme through a hiss of static and the odd burst of negative feedback: 'The oligarchs who dominate the' – *hiss-hiss-hiss* – 'to strangle us, to suffocate us. They are cutting their' – a long, ear-piercing shriek – 'so the shops run out of goods. But Chavismo will rise above . . .' *hiss-hiss-hiss*. Nothing worked in Venezuela anymore; not even the cawing of power.

On the other side of the steeply tumbling street, the people queuing for hours at the state-subsidised co-op on the rumour of toilet rolls, eggs, rice, aspirin, cooking oil, soap, cheese, washing powder, beer, chicken, whatever, found the old slogans unimpressive. One old man spat on the ground; a woman formed the fingers of her free hand, unencumbered by shopping bags, into a quacking mouth. The Chavista saw the gesture and started yelling into his megaphone: 'See the ducks spout their rubbish for the oligarchs.'

The queue, mutinous now, gave him the finger, and with a squeal of tyres he accelerated away, up the hill, in search of a less fractious audience. Once, Chavismo had held so many in his thrall. El Presidente had gone to the United Nations in New York and sniffed the podium just vacated by George W. Bush and smelt sulphur. And now? His corpse was guarded in a fancy mausoleum by four chocolate soldiers in Bolivarian fancy dress, all tights and shakos, but the old slogans of his movement sounded like the tired routines of an elderly comedian.

Joe, anonymous in his motorbike helmet, took in the slow-motion revolt, then released the clutch on his Triumph Bonneville and slipped slowly, delicately down the steep slope. At the very bottom, he came across what he was looking for, a noxious stream, chock-full of rubbish, smelling of shit, slowly treacling towards the Atlantic. This was the real crime of Chavismo – that he and his cronies had taken the nation with the world's greatest oil reserves and made it poorer, so poor that obtaining the ordinary essentials of life – clean water, food, the simplest medicines – had become a wretched struggle for millions of people.

Joe stopped the Triumph and debated taking off his helmet but thought better of it. He'd been trained to kill by the North Koreans and was not a timid man, but in his two days in Caracas he'd heard too many stories of people being mugged at gunpoint – or worse, at the end of a hypodermic syringe loaded with someone's infected blood. Security lay in anonymity; on his elderly motorbike, the red paint on the petrol tank grazed by a previous accident, the pillion seat slashed and repaired by cheap black sticky tape, he could be a local. If he took his helmet off, he would stand out as a gringo and, in this barrio where the police only dared come in strong daylight, he would be ripe for the picking.

Not too far away, someone let rip a round of automatic fire. The gunfire was taken up by the foothills of the Andes, making the sound ricochet around the concrete breeze blocks of the barrio. They said that Caracas was now the murder capital of the world. Nobody knew for sure because nobody dared count. So, rivulets of sweat pouring off his face, Joe kept his helmet on while his fingers dug out the little map scribbled onto a sheet of paper by his informant – snitch, more like – showing the toxic sewer-stream running along the bottom, a wooden bridge across it and, up on the other side of the slope, finer houses, a better class of slum-dweller.

The house he was looking for was as described, an orgy in cerise, its windows shuttered and barred so that it had the appearance of a mini-prison. He killed the engine of the Triumph, put the bike on its arthritic stand, and walked up to the door and knocked loudly. The time for reckoning had come.

Only the door wasn't opened by the man he was looking for but a little black girl, maybe seven years old, wearing a white dress, her frizzy hair neatly done up in Minnie Mouse bunches.

Joe's Spanish was so-so but he had no choice. He asked to speak with the little girl's father or mother. She shook her head. He told her that he was looking for a man called Caesar. She nodded, and said that was her papa, that he was in the big hospital. Why was he in the hospital, asked Joe.

'Zika,' she said, and Joe thanked her and left.

The hospital was an even more pitiless indictment of Chavismo's sloppy posturing than the stinking river. The power had gone, so the metal detectors at the main entrance – there to ensure that gang members did not pack heat when they visited the sick – weren't working. Joe shuffled forwards in the queue and was searched pretty effectively by an old guard. No power meant none of the lights were working, so the hospital festered in gloom, and nor was the air conditioning, so its 1970s concrete structure breathed out a prickly heat, suffused, it felt to Joe, with infection; nor were any of the elevators working. The Zika ward was on the seventh floor, fourteen flights of stairs in all, and Joe felt a very old man when he made it. In any kind of well-run country, it should not have been possible for a stranger tracking down a debt to enter the ward treating the world's most terrifying infectious disease, but this was Venezuela.

Caesar lay at the far end of the ward, where some daylight seeped through grimy windows. He was mixed-race, thin, almost scholarly, with a high forehead and an honest, or honest-seeming, face – an accident of birth that had helped him through a dozen confidence tricks, maybe more. The whites of his eyes were locked on the ceiling; his body lay awkwardly, wrongly immobile, on the filthy sheets. A fly landed in the corner of his right eye and feasted on the liquid to be found there before his wife, a sweet-looking, mixed-race woman way too good for him, shooed it away with a none-too-clean cloth.

'Paralysed?' asked Joe in Spanish.

The woman crossed herself and told him that Caesar had been paralysed for two weeks now, and the doctors – the hospital – had no medicine to treat him, but they said there was very little they could do for him anyway. Joe had read that the Zika virus frequently paralyses the central nervous system; most people recover, though some faculties are impaired; a minority of cases die because the patient's lungs stop working. Caesar looked touch-and-go. At the bottom of the bed lay a cot, and in it an infant girl in dayglo pink, fast asleep.

Caesar Umbrio or Red Narayan or Ken Fox had an interesting collection of aliases. He had run off with one million dollars – give or take a dollar or two – of money belonging to a syndicate fronted by Jerrard Drobb – 'JayDee' – a flaming-haired, half-Swedish, self-certified multimillionaire reality TV star, entrepreneur and candidate in the US presidential election. Team Drobb had flown Joe from LA to New York, economy. When Joe had got a cab from JFK, Drobb's people had told him that it was assumed that he would have taken the subway, and would only recompense him for that route. Joe didn't have a mean bone in his body but the chiselling struck him as odd. As Joe ascended in an Aztec silver-lined elevator in Drobb Domus, the billionaire's signature skyscraper in Manhattan, he reflected that either Drobb was pathologically tight, or he wasn't quite as rich as he said he was. Or both.

Joe had been ushered out of the elevator by a female flunkey in a business suit, dark-haired, long-limbed, her youth and beauty marred by some unspoken but noxious anxiety scribbled on her face. She turned and walked him through a penthouse suite the size of a small cathedral, with a view to die for over Central Park, and into a small side room with no windows, furnished by a silver-effect sofa of a certain age, marked by a dark stain the shape of Lake Superior. The little room's walls were decorated solely with photographs of America's great white hope: JayDee on the stump, JayDee laying concrete on some of his buildings, JayDee snipping ribbons, JayDee pressing the flesh, much of it female. Joe felt locked inside someone else's narcissism, a self-love so vast it knew no horizon.

Drobb had kept Joe waiting for four and a half hours. Rich people, like border guards and policemen, confuse other people's time with something of no value. Joe considered walking but stayed. He didn't need the money but he did need the distraction.

Close on five hours in, Miss Anxiety returned, paddling her hands to suggest that Joe should stand to attention and then come out into the suite, like an aircraft handler guiding a jumbo. She paddled him through the cathedral to an office overlooking the great city of New York and there was JayDee: marmalade skin, tangerine hair. It was whipped up and piled over his scalp like an ice sculpture. He was tall, taller than Joe, and heavy. For a man with such heft, his hands were curiously small, like the flippers of a salamander or early lizard.

'Great honour, Joe, great honour to meet you.' His voice was soft, almost girlish.

For the rich son of a rich man, Drobb in the flesh seemed awkward, insecure, keen – no, desperate – to win Joe's good opinion. Joe's nostrils twitched. There was the memory of a scent in Drobb's office, something that troubled his mind's nose. He couldn't quite trace it.

'So glad you could be here today, Joe,' continued Drobb. 'I've heard so much about you.' The sincerity of the compliment was real for that moment; but the moment passed very quickly. Miss Anxiety hovered, some unspoken agony in her eyes.

'What's eating you up, Flora?' It was hard for Drobb to snarl given the light zephyr of his voice, but he managed it.

'What shall I do about Mr Richards? He's been waiting to see you for two and a half days, Mr Drobb.'

'Let him wait a while longer.'

'But Mr Drobb . . .'

'Entertain him, show him your pussy, whatever.' Her face twitched and she exited, the two men watching her walk out of the office.

'Nice ass, but a nut job,' said Drobb.

Joe said nothing but reflected inwardly that the problem of being a private detective was that the rich people who could afford to hire him made him feel ill. He thought hard about giving this job up, there and then, and telling Drobb to shove it. But something stayed his tongue.

'You wanna know why you're here?'

Joe nodded.

'Ken Fox or Caesar Umbrio, whatever his name is, he's a bad hombre, soldier. I had a Drobb project in the Caribbean. Investors piled in, they see the Drobb name, they know they're getting a good deal, a fantastic deal. Ken took the money and ran. I want you to hunt him down and I want you to break him into little pieces.'

Joe wondered whether Drobb wrote his own words or had them scripted.

'Ken stole from me. I trusted him and he took me for a ride. I want you to find him and clean him out and make him suffer, so that neither he nor any other wetback will dare rip me off ever again. Flora will handle the details. Great to meet, great to spend time with you.' And then Joe felt his presence was no longer required.

Joe had backed away, talked through money and expenses with Flora, re-entered the Aztec silver elevator. Halfway down he slid a key against the silver lining. It was plastic.

And now, in a hospital in Caracas, Caesar's wife was staring up at him. And then Joe remembered the lingering odour in Drobb's office: lavender. Grozhov had been in Drobb's penthouse. It was strange, thought Joe, how the memory of a smell could force a decision.

Joe didn't take kindly to conmen like Caesar. They used their weasel ways against victims who found it incredibly difficult to realise that their trust in a fellow man could be so horribly misplaced. But he took in the paralysed man, the nursing wife, the infant at the bottom of the bed and, back home, the little girl in the white dress with the Minnie Mouse bunches. And the scent of lavender in Drobb's office.

'Caesar . . .' Joe started, then stopped. He had to phrase this delicately and his Spanish wasn't up to it. 'Some money went missing in the Caribbean.'

'*Si*,' said the woman, her face wreathed with anxiety that Joe, who towered over her, had come to do a shakedown.

'A man is looking for Caesar.'

'A priest?' asked the woman, a look of genuine fear etched on her face.

'Maybe he thinks he's some kind of a god, but he's no priest,' said Joe, who, as a lapsed Catholic, was confident in this territory. 'The man wants to destroy Caesar.' He walked around to her side of the bed and crouched down so that his face was close to hers. He didn't want any of the other patients' families to overhear what he was going to say next: 'This man, he's called Jerrard Drobb. He's rich, he's powerful, he may yet become the President of the United States. He's going to ask me where the money is that Caesar took.'

'*Si*,' she said, her eyes wide with unease.

Joe held the palms of his hands out flat, bidding her to stay where she was. He walked to the station at the head of the ward where the nurses hung out morosely in the gloom. Twenty dollars did the trick, and he knew he had been ripped off. He returned with a piece of paper, dated and signed. Joe took out his phone and took a picture of the paper and then handed it to the woman.

'What is this?' she asked, the fear in her voice turning her words to dry husks.

'It's a death certificate. Caesar passed away a few minutes ago. He died of Zika' – who knew, it could well be true in a few days – 'but you need to have a funeral.'

'A real funeral?' The anxiety hardened her face. Joe smiled his slow, slow smile and replied, 'A pretend one. I can't get money off a dead man. Even Drobb will understand that.' He palmed her five hundred dollars. 'But pretend the funeral well. If Drobb ever finds out that I faked Caesar's death, then I'll be in big trouble.'

'Thank you, sir.'

'Good luck. You'll need it.'

'Thank you, mister,' she said in English to Joe's retreating back. 'Thank you. You are a good man.'

*No, I'm not*, thought Joe. *I kidnap children for money.*

# CARACAS, VENEZUELA

Joe walked back to the stairwell, the top of which was lined with windows, open to the sky, and glanced at a parallel stairwell at the far end of the hospital building. There he saw, three storeys below him, a dead man descending the steps.

What Joe did next was beyond stupid. Instead of using caution, quietly following the target and then running him to ground, he yelled out the name of the man he'd last seen slumped in a pool of his own blood, dead, in Damascus: 'Humf!'

Humfrey DeCrecy looked up, startled, clocked Joe – their eyes locked – and then he started to really shift, jumping down the seven steps of a half-landing in one go, again and again. The race had started with Humfrey six flights ahead of Joe, and he was by far the lighter, leaner man. But Joe had been wrestling with his conscience for a month now, ever since he'd kidnapped Ham. He suspected something big was wrong, something missing in the story he'd been told.

And now a corpse was running from him, fast.

Joe took the stairs at a run, gripping the iron balustrade on the inside of the stairwell to pivot on each landing. Two landings down and his way was blocked by a family who, judging from their melancholy, had just lost a loved one; he did his best to ease past them, then accelerated down to the bottom of the stairs. On the ground floor, there was no sign of Humfrey. Joe jogged towards the hospital entrance, diving left to avoid a gurney racing towards surgery, bearing a gunshot victim cratered in blood, and zig-zagging between knots of relatives, bleary-eyed, despondent, slow to move.

Outside, the sun's glare bleached out all detail until an immense rain cloud blotted it out in turn. Squinting into the shadows, he spotted a blur of movement, then clocked a cream Land Cruiser tearing out of the car park. Fat spots of rain began to fall and then thunder rumbled, and with a suddenness that Joe found bewildering, a wall of water was descending from the sky: Andes rain. The Cruiser slowed to exit the security cordon – a thick metal chain untied and then tied to a thick brick archway by a white-haired, frail guard who was in no hurry to get anything done – and Joe caught through the rain a glimpse of a thin, blond-haired man in the Cruiser's oversize side mirror.

Joe raced to his Triumph, jumped on the bike, turned the key and fired up the engine. The rain fell in stair-rods, soaking Joe to the skin, making him blind. Although every second counted, he forced himself to don his helmet, its peak helping to screen the worst of the rain from his sight. Now he could see better, he realised the Cruiser was through the security cordon, the old man tying up the chain even though a funeral hearse and two ancient Chevrolets had just pulled up behind it. If he went the correct way and waited his turn, he'd lose the Cruiser.

To his left was the ghost of a garden, more a bank of earth turning liquid by the moment, that led up to a brick wall. Joe gunned the bike up the bank, his rear wheel spinning in the mud, and revved the machine to the max so that it crawled onto the wall's top; once on solid brick it powered along, almost plunging off the wall. He squeezed the brakes, regained control, and zipped over the arch where the guard was inspecting the coffin in the hearse. On the far, public side of the wall was a kiosk with a sloping, corrugated-iron roof that dropped down to road level, a man selling soft drinks inside. Joe hit the brakes again and cut much of his speed, hoping that the roof would bear the weight of the Triumph. The metal creaked but held; he was down, and he flipped his wrist so the bike sashayed in and out of the traffic as the road turned into a flowing river. Ahead, through the blur of raindrops, he made out the Cruiser taking a very brave and very unpopular right at the lights. The road swivelled and careered uphill extraordinarily steeply, so that Joe thought he was riding up a waterfall. The Cruiser had the advantage of him: its wheels could grip, it had traction, while the Triumph slipped and slid as it would on an ice rink. Joe just, but only just, escaped going under the wheels of a water truck reversing towards a standpipe, but now the road switchbacked downhill and the Cruiser's weight paid against it. Once, twice, the Cruiser almost lost control, clipping a telephone pole and taking out a chunk of the bumper of an Oldsmobile parked by the side of the road. Then it took a corner too fast, its wheels spinning helplessly, and it reared up and fell, the driver's side wheels plunging into an ever-deepening ditch.

Humfrey, stunned and half-blinded by the crash, was struggling to open the passenger door to get out of the stranded Cruiser when he felt himself being lifted clean out of the vehicle. That was the end of the good news.

He didn't see the punch coming. But he felt his arms being wrenched high up behind his back, so that his fingers were almost touching his neck, and then, terrifyingly, he felt his weight being pivoted so that his mouth was in the ditch, and he was held there for ten, twenty, thirty seconds.

Only then did the human see-saw swing back. Humfrey, gasping for air, gabbled but couldn't speak.

'Please . . . go . . . you're killing me, you're going to kill me, you Irish psycho!'

Over the sound of the rain and the rush of blood in his ears did he hear the reply: 'That doesn't matter, because you're dead already.'

Humfrey's face was shoved down into the torrent again, he was going to drown, and then it stopped, and just above the rasping of his breath he heard that soft Irish voice say, 'Humfrey DeCrecy, just a word of advice. Don't make me angry. You won't like it if you make me angry. Talk.'

Humfrey did. It had never been planned, not as far as he knew. It was just an opportunity that had presented itself. He'd known and loved Jam, that was all true. He'd wanted to help her and when Joe had got in touch and asked about her being in ISIS, he'd made a phone call.

'That is the one thing I told you not to do,' said Joe. 'Who did you call?'

Humf spat it out: 'The CIA.'

'Bullshit,' said Joe.

'The truth,' said Humfrey. 'They use me, very occasionally. I have a skill.'

'And what might that be?'

'I play dead people, remember. I'm the man who dies in the first five minutes. I'm good at it. From time to time, the Agency, they call me in, to play dead, in Paraguay, Antigua, Mozambique.'

'Who in the CIA?'

Humfrey held his tongue.

'I forgot to tell you,' Joe continued. 'When I was in the Rah, they sent me to do mortal combat training in North Korea. I was such the star student I killed the instructor. Who did you call in the CIA?'

'I called a number. Then someone called me back, wanting to know more.'

'Who called you back?'

'I can't say.'

'You can't say.'

'No.'

Humfrey felt the mass of Joe's strength on the small of his back, his mouth pivoting back into the stream so that he began to inhale water all over again. He stayed like that for thirty seconds, forty, fifty. When he came up, he was retching for air.

'You can't say?' said Joe conversationally.

'Zeke Chandler,' said Humfrey.

'Did you meet him?'

'Yeah.'

'What did he look like?'

'An old guy, gap between his teeth. Looked stupid but wasn't.'

'You sure it was Zeke?'

'Yeah.'

Humfrey stayed level for thirty seconds, a minute. He liked breathing air so he didn't make a formal complaint.

'So you play dead in the courtyard,' Joe said. 'Mansour kicks the crap out of you. And then what?'

'Then I'm with the goons and I'm blindfolded, and someone puts headphones over my ears, loud, so I can't hear a damn thing, and they take me up to a villa someplace in the hills overlooking Damascus. Then I'm switched, put into another car. These guys drive me to a harbour and it's two days, three days in a sailboat, and then I'm in Cyprus and I'm given a ton of money and a one-way ticket to Caracas.'

'Their choice?'

'My choice.'

'And the purpose of the charade? Mansour pretends to shoot you, kicks the shit out of Qureshi. He's in on the act, too?'

'I was given a kind of script. I was told to take the scimitar off the guy with the scarlet head-cloth; the others all wore black. Then some guy would shoot me. I get to do my bit, then it's off to the Oscar party.'

'You bastard,' Joe growled. 'I thought you were dead . . . When I got back to the States from this trip, I was all ready to break the news to your sister in Arkansas.'

'Heh, it's just showbiz.'

Joe ignored that, but asked a question that was now troubling him greatly: 'So Jameela, she was in ISIS, for sure?'

'I don't know.'

'There's something I didn't tell you,' said Joe. 'The job I had, it wasn't just to trace Jameela, find out that she was safe and well. It was to get her son back to the father, name of Dr Dominic Franklyn. I did that, I kidnapped her son while she wasn't looking. I can still hear her screaming her boy's name, in the fog, on a hillside in the middle of nowhere in northern Hungary.' Joe's voice went softer. 'Thing is, Humfrey, I stole a child from his mother, stole him because I was told that it was the right thing to do by two people in the CIA, one of whom I trust with my life, and all of it – well, your part in it, anyway – turns out to be a lie.'

'So what are you going to do?'

'I'm going to make my confession.'

'You mean, in church?'

Joe shook his head. 'No. I'm going to make my confession. But not in church. Then I'm going to kill someone I trusted, someone who lied to me. Confessing in church then killing would not be right.'

Humfrey nodded in agreement: killings and church confessions didn't go well together.

Joe looked at him. 'You lied to me, too,' he said. 'You put on quite a show. Stay away from me. If I ever see you again, I will break your back. Understood?'

Once again, Humfrey nodded.

# NORTHERN HUNGARY

Autumn sunlight washed through high windows, making the bleak scene somehow less grim. The room in the old convent was bare, white-washed, cool, spacious, floored with red tiles. In its centre sat a stout wooden chair fixed to the floor by steel battens, in the chair the patient, trussed up in a grey straitjacket, her feet tied loosely to the chair legs, her black eyes scowling directly at the steel door.

Joe eased back from the eyehole and said in English, 'She looks pretty harmless to me.'

The nurse, Zsofia, had hair dyed blue and was becoming too fat for her uniform. She spoke good English and translated Joe's remark for Viktor, her male counterpart, a massive man, his skin the colour of a carrot. Viktor sniggered unpleasantly and Zsofia took up the laughter. Joe smiled thinly at them, signalling that he could enjoy a joke at his expense, but inwardly he felt unease, that he would not like to be trussed up in this place.

'Every time we let her out of the straitjacket, she bite,' said Zsofia. Joe was heftier than both of them, knew how to handle himself.

Viktor unlocked the door with a massive iron key and the patient hissed at them. The quiet intensity of the hiss unnerved Joe. This was not what he had been expecting. Nevertheless, he held his nerve and said, 'Get her out of that thing.'

'She bite, she bite,' said Zsofia.

Joe palmed her thirty thousand forints, worth about one hundred dollars, and the two of them gingerly undid the straps of the straitjacket and the leather ties securing her ankles to the legs of the chair. The patient made no move; her eyes were closed. Zsofia backed out first, then Viktor. Then Joe heard the door closing and the key turning in the lock.

The moment the lock clicked, Joe spoke: 'Jameela, I kidnapped your son. I am sorry . . .' But that was all he managed to get out before she came at him, a snarling, biting, scratching whirlwind of hate. He grabbed hold of one arm but she sank her teeth into his hand and bit him hard, drawing blood. He roared in pain, but now she was clawing at his eyes. To defend himself, he had to hurt her, badly. He used his heft, locked both hands onto her right arm and spun her viciously hard against the wall; the air was knocked out of her for a few seconds, so he grabbed hold of the other arm and held both behind her and lifted them high, towards her neck. Her legs were still thrashing so he sat on her with a thunk. Now she was banging her jaw against the tile floor, a terrifying act of self-harm. Joe wrestled with her so that she was locked in some kind of stasis, her arms high behind her back, her stomach fixed to the floor by Joe's weight. Even so, it was with relief that he heard the door unlock and Viktor come in, holding a syringe high and jabbing the needle into her buttocks. After half a minute, she stopped writhing and went limp under Joe, and the two nurses strapped an unconscious Jameela back in the straitjacket and retied her ankles to the chair.

Once Jameela was secure, Viktor winked at Joe and said something not very nice in Hungarian. Joe didn't understand a word, but Viktor's contempt for the patient needed little translation.

'Tell Jameela I'll come tomorrow,' said Joe and he left, nursing the puncture wounds on the back of his right hand.

The second day, the two nurses left the straitjacket on. Joe brought in a chair, sat opposite her and tried to talk to her, tried to explain what had gone so terribly wrong. After the second or third sentence, she spat at him, accurately, hitting his skin just below his left eye. Disgusted, he got up and grimaced, but thought better of saying something and walked out.

On the third day, she remained trussed up in the straitjacket again; her two black eyes stared out at him, full of hate. He brought in the chair, a copy of *Vogue*, a half-bottle of Bushmills and two glasses. He parked his chair beyond spitting distance, flicked through the magazine for a time, got bored by the glossy adverts of fancy men and fancier women banging the stick against the bucket of pigswill, as they didn't call it in the chic advertising houses, poured a good measure of the spirit of life into each glass, and raised one and said: '*Sláinte.*'

He downed his drink in one. 'It means good health in Gaelic,' he said conversationally.

She hissed at him, a long, sibilant eruption of sound.

'Well-brought-up young ladies don't hiss. Didn't anyone tell you?' She hissed again.

'Listen, what I did was wrong, very wrong. If it's any consolation, and I'm sure it isn't, I was lied to. Not just lied to, but the victim of an elaborate play in which a man who I thought was my friend was shot dead. Only it turns out he wasn't shot dead. It was just a game. They told me that you had kidnapped your son, that you had joined ISIS, that you had signed up your boy for the suicide bomb class at school. And then you went on the run to Europe and Little Miss ISIS doesn't look after her boy properly and he breaks his jaw and – guess what? – she takes him out of hospital. So I kidnap your son and everything ends happily ever after. But the reason I'm here, Little Miss Hissy, is that none of this adds up. I think I've been played, conned, part of some horrible little intelligence game by the CIA, by some creepy doctor you once shacked up with, by . . . I don't know who. So I've come here to try to find something, and all you do is fucking bite me and hiss at me.'

The black eyes stayed on him, but she didn't hiss.

'So I'm a thick Irishman that everyone plays like a patsy,' Joe said. 'I spend a bit of time in a hole in the ground, a tomb so deep your ears popped, a guest of your President Zarif. Fun times were had by all, so long as you forget about the blowtorch.'

He picked up the other drink and gulped that down in one, too. Something in her black eyes changed; the ferocity in them dimmed, a fraction, at Joe's mention of him being detained in Zarif's underground prison.

'But you know what? That shit comes with the territory, it's part of being who I am and what, God help me, I do. But kidnapping a child from his mother on a lie – that's something I can't live with. I can't sleep at night. All I can hear is your voice in the fog, screaming "Ham, Ham, Ham!" I've come here to say sorry but not just that. I've come here to help you. I can get you out of here. All you have to do is stop hissing at me.'

Joe looked down at his empty glass and poured himself a third slug. 'You know, you're an excellent drinking partner. You don't fuss, you don't complain.'

The black eyes studied him, silently.

'*Sláinte*,' said Joe.

He downed the whiskey, smacked his lips and continued: 'My father was shot dead by the Rah – the Irish Republican Army – when I was seven years old. And then I was *so* brainwashed by hate, by the hate of some of my own people, that I joined the very organisation that had murdered him so I could kill yet more people, so that yet more sons could weep at the loss of a father, so that mothers and fathers could weep at the loss of a child. You don't have to tell me anything about terrorism. I did it. I was a terrorist. I used to kill people, or try to kill people. And then I became aware of the evidence of my own eyes. You want to know where I was? North Korea, in a terrorist training camp north of Pyongyang. And it was only there, in that godforsaken prison, that I realised that the people there were brainwashed and – guess what? – so was I. So you were in ISIS and I was in the IRA. They'll tell you that the two things are quite different and so they are. But if your child is a kid in a pub in Birmingham and gets blown up, well, what's the difference between that and your child being a sweet nineteen-year-old in Paris shot at a rock concert? "My child died but that's OK because at least the terrorist organisation responsible was slightly more enlightened and phoned through a warning . . ." It's all the same shit. It's driven by hate and it's wrong, just wrong.'

'I was never in ISIS,' Jameela said flatly. 'I hate ISIS. They tried to kill me, my son, the man I love. They're killing my country, my religion. I hate ISIS with every sinew of my being.'

Joe unbuttoned his top pocket and took out a photocopy he'd secretly made of Franklyn's photograph of Jameela and Ham wearing their suicide vests in front of seven black-clad fighters, the ISIS flag at the centre.

'This picture says you're lying. Or have I got it wrong? Who are your pals? The Sea Scouts?'

Jameela smiled, a little, to herself. 'The picture is fake news. The men in the picture were a unit of the Free Syrian Army, funded by your CIA, who pretended to be in ISIS. The head of the unit allowed Ham and I to be photographed with them because . . . because he was, is, my lover. It was a convenient lie because I wanted to break, totally, with my past.'

'Prove it,' said Joe.

'Well, look at the photograph for a start. In it, I am only wearing a headscarf. For ISIS, that's forbidden, *haram*. A woman who shows her face, who doesn't wear two veils, who doesn't wear gloves, will be stoned to death. Anyone who knows the merest thing about ISIS would know this picture is a fake.'

Joe studied the photocopy for a long time in silence and then said, 'You're right. Dear God, please forgive me.'

She didn't say anything, but she didn't hiss.

———

The light shimmered off the lake, turning the still waters a burnt ochre, then a deepening scarlet. From the little wooden house, the woman sat in a rocking chair watching the lone swimmer go far out, so distant that she lost sight of his head, a dot breaking against the reddening waters, fading to black. The stars came out, the plough forging its furrow, Mars twinkling red. A moorhen hooted, the reeds on the edge of the lake rustling in the lightest of breezes. Jameela lit a candle and sat waiting until a lesser darkness emerged from the night.

'So, Irishman, why swim so far?' Her voice was quite different from before, soft.

He dried his back with a towel and smiled. 'Out there, I turn on my back and watch the stars and float and think about infinity and then, somehow, all the terrible things we humans do to each other in the name of our gods seem, somehow, less terrible.'

The candlelight was feeble and he had to squint to make sure that he was seeing right. 'Are you wearing my clothes?'

'I am.'

'Has fashion changed since I started my swim?'

'*La.* I hated everything they gave me in that place.'

Jameela had borrowed his oldest black jumper, a dark-blue cotton shirt and a pair of his shorts, cinched at the waist with a belt. He was more than a foot taller than her and twice her bulk. A less beautiful woman would have looked absurd. She still did, a little.

'Tell me,' she said, 'how did you get me out of that place?'

'Ah, you don't want to know all my secrets.'

'No, tell me. I want to know.'

He disappeared to his room, came back wearing a pink cotton shirt and black jeans, and sat down at the bare wooden table opposite her. Outside, the light had gone.

'I told them that I was Sigmund Freud, professor of psychiatry at Ian Paisley University, Belfast. I emailed them a link to the aforesaid university's website and a contact telephone number. They called the number and were assured that I was indeed exactly who I said I was by the dean of the university.'

'And who was the dean?'

'My brother Seamus.'

'Is he the dean of the Ian Paisley University?'

'He would be the first-ever Catholic to hold that position.'

'Can you answer my question?'

'Not exactly.'

'Not exactly? Is he the dean of the Ian Paisley University?'

'No.'

'What does he do, if he's not a dean?'

'He runs a pub in Donegal. I owe him a pint of Guinness.'

'Tell me about your brother.'

'He's a good citizen, these days. His pub is in the wild north-west of Ireland, where the Atlantic crashes onto the rocks and you can't sleep for the roar of the sea. He's much-loved by his regulars and he looks after them, sorts out their problems. He did the same for my mother and me, after our father was killed. He's always done his best to look after me. Little Joe, he still calls me, some of the time. And . . .'

Joe paused, lost in his thoughts.

'And?'

'He's in a wheelchair because someone wanted to kill me and I'd vanished so they shot him instead.'

They ate fish soup and bread, washed down by a rough red wine.

'So, your turn, Jameela. To fake a connection with ISIS, that's . . .'

'Crazy?' She completed the thought. 'Yes. Dominic drove me mad, literally so, so I ended up in a straitjacket.'

'Why? Why do that? You were playing . . . you were playing with evil.'

'To fight another evil which, to me, at that time, was the greater evil. It still is. Thanks to you, he has Ham, he has my son.'

Joe froze. Outside, the wind, freshening, soughed in the reeds. He stared into his soup, consumed with melancholy, and then with a tangible physical effort he raised his gaze and met her cold black eyes. 'Jameela, I made a terrible mistake. I was lied to. It wasn't a simple lie. It was an orchestrated deceit. To understand the nature of that lie, I need to fathom why you did what you did. If I can work that out, then it's a start.'

'A start to what?'

'To getting Ham back to you, to reunite mother and son, to reverse what I've done.'

'I miss him every second of every minute of every day. I miss him so much. He's a brave, funny, weird boy.'

'Like mother, like son?'

'Did it hurt when I bit you?'

'Yes, very much.'

'Good.' Jameela smiled to herself, then shook her head, banishing the thought. 'I was so angry with you, so beyond ordinary emotion. It is an animal thing when a child is taken from a mother.'

She paused, and then said with a formality he didn't quite believe, 'I am sorry I bit you.'

'Really?'

'No, not really.' She smiled to herself and refilled their glasses, and as she poured wine into her own glass he gave her a mocking look.

'I drink wine, I show my hair, I don't eat pork, I pray to God sometimes, not often but enough for me. I'm not a good Muslim but I'm Muslim enough to know that ISIS is an abomination unto God. There are many worse things in life than having a drink or showing your hair. Taking life, for one. That is forbidden by a verse in the Quran.'

'Tell me what happened. Tell me what he did to you, why you ended up in the photograph wearing suicide vests, pretending to be in ISIS.'

Jameela closed her eyes for a moment, then opened them and started: 'In the beginning, Dominic and I, it was wonderful, magical. I'd had fun in LA, too much fun. I was a wild child, away from my home in Aleppo – alone, enraptured by everything Hollywood had to offer. Then I woke up one morning feeling wretched, and there were horrible stories about me and another man.'

Joe said nothing about knowing Humfrey, not wanting to stop her flow.

'It wasn't just the shame. It was also a feeling that I was part of LA, part of Hollywood, part of the emptiness of the American Dream. I felt hollow inside, empty. What is the line from Browning?'

'Browning, the guy who made the good automatic?' Joe asked.

'No, fool, the poet Browning. *"What of soul was left, I wonder, when the kissing had to stop?"* I thought I needed to see someone – a shrink, someone like that. That's how I met Dominic. I started to work with him, became his nurse. He was, then, inspiring, a man with a mission. With him, I felt I could change the world. To begin with, Fort Hargood out in the desert, it felt pure, ascetic. Dominic's goal was to conquer addiction: drugs, alcohol, sex. I was doing all three. For Dominic, I was the perfect person to test out his technologies. He would experiment on me. In the beginning it was fascinating, truly absorbing. And then it became darker – much, much darker.'

'This is all hippy-dippy talk to me,' said Joe. 'TMI, they called it, or plugging-in. I don't get it. It's bullshit, isn't it?'

'There isn't a mousetrap in the world that doesn't have good cheese. And it isn't all bullshit. It kind of works, or at least there are some people who are willing to pay Dominic a lot of money for his magic box of tricks.'

'I don't understand what TMI is or how it's done.'

'It starts with control over what you do. It ends with control over what you think. You get habituated to knowing he knows what you're thinking. Fort Hargood is full of tiny pinhole cameras, picking up sound and vision.'

'I still don't get it. Help me understand.'

'Dominic read a lot of books by the Scientology founder, L. Ron Hubbard. He thought Hubbard was onto something. He keeps a naval hat in the long room at Fort Hargood as a tribute to Hubbard. But Dominic reckoned that he and Scientology had somehow lost their way. Strip away the space-alien stuff, and what you do if you're a Scientologist is hold cans wired to a meter and confess your sins. You're a Catholic, aren't you?'

'I'm lapsed.'

'What does that mean?'

'It means I'm a Catholic but my batteries have been taken out.'

'Imagine going to Confession but if you lie, that shows up on the meter. Imagine the power that gives your priest, whatever you call him. But Scientology uses 1950s technology. Dominic is doing something with twenty-first-century tech. He looks at your brainwaves, your hot centres of emotion, your buttons. Then he switches on the stimulus to change those brainwaves, so that he can control your buttons.'

'What stimulus?'

'Dominic uses mind-mapping technology to work out what you're thinking. Then, if he doesn't like your thoughts, he hits your buttons to alter them. To change the way you think.'

'That's mind control.'

'It is.'

'How does it work?'

'First, he places you in a room and you go online; you're encouraged to do whatever you fancy. Me, I looked at clothes, houses, swimming pools, then a few guys, discreetly, in the background of the normal ads, then back to shopping, back and forth, to and fro. Then it gets more intense. You wear a skull cap with wires coming out and you're shown thousands of images on a screen, and the air is scented with dozens of different smells, different sounds. The algorithms . . .'

'The algorithms?'

'You cannot defeat the algorithms. They log what excites you, what disgusts you, and they grade everything, so pretty soon the algorithms know the secrets of your soul. They calibrate exactly what you like and then they give it to you, exactly the way you like it. To begin with.'

'To begin with?'

'The first stage is the cheese in the mousetrap.'

'And the second stage?'

'Dominic is a dentist.'

'He's a doctor, no?'

'A doctor of dentistry. The "client" has two big molars taken out, one on either side of the jaw. In their place go two fake teeth, in them two receptors that, with the help of the algorithms, can read your brainwaves and then transmit them to external monitors controlled by Dominic. If they detect particular patterns of thought, the teeth emit an electromagnetic pulse to the optical part of the brain, generating phosphenes.'

'Phosphenes?'

'Flashes of light. So you think good thoughts and nothing bad happens. You think bad thoughts and your brain sees phosphenes. After a time, the flashes get stronger and stronger and your head hurts. You stop thinking the bad thoughts and think nice, the flashes stop. You're a gay film star who is pretending not to be gay. You start thinking bad, the lights flash, you stop it and – hey presto! – you're not gay anymore. You think really bad stuff – that, say, ISIS is good, bombing America is good – that gets you more and more phosphenes, so many flashes of light you go blind. At the top of the dial for too long, the TMI can kill.'

'Luke McDonald, the film star. I saw him on the road to Fort Hargood, driving fast, he almost ran me off the road. Is he a client?'

'Uh-huh.' Jameela gave a bitter smile. 'Everyone says he's gay. He says he's not gay. I know he's gay because I used to select the images, thousands of them, prior to him being plugged in. And I know exactly what floats Luke McDonald's boat. Men. So Luke pays good money, millions and millions of dollars, to look at pictures of hunky men, and then the algorithms start hurting him so that he is forever seeing lights in his head, he's smashing himself against a wall of pain. Then he looks at beautiful women, the kind he sleeps with in his films, and the lights go out and his head doesn't hurt and Luke gets turned on by women, even without being zapped. Through Luke's recommendation, Dominic is beginning to get TMI into Hollywood.'

'There was a black guy. Samson?'

'Samson is a prize specimen for TMI. He was a gang member in East LA, a psycho, killed four or five men, always no witnesses. The LAPD gave up trying to nail him. And then he got introduced to Dominic, got plugged in and now he's the perfect citizen.'

'Too perfect. I only met him briefly but, and maybe I'm exaggerating this, I felt there was something wrong, a suppressed hysteria about the man.'

'Plugged in, see? Samson became a secret friend, an ally. He wants out but doesn't know how to get unplugged.'

'But you got out?'

She lowered her eyes. 'It was because of Ham. It was all right when he was a baby, an infant, but he was growing up fast and soon I feared that Dominic would have him plugged in to TMI. So I became a secret rebel. I spied on Dominic, I started to learn about Komodo.'

'What's Komodo?'

'Well, you should know. You work for them, don't you?'

'I work for no one but myself.'

'You work for the CIA, I'm sure of it.' Something dark crept into her tone, an edge, not quite there yet, of a paranoid suspicion.

'No, that's not right,' Joe said. 'I have never worked for the CIA. I used to be in the IRA and then I woke up from my brainwashing. I became a special needs teacher in London, that's as far away from being some kind of James Bond as I can imagine. My background dealing with difficult kids was one of the reasons I was selected by Dominic.'

'But you know them – you know the CIA?'

'There's a man I know, who used to be a friend of mine, he's in the CIA. He gave me a reference which Dominic picked up. Because I spent so long on the run from the IRA, I know how to hide. That gives me my one skill, finding people. I can step into the shoes of someone who doesn't want anyone to know where they are.'

'You found us and you stole my son.' Again that edge of darkness in her voice.

'What I did was wrong, so wrong that I have come from the far side of the planet and, at the risk of being arrested for practising psychiatry without a licence in Hungary, got you out of the nut farm.'

'You did that.'

'So tell me more about Komodo.'

'Dominic mind-bends gangsters, movie stars . . . losers like me.'

'You're not a loser.'

'So he went to Virginia and knocked on the door of the CIA and said, "I hear you've got a problem with lowlifes getting brainwashed into joining ISIS. Give me a lot of money and I can help you."'

'And they did.'

'They did.'

'How much?'

'The development budget for the Komodo programme is 1.2 billion dollars.'

Joe whistled. 'Holy Mary, Mother of God,' he said.

'But it's a con,' said Jameela. 'You think bad, you get maxed out. That works, that bites. You think nice, for a time. And then your body learns to lie to the algorithms. It tapers off. Luke, the gay film star, he's still gay. Samson the sociopath, he still wants to kill people. Me, I'm still a crazy bitch determined to save my son. Once Komodo got going, Dominic spent more and more of his time in what he told me was Luxembourg. I know the man's mind; I'm the mother of his son. He adored me, once. So I work out some of his passwords and I discover that he's running Komodo so that everything is deniable. It's not in the US jurisdiction, not on any budgetary platform anyone can find.'

'So he's un-brainwashing ISIS wackos in Luxembourg?'

'Albania. He pretends he's in Luxembourg, but he's at this secret facility in the wilds, near some place called Tropojë. And then I get lucky. I use one of his passwords I've guessed and discover he's got two logbooks: one of all the cases that have worked, showing that the clients have been reverse-brainwashed into thinking that the West is cool and ISIS are bad; and a second logbook, showing all of the bad cases, the ISIS psychos who stayed psycho. And the people in the second logbook, he maxes them out, they die.'

'Shot while trying to escape?'

'Natural causes.'

'And the ratio of good to bad?'

'Over its first full year, twenty-three bad, none good.

'So Uncle Sam is paying Dominic 1.2 billion dollars for murderous batshit?'

'Correct. Bullets are so much cheaper. I put together the evidence that Dr Dominic Franklyn is defrauding the US taxpayer by staging a con game and killing people – bad people, maybe, but nevertheless killing them – to perpetuate the con. So I go to the FBI.'

'And?'

'The FBI agents get shut down by someone high up. And then Dominic appears, in the middle of the night, back from "Luxembourg".

He turns the dial full on, and zaps me, eleven hours straight. That's the video that shows me screaming and screaming and screaming. Then there's some big panic and I'm entrusted to Samson while Dominic has to go back to "Luxembourg". Samson is ordered to keep me in lockdown but he lets me be, and then I unlock more secrets and it gets really bad. The ISIS guys, they're smart. They've worked out how to void TMI.'

'They can void a 1.2 billion-dollar programme?'

'Uh-huh.'

'And the magic bullet is?'

'You hang on to a piece of metal and stand in an exposed place in the middle of a thunderstorm. With a lightning bolt comes an electromagnetic pulse, an EMP. Scissors cut paper, EMP cuts TMI.'

'You sure?'

She unrolled the sleeve of her right arm, and on it was a fine red tracery. 'That's what you get if you're struck by lightning,' she said. 'The only way I could escape from Fort Hargood was to stand in the middle of the desert holding a garden fork in my hands, high above my head. The lightning strike burnt my arm, knocked me twenty yards off my feet, but it short-circuited the TMI receptors in my teeth.'

'Why didn't you just get your teeth pulled?'

'Dominic is no fool. You pull your teeth, you get zapped to the max, you die.'

'So you risked being fried?'

'To become free, to get your own thoughts back – it's worth the risk. I got hit by a billion volts to become free. It was the most frightening thing I've done in my whole life, worse than going to Raqqa, but I'd do it all over again, no question. I owe my freedom to Dominic's fastidious attention to detail. Without him listing a series of suicidal attempts by plugged-in ISIS guys frying themselves during thunderstorms, I would never have known how to void Komodo.'

'And then?'

'Then I take Ham and I run. Dominic has a lock on the government in the USA. The only other place I know, apart from LA, is Syria, but Syria in the old times, not now. In Damascus I bumped into my old high-school flame, Rashid. He's cool, he's a doctor, he's saving lives. Rashid, he does his own thing, but he's working with the Free Syrian Army against Zarif, against ISIS, with a rich guy called Qureshi, who runs it – what's left of it, anyway. Rashid keeps the power on in Syria, that means hospitals have electricity, people can eat, see at night. That means he deals with both sides. To do that, he and his boys dress up as ISIS security, the Amn. The CIA know all about it. They pay for it.

'Rashid and I, we hook up. I know Dominic will try to come for me – or rather, send someone like you to find me, so we make the video in Damascus, and Rashid's men play spear-carriers. The message is simple: *Don't follow me.* But then Zarif's people come for Qureshi and lock him up, and Rashid is on the wrong side of the wire, in Raqqa. Qureshi sends word to me to get him out, but by the time I get there, Rashid's already in a cage. We end up in a cage too, Ham and I. And then an ISIS man, someone who had grown sick of evil, he gets us out, he lets us go free.'

'Where's Rashid now?'

She let out a long, low sigh.

'He went back to Aleppo. He's a surgeon; they need him. When we were at school together, we were sweethearts, but I dumped him because I thought he was too pious, too conservative. He never took any risks. I've never been more wrong about someone in my whole life. Well, I was wrong about Dominic, too. I thought he was a good man and in reality he was a monster. And I thought that Rashid was boring, but he is a hero.'

Her eyes were wet. She paused to wipe them, then continued: 'The ISIS man who saved the three of us, he cut my hair, glued a great beard onto my face and dressed me up as a Hisbah. I looked good as a religious policeman. We hightailed it on a motorbike to the Kurdish lines.

They almost shot us dead, we'd forgotten that we looked like ISIS. I hit the brakes on the motorbike, ripped off my beard and said, "I'm a woman, you idiots." The Kurdish fighters couldn't stop laughing, they said it was the funniest thing they'd seen in their whole lives. Rashid and Ham were laughing so hard they were almost sick. Rashid went to Aleppo and Ham and I carried on through Turkey. We almost drowned crossing the Med – many, many others did. We struggled through the Balkans. Ham's jaw was broken when a van reversed into him. We almost got to Austria. But then you stole my son.'

'We'll get him back.'

The black eyes held Joe's, not believing him.

'We'll try our best to get him back.'

'To kidnap him?'

'No. Dominic's got too much money, he's too well connected with the Agency.'

'With your Agency.'

'I'm not CIA and the people I know in it, they're at the back of the class right now.'

'So we lose.'

'So we fight. We go back to the States and take Dominic to court and try to get Ham back. Fighting is better than despair.'

'I've got no money. You cannot defeat the algorithms.'

'We'll get Dominic's algorithms to fight among themselves. He paid me well. I'll get you a lawyer. I'll pay for it.'

'Why?'

'So I can sleep at night. I kidnapped a boy from a good mother and returned him to a bad father.'

She looked miserable. 'But the mother was mad.'

'The mother was a bit mad, but mostly she was good. But the father, he was bad-bad.'

'It's not going to work. We'll lose.'

'You're probably right,' Joe said, stretching. 'But this way maybe you and I get to sleep at night. If we don't fight, you don't get Ham back and I can't sleep out of shame, out of guilt over what I did.'

———

They went to their separate beds, Joe, for once, not troubled by nightmares but lost in a deep and seamless sleep. Who knows what woke him? Perhaps some atavistic awareness of threat; perhaps a tread on a creaking step. The knife glinted in the moonlight.

Maybe she didn't mean to kill him, maybe she did.

'You can kill me,' said Joe, his voice still slurry with sleep. 'I won't stop you. I don't love life; I hate myself too much to love life. But if you do kill me, you stand no chance of ever getting Ham back. They don't return children to convicted murderers.'

The knife fell on the wooden floor with a clatter.

# LOS ANGELES DISTRICT COURT HOUSE, CALIFORNIA

Under the glare of the strip lighting, the court usher's black toupee rainbow-shimmered as naturally as a slick of diesel oil in a mountain stream. He was middling-old, slender, conservatively dressed in a brown suit, had a wicked underbite and a pale moon-face. His demeanour was that of a mourner who'd realised he'd gone to the wrong funeral. He came out into the vestibule and gave the nod, and the two parties filed solemnly into the courtroom, treating the other side as if they weren't there. Next to the father sat his two principal case lawyers, and behind them a further thirteen associate lawyers and sundry experts. Behind the banks of lawyers sat Luke McDonald, one of the most famous film stars in America, his agent, his agent's private eye and the star's three-strong personal protection team. Behind them were two government agents – and behind them, three government lawyers.

Next to the mother sat one lawyer. Five rows back, on the mother's side, was just one more person, Joe Tiplady. By mutual consent, the hearing was private, so there was no public, no media.

Once the usher had closed the doors, he also sat on the father's side.

Her Honour Ernesta Mujillos tapped her gavel tentatively – she had a distaste for histrionics in her courtroom – and the summing-up began: 'There is no decision by this bench more fraught with difficulty than choosing between competing narratives from a loving father and a loving mother over custody of a child. Both sides have set out evidence that the other is some kind of monster, and this bench has the duty to make a ruling which will deeply and profoundly affect mother, father and child for the rest of their natural lives. For the benefit of the court record, I shall now rehearse the competing arguments made by both sides . . .'

After an ocean of time, Joe stood up, nodded at the bench and walked out for a coffee from the courthouse vending machine. The courthouse was twenty-two storeys up, and the vestibule boasted a view of miles of metal and glass threading this way and that on the freeway below, as well as the flat dullness of the LA burbs drifting towards the foothills. The sky was grey, overcast. One dollar and twenty cents bought him a plastic cup containing liquidised cardboard, but it was better than listening to the judge's rehash of the legal argy-bargy. Time and again, the truth had been chiselled into dust. The story was both hideously complicated – that was the way of it when the lives of ordinary people got tangled up in the world of spies, of play and counter-play, of feint and counter-feint, of cross and double-cross – and all too simple. But very little of it had been heard in this court.

He fished out his phone, switched it on and flicked through the news. In France, an ISIS fanatic had beheaded an elderly priest while he was serving Mass in Normandy. More grim news – not just for the world, but also, he feared, for the interests of justice in the courtroom he'd just left. He finished his coffee with a grimace and returned to listen to the verdict.

Ernesta Mujillos tapped her gavel gently and called the courtroom to order. But there was nothing gentle about her determination of the facts: she found that Jameela Abdiek had lied repeatedly under oath;

had repeatedly endangered her son, Ham; had constructed a series of monstrous fabrications about her estranged husband, Dr Dominic Franklyn; had failed to provide a scintilla of reliable, independent evidence to support her fabrications.

'Therefore, it behoves this court to come to the ineluctable conclusion driven by the weight of evidence. This court finds against Jameela Abdiek and in favour of Dr Dominic Franklyn. This court rules that Dr Dominic Franklyn should have custody over his son, Ham Franklyn, in perpetuity, and that Jameela Abdiek should have no visitation or access rights whatsoever. Costs are awarded in full to Dr Dominic Franklyn.'

'All rise,' said the court usher with the iridescent toupee and the pronounced underbite. Everyone in court stood up apart from Jameela, whose body was locked in shock. The judge left the court and Jameela's lawyer, a woman who had fought hard – as best as she could, with no serious evidence to submit to the court – to no avail, got her client to her feet. Slowly, the two women, arm in arm, walked down the central aisle of the court. As Jameela passed Joe, she stared at him and hissed, 'You stole my son.'

Joe closed his eyes and bent his head. He had nothing to say to that.

Then it was the turn of the other side to make their exit. First, the government agents and lawyers filed past Joe, then the experts, then the lawyers, until there was only Dominic Franklyn, Luke McDonald and the private investigator, Rocky Montefiore, left.

It had ended exactly as Jameela had always feared it would end, in total and abject defeat. The truth of it was: everything she said would happen, happened. The algorithms, the money, the secret power of Dominic's connections with the Agency, they had trumped the pitiful attempts of a Muslim immigrant from Syria to prove them wrong.

As the victors filed past Joe, he lifted up his head like a bull beginning to take notice, looked Franklyn directly in the eye and said, 'This isn't over.'

Franklyn smiled indulgently to himself, saying nothing, but Luke McDonald halted, ran his fingers through his thick, lustrous blond locks and retorted: 'Mommy takes the boy off to ISIS summer camp, what do you expect?'

'You fuck beautiful women, but deep down you want to fuck pretty men. Nothing wrong with that, but you pay Shorty over here' – he nodded towards Franklyn – 'to zap your brain to make it behave, and you pay Rocky to kidnap other people's kids to keep the lid on it when your dick misbehaves, because what you lust for doesn't sit well with the box-office receipts. You're a fake, Luke, and Shorty is a torturer and Rocky is a slimeball. Jameela fought ISIS, through and through. Today, power and money won, as it so often does in the courtrooms of the United States. The three of you defeated a good woman and mother who happened to be born in Syria. But your power and money stinks. As I said, this isn't over.'

Joe brushed past them and walked out of the courtroom, taking the stairs, all twenty-two storeys of them, because the thought of being trapped in an elevator and sharing oxygen with them sickened him to his core.

———

The men with baseball bats came for Joe two days later. He'd just parked his car in a basement car park. They did their work deftly, not touching his face once, leaving him gasping with pain. He pissed blood for a week, but even as they hit his kidneys, again and again, he knew that what he had said in the courtroom had touched a chord, and that made it – kind of – worthwhile.

# SANTA MONICA, CALIFORNIA

The door was locked, a mess of letters and community newspapers jammed in the mailbox. It was early morning, and Joe had come the first day he was able to walk without a stick since his beating. Down the street a woman was walking her dog, eyeing the big stranger with the limp at her neighbour's door without trying to look nosy. Joe ignored her and put his shoulder to the door. That didn't work, so he returned to his car and fetched a big screwdriver, which he jammed in the doorframe and leant on it, hard, so the door popped out of its frame. He'd pay for a new one down the track.

The door opened onto her tiny kitchen, which was empty; so was her bedroom. In the small dining room there was a note written in Jameela's rather beautiful handwriting: *I've gone home to Aleppo. Don't try to find me.*

Joe slumped against the wall, not knowing what to do. Returning to Aleppo was a kind of suicide. Jameela's mind had been broken by power and money; broken by a legal system that treats rich and poor alike, or so it lies; broken by Joe, who'd stolen her son; broken by the pitilessness of her ex-husband; broken by the Agency that funded his hideous experiments; broken for committing the twenty-first-century crime of being Syrian.

More than anything, he wanted to sleep at night without suffering his recurring nightmare of kidnapping the boy in Hungary and hearing his mother's haunted cries pierce through the fog: *Ham . . . Ham . . . Ham . . .*

To achieve that goal, he knew what he had to do – and where, eventually, he would have to end up – and even though he was not a timid man, the fear of that made him retch violently.

# BEAR LAKE, UTAH

The Stars and Stripes flapped in the stiff breeze as clouds scudded across the blue sky, the snow-tipped peaks of the Rockies above, Bear Lake below. The trees were turning, a cold snap in the bright morning air foretelling that soon fall would give way to winter. The simple wooden cabin hadn't changed since Joe had last been here, when Katya had been shot. Woodsmoke spiralled from the stone chimney before being scattered by the wind, and Joe wondered if Zeke might, after all, be home. He skipped up to the deck and knocked on the wooden door. After a short while it swung open to reveal a woman in her sixties – petite, lithe, her grey hair piled up in a bun, wearing blue jeans and a cream shirt. Beyond middle age as she was, you could tell in an instant that she had been a ravishing beauty in her youth, and there was still a fiery sweetness about her that Joe found beguiling.

'Joey? How are you, stranger?' No one on this earth was allowed to call Joe by that silly name; no one, that is, apart from Mary-Lou, Zeke's wife for so many years. The old lady held him by his hands, giving him the once-over.

'You look pale, Joey. Not enough sun.'

'It's the dissolute life I lead, Mary-Lou. Hanging around in bars, the bad life.'

'Oooh, take me away, take me there.'

'I don't think old Zeke would like that.'

At the mention of her husband's name, her face crumpled. She put her hand to her mouth, turned away and said, 'You'd better come inside.'

They sat in the kitchen in an edgy silence while she fussed around brewing fresh coffee – she didn't take a drop, on account of her being a Mormon – and providing Joe with a plate piled high with homemade cookies. Eventually she sat down opposite him as he sipped his coffee.

'So Zeke's not here?'

'No, he's not, Joey.'

'Can I ask . . .'

Her face crumpled once more, and she ran off to the bathroom and found herself some tissues, and blew her nose and wiped her eyes and returned, sniffling all the while. 'Damn that Ezekiel Chandler, damn him, damn him, damn him.'

Joe opened and closed his mouth several times, like a goldfish lapping in his bowl, but no sound came out. For the life of him, he didn't know what to say. Marital discord, it's what you did when you'd been married for four, five years, not decades.

'Mary-Lou, I don't know what's happened.'

'Oh, Joey, he's gone out of my life.'

'Mary-Lou, I am so sorry. The thing is, I need to talk to Zeke. I need his advice; I need to get in touch with him. There's a court case I'm involved with, and the bad people in the CIA, they're running rings around us. I need Zeke's help.'

'That's the problem, Joey. I don't know where he is. I believe he's in trouble with the CIA' – she pronounced all the initials long, so that she made it sound like a children's nursery rhyme – 'and they've told him to skedaddle, to lie low for a while.'

'Mary-Lou, you know Zeke better than anyone else alive. Where do you think he might have gone?'

The wind stiffened, rattling the cabin's windows. She looked up and out at the stunning panorama, as if Zeke might be hiding in the mountains on the other side of the Utah–Idaho line.

'He can't go to the badlands, him being a CIA man and all. So not Russia, China, Cuba, Venezuela, Eritrea, Syria, North Korea, South Sudan.' She'd clearly put some thinking-time into it. 'The rest of the world is his oyster. He speaks twenty languages fluently. He could be anywhere.'

'Give me some clues.'

'All right. He's vain about his gift for languages and he doesn't want the CIA knowing where he is, so I don't think he would hole up in any Anglophone country – that rules out Britain, Canada, Australia, New Zealand, South Africa and most of Micronesia. T'other thing is, he's happiest with ancient stuff, unlocking long-dead languages, decoding ancient texts. His hero was an Oxford professor, name of Archibald Sayce, who decoded Hittite, whatever damn thing Hittite is.'

'I don't know either,' said Joe.

'The best place to find out where he might be is to go into that graveyard of books he's got in his den, and look at the latest ones he bought before he hightailed it.'

She led the way. The den smelt musty, unused, the memory of woodsmoke from the stove in the air. It was long and thin, walled with books of an astonishing variety of cultures and languages. A long pine table ran along the window and that, too, was stacked high with piles of books, some of which had toppled over onto the floor. At the end closest to his desk and the stove was a fresh pile, with titles on Catharism, Bogomilism and the Fraticelli.

Joe knew nothing about any of these, but he also knew that Zeke wouldn't just disappear without leaving a clue for his friends, in case of emergency. It just wasn't his style. He sat down at the table and started to read while Mary-Lou brewed him some fresh coffee.

'So you now know what a Hittite is, Joey?' she asked, entering with a pot of coffee, milk and yet more cookies.

Joe lifted his head from the books and shook his head. 'Not yet, Mary-Lou, not yet.'

Time wandered by. Joe looked up, his eyes tired, to realise that the sun was going down behind the Rockies. Mary-Lou entered the den and clicked the lights on.

'You'll go blind reading in the dark.'

Joe smiled to himself. He hadn't been fussed over like this for a very long time.

'So what have you learnt?'

'Heretics,' he said. 'They're all heretics. By and large the Cathars were French, the Bogomils Balkan, the Fraticelli poor friars from Italy – it wasn't called Italy then – who went to war against the corruption and obscene wealth of the Catholic Church.'

Joe scratched his head, found a notebook that Zeke had been using, full of his spidery writing. On the last page, a number: *2231*. He dived back into the fattest book about the Fraticelli with an idea of where Zeke might have gone to ground.

# MONTERIPIDO MONASTERY, PERUGIA

Few sounds on earth are more ethereally beautiful than a chorus of one hundred Franciscan monks intoning the 'Ave Maris Stella', a plainsong first written down in the ninth century. The monks walked slowly out of the chapel into the cloisters overlooking the Umbrian hills to the west and the Apennines to the east. Looking at them with a kind of awe was a group of tourists led by a professor with a basso profundo voice and a love of learning.

'In the year 1322,' said the professor, 'a convocation of the most powerful cardinals, monks and friars of the Catholic Church met here in this monastery to deliberate the most pressing question of the day and ruled on the absolute poverty of Christ. This was a thunderclap for Pope John XXII and caused immense turmoil . . .'

The professor led his tour group towards the refectory, but one of the tourists, a big man who looked too pale for his own good, as though he'd been kept out of the sun, peeled off to stand quietly by a column. As one of the last friars walked past him, the pale man stepped out, not quite blocking his path but advertising his presence.

The friar came to a stop, smiling at the pale man with an open, gap-toothed smile, that might, just might, be mistaken for the smile of a simpleton.

'How did you find me?' asked the friar.

'Twenty-two thirty-one sounds like some kind of space movie,' said the pale man.

'But it's one-three-two-two backwards, the year of a broadside against a rich and corrupt papacy. You're not so dumb after all, Irishman.'

'We need to talk, Zeke.'

'Let's go to my cell.'

Aforesaid cell was a plain room, eight feet deep, white-walled, decorated by a black wooden crucifix, a bed and a wooden chair. Set in the wall above the bed was a window looking out on Assisi to the southwest and the green rolling hills of Umbria beyond. Zeke sat on the bed, Joe on the chair, sunlight fell between the two of them.

'So, Mormon to monk. How's that work?'

'To be exact, I'm kind of in training to be a friar, not a monk. I didn't want to leave Langley but, if you're on the run from the most powerful data-wranglers on earth, a fourteenth-century monastery isn't a bad place to hide.'

'Maybe. Reason I'm here, Zeke, is that you set me up for a fool. You played me. You betrayed me. I go to Damascus with a guy called Humfrey DeCrecy. He gets shot, dies in front of my eyes. Bad news for you is that while I'm doing a job in Caracas, I meet the dead man. Humf tells me, after some deliberation, that he was working for you. Why did you play with me like this?'

Zeke hesitated. 'You wearing a wire?'

'No.'

'OK. On my watch, the CIA ran and funded a covert Free Syrian Army operation in Damascus – essentially a sleeping operation until the regime collapsed. That longed-for eventuality didn't happen. Instead, the military intervention of the Russians in Syria changed the balance of the war. The KGB/FSB, under Grozhov – who I've been crossing swords with since Afghanistan in the eighties – started sniffing around. Reluctantly, I took the decision to close our operation down and get as many of our people out before they got boiled alive. This wasn't a case of what's the best we can do, but the least bad we can do in horrible circumstances. You pull people out; you don't want the regime to know you're doing that. You kick sand in their faces. Your friend Humfrey was window-dressing, visible evidence that Team Zarif was cracking down, was killing our guys. The more we fooled around, the safer were our people.'

Joe pressed on: 'So Mansour mock-kills Humf.'

'Qureshi's was one of ours, too. He's safe now.'

'But Mansour gets to torture me. That's real, by the way. No mocking that up. And all the while you're running him?'

Zeke nodded.

'How's that work?'

'Some people we pay. We own them. Some people are doing their own thing and our interests are aligned, for a time. Some people take out an insurance policy, help us every now and then, in case of what might happen in the future. Mansour works for Zarif, but will do us the odd favour, just in case his boss ends up dead sooner than expected. The prize was to convince Zarif's people that Qureshi was finished so that he and his people could get out of Syria. The show was scripted to give Qureshi and the others the chance of a safe exit. Then you, my favourite Irishman, come along, dragging Humfrey behind you. We've used Humfrey before. He's good at playing dead. So we turn this unexpected opportunity to our advantage. Mansour makes a show of beating up Qureshi and pretends to shoot Humfrey – a nice touch. Our plan was that Mansour would arrest you and kick you over the border. But you disappear, then reappear in a regime prison. To keep his cover, Mansour has to give you something of a hard time. Remember, the other side is tyranny. You play straight with those people, everyone dies. I got you out again, at no little cost to my standing in the Agency.'

'Yeah, thanks for that,' Joe's tone was the opposite of warm. 'But somebody else walked into the crossfire too, Zeke. She's called Jameela and she's Syrian and was on the run from her man back in the States, who is a psycho. She'd taken her boy from him because Dominic Franklyn is so freaking weird. But here's the thing. Psycho Franklyn works hand in glove with the Agency. He's doing some batshit crazy re-brainwashing research which isn't really getting ISIS fanatics from seeing the error of their ways. I didn't know any of that when Franklyn hired me to get his kid back. When the game stopped, I snatched her son and psycho Dominic got him. You gave Franklyn a great reference, saying I would be good at finding his boy. So from where I'm sitting, you used me twice, once as a hapless bystander to add necessary credibility to a fake killing; the second time, to do the Agency's dirty work, to get a boy back to a father who is useful to the CIA, but hardly a good guy. So explain to me why I shouldn't break your neck, right here and now?'

'Put it that way, Joe, go ahead. If you seriously believe I did that to you, break my neck. It's an old neck and the head on top of it belongs to a silly old fool. Go ahead.'

Joe didn't move. Zeke started to say something when the monastery bell tolled noon. As the last toll died away, Zeke started again: 'Joe, we've both been played, both been gulled. Since the war in Iraq, the CIA has been under enormous pressure to stop the bad guys, to stop Islamist terrorists. Under that pressure, the Agency has gone to hell in a handcart. To keep us on the straight and narrow, we have rules. To get around the rules, the Agency has fallen in love with black ops. Don't ask, don't find out, don't even look. Strange things were happening in Albania, ISIS men frying themselves in the middle of thunderstorms. I go there to see for myself. I start hearing about a black facility. I lose my security escort, deliberately, and then we're ambushed. The countryside is sprayed with bullets. Shrapnel hits my lung and I would have died were it not for a shepherd looking after me and an Albanian cop who is even more unpopular with his employers than I am. Curiosity did not go well for this cat.'

'Franklyn's facility is in Albania, Zeke.'

'Who told you that?'

'Jameela.'

'Ah.'

Zeke mused that over for a time.

'Is she sure?' he asked.

'She hacked his private passwords. She's sure.'

'Can I meet her? Will she see me?'

'Two weeks ago, a court in LA gave custody of her boy to Franklyn in perpetuity. She thinks the Agency helped him win. So do I. She hates the CIA.'

'I'd still like to meet her. But my influence at Langley is shot to pieces, Joe. I'm here because the Director told me to lie low for six months, to sit it out until the election is over. I need something, some piece of information that will get me back in the game.'

'There's this,' said Joe. He took an airmail letter from the inside pocket of his jacket.

'Postmarked Berlin,' noted Zeke. 'It's in Russian. Sent to a guy called Alf, on Blossom Drive . . .'

'He walks my dog.'

Zeke read on in silence, then, entirely out of character, said the same word three times. The word was 'wow!'

Zeke laid the letter on the bed and looked at Joe and smiled his gap-toothed smile. 'This letter gives the precise coordinates of a secret stash of several hundred kilograms of sarin gas, imported by the North Koreans to a specially constructed tunnel at Palmyra, now taken over by ISIS. This letter was written by someone who is a friend of a man called Timur. Who's Timur, Joe?'

'You could say that he was my brother-in-law.'

'You trust him – you trust this letter?'

'Totally.'

Zeke dipped below his bed, pulled out a smartphone and fired it up and punched in a number. The moment the call was answered,

Zeke spoke: 'This is Ezekiel Chandler, former deputy director of the CIA, currently on extended leave. I'm seeking crash clearance into the Rome embassy citadel for a conference call with Director Rinder . . .' He cupped his hand over the phone and asked Joe: 'Can you give me a ride to Rome?'

'Yeah,' said Joe.

'How long?'

'The roads are terrible. Three hours.'

'Make it two.' He returned to the phone conversation proper: 'In two and a half hours. Code indigo, repeat code indigo, subject Syria nerve gas cache. Chandler, out.' He ended the call. 'You got a sports car, something nice?'

Joe shook his head. 'Moto Guzzi V7 Stone. Fastest machine in Italy.'

'I hate motorbikes,' said Zeke.

'Ain't that a pity,' said Joe.

————

The sarin warehouse near Palmyra was vaporised six hours later.

The moment confirmation came, Zeke got a text from Rinder: *Welcome back, Zeke. Ur still not popular but with intel like this I don't care. U have been missed.*

Zeke showed the text to Joe and smiled his gap-toothed smile.

'Good,' said Joe. 'Now I'd like you to write a special letter on official CIA notepaper.'

'To whom?' asked Zeke.

'A judge,' said Joe. 'But write it in invisible ink.'

And that is exactly what Zeke proceeded to do.

# ALEPPO, SYRIA

Sieges are never vacuum-sealed. If you're rich or mad or lucky enough, there's always a way in and a way out. You can travel economy down a sewer or first-class in a secret-police limousine with smoked-glass windows. It's never easy but it's never 100 per cent impossible.

Joe had been smuggled into East Aleppo the night before, down a 'hot' road at terrifying speed by two gunmen and a boy who spoke bad English. Their car radio had a tape which played The Stranglers' 'No More Heroes' very loudly again and again, but not loud enough to tune out the sound of the tracer fire ahead, behind and at them. They made it somehow, untouched.

It cost Joe twenty thousand dollars, and as sphincter-clenching rides go it had been worth every cent. Part of him wondered how he might market 'The Thrill of Aleppo Experience' to Disney. Nah, they wouldn't be interested. The boy smuggler, a spotty teenager whose attempt at a beard was frankly comic, had sworn to him on his mother's life that they would stay with Joe until he was safely delivered to his destination, the M10 underground hospital towards the centre of what was besieged Free Aleppo. But they'd dumped him as soon as they got to the rebel side in the darkest hour of all, the hour before dawn. Joe had bunked down on a mattress lying on a sea of dust, underneath an overhanging ledge of concrete and strands of steel wire that creaked, unpleasantly, during the night. He woke up at dawn, cold and alone in the most dangerous place on earth.

Death was an ever-present possibility, but the cries of the *muezzins* calling the living to prayer sounded out across the doomed city as they had done for thirteen centuries. He got up, washed his face in a basin of stagnant water and started picking his way, slowly, on foot, away from the front line from whence he'd come. He didn't know where M10 was, but he surmised that it was in the least dangerous place in eastern Aleppo. All he had to do was stay alive and figure out where that might be.

Aleppo was, they said, the oldest inhabited settlement on earth. At first light, Joe realised that the destruction was off the scale. He'd seen nothing like it in his entire life. The nearest, most approximate thing was black-and-white pictures in school history books of Berlin in 1945, where no building taller than one storey stood for block after block after block. But this was in the twenty-first century and in colour. To the west stood the citadel, controlled by Zarif. Here in the east was this city of the dead, a stink-hole necropolis of pancaked apartment blocks, shell-blasted streets, and vast craters filled by foul-smelling sumps in which a quarter of a million people struggled to survive, a day at a time. The craters were the work of Russian bunker-buster bombs, originally designed to take out NATO missile silos, not poorly built residential districts. Aleppo had been scourged by a plague of bombs, bullets and shells, and yet people still smiled at him, the big pale stranger. Kids still played in the streets, leap-frogging shell-holes, playing peek-a-boo in soot-black ruins. He'd brought a backpack with him, in it ten energy bars and three big bottles of water and a small flask of Irish whiskey. The letter he carried in his inside jacket pocket.

Zoba's men had been giving Free Aleppo a very hard time. The people who held the eastern half of Syria's biggest city were with neither Zarif nor ISIS. They had their problems, they had their issues, but they were trying to find a path between tyranny and fanaticism. The punishment for their effrontery was a siege as brutal as anything from the Middle Ages. Instead of trebuchets flinging rocks and dead horses, they were on the wrong end, much of the time, of cluster bombs – a bomb inside a bomb inside a bomb.

The big bomb was unleashed from the Russian air force jet a mile above the ancient city named in *Macbeth* and *Hamlet*. A few hundred metres up, the primary bomb, the size of a large garbage bin, burst apart and thirty or forty bomblets, the size of large grapefruits, would spin out. On contact with the ground, the bomblets themselves burst, blasting ball bearings the size of big peas in a wide area. The American grunts who had watched them being used in Vietnam called them 'firecrackers' on account of the noise they made when they exploded, but folk down on the ground got little warning.

So when the cluster bomb fell on the kids playing out on the street – it being a fine day and quiet, up to that moment – they had no idea that their lives would be broken for ever. Seven kids in all from three families were messing about in the yard squared off by their apartment blocks. The oldest boy received a ball bearing moving at around nine hundred miles per hour directly in his left eye, killing him instantly; the next oldest boy got a ball bearing in the back of his skull, which bored through his brain and came to a stop behind his nose; a girl suffered one laterally through her left lung and heart, killing her; another girl survived intact; another boy, the youngest, also survived, intact; a boy in a stripy T-shirt was hit in the spine, paralysing him; the seventh victim was a teenager who lost his lower jaw.

Joe had been watching them play and wondering, to himself, whether he might dare to engage them in English, to ask them where the M10 hospital was. But his caution was the thing that saved his life. Had he gone forward, he would have been dead. As he considered what to do behind a thickness of wall, watching them play through a shell-hole, the firecrackers descended from the sky. The moment the cluster bombs did their work, he ran to the kids. He had some knowledge of first aid from his time as a special needs teacher in London. Theoretically he knew how to fix a broken leg, to tie a tourniquet; in practice, he knew how to put a plaster on a cut, make a cup of tea and, if it was serious, to call an ambulance. The un-merry hell in front of him now was beyond his capacity, was probably beyond the capacity of any normal human being without five years' medical training. He could hear their parents and loved ones come running, but he was the first on the scene.

As it was, he did his wretchedly bad best. He took off his jacket and ripped his sweatshirt in two, and did his best to tie a tourniquet around the upper body of the girl with a hole the size of a tennis ball in her chest, only realising that by the time he'd completed his hopeless task, she had been dead the whole time. He stopped someone from moving the boy with the ball bearing in his spine, so he did some good. When the White Helmets arrived, he was so drenched in blood that they scooped him up, too, and he arrived in one of their make-believe ambulances at M10. He'd seen photographs of it on the Internet: a steel gate on the outside, a central courtyard within, and a long ramp leading down to the basement and the wards proper. Bloodied as he was, he was carrying the teenager with a shredded mess of blood where his mouth had been, once, down the ramp, when a sharp series of firecrackers behind him told him that the Russians had dropped yet more cluster bombs on Aleppo.

He stood, aghast, as a shiny steel ball the size of a grapefruit rolled between his legs and came to a stop. On the outside of the ball was written in Cyrillic: *ShOAB-0.5M.*

A big-framed Syrian doctor, who must have been, once, almost as hefty as Joe, shaggy-haired, handsome, tired beyond the point of exhaustion, with dark eyes on fire, greeted him with something wry and sardonic in Arabic.

Joe said nothing, but signalled helplessly he hadn't understood a word and didn't know what to do with this bleeding mess in his arms. The doctor said something in guttural Arabic, and three male nurses took the teenager from Joe and placed him on a stretcher; two attended to the injured boy, but the third returned and started dabbing the gore from Joe's face. He winced in pain, and for the first time realised that he, too, had been hit, only a glancing slice of shrapnel to his cheekbone but deep enough.

The doctor tried something in Arabic to which Joe replied blankly. At the edge of his sight, a security guard, unarmed but handy, started to take interest in the scene.

'You're a lucky man. Sometimes the cluster bombs go off.'

Joe looked down at his feet where the cluster bomblet, in its second stage, glinted in the light malignantly.

'Who are you?' asked the doctor, this time in English.

'My name is Joe Tiplady . . .'

'You are the crazy Irishman,' said the doctor. 'Free Aleppo welcomes you, Mr Joe.' He hugged him and then shouted out something in Arabic, and a nurse hurried into the ward and put up two X-rays above the beds of two of the children hit by cluster bombs. You could clearly see the hard-etched metal of the ball bearing against the ghostly grey of the spine in one; in the second, the ball was lodged up against the boy's nose.

It took quite a few moments for Joe to realise that the nurse with the X-rays was the same woman whose son he had stolen. Jameela beamed at him as if he had passed some kind of test, frankly the only test of humanity worth passing.

'First, we do our best with the patients, Joe,' said Jameela, 'then we talk.'

Joe nodded at the big doctor.

'That's Rashid,' said Jameela.

'Ah,' said Joe.

Joe sat down and began to make sense of the hectic activity around him: there were far too many patients and nowhere enough doctors and nurses to cope. The floors of the hospital were slippery with blood; in the corner, Rashid and two other doctors were kneeling on the ground, bending over a patient's head. Only after a while did he realise they were carrying out emergency brain surgery. He made himself busy picking up the medical detritus, wiping the blood from the floor with a dirty mop. He looked around for a bucket and a mop and found them, but, for the life of him, he could not locate a working tap. As he tried to coax some water from the last remaining tap in the hospital, a doctor with the name Abu Khaled taped on to his uniform told him, 'There is no water, Mr Joe. They bombed the reservoir.'

After he had finished cleaning the floor, as best as he was able to with no water, Joe sat down and rested his head back against the wall. The last thing he could remember was watching Abu Khaled placing a smartphone close to where Rashid was operating on the boy with no jaw, and hearing, to his utter astonishment, a clear voice in English say, 'I want you to make an incision, laterally, below the nipple . . .'

But he was so exhausted he fell asleep and missed the world's first jaw-reconstruction surgery talked through via Skype from London.

———

Sometime in the middle of the night he was shooed awake and helped to stagger a short distance, and he found himself the next morning lying on a mattress under a sheet. After some time, Jameela came to him with a cup of sweet mint tea.

'So, Joe, you are famous throughout the whole of Aleppo – well, this part of Aleppo anyway.'

Joe took a sip of the tea and eyed her suspiciously, knowing that he was about to be mocked. 'And why is that, Jameela?'

'Because you fight your way through the siege to help us, only to fall fast asleep the moment you get here. Even so, everyone is pleased to hear of the crazy sleeping Irishman.'

Joe laughed quietly to himself. Close – to him, terrifyingly close – a stick of bombs fell, shaking the earth. Jameela didn't register them; she did not even adjust her gaze.

'Joe, I want you to know that I have forgiven you for taking Ham,' she said. 'I've seen such terrible suffering here, with my own eyes, that in a funny way it makes me realise that what I have been through, bad as it is, is not the end of the world. Ham is still alive and, physically, he's safe. So it's OK.'

Joe said nothing, but fished out an envelope from his jacket. In it were two sheets of paper – one a general letter in Arabic explaining that he was in Syria on a humanitarian mission; the second was blank. He found a box of matches in his jacket, lit one, and held the heat of the flame close to the blank sheet, but not so close that it caught fire. Within an instant the sheet curled in the heat, but as it did so a man's handwriting became clear. The letter read:

CONFIDENTIAL FOR YOUR EYES ONLY
To the Judge of the US Superior Court, Los Angeles, California. Your Honour, I am the Deputy Director of the CIA for Counter-Terrorism and it has come to my attention that in child custody proceedings in a lower court in LA it was asserted that one Jameela Abdiek was an active supporter of so-called Islamic State and therefore the aforesaid Jameela Abdiek would be wholly unsuited to care for her son, Hamal

Abdiek-Franklyn. Nothing could be further from the truth. Jameela Abdiek is an enemy of ISIS and through her actions has given great service to the war against ISIS, including helping the CIA in a mission of great national security. Any evidence asserted to the contrary I know to be false and, if necessary, I will be willing to testify to this effect whensoever I am needed.

Yours truly,

Ezekiel Chandler, Deputy Director, CIA.

Joe felt Jameela's dark eyes boring into him.

'Jam,' said Joe imploringly, 'come back to the States with me and appeal the decision. This letter changes everything. This letter means you can get Ham back. Zeke's a stubborn bastard, but once he's convinced that something is true, no power on earth can make his change his mind. Get out, come home, look after your boy.'

'I am not leaving Rashid.'

'Yes you are, Jameela.' The voice belonged to Rashid, who had emerged from behind a wall as if he were some kind of magician. 'You're going back to the United States with the sleeping Irishman and you are going to get your son back, and then you are going to buy you and me a lovely condo with a pool overlooking the Pacific. And we will invite Joe over and he can fall asleep the moment he arrives, just as he did in Aleppo.'

'No, Rashid, you need me.'

'No, Jameela. The chances of anyone here surviving for much longer aren't great. I'm staying. But you go back. Your boy needs you. Do that, Jameela. But before you leave, you need to do one thing.'

'What's that?'

'Marry me.'

Joe, as a rule, preferred funerals. This wedding, however, under siege, under Zoba's bombs, was the best wedding he had or would ever attend, ever. They timed it perfectly so that it took place inside a Zoba-decreed ceasefire, all eight hours of it. Hell, Joe even managed to stay awake for much of it.

# LOS ANGELES SUPERIOR COURT, CALIFORNIA

Joe and Zeke watched as the court custody officer returned Ham to Jameela. Mother and son held each other in their arms, cuddled, and then they went off to their car, got in and drove slowly out of the lot. Ham waved madly at the big Irishman and the little old man with the Abraham Lincoln beard standing next to him as they passed by. The two men waved back and Jameela tooted the horn, and then their car was swallowed up in the dragon's tail of traffic on the Pacific Highway.

'If this was an opera,' said Joe, 'a fat lady would come on and sing a song.'

'It's not an opera,' said Zeke.

'Pennsylvania, Ohio, Michigan, Wisconsin. Drobb won the states Grozhov spoke about in the fingernail palace back in Damascus, Zeke. He won the election.'

'Some of us are greatly concerned about that, and we are asking our friends in the FBI to look into it.'

'*It?*'

'The possibility that the Kremlin fixed the whole thing.'

'Why would they do that?'

'Because the Russians might have something on Drobb. You over-heard Grozhov talk about *Kompromat*. They could be blackmailing him.'

'And in the meantime?'

'We hold the line. We defend America, we defend democracy, we defend the Constitution.'

'That's fine and dandy,' said Joe. 'I'm going to get drunk and—'

His phone rang. Joe listened attentively for a while and then said pithily, 'Go fuck yourself,' and hung up.

'Who was that?' asked Zeke.

'The next President of the United States.'

'Why would Jerrard Drobb want to spend his time picking a fight with a crazy Irishman?'

'He lost some money to a conman who holed up in Venezuela. I faked his death and now, it seems, Drobb's found out and he's not best pleased with me.'

'So when I fake a death it's the end of the world,' mused Zeke, 'but when you fake a death, it's just one of those things?'

Joe suppressed a smile. 'I'm going for a drink,' he continued, 'and then I'm going to sleep for a month.'

'A week. When I got you out of that prison in Damascus, you said thank you, and it was kind of left in the air that you owed me one.'

'What?'

'That you owed me one. The Agency would like you to return to somewhere you've been, to do something that might help us understand if – or rather how – our democracy has been attacked.'

'And where's that, Zeke?'

'Pyongyang.'

Joe stared at Zeke for a long time. 'Why the hurry?'

'Because Jerrard Drobb takes office in a month's time. Leave it a month and the new man in the White House may not want to know the answer to our question.'

'I need a drink,' Joe said finally.

He left Zeke standing there and walked off in the direction of the nearest bar. It wasn't a yes, but nor was it a no.

# AUTHOR'S NOTE

*Road*, like its predecessor *Cold*, is a work of fiction inspired by stories I've covered as a reporter. I have just made a short film for BBC *Newsnight* about the nerve agent attack on Khan Sheikhoun, which killed maybe one hundred people, maybe more. To make the film, we had to look at images and video of the dead and the soon-to-die. These following scenes are burnt into my mind's eye: seven dead boys lying in a room, one with his fingers grotesquely locked in the air in a frozen spasm; a dead man on the bed of a truck, his beard flecked white with foam; a video of a man lying in a pool of water, shivering and incapable, as he struggled, helplessly, to breathe. The regime blamed the rebels for some kind of own goal. This is not likely. The scenes in *Road* in which people die of a nerve agent in Syria are grim. I made them up. But in Khan Sheikhoun cruel fact outdid my fiction.

Journalists, by and large, have not been able to go to the heart of the war in Syria lest they be weaponised against their own cultures by so-called Islamic State. But we can read books. I recommend Andrew Hoskins's *Empire of Fear: Inside the Islamic State* and *Hunting Season: The Execution of James Foley* by James Harkin; also Graeme Wood's magisterial article 'What Is The Islamic State?' in *The Atlantic*, March 2015.

Aside from the *Newsnight* piece on Khan Sheikhoun, I've made a number of films for the BBC that I've drawn on for *Road*: in 2015, a *Panorama* documentary about Europe's refugee crisis called 'The Long

Road', a short film for *Newsnight* – 'Finding Azam' – and a second *Panorama*, 'Paris Terror Attacks'. In 2016, I made three short films for *Newsnight* about Russian and Syrian regime bombing of the M10 hospital in Aleppo. I went to Syria several times before the war, but the nearest I got to the war zone was sitting in the office of London surgeon Dr David Nott filming him conduct the rebuilding of a jaw in Aleppo via Skype and WhatsApp. If you want to know more about the amazing Dr Nott, here's a link to his foundation: http://davidnottfoundation.com/.

North Korea raised its ugly head in *Road*, supplying chemical weapons to the regime. The North Koreans have been caught, twice, trying to ship chemical suits to Syria. The evidence that the Syrian regime has used chemical weapons against its own people is damning. If you want to know more, you might care to take a look at my non-fiction book, *North Korea Undercover*, which also tells something of the backstory of the IRA man who really did go to North Korea to learn how to kill the British back in the eighties, and realised that they, the North Koreans, and he, as an IRA man, had been brainwashed.

*Road* is dedicated to two people and the surgeons of what was, once, Free Aleppo. The real Agim Neza was our tour guide in Albania in 1990 when a group of journalists pretending not to be journalists invaded Albania. Agim was witty, dry and civilised then and throughout his life, which ended tragically too soon in the summer of 2016. It's been a pleasure to base the character of a good Albanian cop on the real Agim. The late Marie Colvin was, so her family believe, specifically targeted by the Syrian regime. Marie was a brilliant journalist whose life was a mirror that glittered as it showed truth to power. The third dedication is to the doctors of Free Aleppo when it existed, and specifically the doctors who worked in the M10 hospital as it was bombed repeatedly by the regime and the Russian air force. Bombing hospitals is against the rules of war. To do so repeatedly is a war crime.

For the name of my main character I must thank the family of Joe Tiplady, a wonderful Londoner who died of a heart attack when he was far too young. For getting me to write this series, thanks to my agent Humfrey Hunter and my publisher Jane Snelgrove. For putting up with me, thanks, foolish as this seems, to my dog Bertie and, not foolishly at all, my family.

John Sweeney

London, April 2017

# ABOUT THE AUTHOR

John Sweeney is a writer and journalist who, while working for the BBC, has challenged both Donald Trump over his association with a Russian-born gangster – Trump walked out on him – and Vladimir Putin over the war in Ukraine. Sweeney became a YouTube sensation in 2007, when, while filming 'Scientology and Me' for *Panorama*, he lost his temper with Tommy Davis, a senior member of the Church of Scientology. As a reporter, first for the *Observer* and then for the BBC, Sweeney has covered wars and chaos in more than eighty countries and been undercover to a number of tyrannies, including Chechnya, North Korea and Zimbabwe. He has helped free seven people falsely convicted of killing their babies, starting with Sally Clark and Angela Cannings. Over the course of his career, John has won an Emmy, two Royal Television Society Awards, a Sony Gold Award, a *What the Papers Say* Journalist of the Year Award, an Amnesty International Award and the Paul Foot Award. Sweeney's first novel, *Elephant Moon*, was published to much acclaim in 2012. His hobby is annoying the Church of Scientology.